D0361383

THE
WARRIOR
PRINCESS

ALSO BY K. M. ASHMAN

THE
WARRIOR
PRINCESS

K. M. ASHMAN

THOMAS & MERCER

This is a work of fiction. Names, characters, organizations, places, events and incidents are either products of the author's imagination or are used fictitiously.

Text copyright © 2017 K. M. Ashman
All rights reserved.

No part of this book may be reproduced, or stored in a retrieval system, or transmitted in any form or by any means, electronic, mechanical, photocopying, recording, or otherwise, without express written permission of the publisher.

Published by Thomas & Mercer, Seattle

www.apub.com

Amazon, the Amazon logo, and Thomas & Mercer are trademarks of Amazon.com, Inc., or its affiliates.

ISBN-13: 9781612185781
ISBN-10: 1612185789

Cover illustration by Chris McGrath

Cover design by Richard Augustus

Map illustration by David Woodroffe

Printed in the United States of America

MEDIEVAL MAP OF WALES

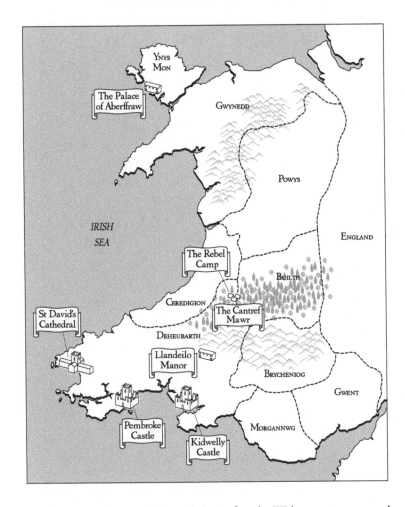

Though the borders and boundaries of early Wales were constantly changing, for the sake of our story, the above shows an approximation of where the relevant areas were at the time.

Character list

Although correct pronunciation is not really necessary to enjoy the story, for those who would rather experience the authentic way of saying the names, explanations are provided in italics.

THE HOUSE OF ABERFFRAW

Gruffydd ap Cynan: King of Gwynedd – *Gruff-ith ap Cun-nan*
Gwenllian ferch Gruffydd: Daughter of Gruffydd and wife of Tarw

The 'll' can be difficult to pronounce in Welsh, and is formed by placing the tongue on the roof of the mouth while expelling air past the tongue on both sides. Non-Welsh speakers sometimes struggle with this – audible representations are available online.

THE HOUSE OF TEWDWR

Gruffydd ap Rhys: Youngest son (known as Tarw) – *Tar-oo (roll the letter 'R')*
Nesta ferch Rhys: Daughter – *Nessa or Nest-A*
Emma: Maid of Nesta

OTHER CHARACTERS

Henry Beauclerc: King Henry I of England
Stephen de Bloise: Successor to Henry
Wilhelm Berman: Flemish knight and ally of the English
Rowan Handlestein: Flemish knight and ally of the English
Heinrich of Saxony: Saxon mercenary and ally of Gwenllian
Hywel ap Maredudd: Lord of Brycheniog and victor at the battle of Gower – *How-ell ap Mar-ed-ith*

PEMBROKE CASTLE

Gerald of Windsor: Castellan of Pembroke Castle
John of Salisbury: Constable of Pembroke
Walter de Calais: Ally of John of Salisbury

KIDWELLY CASTLE

Maurice de Londres: Castellan of Kidwelly
Lady Marion: Wife of Maurice

THE REBEL ARMY

Taliesin ap John: Leader of the rebels in Gwenllian's absence – *Tally-es-in*
Dog: Taliesin's right-hand man and paid mercenary
Robert of Llandeilo: Gwenllian's trusted right-hand man
Bevan ap Maldwyn: Lord of Llandeilo and loyal to the Rebellion

PLACE NAMES

Aberffraw: *Ab-er-frow*
Brycheniog: *Brick-eye-knee-og*
Deheubarth: *Du-hi-barrth (roll the letter 'R')*
Dinefwr: *Din-e-foorr (roll the letter 'R')*
Gwynedd: *Gwin-eth*
Kidwelly: *Kid-well-ee*
Pembroke: *Pem-broke*
Carmarthen: *Car-mar-then*

Prologue

Wales AD 1135

In the years leading up to 1135, English interests right across the kingdom of Deheubarth in the south of Wales were subject to a targeted and brutal war of attrition led by a powerful group of rebels operating out of the Cantref Mawr, a vast and inhospitable wooded area in the north of the kingdom. At their head was the last true prince of Deheubarth, Gruffydd ap Rhys, commonly known as Tarw, and at his side rode his beautiful warrior wife, Gwenllian ferch Gruffydd, the daughter of the most powerful king in Wales.

Together, and with a fearless band of warriors at their backs, they harried the English at every opportunity, forcing the Crown to commit valuable resources to protecting its interests across the country.

Many died on both sides of the bloody struggle, but when Tarw was killed, Gwenllian disappeared without trace and, without their inspirational leaders, the resistance fell apart. The rebel army disbanded and many left the camps amongst the forests to return to their farms and cottages. Though some decided to carry on with the struggle, their numbers were few and they posed little threat to the might of the English Crown.

For the next ten years or so, Wales was relatively peaceful, with many treaties, both formal and informal, being signed between kingdoms in an effort to avoid costly and unproductive wars.

In the south, Gerald of Windsor had been castellan of Pembroke Castle for many years and was a favoured knight of King Henry. He was also known as a gifted politician and a fair governor. This was in no small part due to his marriage to Nesta ferch Rhys, the daughter of the last Welsh king of Deheubarth and mother to the bastard son of King Henry himself.

Gerald governed Deheubarth on behalf of the Crown with a firm yet fair hand and, consequently, the English occupying forces enjoyed the most profitable and dominant position they had seen for a generation, safe in the knowledge that there was no prospect of ever facing the Welsh in battle again.

Or so they thought . . .

The Carmarthen Road

December 6th, AD 1135

A wayside tavern wasn't a normal haunt for a shepherd and two of his flock but the inviting firelight seeping through the shutters had been too enticing for even the toughest of men in the snowstorm ravaging the hills of southern Deheubarth.

Outside the wind tore at anyone stupid enough to brave the storm's fury but in here, amongst the bustle and noise of the single crowded room, the heat of the log fire and the warmth steaming from the fleeces of so many tethered animals mingled with the smell of man-sweat to wrap a welcoming blanket around any weary traveller.

In the corner of the tavern, the shepherd sat alone, minding his own business, with two yearling rams lying at his feet, both animals staring nervously at the many dogs seeking titbits amongst the forest of table legs and stools. A tankard of hot ale stood on the trestle before him, the second he had enjoyed since seeking shelter, and he looked around with feigned disinterest, taking in the many characters such a place attracted. Most were known to him – men of the local villages who frequented the isolated tavern seeking release from overbearing wives or the rigours of their hard existence. Others, as was often the case, were strangers, and though his gaze wandered as freely as his flocks upon the hills, his attention was focussed, listening out for anything that could benefit him or his masters.

The Drover's Rest was a popular watering hole on the road to Pembroke, not just for the service its name implied but also as a source of information for anyone wishing to know the latest news about the politics of the day, both local and national. Its reputation meant that many men made it their destination of choice, and spies of all loyalties played their games in the tavern's cloying warmth – offering rumours and news of their own in the hope of gleaning something more important in return.

Such was the case on this night, when a caravan bringing salted pork from Gwent to Pembroke Castle sought shelter from the heavy storm. After the exhausted horses had been fed and rubbed dry in the attached barn, men and dogs alike filed into the steamy room for much-needed rest from the elements.

'Master Steffan,' shouted the sweating landlord over the noise of the busy tavern, 'I haven't seen you for many weeks. Good to see you again.'

'Indeed,' said Steffan, stamping the snow off his boots. 'I thought I had seen my last caravan before next spring but that goat of a man Besford went and got himself killed by brigands a few weeks ago and there was no one left to bring the salt-pork to Gerald.'

'Then let's just be thankful you are in gainful employment and drink to your fortune. Come, I will find you a seat by the fire.' The landlord turned and waddled across the room, his breath coming in laboured wheezes as he pushed men of a smaller stature out of his way. Few complained for in addition to being a man of enormous girth, he had a vicious temper and many men had disappeared after upsetting him, never to be heard from again.

Steffan grunted and looked around the room. As expected, there were the usual rascals who seemed to hover around the tavern like flies around filth but there were other faces, men he had never seen before, and that always promised an interesting night. He walked over to the fire and waited as the landlord hauled a drunk from a chair and dragged him over to a bench near the door.

'You're warm enough, Weasel,' he growled. 'Time to let a gentleman have your seat.' He returned to the fireplace and wiped the piss off the chair where the drunk's bladder had let him down.

'Sorry about this, Master Steffan,' he said, throwing half a tankard of ale onto the seat. 'I'll have it as clean as a priest's conscience in just a moment.'

Steffan waited until the seat was dry then, removing his cloak, sat down to stretch out his hands before the fire.

'Ale or wine?' asked the landlord.

'Ale,' said Steffan. 'And a bowl of whatever is in that pot.'

The landlord glanced at the huge cauldron of pottage sitting in the alcove to the side of the flames.

'I can do better than that,' whispered the landlord, leaning forward to speak quietly into the cart master's ear. 'How about a steaming hot beef pie with greens, gravy and a hand of bread? Freshly baked just this morning, it was.'

'A pie, you say?' said Steffan, his interest piqued. 'And how much will you fleece me for such a treat?'

'You insult me, my lord,' said the landlord, standing up with feigned shock. 'The pie was my own, kept behind for my supper, but you can have it for a mere two pennies, the exact same price it cost my good lady to bake.'

The cart master sighed, suspecting that the landlord could probably bake ten pies for two pennies, but he was cold, his belly was empty and a hot pie sounded like exactly what he needed.

'Throw in the ale and you have a deal,' he said.

The landlord grumbled something about being robbed before turning to one of the serving wenches, who was sitting on a customer's knee trying to sweet-talk him into extra business in the back room.

'Oy, Fira,' said the landlord, 'put him down for a minute and go and get that platter of food I set aside earlier. Place it over a pot of boiling water and when it's hot, serve it to that gentleman there.'

'Really?' said the woman, wiping wisps of unruly hair from her face. 'What's so special about him that he gets the pie?'

'First of all, he's paid me a good price,' whispered the landlord, 'but more importantly, he is a good contact to have and, if I play my cards right, I may come out of this with something far better than stale pastry.'

The girl looked back at her punter and smiled. 'You just stay there, my sweet, and hold that last thought. I won't be gone longer than a few minutes.' She stood up and made her way out into the only other room of the tavern to find the lidded bowl the landlord had referred to.

'So,' said the landlord, returning to the fire, 'what else is so important that you risk the horrors of the storm to deliver it?'

'Nothing special,' said Steffan. 'Just salted pork and other such goods. It seems that the English have finally understood that the winters can be much harder down here and they don't want to get snowed in without plenty of meat to warm their bellies.'

The landlord laughed and sat down beside the cart master, unaware that just a few tables away, the shepherd was listening intently to the visitor's every word.

Five leagues away, another door opened and another snow-covered man stamped his feet to rid his boots of the winter slush and mud.

'Master Carwyn!' gasped the maid, running across to meet the steward of Llandeilo Manor. 'Look at the state of you. Come in quickly before you catch your death of cold. I'll have the kitchens prepare something warm.'

'Not for me,' said the steward. 'I'll be going home to sup with my wife soon.'

'Of course,' said the maid, and she scurried away to the kitchens as Carwyn looked around the minor hall, taking comfort in the roaring flames in the fireplace. He walked over to the fire, and after picking up a wooden tankard from a table, ladled warm wine from the open pot hanging from a side frame.

'Ah, that's better,' he said quietly to himself as the soothing liquid reached his stomach.

'Stealing my wine again?' roared a voice, and Carwyn turned to see the lord of the manor striding into the hall.

'My Lord Bevan,' said Carwyn with a smile. 'Alas, I have been caught red-handed.'

'Then let me also redden my hands,' said Bevan with a grin, 'for there is far too much for just one man.' He filled a second tankard and held it up in a toast. 'To Mother Nature and her glorious cloak of white.'

Carwyn laughed and looked down at his still sodden clothing.

'Perhaps a curse would be more appropriate than a toast,' he said, 'but I would never refuse any chance to relieve you of your hospitality.' Laughing, both men drank from their vessels before placing them on the table before the fire.

'Come, sit,' said Bevan. 'I would hear all about your journey. Was it successful?'

'Aye,' said Carwyn, 'to an extent. Master Jonas has agreed to sell you the farm though he asks for a far steeper price. I tried to reason with him but he is as entrenched as a thousand-year-old oak.'

'Hmm,' said Bevan. 'That man is as stubborn as a mule, always has been, but I see no reason to pander to his demands. I hear he already struggles to service his debt and it is only a matter of time before his creditors involve the constable.'

'That may be so,' said the steward, 'but let's not lose sight of the fact that he has a family and several young mouths to feed.'

'All the more reason to call his bluff,' said Bevan. 'As this winter bites he will realise my offer is more than fair. Hunger is a powerful mistress.'

'Indeed,' said Carwyn. 'But can I suggest there may be another way?'

'And what is that exactly?'

'Perhaps we can strike a deal before there is any chance of him being carted off to face a debtor trial.'

'Why should I do that?'

'Because if he is convicted he will forfeit his lands and as he pays liege to no lordship, his farm could be sold to the highest bidder on an open market. The last thing we want is to become embroiled in a bidding war. It could turn out to be more expensive than the price he currently asks.'

'So what do you suggest?'

'What if we offer to pay his debtors off and allow him to keep his farm?'

'I can see no reason whatsoever that would encourage me to do such a thing.'

'Wait,' said Carwyn. 'I haven't finished. Obviously there would be conditions otherwise it would indeed make no sense. What I was thinking is this: he gets to stay on his land for as long as he lives but only if he signs a document saying that on the day of his death, the ownership of his farm and all its associated holdings, including the land, tools, stock and indentured servants, transfer to your estate. In the meantime, he works the farm on your behalf for a fair price with all profits coming to your own treasury. That way, he need not worry about his debt, feeding his family or his children's future and your estate benefits from the expansion you desire.'

'And what about his heirs?'

8

'He has no sons, my lord, only daughters.'

'At the moment.'

'Perhaps, but we can build that eventuality into the agreement. Promise him that any future sons will benefit from a position here in the manor, or something similar, and he should see reason.'

Bevan thought for a few moments, contemplating the proposal. 'I still can't see how this benefits me,' he said. 'Only property I own can be entered against the value of my estate. By doing this, Master Jonas will still legally own the farm until the day he dies.'

'True, but ask yourself this: why are you growing your estate each year even though you cannot take it with you when you die?'

'Because it will be my legacy for future generations of my family.'

'And therein lies my point. It could take years or even decades for Master Jonas to die but in the end your estate and your sons will benefit. Time is not the issue here; your legacy is. Buying the farm would cost ten times as much as settling his debts so, by doing so, you not only save an enormous amount of money but also invest in the future while pocketing any profits the farm makes. In addition, you will be seen as a kindly landlord who has helped a fellow man in need, irrespective of his position.'

'And you think he will do this?'

'I'm sure of it.'

'How?' said Bevan slowly, his eyes narrowing with suspicion.

'Um, because I have already floated the suggestion,' said Carwyn.

'And his response?'

'He is mulling it over.'

For a few seconds, Bevan stared at Carwyn, then he suddenly sat back and burst into laughter.

'Master Steward,' he said, 'you have the cheek of the devil himself yet I admire your audacity.'

'That's why you hired me, my lord,' said Carwyn with a smile.

'Well,' said Bevan, his laughter abating, 'that's one of the reasons.'

'Indeed, but let us not dwell on such things. Those days have long gone.' He took a swig of his wine before continuing. 'So, shall I pursue the deal?'

'If that is your recommendation then I will leave the details in your hands. I trust you with my life, Master Steward, so please proceed accordingly.' Both men raised their tankards and drained them dry.

'Another?' said Bevan.

'No, my lord. I promised my wife I would dine with her and our sons this evening and I am already late. If you don't mind, I will be away.'

'Of course,' said Bevan, standing up. 'Give my regards to your lovely lady and keep me updated as to how goes the transaction.'

'I will,' said Carwyn, bowing slightly.

'I've told you before,' said Bevan. 'Please don't do that. It makes me uncomfortable.'

'I know,' said Carwyn with a wink. 'Why do you think I do it?'

'Be gone, varlet,' laughed Bevan, 'before I head over to your lady's bedchamber myself.'

Carwyn smiled and donned his cloak before leaving the hall. The day had been long and he was exhausted, yet the satisfaction of achieving a fair outcome to the benefit of all parties made every sodden minute worthwhile. They were living in strange and dangerous times so every victory, no matter how small, was to be celebrated.

Back in the hall, Bevan stood at the window sipping his wine as he watched the steward walking across the courtyard, leaning into the vicious storm. His relationship with Carwyn was one of mutual respect, and there was hardly a day went by when the steward's intelligence, loyalty and ability didn't make life in the manor as easy as it could be and he knew that if circumstances were different, Carwyn was capable of being so much more.

A few minutes later, Carwyn walked into a small house situated within the courtyard of the manor. His wife was on her knees, adding a log to the fire, and she turned to smile as she heard him enter.

'Carwyn,' she gasped, scrambling to her feet. 'Thank the lord.' She ran across the room and embraced her husband, holding him tightly.

'A wonderful welcome indeed,' said Carwyn, returning his wife's embrace. 'What causes such emotion?'

'You are late,' said Branwen, stepping back to look up at her husband. 'And the storm is fierce. I thought you may have been caught in the midst of it.'

'I'm sorry, Branwen, but the journey was far harder than I anticipated, and if truth be told, there was a while when I too thought we would have to camp.'

'Well you are here now,' she replied, 'but you look exhausted.' She looked into his eyes with concern. 'Are you hungry?'

'As a wolf,' said Carwyn.

'Then come,' she said, taking his hand. 'I have two venison steaks waiting to be cooked and bread still hot from the oven. The boys have already eaten so there is plenty to fill your belly.'

'Venison!' exclaimed Carwyn as he removed his heavy cloak. 'I am in danger of being spoilt.'

'A gift from Lord Bevan's kitchens,' said Branwen. 'And, anyway, you deserve it after working so hard. Take a seat while I bring the griddle.'

'In a moment,' said Carwyn. 'First I would see the boys. Are they awake?'

'Rhys is fast asleep but Rhydian may be awake.'

'I'll have a quick look,' said Carwyn, and he crept up the stairs to peep through the door of his children's bedchamber.

As the lord of the manor's steward, Carwyn enjoyed a position of privilege and was lucky to have a very generous house within the manor walls. The main living area on the ground floor had direct access to its own stockroom at the rear, as well as a cold store and a latrine. Upstairs consisted of two more rooms, each used as bedchambers, one for Carwyn and his wife and the other for three of their four sons – Maelgwyn aged sixteen, Rhydian aged five and, the youngest of them all, Rhys aged two. The fourth and oldest son was Morgan, a nineteen-year-old, hot-headed young man who lived in the soldiers' quarters above the stables along with the half-dozen men-at-arms tasked with guarding the manor's interests.

To any outsider, Carwyn's life was the model of perfection. He had a beautiful wife, a position of status and a family of four healthy boys, each assured a position within the manor as they grew older, yet his mind was troubled. As part of his duties he often travelled the breadth of his master's lands on business, and the more he talked to people, the more aware he became of the rebellious undercurrent flowing beneath the surface of those suffering hardship under the control of the English. As a passionate Welshman his heart ached at the suffering of his countrymen yet he knew there was little anyone could do – the English were far too strong and the days of conflict in the past.

In the middle of the boys' room was the enormous bed that Carwyn had made with his own hands almost ten years earlier, and on the table stood a burning candle, a comfort oft demanded by Rhys before he went to sleep. At the table, Maelgwyn sat reading a document in the small circle of light. Carwyn gently placed another heavy blanket over his youngest two children, fast asleep in the bed, before walking over to peer over his older son's shoulder.

'Father, you're back,' said the boy quietly.

'Aye,' said Carwyn, placing his hand on the boy's shoulder, 'it was a tough journey, sure enough, but it is done. Woe betide any man stuck out in that storm tonight.'

'Have you tended to your horse?' replied Maelgwyn, sitting up. 'I can do that for you, if you like.'

'No, you stay there. Robert has it in hand. Anyway, it's horrible out there. Tell me, what are you reading, the Bible?'

'No. It's a very rare document – an account of the life of Hywel Dda. I was given it by Lord Bevan this very afternoon.'

'Were you indeed?' said Carwyn. 'Well, I'm happy you are taking such interest in the life of the lawmaker but be aware that many of his decrees no longer hold sway in these lands and we are bound by English law. Henry and his predecessors have seen to that.'

'I know,' said Maelgwyn, 'but it seems so unfair. Why can we not rule our own lands, Father? Surely we should be free to walk our own hills without being beholden to the whims of a foreign king?'

For a few moments, Carwyn looked at his second-eldest son and his eyes glazed over. Deep inside he felt the familiar pangs of patriotic fervour threatening to come to the surface, but the feelings were quickly quashed as his self-imposed discipline refused to let such thoughts colour his thinking. The road of resistance was for other men; his path consisted of doing whatever he could to protect his family.

'Father,' said Maelgwyn, staring at the blank look on Carwyn's face. 'Is there something wrong?'

Carwyn took a deep breath and looked down at his son. 'No,' he said. 'Everything is fine. Just be careful what you say, Maelgwyn, for such words are likely to get you in the stocks if they reach the wrong ears.'

'I know,' said Maelgwyn, 'but I only voice such things within these walls and, besides, Morgan said—'

'You have been talking to Morgan?' interrupted Carwyn. 'I should have guessed.'

'Father, you don't understand,' replied Maelgwyn. 'He only reinforced what I already believe to be true in my own heart – that we should be free to govern our own fate.'

'Your brother is an angry young man, Maelgwyn, and needs to curb his tongue else we could all get in trouble. Now, your mother is about to put a couple of venison steaks on the griddle and I'm not sure I can eat them both. Perhaps you can help?'

'Aye,' said Maelgwyn, closing the book. 'It has been a while since I tasted venison.'

'Then come,' said Carwyn, 'before we waken the boys.'

Together, father and son descended the stair. Branwen was crouched near the fireplace, turning the sizzling steaks over on the flat-iron griddle amongst the flames.

'Still awake?' she asked over her shoulder.

'Aye,' said Maelgwyn, 'and Father said there may be a venison steak going spare.'

'There is,' she laughed, 'but where you put it all, I'll never know. You've already emptied the stew pot.' She looked over to her husband. 'Carwyn, could you pass me some more wood, please?'

'He's a growing boy,' said Carwyn, walking over to the woodpile in the corner, 'and will need all the meat we can spare.'

Maelgwyn grabbed two tankards and filled them from a flask of ale before sitting at the table.

'Father,' he said eventually, 'I was with Morgan and his comrades earlier and they were talking about a prince who once rode in these parts as a brigand. Tarw, they called him. Did you know of such a man?'

Carwyn paused and stared at the log in his hand for a moment, recalling memories still raw in his mind despite the passing years.

'Father?'

'Aye,' said Carwyn, resuming his task, 'I knew of him. Why do you ask?'

'One of Morgan's fellows said you may have once ridden alongside him as a rebel. Is that true?'

Branwen looked over and saw her husband turn to stare at his son, a hint of anger in his eyes. She stood up and quickly walked over to the table with the two steaks hanging from the blade of a knife. Carwyn lifted the tankard and took a long draft, deliberately ignoring his son's question.

'Aye,' intervened Branwen as Carwyn drank, 'there is an element of truth in the tale but we don't speak of that man around here anymore. He is long gone.' She placed a steak on each trencher and pushed one across the table to her son. 'Here, eat up while it's hot. I'll get you some bread.' She turned away but stopped in her tracks as her son continued the unwelcome line of questioning.

'So where did he go – this man called Tarw?' asked Maelgwyn, his mouth full of meat. 'Was he captured by the English?'

'He is *dead!*' shouted Carwyn, slamming his tankard down hard onto the table. 'And that's all you need to know.'

Maelgwyn stared at his father in shock. Rarely did Carwyn raise his voice but when he did it was better not to risk further admonishment.

'I'm sorry,' muttered Maelgwyn. 'I was just interested.'

'Don't be,' snapped Carwyn. 'That man's name is not welcome around here, at any time. Now eat up and go to bed. Your mother and I have things to discuss.'

'Of course,' said Maelgwyn. 'My apologies.'

Ten minutes later, Maelgwyn was back in his bedchamber while his father was still downstairs, sitting in the chair before the fire. His venison lay untouched upon the table.

'Don't be too hard on him,' said his wife, rubbing away the tenseness in the back of his neck. 'He knows not of what he speaks.'

'Aye,' sighed Carwyn, 'I know, and I was out of order to react so. I'll make it good with him on the morrow. It's just that this whole situation is so frustrating.'

'Let it go, Carwyn,' said Branwen. 'Those days have long gone.'

'Have they, Branwen?' asked Carwyn. 'Have they really or are they still wrapped around us like a great, unseen cloak? For I tell you this: something is stirring out there, something big, and if it is what I think it is, then I fear for the future of our sons.'

Pembroke Castle

December 7th, AD 1135

Nesta ferch Rhys sat at the long table in the main hall alongside four of the castle ladies with whom she shared a close friendship. As the wife of Gerald of Windsor, the castellan of Pembroke castle, she enjoyed the privilege of sitting on the seat at the head of the trestle table while the other four ladies sat at the sides, though all in reach of the tapestry lying before them. To one side sat Emma, Nesta's maid and closest confidante. Emma had been with Nesta for many years, and even though she still held the humble title of lady's maid, she enjoyed privileges of which most servants could only dream. As the ladies chattered like the women of the markets, Emma busied herself sorting out the threads needed to feed their love of embroidery.

Emma's eyes were not what they used to be but, despite struggling to thread the needles, she persevered, not helped by the raucous gossip and laughter coming from those who, in her mind, should show more decorum.

'I am telling the truth,' said one of the ladies, particularly loudly to better the laughter from her friends. 'Her husband came back early and Master Clive jumped from the window without a stitch of linen upon him.'

'Naked?' asked one of the ladies. 'Surely not.'

'As the day he was born. I know for I saw him with my own eyes.'

'Lady Cerys!' gasped one of the others. 'Are you telling us that you did not avert your gaze?'

'Certainly not,' said Lady Cerys looking around her laughing friends. 'I have heard that the stable master has been particularly blessed and I was inquisitive as to whether the stories are true.' Again the women broke down in laughter as they pictured the scene.

'And is he?' gasped Nesta, wiping away her tears of mirth. 'For we are all anxious to hear.'

'Well, I am not one to tittle-tattle but let's just say I now know why the Lady Delyth is so happy these days.'

The women again collapsed in laughter as Nesta turned to address Emma.

'Oh dear,' she said, trying to gather her sensibilities, 'I fear this tapestry will never be done. Emma, would you be so kind as to arrange a fresh flask of wine?'

'Of course, my lady,' said Emma, getting up from her seat. 'I will send a boy straight away.'

'Emma,' continued Nesta, stopping the woman in her tracks, 'why not bring another goblet and join us at the tapestry?'

'I think not, my lady,' said Emma with a smile. 'You know what the master is like.'

'Oh, you leave him to me,' said Nesta. 'Join us at the tapestry and rest for a while. You work too hard.'

'If you will forgive me, my lady, I would not be comfortable and, besides, I have to see the stable master later on and if I hear any more secrets about him I swear I will swoon from embarrassment the very moment I see him.'

All the women laughed again as Emma left the room and Nesta took a deep breath before returning her attentions to the tapestry.

———⌣———

Emma walked down a narrow corridor towards the kitchen, frustrated that the page was nowhere to be seen. 'I'll box his ears when I see him next,' she muttered, retrieving a flask of wine from a shelf in the cold store. On the way back, a door opened to one side and she paused to avoid walking into the constable. She kept quiet, hoping he wouldn't notice her in the gloom. John Salisbury was a man of few redeeming features and the last thing she wanted to do was antagonise him. The constable locked the door and was about to walk away when he sensed someone was behind him and turned to face the maid.

'Good evening, Master Salisbury,' said Emma with a slight nod of the head.

Salisbury took a few steps towards her, looming tall in the gloom.

'Well, well, well,' he said, 'if it isn't Nesta's favourite slave. What, no curtsey for your betters?'

'Such salutations are reserved for Master Gerald and my lady,' replied Emma. 'As you well know.'

'Hmm,' said Salisbury, placing two fingers under her chin to lift up her head. His cold eyes stared into hers for a moment before she looked away and he dropped his hand. 'You are getting stubborn in your old age, woman,' he said. 'But you're not so old that you won't get a flogging if you keep treating me with such disdain.'

'Only the Master can authorise such a thing on a member of his household,' replied Emma, turning her head to face him again, 'and he would never allow it.'

'Well, you had better hope that he sticks around,' said Salisbury, 'for I would take great amusement in opening that old crone skin upon your back.'

'The Master is going nowhere,' said Emma.

'Really?' said Salisbury. 'No man lives forever, wench.'

Emma just stared in silence, knowing that she could never beat him in an argument.

'Is there anything else?' she asked eventually. 'For I am on an errand for my lady.'

'Are you really?' he replied. He looked down at the contents of her basket. He picked up the flask and removed the cork stopper before smelling the contents. To Emma's disgust he lifted the flask to his lips and took a mouthful, all the time his evil eyes never leaving hers.

'That's good wine,' he said, wiping his mouth with the back of his hand. 'Perhaps I should take it myself.'

'Why are you doing this?' asked Emma. 'You never used to be so hurtful but these days it is as if you have the devil himself within you.'

'A man changes, Emma,' said Salisbury, 'as does his ambitions. Now, away with you and I will see Lady Nesta gets her wine.'

'But . . .'

'Off with you, Emma, or you will indeed feel my ire.'

Emma turned away and walked back towards the kitchens. She may have enjoyed a certain level of privilege at the castle but Salisbury was powerful and she knew she could only push back so hard.

'You forgot this,' shouted Salisbury as the empty basket hit her in the back. With a sigh she picked it up and continued on her way, upset by the sound of his laughter behind her.

As he watched her go, John Salisbury took another swig of the wine, though this time he just swilled it around his mouth before spitting it carefully back into the flask. After replacing the stopper, he made his way up to the hall and threw open the door with vigour, deliberately causing it to crash into the wall. All the ladies jumped and turned to stare at the constable as he strode across the hall.

'My apologies,' he said with a grin. 'Sometimes I underestimate my own power.'

'Master Salisbury,' said Nesta, any trace of mirth draining from her face. 'This is a surprise, I thought you were out on an errand.'

'I run no errands, my lady,' said Salisbury. 'I carry out the business of the king on behalf of the castellan, as you well know.'

'My apologies,' said Nesta. 'But nevertheless, your appearance here surprises me. Surely it takes up more than a few hours to capture a brigand?'

'Perhaps, but my quarry was an idiot and hid in the woodpile of his father's farm, who, by the way, is now in the gaol awaiting trial for offering succour to a known thief.'

'And his son?'

'Already hanged,' said Salisbury. 'Do you mind if I join you?' Without waiting for an answer he dragged a chair over and placed it next to Nesta. The women glanced at each other – more disturbed at the overfamiliarity of the constable than at the offhand way he dismissed the execution of a young man.

'Master Salisbury,' said Nesta, with a false smile. 'Surely the simple activities of the castle ladies are below a man of your station?'

'On the contrary,' said Salisbury, pouring wine from the flask into Nesta's goblet, 'I have long been interested to find out what joy such a simple task brings.' He returned her smile and turned to the rest of the women, offering up the flask. 'Ladies?'

Two of the ladies handed over their goblets while the others politely declined. An awkward silence fell around the table, a situation that Salisbury was revelling in.

'So,' he said, turning his attention to the tapestry spread out across the table, 'how do we go about this?'

Before anyone could respond, the outside door at the far end of the hall opened and a boy burst in to run across the hall. His sodden riding cloak still hung about his shoulders and he was bedraggled from the harsh winter weather.

'Hold there,' shouted Salisbury, jumping up from his seat. 'Who are you to burst into the hall unannounced?' His hand went to the hilt of his sword and the boy stopped dead in his tracks.

'My lord!' gasped the boy. 'My apologies, but there was nobody to introduce me and I need to see the castellan immediately. Are you he?'

'No, he is not,' said Nesta quickly, she too standing up. 'My husband is not here but I can take a message on his behalf. Declare yourself and your business.'

'My lady,' said the rider, 'I am Iain Waters, a rider in the employ of the castellan at Carmarthen. I have a message for your husband's eyes only, received yesterday from London.'

'What is this message?' asked Salisbury, leaving the table and striding towards the messenger.

'I have been instructed to pass it to the castellan only,' stuttered the boy, 'on pain of punishment.'

'Hand it over,' said Salisbury, his voice lowering in warning, 'or the punishment you fear will be nothing compared to what you will receive at my hands.'

'My lady,' said the messenger, looking across at Nesta with a pleading look on his face. 'Is your husband anywhere near?'

'I will send for him,' said Nesta, walking towards the frightened boy. 'Master Salisbury, stand down, can't you see he is only doing his master's will and since when is that a crime?'

Salisbury didn't answer but kept his hand on his sword.

'Come to the fire,' said Nesta, turning to the scared boy. 'Let's get you warmed up; you look freezing. Lady Margaret,' she continued as she led the boy across the hall, 'I'm afraid Emma seems to be detained elsewhere. Would you be so kind as to find a page and send him to find my husband?'

'Don't bother,' snapped Salisbury. 'He is in the treasury. I will bring him myself.' He strode out of the hall leaving the rest staring after him.

'Such an unpleasant man,' said Lady Margaret, joining Nesta and the messenger near the fire. 'Here, you must be frozen to the core.' She gave him her goblet of wine and he drank it down eagerly. 'I'm afraid it's not warmed,' said Margaret, 'but it may defrost your innards.' She turned to Nesta. 'Shall I go to the kitchens and arrange some hot food, my lady?'

'Yes. That would be good. Thank you.'

Margaret left the room while one of the other ladies brought over a chair.

'Take that sodden thing off,' said Nesta. 'And your jerkin. Quickly now, before you catch a chill.'

'My lady,' replied the messenger, 'I will be bare-chested if I was to do such a thing, and that would never do in such fine company.'

'Nonsense,' said Nesta. 'I have sons of my own and all are around the same age as you.'

'What about them?' asked the boy, nodding to the other ladies.

'Trust me, they have all seen their fair share of naked chests before.' She looked around and walked over to retrieve a cloak from the back of a chair.

'Lady Nesta,' said one of the other women, 'that is my second-best cloak.'

'Oh, hush your concerns,' replied Nesta. 'Can't you see the lad is shivering? I will have my maid clean it for you if it bothers you so.'

Her friend wasn't happy but allowed her to continue.

'Here,' said Nesta, handing over the fine cloak. 'You strip off and wrap yourself with this. I will arrange for your clothes to be dried before you return to Carmarthen.'

'Thank you, my lady,' said the boy.

All the women returned to the table as the boy got undressed and soon he was wrapped in the fur-lined cloak, sat in a chair before the fire. Margaret returned, followed by Emma carrying a tray with a bowl of soup and a loaf of bread.

'Please excuse me, my lady,' said Emma, pushing past Lady Margaret, 'I will take it from here.'

'Thank you, Emma,' said Nesta. 'Once he has completed his task, perhaps you can find him a cot until the storm subsides.'

'Aye, that I will,' said Emma as she knelt on the floor alongside the boy's chair. She placed the tray on the table at his side.

'You are in luck,' she said gently. 'There was a fresh pot of chicken stew on the fire for the staff's supper. Now, eat up but be careful, it is a bit hot.'

'Thank you, miss,' said the boy and, foregoing the spoon, he lifted the bowl to his lips, blowing it gently before taking a sip of the warming stew.

'It's a fair stew, my lady,' he said after the first few mouthfuls.

'Good, now take your time and dip some of that bread into the juice. We'll have you warm before you know it.'

The doors opened again and Sir Gerald of Windsor walked into the room, closely followed by John of Salisbury.

'I hear there is a message for me,' said the castellan, striding across the hall.

'Indeed,' said Nesta, walking across to greet her imposing husband, 'but first, let me take your cloak.' She undid the ties around his chest and handed the garment to Emma, who exchanged it for a goblet of wine. Gerald emptied the goblet in one draft and handed it to Salisbury. The constable was annoyed to be used as no more than a mere servant but comforted himself with the knowledge he had already tasted and spat out the very same wine now circulating in the castellan's gut.

'So where is he?' asked Gerald, looking around the room. 'I still have business to attend.'

'Here, my lord,' said the boy, standing up from the chair. He bowed slightly and clutching at the cloak with one hand to keep it closed, reached for the leather saddlebag on the floor beside the chair. Salisbury strode forward and snatched the bag from him before delving inside and retrieving a note contained in a leather pouch. The pouch was sealed with the seal of the king.

'Where has this come from?' asked Gerald looking at the pouch. 'Surely you haven't ridden all the way from Windsor?'

'No, my lord, but several of these were delivered to Carmarthen two days ago and have been sent out to all the castellans of Deheubarth. I was instructed to deliver this with all haste and to stop for neither food nor ale.'

Gerald took a blade from his belt and cut the bindings along with the wax before retrieving the folded parchment within. Quietly he read the note and Nesta was shocked to see the colour drain from his face.

'Gerald, what is it?' she said.

'Emma, gather the staff in the lesser hall,' he replied, his voice shaking, 'there is something they should know.'

'At once, my lord,' said Emma and she ran from the hall.

'Well,' said Nesta, 'are we to wait like common servants or are you going to tell us what shocks you so?'

'Aye, I will tell you,' said Gerald. 'But the news is not good, Nesta, and you should prepare yourself for the worst.'

'Just spit it out, Gerald,' said Nesta. 'For every breath you linger makes me burn with fear.'

'Has he declared war on these God forsaken people at last?' said Salisbury. 'For if he has, I, for one, will shed no tears.'

'No,' replied Gerald, turning to stare at Salisbury, 'he has not declared war, nor is he ever going to. Our monarch has succumbed to illness. My friends, the king is dead.'

Pembroke Castle

December 8th, AD 1135

Nesta stood at the window in her quarters, staring out over the town below the castle. Her tears had long dried, and though she had lain in her bed for many hours, sleep had evaded her as she realised an important phase of her life had come to an end.

Despite her age, she knew that she was still a beautiful woman. Her dark hair, a source of pride in her younger years, was just as thick and as long as it had always been, and though the glow of youth had long gone, when she looked in the mirror these days, in its place she saw a woman who had lived an eventful life but had survived with grace, intellect and perhaps also, still, beauty.

But it had not been easy and she was in a reflective mood since having heard the news about Henry. Though it had been many years since they had been together, his death reminded her how far she had come since those days. As a young woman she had been a firebrand and, there was no doubt, a risk to the English should the native Welsh of Deheubarth have rallied in her name. The move to London after the death of her father had been the one thing that had changed the course of her life.

No longer part of Welsh society, she and the young French prince Henry had fallen deeply and madly in love. But it had soon become clear that the politics of the Crown meant she could never become his queen. The loss of Henry had been a hard time for her, not least because she had been pregnant with his child. But things had become a little easier with her marriage to Gerald of Windsor, the castellan of Pembroke. The move had helped ease the tensions between the English and Welsh of Deheubarth, her family's ancestral home.

She reflected now, as she turned to look in the mirror, that her life with Gerald had been good, although not without its troubles. It still pained her to remember the two years she had spent as a rebel with the Welsh prince Owain.

Despite this, Gerald had remained loyal to her, never giving up on her, and when she was finally rescued, reality hit home and she knew she could not live the life of a rebel. All in all, she knew that, though as a child she had seen her life differently, she was – so long as Gerald lived and loved her – the wife of an English knight.

A knock came on the door and she turned, expecting to see Emma but, surprisingly, it was her husband, Gerald.

'Can I come in?' he asked.

'Since when have you had to ask permission to enter my bedchamber?' she asked with a smile.

'I know, but this is different. I thought you may want to be alone.'

Nesta sighed deeply and walked over to her husband, placing a kiss upon his cheek. The past few years had treated them well and they had grown closer as they had grown older. It hadn't always been this good, for when she had first been rescued from Owain ap Cadwgan years earlier, the relationship between them had been cold and unyielding. However, this coldness soon thawed and when she gave birth to Gerald's second son, they had decided to try to make the relationship work, if only for political reasons and for the sake of their children. Since then they had each managed to forgive the other, and as the years had passed, a love grew between them that neither had expected.

'It is very good for you to think that way, my love,' said Nesta, 'but my relationship with the king was a very long time ago. My tears are for my son, only, for he has lost his father.'

'Still, you must have had feelings for Henry when you were with him?'

'Remember, he was not the king at the time and we were both very young and without fear and thought of consequence.'

'Have you heard from young Henry?'

'Not for a while. The last I heard he was in London so I expect he is fully aware of his father's fate. I just hope he doesn't get caught up in any political manoeuvring as the scramble for the throne begins.' Nesta walked over to her bed and picked up a hairbrush, drawing it slowly through her long thick hair as she stared unseeingly into the mirror fixed on the wall panelling.

'What makes you think there will be manoeuvring?' asked Gerald, walking over to the table to pour himself a drink. 'Henry has made it clear that his daughter is his heir and will reign as queen.'

'A woman on the throne of England?' said Nesta with a laugh. 'Can you really imagine such a thing? I don't think any baron worth his salt will allow it to happen – despite the sworn oaths. No, Matilda may be a formidable woman, Gerald, but I can't see her ever being queen.'

Gerald walked over to the door and slid across the bolt. 'Perhaps your son may have a claim.'

'No, he doesn't have a powerbase. Whoever it is going to be will need the support of the church, a will of iron and an army to back him up.'

Gerald sat on the bed beside Nesta. He took the brush from her hand and proceeded to brush her hair for her, each stroke slow and considered.

'What will become of us, Gerald?' she asked quietly. 'You were Henry's favoured knight. With him gone his successor may not see you in the same light. Is there a chance we may be in danger?'

'I do not know the answer,' said Gerald. 'But I will say this. Any new monarch can ill afford to estrange any of his castellans or barons, and to do so invites open rebellion. We should sit tight and let the dice fall where they will. When the new king or queen is crowned, I will make representations to avow our loyalty. Hopefully, we should see no difference to our situation.'

'I hope not, Gerald,' said Nesta, 'for, if truth be told, I don't think I have ever been as happy as I have been these past few years.'

Gerald smiled. He felt the same and had long forgiven Nesta for the two years she had spent with Owain. After all, she was still the mother of his children.

'Nor I,' said Gerald and he kissed her gently on the back of the neck.

Nesta twisted her head around to return the affection, but as she did, a loud knock came on the door, interrupting the intimate moment. With a laugh of resignation, Gerald called, 'Who is it?'

'My lord, it is Emma. I have an urgent message for you.'

'Can it not wait?'

'No, my lord.'

With a sigh Gerald turned back to Nesta. 'I'm sorry, my love, I don't think we are meant to have peace this day, the world is too busy sending messages.'

'See to it, Gerald,' she said. 'I am going nowhere.'

The castellan walked over to the door and threw back the bolt. Emma stood outside, her face ashen.

'Emma, you look shaken,' said Gerald. 'What worries you so?'

Before she could answer, Emma burst into tears and Gerald looked down to see a large dark stain spread across her usually spotless apron. 'Emma, is that blood?' he gasped. 'Are you hurt?'

Behind him, Nesta jumped from the bed and ran across the room. 'Emma, what have you done?'

'Fear not, my lady,' said Emma through her tears. 'The blood is not mine but there are two injured men in the stables. Their wounds are grievous and I fear one won't survive this day.'

'What do you mean injured men?' asked Gerald. 'Who are they?'

'They suffer the wounds of warfare, my lord, received defending one of your caravans from brigands. One is the son of James the Taylor. He grew up here as a boy but left to seek employ in the ranks of the garrison at Carmarthen.'

Gerald's face fell and he turned to face Nesta.

'Go,' she said, before he had time to speak, 'and do whatever it is that needs to be done. I will look after Emma.'

Gerald pushed past the maid and ran down the wooden stairs. 'You two,' he shouted as he passed the guardroom, 'come with me.' The two men inside jumped to their feet and retrieved their coifs from the table. By the time they had grabbed their swords Gerald was already down in the bailey and making his way to the stables. He strode inside, passing two grooms attending an exhausted horse. Inside he saw a group of people standing around two men lying on blankets, one of whom was being attended by the garrison priest.

The priest looked up as he approached, shaking his head gently as their eyes met. Gerald walked on and looked down at the second wounded man. Two of the castle ladies were busy washing and sewing a large wound on his torso.

'Is this the son of James the Taylor?'

'Yes, my lord,' said one of the women. 'Do you know him?'

'I knew his father well,' replied Gerald. 'Do we know what happened to him yet? Has he said anything?'

'Not yet, he is under the influence of the poppy milk and unable to answer. His arm is broken and he was in so much pain it was the only thing we could think of.'

'It looks like you are doing a fine job,' said Gerald. 'Make him as comfortable as you can. Have you sent someone for the surgeon?'

'Yes, there is a messenger riding to the village as we speak.'

Gerald nodded and beckoned one of the other women to step to one side so his next question would not be overheard. 'Tell me truthfully,' he said quietly, 'do you think this man will live?'

'Possibly, if infection doesn't set in but, alas, his comrade is beyond help.'

Gerald looked back at the other man who was being administered the last rights by the priest. He watched as the man succumbed to his injuries, before continuing. 'Listen, it is important to keep this one alive for as long as possible. I need to find out what happened and if he is the only survivor then there is no other possibility of finding out who did this. Do you understand?'

'We will try our best, my lord,' said the woman. 'Once the surgeon comes, he can set his bones properly.'

'Good, but no more poppy milk until then. I need him able to talk.'

'But . . .'

'Just do as I say,' said Gerald. 'I need him conscious.'

'Understood,' said the woman.

Gerald turned to the guard at his side. 'Have you seen the constable?'

'Not for hours, my lord.'

'Send someone to find him immediately.' He turned to speak to the second guard. 'Alert the garrison and secure the gates. I don't know if there is some sort of attack planned on the castle but I'm not taking any risks. I want every able man fully armed and manning the ramparts.'

'Aye, my lord,' said the guard, and he ran out of the stable towards the barracks.

Back in the bedchamber, Emma was sitting in Nesta's chair sipping a glass of honeyed water. Nesta knelt at her feet, holding the maid's free hand between her own.

'I know I'm being foolish, my lady,' sobbed Emma, 'for I have seen death in all its forms, but to see young Master Taylor fall from his horse with blood pouring from his wounds just caught me unawares. I was good friends with his mother and held the boy on my knee many an evening when he was a child.'

'You're not being foolish at all,' said Nesta. 'These things always hurt more when the victim is someone we know. Take your time and when you have calmed down, perhaps we will go and see how he is. Does that suit you?'

'Thank you, my lady,' said Emma. 'I'll be fine in just a few moments.'

Nesta stood and walked over to the pegs on the wall to select one of her cloaks.

'First the king,' she said quietly, 'and now this. What other horrors does this day hold?'

———

Five leagues away, a column of desperate men ran as quickly as they could through the forest, each weighed down with sacks of salted pork. Behind them, the smoke from the burning carts rose into the air, buffeted by the remnants of the storm winds. Snow, freshly laid less than a few hours earlier, now lay muddied and reddened with human blood while all around the road, victims and assailants lay side by side, each equal in death's embrace. Most of the corpses had been stripped of anything valuable, including weapons, clothing and any coin or jewellery they happened to have, and the two women who had been riding in one of the carts, lay naked in the mud, the subjects of multiple rapes and a brutal death. No one had been left alive, not even those who may have survived their wounds. There was no place for prisoners amongst the brigands, for winter was a hard mistress and they already had too many mouths to feed.

Taliesin ap John waited on the ridge, counting his men as they passed. His beard was white with frost and his wolf-skin cloak fought hard to keep out the worst of the winter winds.

Five had been killed in the ambush, including one he counted as an old friend. For a few seconds his thoughts were clouded with regret but as the last of his hungry and exhausted men struggled over the ridge, he came back to reality. Times were hard and every man operating out of the Cantref Mawr had a price on his head. This may not have been the life they would have chosen but it was better than the hangman's noose or the executioner's blade. Those outside the law had little option but to resort to desperate measures and this was such a time. Finally, the last of the column crested the ridge, and as one of the few mounted men rode past, Taliesin bid him stop.

'Tomas,' he said. 'I hear you fought well today.'

'My hungry son means there is no other way to be,' said Tomas Scar, a man named for the wound across his face.

'I understand,' said Taliesin. 'And I know you want to get back to him but first there is a task I would have you do. I will see you are well rewarded.'

Tomas nodded. Any way of earning extra food or money was always welcome. 'Name it,' he said.

'I want you to ride to the sheepfold on the hill above the Drover's Rest and leave a sack of salt-pork behind the southernmost wall.' He reached inside his cloak and retrieved a leather purse of coins, tossing it over to the other rider. 'Put this beneath the sack. It is the price agreed for the information regarding the caravan.'

Tomas weighed the purse in his hand before tucking it inside his own jerkin. 'It feels like a pretty price to pay for information,' he said.

'Coins I can steal,' replied Taliesin, 'but when hunger claws at our bellies, food is much more difficult to find. This haul will last us the best part of a month and, if truth be told, that information was worth ten times the purse agreed. Just make sure he gets every penny. I am known as a man who pays his debts and the day that reputation ends, is the day our own people turn upon us.'

'Anything else?'

'No, that is it, but take care, for Gerald will not take this attack lightly and there will likely be patrols along the road as soon as he receives the news.'

'Aye,' said Tomas.

'The rest of you,' said Taliesin, turning to the other riders, 'continue back to camp with the rest of the men. 'I will be back in two days and will ensure the share-out is equal amongst all.'

'Where are you going?' asked Tomas.

'I have business to attend to. Now, be gone and make sure you are not followed.'

Back in the castle, John Salisbury paced the floor of his own quarters. The door was locked and his mind was racing.

Since the rebellion had ended, the constable had become a powerful man in his own right and his cruelty was feared across Deheubarth. He knew that, given the opportunity and resources, he was more than able to crush any lingering Welsh defiance once and for all but his ambition was constantly tempered with the castellan's tendency for so-called fairness and justice, a trait that Salisbury saw as nothing more than weakness.

Up until now there was little he could do, but with the death of the king the rules of the game had been drastically changed. The changes in the politics of London would be seismic and, with a bit of manoeuvring, a clever man could climb the ladder of royal favour quicker than at any other time.

The opportunities were there, they had to be. Any new king would distrust old allegiances and be open to new. All he had to do was work out a way.

He looked out of his window at the castle courtyard. It was all a game to him, each person a real-life chess piece and all sacrificial in his quest for power. Power was everything to him and he wanted it all. The position, the castle, the wealth and the woman, all were there for the taking. Ah, yes, Nesta, the most beautiful yet unreachable woman he had ever set eyes on. Warm yet aloof; endearing yet majestic. Each night he dreamed of the day she would warm his bed and though he knew she thought little of him, he also knew that, one day, whether she liked it or not, it would be he that she called master, not the weakling Gerald.

Mentally exhausted, Salisbury sat down and reached for the wine jug on his table. Foregoing the tankard, he drank straight from the jug and the more he thought, the clearer his mind became. The death of King Henry was not the disaster that everyone made out, at least not for him. Indeed, it was an opportunity to be exploited and the opportunities were many and varied. He could wait for the politics to play out and make an early representation to the new monarch promoting his own skills and loyalty, but that relied on whoever was crowned holding bad feeling towards Gerald and there was no guarantee of that. No, there had to be a way to make the dice fall in his favour so that when he did make the representation, the new king would have no option but to see the sense of his argument.

Over and over he played out the different scenarios in his mind, each time coming to the conclusion that every outcome was too uncertain and each time returning to the one situation with the best hope of success.

Finally, he allowed himself to face the thought that he had avoided for the past hour. As constable, he was the natural successor to Gerald but he could never achieve that role until either the castellan was posted elsewhere or he died, leaving the position vacant.

He replaced the wine jug on the table but cursed as he knocked it over and the contents spilled across the floor. He reached down to retrieve the jug but paused as the scarlet liquid flowed across the stone slabs, as if mimicking the flow of blood from a fatally wounded enemy.

At that exact moment, Salisbury knew for certain what he must do. Gerald had to die, that much was certain, but rather than wait for events or nature to take their natural course, there was only one way to ensure the outcome was final. It needed his involvement.

Decision made, he picked up the jug and walked over to the window again. Down in the courtyard he could see the man who stood in his way. Gerald stood with one of the officers and, though Salisbury knew the castellan couldn't hear or see him, he spoke to him directly.

'Enjoy it while you can, Gerald,' he said quietly. 'Your days are coming to an end.'

Lifting the jug to his lips he drained the last of the dregs before tossing it into the fireplace to smash against the stone hearth.

There was no more time for drinking; he had plans to make.

Pembroke Castle

December 8th, AD 1135

Nesta stood alongside her husband's horse, holding the reins while he adjusted his saddle. All around the bailey, armed men carried out similar tasks as they prepared to ride from the castle in search of the brigands who had devastated the supply caravan. The smell of the animals was strong and many pawed the ground, impatient to be gone.

'Are you sure you really need to do this?' asked Nesta. 'I don't think we have seen the worst of that storm yet and you don't want to be caught in its wrath.'

'We have to,' said Gerald, tightening the girth strap, 'or the trail will be cold. This assault was the worst in years and if we don't react with the full force of the Crown's might then others may be encouraged to attack our columns. Before we know it we could be back to the days when no man could ride the road without fear of being attacked.'

'But you don't even know who they are.'

'Perhaps not, but the tailor's son told me only a few were mounted so that means they can't have got far, especially laden with their ill-gotten goods. We will ride back to the site of the attack and then hope-fully track them from there. If God is with us, we can hunt them down, retrieve our goods and be back before this storm has chance to regather its strength.'

'I hope you are right, Gerald,' said Nesta. 'It has been a long time since any of you faced a skirmish of any kind and these rebels may be desperate.'

'They are rebels in name only, Nesta,' said Gerald, 'and are no more than thugs and murderers.'

'My brother was no murderer,' said Nesta.

'I did not say that,' said Gerald. 'I am referring to this current lot that hide away like frightened rabbits. Your brother, despite his unfortunate choice to oppose the Crown, was a gentleman and a fierce warrior. If he had just embraced the king's offer of amnesty, then I would gladly have ridden alongside him as a comrade knowing my back was secure.'

'He was a proud prince of Deheubarth, Gerald, and could never have accepted the king's coin. You know that.'

'Well,' said Gerald, 'those days are far behind us now so let us move on. My men are well trained and more than a match for anyone operating out of the Cantref Mawr. Don't worry, Nesta, we will be fine. Besides, I have to get back soon as I suspect we will be summoned to London for the coronation of the new monarch – whoever that may be.'

'Just be careful, Gerald,' sighed Nesta, and she tiptoed up to kiss him on the cheek.

Gerald mounted his horse and gave the signal to his captain of the guard to open the gate. The rest of the men mounted their own horses and as one of his lieutenants led the column out through the outer palisade, the castellan stopped below the gate towers and looked up at the constable, standing on the ramparts above.

'The castle is in your hands until I return, Master Salisbury,' he shouted. 'I will hold you responsible for the safety of these walls and all who dwell within them.'

'They are in good hands, my lord,' replied Salisbury. 'God's speed and I hope you put this viper's nest to the torch.'

'Aye, we will,' said Gerald as he kicked his heels into his horse's flanks to urge her out of the castle.

'Close the gates,' called Salisbury as soon as the castellan was clear. 'Captain of the guard, attend me in the lesser hall.'

'Aye, my lord,' replied the captain.

Nesta stayed where she was until the bolts were finally thrown across the gates, before walking back to the motte.

'My lady,' said a voice, and she turned to see Salisbury striding up behind her.

'Master Salisbury, it seems my husband has placed a great responsibility upon your shoulders. I hope you are up to it.'

'Worry not for your safety, my lady,' said Salisbury. 'The time of Gwenllian terrorising the roads from here to Ceredigion are long gone. These men who claim the title of rebels in her memory are no more than an irritation in comparison. Your husband is more than capable of dealing with their threat and, until he returns, I will personally ensure nothing untoward befalls your person.'

'I am quite sure that eventuality is not going to come to pass,' said Nesta. 'I was thinking more of you keeping the rest of the garrison alert and engaged while the castellan is away.'

'Such things are not for the minds of ladies,' said Salisbury, 'especially those as pretty as you, but if you are concerned as to my suitability, perhaps I could allay your fears over the evening meal tomorrow evening?'

'Thank you, Master Salisbury, but I will be dining alone while my husband is away.'

'Nonsense,' said Salisbury. 'It would be very rude of me to allow such a thing. So, as the host of this castle, I'm afraid I must insist.'

Nesta's eyes narrowed in suspicion. 'Master Salisbury, may I remind you that my husband is still castellan of this place and by implication that means that I, as his lady, am the official host here. If there are any feasts or celebrations of any kind to be arranged, then it is I who will be the one to instigate them.'

'Ah,' said Salisbury. 'Ordinarily that would indeed be the case, but I think you will find that in times of conflict, military law overrides the quaint customs of courtesy, and outright command goes to the senior officer present. As your husband has now vacated the castle, that means I am now in charge.' He gave a smile that sent chills deep into Nesta's heart. 'So,' he continued, 'I will arrange the evening meal to be served in the main hall tomorrow evening. You and the rest of the ladies will attend, and we will toast the health and life of your husband.'

Without waiting for an answer, Salisbury bounded up the steps, leaving Nesta staring at his back. His very presence made her skin crawl and she feared that the next few days were going to be particularly unpleasant.

Llandeilo Manor

December 9th, AD 1135

Carwyn and one of the manor grooms walked along a line of horses outside the stables, inspecting the teeth and hooves of each animal as they passed. The groom ran his hands along their sides and pressed his fingers into the muscle mass at the top of their legs, judging the strengths and weaknesses of each animal. Behind them followed a scribe, noting down any comments they made. To one side stood the selling merchant, waiting nervously to see how many of his animals would pass the stringent inspection. When he had finished, Carwyn, the groom and the scribe talked quietly amongst themselves before the steward finally walked over to the merchant.

'Master Trystan,' he said. 'We seem to have a mixed bag here.'

'In what way?' asked the merchant, instantly on the defensive. 'I can assure you they are all well bred and some even have battle experience.'

'I can well believe it,' said Carwyn. 'But we are both busy men so let's not waste time in haggling. I will make you an offer and one offer only. If it is not to your liking, you are free to leave.'

'That puts me in a very unfortunate position,' said the merchant.

'We are not brigands, Master Trystan, and the offer will be fair. However, it is obvious some of these beasts are not up to the standard we expect.' He turned to the scribe. 'Please share our findings.'

'My lord,' said the scribe. 'Of the twenty-one animals, thirteen are good and another four can be expected to be returned to good health. However, a further three are lame and one is fit only as meat for the dogs. In all, I judge the true value to be no more than two thirds of the asking price.'

'Two thirds,' snapped the merchant. 'That is daylight robbery.'

'It is a fair offer,' said Carwyn. 'Take it or leave it.'

The merchant stared at the steward, trying to see if he was bluffing, but saw only steadfastness.

'I will take the offer,' he said. 'But I will take the matter up with Lord Bevan the next time we meet.'

'You are free to do so,' said Carwyn, looking over to the other side of the courtyard where his wife was talking with one of his sons. 'Now if you will excuse me, I have other matters to attend to. Please arrange the transaction with the purser – my scribe will take you to him shortly.'

'Of course,' said the merchant, but Carwyn was already walking away.

'Branwen,' he said as he neared his wife. 'Is there a problem?'

'I'm not sure,' said Branwen. 'I sent Maelgwyn to ask Morgan if he would dine with us this evening but he says he is not here.'

'What do you mean, not here?' asked Carwyn, turning to his son.

'I went to the barracks,' said Maelgwyn, 'but they said he left the manor several days ago.'

'Where has he gone?'

'No one knows,' said Maelgwyn.

'Has his horse gone?'

'I am unsure. Perhaps we should check.'

Carwyn turned and saw the groom still by the newly acquired horses. 'Master James, attend me,' he called.

The groom turned and ran across the courtyard. He looked nervously between the steward and his wife.

'Is my son's horse still in the stable, Master James?'

'Which son?' asked James.

'Morgan.'

'No,' said James. 'He took his horse not three days since. I thought you knew?'

'No,' said Carwyn. 'Do you know where he has gone?'

'He didn't say, though he took enough grain to feed his horse for three days.'

'Where could he possibly be going that will take three days?' asked Branwen.

Carwyn turned to Maelgwyn. 'You saw him last. Did he say anything about going anywhere?'

'Not that I recall,' said Maelgwyn. 'We spent most of the night talking about the rebels in the Cantref Mawr.'

Carwyn stared at his son, realising the hotbed of rebels and brigands was almost exactly three day's ride away. 'What did he say exactly?' snapped Carwyn, grabbing his son's arm. 'Think hard.'

'Many things – but he had drunk a lot of ale and I thought he was jesting.'

'About what.'

'About joining the rebels!'

Back in Pembroke, Gerald's column had made good progress in pursuit of the brigands who had ambushed the caravan. The break in the weather meant the tracks in the snow were still visible and, though the perpetrators had a few days' head start, it soon became obvious that most were on foot and were making slow progress. Encouraged, Gerald pushed his riders harder until soon his scouts returned to tell him there was an encampment no more than a few leagues northward.

'Is it the men we seek?' asked Gerald.

'Aye, it is,' said the lead scout.

'Are you sure?'

'Well, their camp fires spit from the fat of salt-beef and, unless there is a surplus of such treasures in these parts, I suggest it is the cargo from the caravan.'

'Noted,' said Gerald. He looked up at the sky. 'It will be dark soon so we'll make camp here for tonight.' He turned to his second in command. 'Sergeant-at-arms, get the men under cover but I want them ready to move before dawn's first light.'

'What about the brigands?' replied the sergeant. 'Are they not at our mercy?'

'Perhaps so but we have ridden our horses hard and I want them well rested for the assault. Besides, if our quarry are so engrossed in their ill-gotten gains, I suspect they will not be headed anywhere anytime soon.'

'Understood,' said the sergeant, as Gerald turned to the scouts.

'You have done well,' said Gerald, 'but I want you to return to the enemy camp and set up a watch. I want to be briefed about everything there is to know: strength, armaments, routes in and routes out. Make sure you are not seen and report back to me at midnight so we have time to set our plans.'

'Aye, my lord,' said one of the scouts. 'We'll just feed our horses and be on our way.'

Gerald nodded and turned to join the rest of the column now dispersing into the trees at either side of the road. 'No fires,' he called as he dismounted. 'Tonight we will eat biscuit only. Let's not give anyone the opportunity to know we are here.' He walked his horse between the trees before finding two that were of a suitable distance apart to suspend his canopy for the night. It would not be windproof but it would keep off the worst of the weather should it turn bad.

'My lord,' said a voice. 'Can I help?'

Gerald looked over at one of the younger archers who was standing to one side.

'Do you not have your own shelter to build?' he asked.

'Aye, but I'm sharing with two others and too many hands make a muddle. Usually I would be making the fire but as that is not necessary, my hands are spare.'

Gerald nodded and rolled out the waxed blanket on the snowy forest floor.

'Take that rope,' he said, 'and tie it at head height around that tree.'

The archer removed his arrow bag from his waistband and placed it against a tree along with his unstrung bow. Taking the far rope, he did as he was instructed and waited as Gerald did the same on the opposite end. When the ridge of the cover was taut, they spread out the other three lengths of rope along each side and drove wooden pegs into the ground to form a rudimentary shelter.

'That will do,' said Gerald.

'Is there anything else, my lord?' asked the archer.

Gerald paused and looked at the young man. He couldn't be more than sixteen years old but the muscles in his right shoulder and forearm bore testament to the fact he had been taught the art of the bow from a very early age.

'What is your name, boy?' he asked.

'Colin, my lord. Colin of Monmouth.'

'Well, Colin of Monmouth, you could take my mount over to the horse master and see she is taken care of.'

'Of course,' said the boy. 'Thank you, my lord.'

'Off you go,' said Gerald. 'I'll be watching you from now on.'

The boy beamed and walked away to Gerald's horse.

'Wait,' shouted a voice and Gerald turned to see the sergeant-at-arms striding from amongst the trees.

The boy froze and stared at the frightening warrior.

'You,' continued the sergeant. 'Your name is Colin, is it not?'

'Aye, my lord,' said Colin.

'And what is your role amongst my men?'

The boy stared at the sergeant-at-arms in confusion. The sergeant knew full well what his role was, as he did with every man under his command.

'Archer, my lord.'

'Is it?' asked the sergeant.

'Yes, my lord.'

'Then where is your weapon?' snarled the sergeant.

The boy's hand went to his shoulder before realising it was still against the tree. He gulped hard and stared at the sergeant.

'My lord, I was . . .'

'I know what you was doing,' replied the sergeant, 'but who gave you permission to abandon your bow? Was it the master here?'

'N-no,' stuttered the boy, 'I just thought . . .'

'We are on campaign, Colin of Monmouth, and I should have you whipped for your stupidity.'

'My lord,' said the boy, his eyes darting between the sergeant and Gerald, 'my apologies, it will not happen again.'

'No, it won't,' said the sergeant, picking up the boy's bow and arrow-bag. He tossed them over to land in the snow before him. 'Pick them up,' he said, 'and henceforth they will never leave your side until you are stood down within the walls of Pembroke. Understood?'

'Yes, my lord,' said the boy.

'Make sure you do for if you are seen without your weapon again, I will have the hide from your back. Now be gone and make sure your aim is good on the morrow.'

'Thank you, my lord,' said the boy, and he ran into the trees. The sergeant watched him go and turned back towards Gerald.

'A bit harsh, methinks,' laughed Gerald. 'He was only helping his master.'

'There is no room on campaign for stupidity,' said the sergeant, 'as you well know. You have my gratitude for not contradicting my admonishment.'

'I am not about to undermine your role, Sergeant, especially on the eve of battle.' He reached to his belt and retrieved his leather flask. 'Wine?'

'Not yet, my lord, I have things to do. I have just come over to check your plans for the morrow. Is there a strategy I need to know?'

'Not as yet. I intend to approach the enemy camp under the cover of darkness and be in place by dawn but, as far as the details are concerned, we have to wait for the scouts' reports. How do we fare with the men?'

'The men are fine,' said the sergeant, 'but the horses, less so.'

'What do you mean?'

'There are over a dozen with leg strains or hoof problems. They will have to stay here.'

'I suppose that's what comes from riding through the undergrowth for so long. It matters not. We will be approaching on foot so the horses will have a chance to rest before the journey back.'

The sergeant was about to respond when a noise from the forest made them both turn and reach for their swords. Two men burst from the trees pulling a third between them. The prisoner managed to drag himself free from one of the captors but was knocked to the floor with a mailed fist before he could escape. A kick followed the punch and the prisoner fell into the mud, his nose pouring with blood.

'Who's this?' demanded the sergeant.

'My lord,' said one of the men, 'we were posted as rear guard and saw this man following us through the forest. We hid away and waited to see if he was alone before taking him prisoner.'

'And was he?' asked Gerald.

'Aye, my lord,' said the soldier. 'He's obviously a spy so we brought him straight here so you could question him.'

The sergeant walked over and placed his foot under the wounded man's chin. He lifted it up and stared into the prisoner's eyes. 'Who are you?' he asked. 'And why are you following us?'

The man pulled his head away and spat a mouthful of blood onto the floor before answering. 'My lord,' he gasped. 'I am no spy. I am just an honest man looking for work.'

'Liar,' snarled one of the guards. 'He was trying not to be seen but we spotted him through the trees. Do you want us to beat the truth out of him?'

'No,' said Gerald before the sergeant could answer. 'Take him to the supply carts and tie him securely. Sergeant, stand to the men. The last thing we need now is to be caught unawares.'

'Aye, my lord,' said the sergeant, and he drew his dagger from his belt. He grabbed the man by the hair and dragged him to his feet. 'You come with us,' he snarled, 'and the slightest step out of place will see my blade in your heart, understood?'

'Understood,' said the young man, the fear evident on his face.

'Good. Now start walking.'

The atmosphere was tense for the next few hours as the column adopted defensive positions around their horses. The silence was total as men peered through the trees, expecting an assault at any moment. One of the sergeants walked quietly between each position, checking his men stayed alert and whispering encouragement to those new to campaigning. When he was done, he returned to the brow of a slope that overlooked a vast wooded valley below.

'See anything?' he asked quietly as he dropped beside the two men lying amongst the undergrowth.

'Not a thing,' said one of the young men.

'Well, keep watching,' said the sergeant. 'Heaven knows what those trees conceal.'

'Is that the Cantref Mawr, Sergeant?' asked one.

'The Cantref Mawr is all around us,' said the sergeant, 'and is no more than a lair for filthy murderers.' He pointed down the slope to the treetops stretching away before them. 'That valley there was the black heart of the rebel's hideout when I was your age so make sure you don't fall asleep. I would wager a month's wages there are brigands behind every tree.'

'Did you ever go down there?'

'Aye, on many occasions, but we never found anyone. Oh there were camps and smouldering campfires aplenty but any rebels had always long gone by the time we arrived.'

'How did they know you were coming?'

'Some people say they had spies everywhere but others said that they were led by a witch.'

'Gwenllian?'

'Aye, that was her, but she was no witch, lad. She was a warrior and, though it hurts me to say it, her skills in battle were as good as any man.'

'You saw her fight?'

'I did, once, and thank the lord that it was from a distance.'

'What happened?'

'I was a guard on a caravan bringing weapons to Pembroke when we were attacked by a column of rebels led by Gwenllian, and I'm not talking about the sort of men we seek now – peasants and murder-ers – but real men, hardened from battle and each fighting for their country. They were well-trained, fierce warriors but more than that, they fought for their leader, a woman who led from the front with sword in hand. Nobody could match her and, though our numbers were strong, the mere sight of her was often enough to affect a man's judgement. She struck ice-cold fear deep into the heart of any man laying eyes upon her.'

'I heard her ghost still haunts these forests?' said the young man looking around nervously.

'It's not the dead you should be worrying about, lad, but the living. You just keep your eyes fixed on those trees down there in case anything moves.'

'But what if it's true?' asked the other man. 'What if she is still alive and waiting to come back to kill us all?'

'Trust me,' said the sergeant, getting to his feet, 'if she was alive, you'd already have a bloody smile from here to here.' He drew his hand slowly across his own throat before turning away and heading back down the slope, leaving two scared but wide-awake foot soldiers behind him.

———

Eventually the tension eased and when a patrol returned to report the area clear Gerald allowed every second man to stand down before bidding the sergeant to bring him the prisoner.

The sergeant ordered two men to drag the captive from a cart and forced him into the clearing to stand before the castellan. Gerald stared at the prisoner for a while, his eyes narrowing momentarily as he saw something in the boy's face.

'Have we ever met?' Gerald asked eventually.

'I don't think so, my lord,' said the prisoner. 'I am just a poor man out to seek work. I have never been this way before.'

'Hmmm,' said Gerald, staring into the man's eyes. 'For a second there you reminded me of someone but the name escapes me. Anyway, enough of such things. Whether you are known to me or not, it seems you have been caught in the act of spying. So, I am going to ask you some questions and you are going to tell me the truth. If I suspect you are holding anything back, I will allow the sergeant here to beat you to death. Understood?'

'Yes, my lord,' said the young man.

'Good, let's start with your name.'

'Geraint, my lord. I am a farmer's son from Llandeilo.'

'Why were you following us?'

'I did not know who you were, my lord, and just thought I had come across a merchant's caravan. I was hoping I could join it, at least until we cleared the forest.'

'Why?'

'This place is known as a refuge to brigands and I thought I would be safer with other travellers.'

'Where are you headed?'

'Ceredigion.'

'Why?'

'To look for work. I have been told there is good farming on the west coast and strong farmhands are in short supply.'

'Where are your family?'

'All dead, my lord. They fell to the ague not two months since and I have not been able to find work.'

Gerald fell silent and stared at the young man. His story was plausible enough but any spy worth his salt would have a believable tale ready to be told in situations like this. He walked a few yards away before stopping and turning back to face him.

'So what did you see of my men?'

'Nothing, my lord. I was too far away. If you let me go, I will return the way I came and will say nothing to anyone.'

'Hmm,' said Gerald. He motioned to one of the soldiers in the clearing. 'Give me your sword.'

The soldier looked at the castellan in confusion but did as he was told.

Gerald turned and without warning, threw the sword over to the young man.

Geraint reached out and caught the sword without thinking as Gerald drew his own weapon.

'Defend yourself,' snapped Gerald and stepped forward into the attack.

Geraint had no time to think and lifted his sword to deflect the castellan's assault. The blows came quickly but each time he managed to block them with moves of his own. Eventually the castellan stepped back and stared at the boy but this time there was malice in his eyes.

'Did you see that, Sergeant?' he asked over his shoulder.

'Aye, my lord, I did. The boy handles a sword like no farm labourer I ever knew.'

'My thoughts exactly,' said Gerald. 'He has had training of sorts and that says to me that he is not who he says he is.'

Geraint gulped and knew he had been out manoeuvred. He looked around the clearing, frantically seeking an escape route but saw it was useless. He was surrounded by armed men.

'Drop the sword,' said Gerald quietly, 'and I might yet let you live.'

'You don't understand,' said the young man. 'I have had some training, I admit, but it was from my father.'

'Drop the sword,' said Gerald again.

The boy's face showed panic and he stepped towards Gerald.

'*Archers,*' roared the sergeant and six bows strained back, each aimed at Geraint's heart.

'Don't do anything stupid,' said Gerald. 'Now, for the last time, drop the sword and we will talk.'

The boy's hand opened and the weapon dropped to the floor.

'Soldier, retrieve your weapon,' said Gerald.

The soldier walked over to pick up the sword but as he bent over, the captive grabbed him and spun him around as a human shield against the archers. Before anyone could react, he drew the soldier's own knife from his belt and held it against his prisoner's throat.

'Stand back,' he roared, 'or I swear I'll cut his throat.'

For a few seconds there was silence and everyone stared at the young man, knowing he had nowhere to run. Geraint started to walk backward, dragging his hostage with him.

'Don't be stupid, boy,' said Gerald. 'How far do you think you will get?'

'Far enough,' said Geraint. 'Don't try anything or this man dies.'

Again there was silence but seconds later it was broken by the unmistakable sound of a heavy blade being drawn from its sheath. Everyone turned to see the sergeant-at-arms walking forward with his sword hanging loosely from his fist.

'Stand back,' shouted Geraint again. 'Or this man dies.'

'Go ahead,' said the sergeant coldly without breaking his stride. 'He is one man and matters not to me. You, on the other hand, are not going anywhere.'

Geraint panicked and in his moment of hesitation, his hostage broke free, leaving him isolated in the centre of the clearing. Knowing he had been bettered, Geraint threw away his knife and dropped to his knees. 'Please, my lord,' he said, 'have mercy. I swear I am no spy but acted only through fear.'

The sergeant placed his sword under the young man's chin and lifted his head.

'You are very close to dying, boy,' snarled the soldier, 'unless you tell me the truth, right here, right now. Who are you and where are you from?'

'My name is not Geraint, my lord,' gasped the young man as the point of the blade nicked the skin on his throat. 'It's Morgan ap Carwyn and I am the son of the steward of Llandeilo Manor.'

The Cantref Mawr

December 15th, AD 1135

Carwyn and Maelgwyn sat at their campfire deep in the centre of the Cantref Mawr. Behind them, their horses were tethered to a tree, both draped in heavy blankets against the cold. Each animal had a nosebag and a leather bucket of water lay between them.

The past few days had been hard going for Carwyn and Maelgwyn, and they had been forced to seek shelter in a crofter's shack until the remnants of the storm blew itself out, but at last the worst had passed and with a clear sky above they had finally made some good ground.

Carwyn leaned over and stirred the embers before nodding towards Maelgwyn, the unspoken signal that the fire was ready. Maelgwyn lifted the small cooking-pot containing the melted snow and the diced salt-pork and placed it over the flames, suspending it safely from the iron tripod they had brought along with them.

'How long will this take?' asked Maelgwyn.

'A couple of hours,' said Carwyn, throwing in a handful of salt.

'A couple of hours? I'll be dead of hunger by then.'

Carwyn smiled and added in a chopped beet along with a large onion.

'Trust me,' he said, 'it will be worth it. In an hour or so, remind me to add some oats, it'll thicken the stew.' He picked up his blade and gently stirred the pot before retreating to sit on his blanket beneath a tree.

'Father,' said Maelgwyn, dropping onto his own blanket, 'there are still a few hours of daylight left, shouldn't we press on?'

'Pushing too hard kills many men,' said Carwyn. 'Especially in this weather. A few hours' rest and a hot meal in our bellies will ensure we will travel well tomorrow. We wouldn't get much further today anyway. I recognise this place and the path gets much harder once we are over this hill.'

'You have been here before?'

'I have.'

'When?'

'In my younger days,' said Carwyn. 'It is a time I would rather forget.'

Maelgwyn stared at him. On occasion, he had overheard his father and mother talking quietly between themselves and had often heard vague references to their early lives together, but whenever he or any of his brothers had enquired further, they had been given short shrift and the conversation was always changed. Despite this, it had become clear that his parents had a past they would rather remained secret and though it was never discussed openly, the brothers reckoned that their parents had once been involved with the rebels. Maelgwyn looked across at Carwyn, frustrated that his father felt he could not trust his own sons. In a moment of madness, he decided he would push his luck.

'Do you think we are close?' he asked.

'To where?'

'To the rebel camp.'

Carwyn stared at his son.

'What makes you think we are going to the rebel camp?'

'Oh, come on, Father,' said Maelgwyn. 'Can we not end this pretence? Why is it I am deemed man enough to accompany you in the pursuit of my brother yet when it comes to the detail, I am treated no better than an untrustworthy child? It is obvious we are seeking the rebel camp, for where else could Morgan possibly go to join them? What interests me is how you know where to look?'

'There are things better left unknown,' said Carwyn.

'But why? What is it you have done that is so bad? Is it because you were once a rebel yourself or is it because perhaps you have killed men? Either way, why do you keep it to yourself, for neither I nor my brothers will judge you? On the contrary, our respect would increase manyfold if such was the case.'

'Causing the death of any man can never increase respect,' said Carwyn. 'No matter what the reason.'

'Even if caused when fighting for the freedom of a people?'

Carwyn remained silent.

'Father,' continued Maelgwyn, determined to press the point, 'I am a man in a man's world. If you respect me, surely I should know the truth.'

Carwyn sighed and looked up at his son. 'Yes,' he said eventually, 'you should. There are things that are better left unsaid but at least you should know about my past. The truth is, I did ride with the rebels for many years, as did your mother.'

'My mother was a rebel?' gasped Maelgwyn.

'She was,' said Carwyn, 'as were many women. We did not differentiate and as long as someone could fight and ride they were welcome and our group was feared from Ceredigion to Brycheniog.'

'What happened?' asked Maelgwyn, leaning forward.

'The rebellion died away,' said Carwyn. 'After they found Tarw's body at the base of a cliff, his wife disappeared and the heart was ripped from those who had followed her without question. Without Gwenllian at their head, the rebels were nothing. The English started fighting back, and with our children at risk, your mother and I fled the Cantref Mawr to find somewhere safe to raise our family. Through our family's links,

I found work with the Lord of Llandeilo. I worked hard on his estate and a few years later managed to achieve the position I now hold. There, now you know.'

Maelgwyn sat back thoughtfully. 'I seem to recall a lot of different homes when I was a boy and many times when you were away for long periods of time.'

'Yes, we had to be on the move constantly and often you and your brothers were left in safe houses. That is no way to bring up a family so we made the decision to stop.'

'Wait,' said Maelgwyn. 'If I remember such things then surely Morgan has more recollection than I?'

'Morgan is fully aware of our history,' said Carwyn. 'And that is why he feels so much affinity with the rebel cause. It is as if he feels there is unfinished business.'

'He knows you were once rebels?'

'He does.'

'He never once revealed that information,' said Maelgwyn quietly, 'but carried it as his own secret.'

'I would say, more like an unwanted burden,' said Carwyn. 'That's why he had to move out into the soldiers' quarters, he was always so opinionated and critical of why we abandoned the cause.'

'Do you regret leaving the rebels?' asked Maelgwyn.

Carwyn remained silent, just staring over at the flames of the fire.

'You do, don't you?' said Maelgwyn. 'You were fighting for something you believed in yet had to give it up for the safety of your sons. No wonder you hold a grudge.'

Carwyn's head spun around to face Maelgwyn. 'No,' he snapped. 'Don't you ever think I hold a grudge against you and your brothers. The truth is I would give up anything for you, even my life. Yes, I feel there are still things we should do to stop the English from devouring our lands but until all my sons reach the age to make their own decisions, I will do nothing to risk our family. A life of rebellion is harder than you could ever imagine and, with the English now spread across Deheubarth like a bloody stain, there is no way we could ever regain the strength and power we need to make a difference. That's why we must find your brother as soon as possible. He chases a dream, Maelgwyn, those days are over.'

Silence fell again. Maelgwyn walked over to the fire and stirred the pot, his mind deep in thought.

'So, did you know him?' he said eventually.

'Know who?'

'Tarw, the rebel prince.'

'Aye,' said Carwyn. 'I knew him.'

'What was he like?'

'Opinionated. Passionate about his country's freedom, yet deeply flawed.'

'In what way?'

'He thought he could do it all,' said Carwyn, 'and often wouldn't listen to those who knew better until the day it cost him the life of his brother.'

'I didn't know he had a brother?'

'Aye, a man called Hywel and he hated the English more than any man I ever met.'

Maelgwyn returned to his place on his sleeping blanket. 'Why did he hate them so much?'

'Because he had been their prisoner since a little boy, suffering brutality and mutilation at their hands. When he was finally freed he took it upon himself to pay back the horrors with interest. No man English born was safe.'

'So what happened?'

'The Prince sent him to his death, that's what happened.'

'How?'

'By not listening to his peers. He sent him on a mission deep into the heart of English territory against the advice of men who knew better.

Three days later they found his head atop a spike at Poor-man's bridge. Anyway, enough talk. Go and collect some more wood for the fire.'

Maelgwyn stared at his father again. The way he had brought the conversation to an abrupt end signalled that he would talk no more. Still, Maelgwyn was satisfied for it was more detail than his father had ever shared before about his past. It wasn't much, but it was a start. He got to his feet and pulled his cloak tighter about him before walking into the trees.

'Don't go too far,' called Carwyn, 'and make sure the wood is as dry as you can.'

Maelgwyn grunted a reply and looked up the small slope. The trees looked thicker there and any deadfall should be better protected from the weather. Quickly he walked up the hill until it flattened out at the top. He walked further into the trees, tossing whatever wood he could find into small piles for collection on the way back but hadn't gone far when something caught his eye through the trees.

Carefully he walked forward, coming to a halt and staring in horror as the terrible sight became clear. Hanging from the trees were the bodies of dozens of men and women, each with their hands tied behind their back. Some were stripped naked and bore the evidence of having been beaten before they were hanged while others dangled above blood-stained snow, their wounds frozen open in a graphic display of brutality.

Maelgwyn looked at a pile of frozen bodies near a fallen tree trunk and was horrified to see each had been decapitated. He walked over and found the head of each corpse lying scattered on the other side of the log, their sightless eyes staring accusingly as if it was he who had wielded the blade. The scene was devastating and for several minutes, Maelgwyn looked around the site of the slaughter, his heart racing. At last, he started to retrace his steps back to his father and as he left the clearing, he began to run, all thoughts of firewood forgotten.

Back in Llandeilo Manor, Branwen sat at the table in her house, feeding the two youngest of her four sons. Despite them both being of an age where she needed eyes in the back of her head to keep them out of mischief, she couldn't help but be distracted. Her husband had been gone for days, for as soon as he had found out about Morgan's intentions he had immediately gone after him, knowing full well that the life of a rebel held only heartache and pain. Maelgwyn had insisted on joining his father, and it was only when he swore he would set out on his own if denied the chance that Carwyn had relented and allowed him to go. Since then there had been no word and with every day that passed, Branwen became more and more worried. Having once ridden as a rebel herself, she knew only too well the steeliness and commitment needed just to survive in the forests, and that was without the skills at arms needed if it came to a fight. She had seen many men die over the years and as most were far better with a sword than any of her sons, she couldn't help but fear for their safety.

She finished feeding the youngest boy and placed him on the floor to play, when a knock came on the door and one of the manor servants walked in.

'My lady,' she said, with a bow of her head, 'Lord Bevan wants to know if the steward has returned yet, and if so, could he attend him immediately?'

'Master Carwyn is still away,' said Branwen, wiping her hands on a linen cloth.

'Is he due back anytime soon?'

'I have no idea,' said Branwen. 'What is so urgent that demands his presence?'

'I know not, my lady, but Lord Bevan paces the floor like an expectant father.'

Branwen stared at the servant, knowing it was unlike the lord to get so stressed without good cause, and it was even more rare for him to summon her husband at so short notice.

'Could you look after the boys for a while, Gwyneth?' said Branwen. 'I will return as soon as possible.'

'Where are you going?' asked the servant.

'To see Lord Bevan. Perhaps there is something I can do to ease his manner.' She pulled a shawl around her shoulders and left the house to run across the courtyard, entering the manor through a side door near the kitchens. Inside, one of the serving girls curtsied as she passed, her face red from worry.

'Where is the master?' asked Branwen.

'In his chambers, my lady, but he is in no mood for visitors.'

'Thank you,' said Branwen, and she pressed on. Moments later she ran up a wide stairway and stood outside the door to the lord's private rooms.

'My lord,' she said, knocking on the door, 'it's Branwen. Can I come in?'

For a few moments there was silence but then she heard someone walking across to open the door.

'Branwen,' said Bevan from across the room as a page opened the door, 'come in. Is your husband with you?'

'No,' said Branwen, 'but I heard you are of a troubled mind. Perhaps I can help.'

'I doubt it,' said Bevan with a sigh, 'but your opinion is always welcome. Please, take a seat, I will get us a drink.'

Branwen walked into the room and was surprised how warm it was. She removed her shawl and sat on the offered chair.

'It's like a summer's day in here,' she said, looking at the roaring fire in the hearth.

'Aye, but not as hot as my mood, you will find.'

'So I have heard,' said Branwen, glancing over to the page standing silently in the corner. 'Is it something you wish to discuss?'

Bevan also looked over to the boy. 'You,' he said, 'be gone and see that we are not disturbed.'

'Yes, my lord,' said the boy. He ran from the room, closing the door behind him. Bevan locked the door and walked over to the table to pour two goblets of wine.

'At least we can now talk openly,' he said, handing her one of the drinks.

Branwen sipped her wine but noted he remained on his feet.

'So where is your husband?' continued Bevan.

'Out looking for Morgan,' she replied.

'Still no word?'

'None, and I am getting worried if truth be told.'

'It pains me to say this, Branwen, but you may have good reason to be worried.'

'Why?' asked Branwen. 'Is there something I should be aware of?'

'It may be nothing, but I have recently received worrying news. It seems that Hywel ap Maredudd has issued a call to arms to all citizens of Brycheniog.'

'Why?' asked Branwen. 'Is he under threat?'

'I don't think so, but rumours abound that there is unrest about whom Henry named as heir to his throne.'

'Matilda?'

'Aye.'

'Well it was always going to be a contentious issue but I thought Henry made his court swear an oath of loyalty to his daughter?'

'He did, but it seems the barons have rejected the pledge and seek a male to occupy the throne.'

'Why does this involve Hywel ap Maredudd? Surely he does not see himself fighting for anyone involved in the dispute?'

'No, on the contrary, he suspects that there will be a civil war between the interested parties and he gathers his forces about him to ensure the security of Brycheniog should such a thing take place.'

'Surely that is a good thing?'

'Perhaps, but there is more. There is also a whisper that if such a thing comes to pass, he may be emboldened to march against the occupying forces in the south while the Crown is divided.'

Branwen sat back in silence as she absorbed everything Bevan had just said. What he was suggesting was that one of the few remaining Welsh leaders in the south was not only planning a possible rebellion, but doing so on a scale previously unheard of – complete with a strong, well-trained army.

'And it doesn't end there,' said Bevan, dropping into his own chair. 'He has recently sent communication to all the local manors, including mine, requesting pledges of support should the time come.'

'And that is what worries you?'

'No. The request is fair enough, and you know where my loyalties lie in such matters, but the thing is, the letters of communication included the names of everyone he sent them to – everyone whom he suspected he could rely on if it comes to war.'

'*What?*' gasped Branwen, lowering her glass in astonishment.

'I know,' replied Bevan. 'All it takes is for one of those letters to fall into the wrong hands and everyone named will immediately be considered a potential enemy to the English crown.'

'How could he have been so stupid?'

'All I can think is that it was written on his behalf by a scribe without knowledge of the fragility of the political situation.'

'Still, it has the potential for serious damage.'

'Aye it does and the thing is, as steward of my estate, Carwyn will be implicated in any perceived plot. By now that letter could well be in English hands and if your husband should come into contact with anyone already in possession of this knowledge, he is in danger of being arrested and tried as a conspirator.'

The Cantref Mawr

December 16th, AD 1135

Deep in the Cantref Mawr, Carwyn and Maelgwyn rode along the narrow trails, paths known only to those who had trodden them many times before. Since leaving the site of the mass execution, Carwyn had pushed the pace, contrary to everything he had ever taught his sons, and though Maelgwyn had asked his father several times, the boy still had no idea where they were going. He looked around nervously. The trees loomed high above him and, apart from the path, the ground was a tangle of undergrowth, impossible to ride through. The forest became more claustrophobic the further they went and soon it blocked the weak winter sun, leaving them in silent, foreboding gloom, and he knew that if they were attacked now, there was nowhere to go.

'I thought you said it was dangerous to ride hard through the forests,' mumbled Maelgwyn at his father's back.

'It is,' said Carwyn, 'but this is different. Morgan is still missing and I just thank God he was not amongst those poor souls we found slaughtered. To kill so many without trial means something big is happening and we have to find out what is going on.'

'We should have buried them,' said Maelgwyn. 'If the wolves take their bodies their souls will never reach the gates of heaven.'

'You've been listening to too many old women,' said Carwyn. 'God will receive a good man's soul no matter what happens to his earthly remains.'

'So where are we headed?' asked Maelgwyn again.

'To see someone who may know what is going on.'

Maelgwyn was about to respond when a voice echoed from within the trees.

'Hold right there, strangers. Raise your hands above your heads where I can see them.'

Carwyn reined in his horse and did as he was bid.

'Do as he says,' he said over his shoulder, 'and make no sudden moves. There are probably a dozen arrows aimed at our hearts as we speak.'

Maelgwyn raised his arms and strained to see any sign of life amongst the trees.

'State your names and your business,' shouted the voice.

'My name is Carwyn of Llandeilo and this is my son, Maelgwyn. We seek the man known as Brynmore ap Owen.'

For a few seconds there was silence until the voice spoke again.

'Even if there was someone of that name, how do I know you are not a spy or an assassin sent here by the English to slit our throats in our sleep?'

'Just tell him that the steward of Llandeilo Manor is here and he will vouch for me.'

A man stepped out from the undergrowth and walked towards the father and son.

'Dismount,' he said. 'Sit over there against that rock. See to your horses but leave your weapons here.'

Carwyn nodded and lowered his hands.

'Do as he says, Maelgwyn,' he said, 'and remove your sword belt.'

Maelgwyn's heart was racing. The warrior making the demands was wrapped in a heavy wolf-skin and across his arms, cradled like a newborn babe, lay a gleaming curved scimitar, ready for instant use. His hair fell matted around his shoulders, merging seamlessly with his tangled beard, and his weather-beaten face was testament to a life of hard living.

'See anything that interests you, boy?' asked the man coldly.

'Sorry,' stuttered Maelgwyn. 'I was only . . .'

'Just do as you are told and my blade here will go thirsty for yet another day, but cause me the slightest of doubt and she will taste your blood before you have time to think. Understood?'

'Aye,' said Maelgwyn with a gulp and he followed his father over to the rock. 'Who is he?' he whispered as they both turned and looked at the rest of the men now appearing from the trees.'

'If I'm not mistaken, he is called Dog,' said Carwyn. 'A more vicious killer never walked these lands.'

'Where is he from?'

'Nobody knows, but he spent a long time in the Holy Land as a mercenary and they say he left half his mind there.'

'Does he fight on the side of the Welsh?'

'He fights for whoever pays the best purse. He is loyal to his paymasters but his brutality is second to none. Do not cross him under any circumstances.'

'I won't,' said Maelgwyn. 'And besides, he stinks to high heaven.'

'You don't smell too sweet yourself,' said Carwyn. 'And that is after just a few days in the saddle. These men live like this permanently.'

'Are we near the rebel camp?'

'Near? We are deep in the heart of it and have been for several hours.'

Both father and son fell silent as Dog disappeared into the trees leaving several guards to watch over them.

'So, who is this man we seek?' said Maelgwyn after a while.

'Brynmore ap Owen was a close friend,' said Carwyn. 'We fought alongside each other many times in my younger days. I have not seen him for many years but knew he still lived amongst the rebels. He is one of the few men I know I can still trust. If Morgan has indeed come this way, then Brynmore will know where he is. All we can do now is wait.'

Maelgwyn sat back with a sigh and closed his eyes. After what seemed like hours, his father nudged him in the ribs. 'Here we go,' he said. 'Something is happening.'

Maelgwyn looked up and saw Dog emerging from the forest again. He talked to one of the guards before pointing at Maelgwyn.

'You, stay here,' he said before turning to Carwyn. 'You will come with me.'

'I am going with my father,' said Maelgwyn, jumping up.

'Maelgwyn, sit down,' said Carwyn. 'I'll be back as soon as I can.'

'Do as he says, boy,' smiled Dog, revealing the few rotten and broken teeth still in his head, 'and you might just get out of here alive.'

Maelgwyn sat back down and watched his father and Dog head into the forest. For the next hour or so he waited in silence, watching the men still positioned around the clearing. They all looked like they lived a hard life and he wouldn't fancy his chances against any one of them. Eventually it started to get dark but in the gloom he saw his father emerge from the trees along with Dog and another man he hadn't seen before. Though Maelgwyn couldn't hear their conversation it was obvious that his father and the third man knew each other well and as they parted, both grasped each other's wrists in a sign of friendship.

Maelgwyn got to his feet as his father strode across the clearing and it was obvious something weighed heavy on his mind.

'Have the horses been fed?' asked Carwyn as he neared.

'Yes, Father. I loosened their tack and they are well rested. Was that Brynmore?'

'Aye, it was, but sort out your horse. We have to ride right now.'

'But it's getting dark.'

'We have no choice. I've just found out your brother has been captured by the English and taken to Pembroke Castle for questioning.'

'*What?*' gasped Maelgwyn. 'But why?'

'I'll explain as we go,' said Carwyn. 'Now mount up. We have to go.'

Back in Pembroke Castle, the patrol had returned from their foray into the Cantref Mawr and as the grooms ran out to look after the horses, John of Salisbury walked across to greet the castellan. Outwardly his smile offered a warm welcome but. inside, he was deeply disappointed the castellan hadn't been injured or worse.

'My lord,' said Salisbury, taking Gerald's horse's reins while the castellan loosened the saddle. 'I hear the campaign was a total success.'

'Aye, it could not have gone better,' said Gerald. 'We took the enemy camp by surprise and over half did not wake from their sleep. Many are now pleading their case before God or Satan, depending on the trueness of their souls.'

'What about the rest?'

'Most were tried and hanged for brigandry but there are some prisoners in one of the carts. I brought them back for questioning.'

'About the ambush?'

'No. For a while my spies have relayed tales that the rebel strength is growing in the Cantref Mawr and though I have not paid them much heed thus far, this latest affront to our rule in Deheubarth makes me think that perhaps I should be more concerned. Hand the prisoners over to the torturer and see what he can learn.'

'Of course,' said Salisbury.

'Oh, there is one exception,' said Gerald, handing his saddle over to his groom. 'One of them is the son of the steward of Llandeilo Manor.'

'Really?' said Salisbury, his eyes widening with surprise. 'I thought Lord Bevan was an ally.'

'Aye, it disappoints me too but that is the fact of the matter and we need to make an example of him. Send him a message and tell him that we found one of his staff following us in the Cantref Mawr. Inform him that unless he is able to provide any good reason to the contrary, the boy will be hanged as a spy.'

'Understood—' said Salisbury, but before he could continue, Gerald started to talk to one of his armourers. Inside, Salisbury seethed at the dismissal and watched the castellan walk away laughing with the other men. The past few days in charge of the castle had whetted the constable's appetite for more power, and with his resolve hardening he knew there was only one way to achieve the outcome he craved; he would have to take matters into his own hands. He sighed and turned to two of the guards standing near the gates.

'You men,' he said, 'bring the prisoners to the guardhouse and summon Master Chirond. Let's see how brave they are when faced with someone gifted in the art of administering pain.'

Pembroke Castle

December 17th, AD 1135

Gerald sat at a table in his quarters, taking the opportunity to catch up on any dispatches he had missed during his time away. A knock came on the door and his wife entered followed by one of the kitchen servants, bearing a tray.

'Nesta,' said Gerald looking up. 'Didn't I say I was not to be disturbed?'

'You did,' said Nesta. 'But that was this morning. You have gone the whole day without eating so I have brought something up. I will hear no argument, Gerald. You need a break from matters of the state.' She turned to the servant and nodded towards a side table by the window. 'Please put the tray there,' she said, 'and close the door on the way out.'

'Yes, my lady,' said the boy and he soon disappeared back down to the kitchens.

Gerald rubbed his eyes before standing up and stretching. 'Actually, I am rather hungry,' he said. 'And I've lost track of time.' He walked over to the table and looked at the selection of cold meats and hot soup.

'Are you joining me?' he asked as he took a seat.

'I will sit with you,' said Nesta, 'but I've already eaten.'

Gerald picked up a chicken leg and dipped it in the soup.

'Really,' she said with a critical look on her face, 'is that how a man of your station now eats his meat?'

Gerald smiled at her as he chewed the chicken. 'We are not in company, my love, so please allow me my indiscretions.'

'I dread to think what you are like on campaign,' she replied. 'Without me around you must live like an animal.'

'We eat as soldiers,' said Gerald, breaking off some bread. 'No time for the niceties of court life on campaign.'

'So what was it like?' asked Nesta. 'You haven't said much since you returned.'

'No different to any other patrol,' said Gerald.

'But you came back with prisoners. Was there a fight?'

'Not exactly but some men did die, as is often the case in such things.'

'I hear there are to be several executions next week.'

'Aye, when the torturer has finished with them. They chose the path of brigandry so will pay the price such a life often brings.'

'Brigands or rebels?'

Gerald stared at his wife thoughtfully as he chewed a mouthful of soup-soaked bread. 'What do you mean?' he asked, reaching for a piece of sliced pork.

'Exactly what I said,' said Nesta. 'Are your prisoners brigands or rebels?'

'I see no difference between the two,' said Gerald. 'As well you know. Both callings are punishable by death so why differentiate?'

'Because, sometimes, the poor are drawn to live a life amongst those who preach rebellion yet have never raised a fist against anyone. There may be innocents amongst them and you wouldn't want to be responsible for killing innocent men.'

'Unfortunately, sometimes that has to be the way. Would I seek out one rat who eats my corn or kill the whole brood?'

'A strange analogy,' said Nesta.

'Worry not,' said Gerald, picking up a spoon to attack the soup. 'If any innocents die as a result then God will forgive them and welcome them to his side.'

'And what about those that are committed to their cause. Are they all as guilty as each other?'

'Of course,' said Gerald. 'They will be given a fair trial, found guilty and hanged for their crimes.'

'Do you not see the absurdity of such a statement?' asked Nesta.

'In what way?'

'Is not the whole purpose of a trial to ascertain guilt or innocence?'

'Ordinarily, but these men were taken from a rebel camp. They are as guilty as the devil himself so innocence is not an option.'

Nesta sighed and looked at her husband. She had been with him for many years and had grown to love him over time but their relationship was always kept at arm's length by their nationalities. He was English born and loyal to the Crown while she was the daughter of a Welsh king, the last true ruler of Deheubarth, and though it had been many years since her father had died, her feelings for her country were still as strong.

'What is all this about, Nesta?' asked Gerald, placing the spoon back into the bowl. 'It looks like you have something on your mind.'

'Not really – it's just that after so much time, it seems that people seem to be getting killed again. It has been quiet for so many years.'

'You can blame your brother for that,' said Gerald.

'My brother?' said Nesta with surprise. 'Tarw has been dead for ten years, Gerald. He shoulders no fault for what happens in Deheubarth or beyond.'

'His flesh may be dead,' said Gerald, 'as is that of his wife, but their names are as alive as you and I. Do you know how many children are named after them, even now after all these years? Too many. It is a frustrating and dangerous situation for all involved.'

'Why? I don't understand.'

'Because as long as the people of Pembroke continue to cling to their memories they will nurture false hope in the breasts of their own children and that can only lead to more heartbreak. Nobody wants that, Nesta, least of all I. I can understand how your brother and his wife became almost legendary in the people's minds and hearts – they fought a good campaign – but those days have long gone. The people need to move on and accept the law of the English Crown, and the sooner the constable puts an end to such nonsense, the better.'

Nesta fell quiet, knowing it was pointless pursuing the matter. When it came to matters of warfare or politics, Gerald was particularly focussed on administering justice, whether justified or not.

'So, what has happened since I was away?' he asked, reaching for his wine. 'I hear you and Salisbury hosted a feast for the castle ladies and the remaining officers.'

'It was hardly a feast,' said Nesta. 'We just shared our table with others whose partners were on campaign.'

'It sounds good,' said Gerald. 'Did it go well?'

Nesta hesitated, wondering whether to tell her husband about the pass Salisbury had made at her when all the guests had left. She swallowed hard at the memory and subconsciously her hand went to her injured arm, the bruises still purple beneath her sleeve where the constable had forced her back against the wall. For a few moments that night she had feared she was going to be raped but Salisbury was anything but stupid and had eventually backed off, making it clear that if she reported his unwelcome advances to her husband, he would accuse her of making the first move. After her history with Owain ap Cadwgan years earlier, she knew there was no guarantee that Gerald would believe her version over Salisbury's.

'Yes,' she said with a forced smile, 'it was fine but I am glad you are back. It wasn't the same without you at my side.'

'Hmmm,' said Gerald, looking over to the unopened messages still on the table. 'Perhaps so, but I am beginning to wonder if it is less stressful hunting brigands.'

'Why?' asked Nesta, following his gaze. 'Are you in receipt of bad news?'

'Not bad news as such,' said Gerald. 'At least not yet.'

'What do you mean?'

'Just the politics of the Crown,' said Gerald sitting back and wiping his mouth with a napkin. 'As you know, a few years ago, Henry made his barons swear fealty to his daughter should he die without a male heir. At the time there were many grumbles but few opposed him. Now that very thing has come to pass, the barons are backtracking on their oaths and there is turmoil around the empty throne.'

'I have already told you I believed there was never any chance that Matilda would be crowned once Henry died. The role is too great for any woman to hold alone.'

'She wouldn't have been alone,' said Gerald. 'Her husband, Geoffrey Plantagenet, would sit alongside her until their sons came of age. I think that is what has angered the barons so much. They want one of their own as king, especially as the Normans are pushing the case for Theobald de Blois.'

'So what do you think is going to happen?'

'Well that's what is so worrying. It seems that Theobald's brother, Stephen de Blois, has taken advantage of the confusion and landed with his army on the east coast. As we speak he is headed for London to press his case.'

'And will he succeed?'

'Who knows, but I will say this. If he does, Matilda will not take it lightly and I fear we will be forced to choose sides. Civil war is in the air, my love, and if it comes, it will not leave us unscathed.'

The following morning, the sun was high in the sky when Carwyn and Maelgwyn finally crested a hill overlooking Pembroke town. In the distance they could see the formidable wooden palisades of the castle and the sprawl of tightly packed houses below. Both men were exhausted but they knew they could waste no time if they were to help Morgan.

With a kick of their heels, they made their way down to the town and headed for the nearest tavern. Carwyn paid a boy to take their horses to a stable and booked two cots in the back room for two days.

'You're in luck,' the landlord had said when Carwyn had first asked. 'I have two cots left. The rest are all full. It's always a good draw when there's a hanging to be seen. Is that why you are here?'

'A hanging?' said Carwyn. 'Who is the criminal?'

'There are several,' said the landlord. 'All captured in the Cantref Mawr not a few days since. I like seeing no man die but it is good for business.'

Carwyn glanced at Maelgwyn and saw a look of fear in his son's eyes. Both had realised that Morgan was probably amongst those condemned.

'Tell me,' said Carwyn, turning back to the landlord, 'who is running the hanging?'

'The constable of course, a man called John of Salisbury. A cruel man, true enough.'

'Does he have rooms in the town?'

'No, he is based in the castle. Why do you ask?'

'I need to ask him something,' said Carwyn. 'How can I get in to see him?'

'You can't,' said the landlord. 'Unless you are summoned or working there, nobody gets in through the gates.'

'Thank you,' said Carwyn and he turned to Maelgwyn. 'Come on, we have no time to waste.'

Ten minutes later they were in the town square watching a team of carpenters hard at work building a large wooden structure.

'What are they making?' Maelgwyn asked to a man in the crowd.

'A scaffold for the hanging,' replied the man. 'There are a dozen men to swing so the old one was too small.'

Maelgwyn glanced at his father. 'What are we going to do?' he asked.

'First of all,' said Carwyn, 'we will try to do this the right way. Morgan is innocent of all charges and we will try to make representation to the constable.'

'How?'

'By asking,' said Carwyn. 'Come on.' He led the way up to the castle gates but as they neared, the two guards stepped forward and presented their pikes.

'Hold there, my friend,' said one of the guards. 'State your business.'

'I need to speak to the constable,' said Carwyn.

'About what?'

'About my son. He is being held within the castle and is falsely accused of being a rebel.'

'Ah, another innocent,' sneered the other guard. 'If only I had a penny for every rebel who claims innocence as soon as he is faced with the scaffold.'

'This is different,' said Carwyn. 'He was just travelling and was swept up with all the rest. If you allow me an audience with the constable, I can prove it.'

'How?'

'Because I am the steward of Llandeilo Manor and can send for letters of reference from the Lord of Llandeilo. If you execute this man, you will be making a terrible mistake.'

'What do you think?' asked the first soldier to the second.

'Not going to happen,' said the second soldier dismissively. 'All representations for clemency or dispute resolutions are to be made on the last day of the month in an open court. Come back then and he will hear your case.'

'But the hangings are in a few days,' shouted Maelgwyn. 'The end of the month is weeks away. Are you both stupid?'

Both soldiers lowered their pikes into a threatening position.

'Watch your mouth, boy,' said one of the men, 'else you could be joining your brother on the scaffold.'

'Enough, Maelgwyn,' snapped Carwyn. 'Come on, we will try something else.' He led his son back down the timber ramp towards the town.

'We have to rescue him, Father,' said Maelgwyn as they went.

'I know,' said Carwyn, 'but there's no way to get inside that castle.'

'You heard those men. The prisoners have already been found guilty. There's no way the constable will listen to reason.'

'Oh yes there is,' said Carwyn, 'because I have something he will accept in return for Morgan's life.'

'What?' asked Maelgwyn.

'You'll see soon enough,' said Carwyn, 'but let us be gone before those soldiers decide to arrest us for your outburst.'

They walked back down to the town and made their way back to their lodgings. Carwyn's mind was in a turmoil for he could see no resolution to the problem apart from the one he least wanted to do. However, deep inside he knew it had to be done if his eldest son was to survive. With a heavy heart he looked over at Maelgwyn. His hand reached out to his son's shoulder and he squeezed it hard.

'Whatever happens in the next few days, son,' he said, 'never forget I love you.'

Llandeilo Manor

December 20th, AD 1135

Branwen stood in the gateway of the manor walls, gazing out over the fields and slopes leading up to the nearby hills. She still had no news as to the whereabouts of her husband or sons and every day that passed worried her more. She knew that Carwyn could more than look after himself but her sons had been brought up mainly within the confines of the manor walls and were unused to the trials of life in the saddle. She heard someone walking up behind her and turned to see Lord Bevan approaching, his face creased with worry. In his hand he held a letter and instinctively she knew it was bad news.

'Lord Bevan,' she said, 'what is it?'

'Branwen,' he replied, 'I have had correspondence from Pembroke and it is not good.'

'Is it about Carwyn?' she asked.

'No, it is regarding Morgan. Apparently he has been arrested for spying on behalf of the rebels and has been sentenced to hang.'

'*Spying?*' gasped Branwen. 'But he hasn't been gone long enough to even find the rebels, let alone become one of their trusted men.'

'I know, and there has obviously been a terrible mistake. Of course I will send a messenger to beg for mercy but I'm afraid my pleas may not carry much weight with the governor there.'

'Then I must go myself,' said Branwen, her eyes hardening. 'I will not abandon him.'

'Branwen, I know you could lose your son but he has chosen his own path. There is nothing you can do to change the situation.'

'No,' said Branwen. 'Nothing is more important than a mother's son. What will be, will be, Lord Bevan, but while he is still alive there is always hope. If I could entrust my two other children to the servants of the manor, I will be away within the hour.'

'Are you sure?' asked Bevan. 'For this whole mess could see everything you have built here fall apart. If they find out you once rode with the rebels they could still make you pay the ultimate price.'

'It is a risk I have to take,' said Branwen. 'If Carwyn was here he would do the same. I cannot just stand back and let my son hang.'

Bevan stared at Branwen for a few seconds knowing that once she had set her mind on something there was no stopping her. With a sigh he took her hand. 'If you do this,' he said, 'you know that your life will never be the same.'

'I know,' she said quietly, 'but if not to save the life of my son, then what other reason could there ever be.'

Bevan nodded. 'I will arrange an escort for you,' he said, 'trusted men who can be relied on if it comes to a fight.'

'Thank you,' said Branwen, 'but there is no need. Robert will be at my side and there are others whom I can call upon if needed. All I ask is that my other two boys are well cared for in my absence.'

'You know they will be,' said Bevan.

'Thank you,' said Branwen. 'Now, if you don't mind, I have to get ready. I may already be too late.'

Back in Pembroke, Carwyn and Maelgwyn made their way through the crowd to the scaffold. The square was already full of people and the mood was ugly. Twelve ropes hung from the cross pole, blowing gently in the morning breeze. An armed soldier stood at each corner, protecting the platform from any sort of sabotage; in the distance, they could see a line of men being escorted down the hill from the castle gates. Each prisoner had his hands tied before him and they were fastened to each other by ropes around their necks. Many were hardly able to walk such were their injuries and it was obvious they had all suffered terribly at the hands of the castle torturer. Maelgwyn climbed up onto the sill of a window to try to see his brother.

'There he is,' he said. 'The last man.'

'I can't see him from here,' said Carwyn. 'Is he hurt?'

'I'm not sure,' said Maelgwyn. 'It's difficult to see from here.'

'Come,' replied Carwyn. 'We have to get closer to the scaffold.'

Maelgwyn jumped down and they forced their way through the crowd. Soon they were at the front and they waited patiently as the prisoners and the guards drew near.

'Look,' said Maelgwyn, pointing up the path towards the castle, 'that must be the constable.'

Carwyn followed his gaze and saw several mounted men following the prisoners down the hill.

'Aye,' said Carwyn quietly, 'and he is exactly the man we need.'

The crowd parted to allow the condemned men and the guards through. They climbed up to the scaffold and the guards made each of the prisoners stand behind a noose. Behind them came the executioner, a squat man with a broad muscled chest. He was stripped to the waist and his torso was covered with hundreds of tiny tattoos, each forming the shape of a cross, one for each man he had sent to his death. The crowd fell silent as the constable eventually followed him up the steps.

Maelgwyn and his father stared up at the scaffold. All of the prisoners bore the marks of severe beatings and most had at least one broken or dislocated arm. In comparison, Morgan was relatively unharmed. His eyes were blackened and his face swollen but apart from that it seemed he was in far better condition than the others. Carwyn turned his attention to Salisbury, trying to judge the man's mettle. The constable was well known across Deheubarth for his cruelty; but he was also known for his greed and thirst for power, and it was these traits that Carwyn hoped to exploit.

As he watched, the constable walked slowly behind each prisoner, pausing occasionally to twist an already dislocated shoulder or prod an open wound with the point of his blade, smiling as each victim cried out in pain. His narrow face was almost gaunt in comparison to other men and a wispy beard did nothing to hide the bony jawlines sweeping down from each side of his balding head.

'Good people of Pembroke,' announced the constable as he reached the end of the line, 'you have been summoned here today to witness the execution of these twelve men for the crimes of brigandry and murder. Have no compassion for their pain, for each are murderers and are better off dead. Let this punishment send out a message to every man, woman or child who raises a fist against the Crown that such actions will be met with swift and unrelenting justice.' He turned to face the condemned men.

'As constable of Pembroke,' he said loudly, 'it falls upon me to send you to whatever fate awaits you. May God have mercy on your souls. Executioner, carry out the sentence.'

The broad man stepped forward and placed the noose around the first man's neck. As he did, the victim started to shake and tears flowed from his eyes as he realised the moment of death was finally upon him.

'Merciful Father,' he whispered through his tears, 'forgive me for my sins. Accept me into your house . . .'

Before he could finish, the executioner pushed him from the scaffold and the rope tightened as his descent came to a shuddering stop a few feet above the ground. The executioner looked over the edge and saw the victim's neck hadn't broken and the man was choking to death. The smell of faeces filled the air as the victim lost control of his bowels and he twisted and turned at the end of the rope, desperately fighting against the inevitable.

'Move on,' ordered the constable, and with a shrug the executioner moved across to the second man.

'Father, we have to do something,' said Maelgwyn, 'before it's too late.'

Carwyn's mind worked furiously. It was obvious that any attempt at a physical rescue would only result in the injury or death of himself and perhaps Maelgwyn, and he was not about to risk a second son. Without warning he stepped forward to just in front of the line of guards surrounding the scaffold. The soldiers all stepped forward, each alert for any sign of interference.

'Step back,' growled one, 'or I will drop you where you stand.'

Carwyn ignored him and looked up at the constable. 'My lord,' he shouted, 'I bid you wait.'

Salisbury looked over, annoyed at the interruption, but said nothing. Instead he nodded towards the executioner and a second man fell to his death.

'My lord,' shouted Carwyn again, 'please, hear my petition.'

'The time for petitions is done,' answered one of the guards. 'Stand back.'

'What if I was to say at least one of these men is innocent?' shouted Carwyn. 'Surely you have a duty to hear me?'

'These men have been tried before a court of the governor and found guilty,' came the reply. 'Now stand back or I will have you arrested for actions in support of a criminal.'

'But I can vouch for the man's innocence, as can the Lord of Llandeilo. Surely a noble's word should carry some weight.'

'Shut that man up,' shouted the executioner as his third victim choked to death. 'I am trying to do a job of work here.'

'My lord, you cannot hang an innocent man,' shouted Carwyn. 'If you do, all these people will witness that your justice is tainted. How then can you morally demand that the people adhere to the laws when all along they know that fairness does not have a place in your judgement? I thought that Gerald was a better man than that.'

Two soldiers sprang forward and grabbed Carwyn. Maelgwyn was surprised when his father did not struggle and pushed forward to help.

'Stand back,' said Carwyn, making Maelgwyn stop in his tracks. 'I know what I am doing.'

'Wait,' shouted a voice and everyone turned to see the constable staring at Carwyn from the far side of the scaffold. He slowly walked across the platform, holding up his hand towards the executioner as he passed to temporarily halt the hangings.

'Release him,' said Salisbury and he waited as the soldiers stepped back into line. He looked down, his cruel eyes narrowing, trying to remember where he had seen the man before. 'Who are you?' he asked eventually. 'Your face is familiar to me.'

'I am Carwyn, my lord,' came the reply, 'and I am the manor steward at Llandeilo. My master is Lord Bevan ap Maldwyn.'

'Ah, so you are the steward,' said Salisbury. 'That explains your outburst. Indeed, it probably explains why you look familiar. Perhaps that is where I have seen you before?'

'Perhaps,' said Carwyn, knowing full well that it was not in Llandeilo where their paths had crossed in the past.

'I suppose you are here to plead on behalf of your son?'

'You know one of the prisoners is my son?' asked Carwyn, surprised.

'Indeed I do. And you are correct when you say Lord Bevan would vouch for your son, for I have a letter in my possession doing just that. Received this very morning.'

'You do?' asked Carwyn, caught off guard by the revelation. 'How did he know he had been arrested?'

'Because we are not barbarians, Master Carwyn. When your son finally declared his true identity, we wrote to Lord Bevan and gave him the chance to explain why one of his staff was spying for the rebels. We also invited him to speak on behalf of your son.'

Carwyn's mind was in turmoil. If this was true, then Branwen would also know about Morgan's plight and she would be beside herself with fear and worry.

'If you have a letter from Lord Bevan, surely he speaks glowingly on behalf of my son?'

'He does and indeed is full of praise for the boy's character. Alas, that does not give your son amnesty from paying the price demanded when convicted of rebellion. All such criminals are equal in the eyes of the law, irrespective of station or birthright, and I'm sure these people would have it no other way.'

A murmur rippled around the crowd in support of the constable. He was not a popular man but if there were hangings to be done, then all should be treated the same with no favour for station.

'I understand that,' said Carwyn, 'but my son is no rebel. He was just in the wrong place at the wrong time.'

'He was in the Cantref Mawr not three leagues away from a known brigand camp. In fact, it was these very people who robbed a caravan with meat intended for Pembroke and killed all those innocents some of whom were coming home to visit loved ones.' Again a murmur of anger rippled around the crowd and Salisbury knew his approach was winning them over. 'I am sorry, Master Carwyn,' continued Salisbury, 'but your son is responsible for his own actions and even if he was not actually a rebel than it seems highly likely that he was seeking the rebel camp to become one himself. These good people suffer almost daily as a result of brigandry and it is their safety that spurs our need for justice. The decision has been made and the sentence stands. Your son will be hanged.' He turned away to return to the far end of the platform.

'Wait,' called Carwyn. 'There is more.'

'I have allowed your petition, Master Carwyn,' said Salisbury, as he walked away, 'and this conversation is over. Executioner, proceed.'

Another man was pushed from the scaffold and Carwyn knew he was running out of time. He pushed his way along the crowd until he was nearer to the constable and looked up at his son at the end of the line. Morgan's face was hugely swollen and one eye completely closed. His naked torso bore the blisters of dozens of burns and the ends of his fingers were a bloody mess where his fingernails had been torn away.

Carwyn swallowed hard. Every fibre of his body demanded he jump up onto the platform and cut away the ropes, fighting if he had to, but he knew it was pointless. There were far too many guards.

'Father,' mumbled Morgan through his bloody lips. 'Take Maelgwyn away. Don't let him see me die like this.'

'You are not going to die,' snarled Carwyn. 'I swear it.'

'It's too late,' said Morgan. 'There is nothing you can do.'

'Oh yes there is,' said Carwyn as another two men fell to their deaths. He turned to look up at the constable.

'John of Salisbury,' he said calmly, yet loud enough for the constable to hear. 'What you are about to do here is injustice of the highest order but if you won't listen to reason, then I will offer you a price for my son's life.'

Salisbury looked down with a sneer. 'Do you really think I would take a few measly shillings in return for the life of a rebel? The people would never allow it.'

'I don't offer money,' said Carwyn. 'I offer something far more valuable than you could ever imagine, something that would make your name renowned across England as the man who did what no other could ever do, knight or king.'

Salisbury looked down, his interest raised. 'And you are in possession of such a gift?'

'Aye, I am,' said Carwyn, 'but first I want you to swear that in return you will release my son.'

Morgan looked down at his father, realising what he was about to do. 'Father, no,' he gasped. 'Don't do this.'

'What about it, Salisbury?' continued Carwyn, ignoring his son. 'How would you like to go down in the history books as one of the most influential men of our age?'

'Tell me what is on offer, Carwyn, and perhaps we will talk.'

'No,' said Carwyn, starting to sweat. 'Release my son first and then we will talk.'

Salisbury nodded towards the executioner and victim number seven was pushed off the platform, his neck snapping like a winter branch.

'You are in no position to make demands,' said Salisbury, 'and are running out of time. Now if you have nothing more, I have business to conclude.' Another man was pushed from the scaffold, screaming in fear until the sudden jolt ended his cries.

'Wait,' said Carwyn. 'Enough. I will tell you what you want to know.'

Salisbury held up his hand to the executioner and walked over to stand above Carwyn. 'Explain yourself.'

'What if I was to say I can deliver the most wanted man in the kingdom into your hands. A man the king himself would pay a fortune to lay his hands on.'

'And who would that man be?'

Carwyn looked around at the crowd. Silence had fallen amongst those in earshot and he knew they were waiting on his every word.

'Father,' gasped Morgan again. 'Don't do this.'

'The man I speak of,' continued Carwyn, 'is the one who was solely responsible for ravaging Deheubarth for years, causing the deaths of many loyal to the English Crown and untold strain on the Crown's treasuries.'

'There has not been such a man since Gruffydd ap Rhys and his whore of a wife decided to lead these lands into open rebellion,' said Salisbury, 'and he has long rotted in a pauper's grave.'

'Has he?' asked Carwyn. 'How do you know it was him?'

'He was identified by one of the king's own men after a pursuit,' said Salisbury, 'and we hung his corpse to rot in the summer sun.'

'He was identified by a king's man, I agree,' said Carwyn, 'but I know that the witness also had allegiances to his own Welsh heritage and was paid handsomely for the identification.'

'Nonsense,' said Salisbury. 'Nought but the wishful thinking of a desperate man.'

'Is it?' replied Carwyn. 'The pursuit was easily engineered as was the scene of the prince's death. The dead man you found was the son of a farmer who had broken his neck in a fall from his horse. His resemblance to Tarw was uncanny and the plot was hatched to make the English think the prince was truly dead. In truth, he has been living a second life not far from here, right under your very noses.'

Conversation rippled through the front rows of the crowd. If what this man was saying was true, there was a chance that Gruffydd ap Rhys, their last prince of Deheubarth, was alive and well.

Salisbury stared at Carwyn, his mind working furiously. The thought of a wanted prince living as a commoner was ludicrous, yet such was this man's conviction, there may be the slightest of chances that his tale might be true.

'Even if I believe you,' said the constable eventually, 'are you saying you are willing and able to reveal his whereabouts to me?'

'Aye, but only upon the release of my son.'

'Father,' moaned Morgan again, 'don't do this, please.'

'Don't betray the prince,' shouted a lone voice from amongst the crowd.

Salisbury looked around the crowd and saw the mood was changing. The Welsh prince and his warrior wife had been the scourge of the south for many years. Their band of brigands had been fearless and all the castles from Brycheniog to Ceredigion had feared for their supply lines. At one point, Henry himself had offered them an amnesty if they would stop their campaign but they had declined and continued their fight against the occupying forces. Many men died, on both sides, yet their hit-and-run offensive carried on relentlessly until, suddenly, it all came to a stop. The body of Tarw had been found mangled along with his horse at the bottom of a ravine and when it was positively identified as the prince, his wife also disappeared and peace returned to Deheubarth.

Despite the hardships, they had been a popular couple, often redistributing their ill-gotten gains amongst the poor. Their generosity and unfaltering patriotism had garnered them many loyal supporters and Salisbury knew that if there was the slightest chance that this man's outrageous claim might be true, he had a duty to explore it.

He looked at the remaining four men on the scaffold. Each already had a noose around their necks and the executioner stood waiting to finish the job. Without warning, Salisbury walked behind the condemned men and pushed three off the scaffold in quick succession. Voices were raised in protest and all the soldiers presented their weapons against any surge of the angry crowd.

'*Stop*,' shouted Carwyn as Salisbury grabbed Morgan. 'I am telling the truth, I swear.'

Salisbury pushed Morgan close to the edge of the platform and glared down at Carwyn. 'I don't know if you are wasting my time or are simply a madman,' he spat, 'but I will tell you this. I do not negotiate with anyone trying to hold me to ransom. If you are telling the truth and you know where this man is, you will spit it out right now or I swear you will hear your son's neck snap by the time I count to ten. One, two, three . . .'

'All right,' shouted Carwyn in panic, 'I will tell you. Pull him back!'

Salisbury dragged Morgan back from the edge but held him by his hair.

'Spit it out, Carwyn, where is the prince?'

'Can I approach?' asked Carwyn. 'These words are for your ears only.'

Salisbury didn't answer but instead turned to speak to one of the soldiers by his side. The soldier walked down the steps with two of his comrades and searched Carwyn before dragging him up to the platform.

'So,' said Salisbury as Carwyn stood before him. 'Tell me what you know.'

'When you said you recognised my face earlier,' said Carwyn quietly, 'you were correct. We have met before, for we have talked many years ago, before I took the path of a freedom fighter. You know my face because I am the man we are talking about. I am Prince Gruffydd ap Rhys. I am the one known as Tarw!'

For a few moments Salisbury's eyes narrowed as he stared at Carwyn.

'Listen to me,' hissed Carwyn, meeting the constable's gaze. 'Look at my face, listen to my voice. You know I am telling the truth. We met inside this very castle many years ago. Nesta is my sister and she introduced me to you.'

For a few seconds there was silence but, eventually, a thin sneer of recognition played about Salisbury's mouth. 'By Satan's teeth,' he said, 'I do believe you are who you say you are.'

'I am,' said Carwyn, 'and if you need proof, just present me before Gerald, for in the past he and I met on several occasions when he first wed my sister. He will vouch for who I am.'

'Oh no,' said Salisbury, his face opening up into a smile, 'this is not Gerald's victory, this is all mine.'

'Do what you will,' said Carwyn, 'but I have kept my side of the bargain. Release my son and I will walk freely up that hill and face whatever fate you have planned for me.'

'I promise you will meet your fate,' said Salisbury, 'and it will be at the end of a rope but it won't be in the castle, it will be right here, today, alongside your treacherous son.'

'*What?*' cried Carwyn as the soldiers seized him again. 'But we had a bargain.'

'You heard me earlier,' said Salisbury. 'I do not bargain with those who use blackmail as a weapon. You will hang today as payment for trying to free a lawfully convicted rebel under false pretences.'

'You can't do this,' said Carwyn. 'I am Gruffydd ap Rhys, prince of Deheubarth, and I demand a fair trial before a court of my peers.'

'As far as I am aware,' said Salisbury, 'you are nothing more than an idiot with a ridiculous story made up to save the neck of your rebel son. For all I know you could be a rebel yourself.'

'But you recognised me,' gasped Carwyn. 'I know you did.'

'Possibly, but I am not willing to take the risk and, either way, I cannot lose. If you are lying then the world is less one more madman but if you tell the truth, then everyone already thinks you are dead so you will not be missed. Oh, this is good, Welshman. You have truly made me a very happy man.'

'What's happening?' shouted Maelgwyn from down below. 'Release him.'

'Shut him up,' snapped Salisbury and Maelgwyn was beaten to the ground by two soldiers.

'*Executioner,*' called Salisbury. 'Find me a noose. This man is a lunatic and has just admitted riding with the rebels. We will hang father and son, side by side.'

Carwyn stared at Salisbury in defiance. He may have failed in his task but he would not let this man have the satisfaction of seeing any regret or fear in his face.

'Do your worst, Salisbury,' he said, 'and may your soul rot in hell.'

Moments later, Carwyn and Morgan both stood at the edge of the platform waiting for their lives to end. Below them, Maelgwyn struggled frantically but some of the crowd held him back, knowing that if he interfered, there would be three members of the same family hanging from the gallows. Salisbury descended the steps and walked in front of the crowd before turning to face the scaffold above.

'I have a better view from down here,' he laughed, 'and want to see your face as you realise it was all for naught. All the campaigns, all the manufactured heroism, it was all in vain and it all comes down to this, you dancing at the end of a rope at my behest. You may well be who you say you are but it is I, a man of common birth who has worked his way up, sweating blood and tears, who will bring your reign to an end.'

'Don't justify your life amongst honest men,' spat Carwyn. 'You have made your name through deceit, bribery and brutality. I go to my God with a clear conscience, a situation eternally denied to you and your like. Get it over with, Salisbury, being in your presence sickens my soul.'

The constable's face darkened and without removing his stare, he called out to the tattooed man waiting on the platform.

'Executioner, in the name of King Henry and the people of England, I, John of Salisbury, Constable of Pembroke and representative of Sir Gerald of Windsor, hereby condemn this man to death, with execution to be carried out immediately. Deliver him unto the hands of the Lord and may God have mercy on their souls.'

'*Nooo*,' screamed Maelgwyn as the executioner stepped forward but he knew it was too late; his father and older brother were about to die before his very eyes.

Pembroke

December 20th, AD 1135

The executioner raised his hands to push the men to their deaths, but before he could carry out his lethal task, the crowd heard a thud and he staggered backward, staring down at his chest in confusion. In amongst the multitude of tiny crosses was the fletched end of an arrow that had smashed into his body.

The pain still hadn't registered when two more arrows joined the first and he fell back against one of the scaffold supports, looking down at the constable as if seeking an explanation. For a few seconds, the crowd stared in confusion and it was only when the executioner fell to one side that reality kicked in. A woman screamed and everyone turned to see where the arrows had come from, just as the air filled with willow and steel.

'To arms,' roared one of the sergeants. 'Sound the alarm, we are under attack—' But before he could draw a sword, he too fell to the ground, clutching at an arrow through his throat. A horn echoed through the morning air, and up at the castle, the sentries atop the palisade relayed the alarm down into the bailey.

In the square, panic ensued as men fell to all sides and dozens of archers on the nearby roofs released arrow after arrow towards the soldiers surrounding the platform. Carwyn quickly realised what was happening and shouted down to his son, his voice hardly audible above the screams and cries of the panicking crowd.

'Maelgwyn, bring a knife, quickly.'

Maelgwyn drew his blade and forced his way through the throng. He had no idea what was happening, but it was clear he had a chance to save his father and brother.

Further along the square, several guards had managed to surround the constable, each with their shields facing outward. Arrows thudded amongst them but none made it through. Salisbury looked terrified, yet even as they retreated towards the safety of the buildings behind, he still barked out his orders.

'*Kill the men on the scaffold*,' he roared. 'A fortune to any man who takes their lives.'

One of the remaining guards ran towards the platform, his sword drawn. His shield was held above his head, and despite the heavy rain of missiles, he remained unscathed.

'Maelgwyn, look out,' shouted Carwyn, and though his son turned just in time to avoid the soldier's swinging blade he was knocked to the ground by his attacker's momentum. The soldier continued his run towards the scaffold steps, barging people out of his way, and was about to climb up when someone emerged from beneath the platform and plunged a knife deep into his back.

'*Brynmore*,' gasped Maelgwyn, recognising the man his father had met only days earlier. 'What's going on?'

Without answering, Brynmore dragged his blade across the English soldier's neck, slicing deep into his throat. Plumes of blood spurted out, much to Maelgwyn's disgust, and he staggered backward as his face was covered in a fountain of crimson red. Brynmore ran up the steps and within moments had removed the nooses from both Carwyn's and

Morgan's neck before slicing the rope from their wrists. All three men jumped from the scaffold and took shelter from the many arrows landing in the square. All around the crowd, people screamed as the attack continued and some of the civilians had been hit in the confusion.

'Brynmore,' panted Carwyn, as Maelgwyn ran over to join them. 'I don't know what you are doing here, but you have my gratitude.'

'You didn't think I was going to let you ride into this viper's nest alone, did you?'

'This fight is not yours to share. Our allegiance ended many years ago.'

'Some allegiances last forever,' said Brynmore. 'But enough talk. Keep low and make your way to the street of bakers.'

'Father,' said Morgan, staring up the nearby hill. 'The alarm has been raised. Look!'

All four men looked upwards and saw a column of horses streaming out of the castle gates. Carwyn looked towards Brynmore.

'You just get to the horses,' said the rebel, 'and leave the English to us.'

'But . . .'

'My lord,' said Brynmore, 'there is no time to explain – just get yourself and the boys to safety. We will talk later.' He gave Carwyn the sword he had taken from the man whose throat he had slit. 'Now, be gone.'

Carwyn nodded and turned to Morgan and Maelgwyn. 'You heard him. Keep your heads down and follow me. Stop for no man, friend or foe.'

The two young men nodded and Carwyn could see the fear on their faces. Neither had come so close to death before, and despite being trained in the way of weapons, this was the first time they had seen any used in anger. He bent down and retrieved a sword from a nearby dead soldier before throwing it over to Morgan.

'Time to be a man, son,' he said, 'and don't be afraid to use it.' Without another word he ran from the shelter of the scaffold and across the square, dodging the dead and the wounded as he went. 'Keep moving,' shouted Carwyn, as an arrow just missed his head. 'We're almost there.' Moments later he ducked into an alleyway, his two sons close behind him.

'Morgan, you are wounded,' he said, seeing blood running down his son's arm.

'A scratch only,' gasped Morgan. 'Keep going.' Carwyn turned and made his way through the alleyways, trying to remember the street of bakers. Finally, he came to a side lane where the smell of baking bread assured him he was in the right place.

'Down there,' cried Maelgwyn, pointing at a waving man at the end of the lane.

Carwyn and his sons ran down and were relieved to see a row of saddled horses tied to a rail.

'Take what you need,' said the man, 'and get to the Cantref Mawr.'

'Who are you?' asked Maelgwyn.

'Ask no questions of those who help, son,' said Carwyn, mounting one of the horses. 'That way if you are ever caught and tortured, you can give away no information.'

Maelgwyn nodded and mounted his own horse.

'Ride like the wind, my lord,' said the man as he retreated into the shadows. 'We need you alive.' Seconds later he had disappeared into the maze of streets.

Carwyn turned to his sons. 'Ready?'

'Father,' said Maelgwyn, 'that is the second man to call you *my lord*. What is happening here?'

'Nothing that you need concern yourself about,' said Carwyn. 'Now we have a hard ride ahead of us. We need to get going.'

'No,' said Maelgwyn as his father turned his horse to ride away.

'Maelgwyn, do as you are told,' snapped Morgan, 'or we could all die here.'

'Not until someone tells me what is going on,' said Maelgwyn. 'I have asked him over and over again yet he keeps me in the dark like an ill-tempered child.' He glared at his father. 'Well, he continued, 'are you going to tell me or not?'

'Tell you what?'

'Why these men fight for you and why they call you lord?'

'There is no time for this,' said Carwyn. 'Let's get out of this place and we will talk later.'

'No,' started Maelgwyn again, and Carwyn was about to launch into a tirade when Morgan interrupted them both.

'*Just tell him*,' he shouted through his swollen mouth. 'In the name of Christ, can't you see? The time for such secrets is over, Father. He needs to know.'

Carwyn looked at his eldest son, still hesitating to reveal his secret, but before he could speak, Morgan took the option away from him.

'Maelgwyn,' he said, 'our father is not the man you think he is. His name is Gruffydd ap Rhys and he is the last true prince of Deheubarth. That is why those men are risking their lives to save him.'

Maelgwyn stared at his father, slowly shaking his head. 'No,' he said. 'It's not true. The prince has been dead for many years.'

'That man was not the prince,' said Morgan. 'The prince sits astride the horse before you. You are royal born, Maelgwyn. Our father is the prince of Deheubarth.'

Maelgwyn turned to Carwyn. 'Is this true?' he asked simply.

Carwyn looked across at his oldest son. Morgan had always known the truth but he had wanted to shield his three other sons from the threat such knowledge would surely bring. But Morgan was right: that luxury had now come to a sudden and violent end.

'It is true,' he said eventually. 'And I promise to tell you everything. All I ask is we get away from here while we still can. Now, can we do that?'

Maelgwyn nodded silently, shocked at the revelation.

'Good; now follow me.' Carwyn turned his horse and rode it through the narrow streets, heading towards the outskirts of the town. Behind him was Morgan, his aching body crying out at every jolt of the horse, and bringing up the rear was Maelgwyn, his mind ablaze at his father's revelation. If it was true, and at the moment he wasn't sure it was, then his father was one of the most notorious rebel leaders ever to raise a sword against the English: Gruffydd ap Rhys, more commonly known as Tarw, the Bull of Wales.

Pembroke Castle

December 20th, AD 1135

Nesta and Emma sat at a table in the Princess's chambers, both sewing small tapestries held in wooden frames. For the past hour or so they had talked quietly, picking on dried fruit and reminiscing about the days before the English had established such a stranglehold over the whole of the south.

'Remember when young Henry put a mouse beneath my bed covers?' said Emma, lowering her sewing. 'I thought I would truly die that night.'

'Oh, yes,' said Nesta with a laugh, 'and the time he placed a rotting sheep's head in Lady Elspeth's window.'

'He was so naughty,' said Emma with a sigh, 'yet so loveable. I do miss him so.'

Nesta smiled and put her sewing down on the table alongside Emma's. 'I do, too,' she said. 'I always knew his place was at court, but it still wasn't easy to see him go.'

'Do you hear from him?'

'Not much. I have the occasional letter but apart from that I think he finds the wonders of Westminster too distracting for such simple pastimes and, besides, the palace is far more comfortable than the draughty walls of a wooden Welsh castle.'

'Don't you mean English?'

'It was Welsh long before Gerald and his men claimed it for the Crown all those years ago, Emma, and though the fortress that once stood upon this site bore little resemblance to what it is now, to me, it will always be a part of our heritage. I am Welsh and, despite what you may think, my allegiances are always with my people.'

'I have often wondered how you make that work, my lady.'

'What do you mean?'

'Well, you make no secret about your passion for your heritage, yet here you are, married to an English knight, the mother of two of his sons and also the mother to the bastard son of an English king. It seems quite a situation to be in for someone who professes to hate the Crown so much.'

'I hate the thought of the Crown,' replied Nesta. 'I hate the thought of my people being oppressed and I hate the thought of never walking these hills again without armed bodyguards at my back. What I don't hate is any individual who is just as much a victim of the situation as I am. I include Gerald in this stance, for though he was not my first choice as a husband and I know it was no more than a political arrangement, he has forgiven me more than any man should ever have to. We both love our sons and Gerald has brought Henry up as if he were his own. No mother could have asked for more, and though he represents a system I hate, he is not responsible for that system.'

'Do you love him?'

Nesta hesitated, shocked at the bluntness of the question.

'Your hesitation speaks for you,' said Emma.

'On the contrary,' replied Nesta. 'I was just taken aback and it is a very difficult question. I never used to but, now, I think I do. I would certainly never do anything to hurt him and he has my undivided loyalty for as long as I am his wife.'

'But what if that situation should come to an end?'

'What do you mean?'

'It is a dangerous world out there, my lady, and the master has many enemies. Surely it has crossed your mind that one day he may fall foul of an assassin's blade, or even fall in battle.'

'I hope that day never comes, Emma.'

'As do I, for he has always been kind to me, but if it does, who will demand your loyalty then?'

Nesta stared at the maid for several moments. For a woman with no education, Emma was very astute politically. 'All I will say, Emma,' she said eventually, 'is that if I am ever widowed, then any loyalty I had to Gerald will come to a natural end and any subsequent actions will be to suit my own mind, not the minds of others, be they a pauper or a king. I am older and wiser than the girl they sent to Westminster all those years ago; if I had known then what I know now, I probably would not be sitting within this keep talking about what might have been.'

'Where do you think you would be?' asked Emma.

Nesta took a deep breath and turned her head slowly to the window. 'I'm not sure,' she said eventually, 'but I do know this. It would be somewhere out there with the wind in my hair, the sun on my face and with freedom in my heart. With those three things, Emma, I would be the richest and happiest woman in the world.'

The maid smiled and reached out to take her mistress' hands. 'Who knows, my lady, there may yet come a day in our lifetime when all three will be yours to enjoy.'

For a few moments both women sat in silence, each dreaming of their own versions of freedom.

'Anyway,' said Nesta suddenly, 'enough of such nonsense. I have to see the steward and my husband about the new tapestry. Could you clear this away and I'll see you at the meal this evening?'

'Of course, my lady,' said Emma, and as the maid started to clear away the sewing, Nesta headed out of her room and down the keep stairway.

———— ⌣ ————

In the lesser hall, the steward was talking quietly to the treasurer while Gerald sat at a table placed near the fire. Upon the table was a leather bag containing dispatches from London. His face creased with concern as he read one in particular. The door to the hall opened and Nesta walked in.

'Nesta,' said Gerald, looking up. 'Forgive me. I forgot we were supposed to be meeting. I believe you want to commission a new tapestry for the wall of the great hall, is that true?'

'It is,' said Nesta, seeing the strain upon her husband's face, 'but if it is a bad time, we could discuss it later.'

Gerald sighed and rubbed his eyes.

'It would help, if you don't mind.'

'Is there something I can do?' asked Nesta.

'Not this time,' replied Gerald. 'Some of these matters are beyond even my influence.'

'Such as?'

'Well, for one, it looks like the succession may not go ahead as we thought. Stephen de Blois is already in London, and it seems he has the support of the nobles and many of the bishops for his claim to the throne.'

'And what do you think of this?'

'I admit that the thought of a queen on the throne is a strange one but Matilda is a strong woman. Stephen, on the other hand, is reputed to be weak and perhaps that is not what England needs at the moment. Whatever the outcome, it is out of my hands.'

Nesta sat on the second chair and reached out to take her husband's hand. 'You look tired and should take some rest.'

'I can't,' said Gerald. 'I have to ride to Kidwelly as soon as possible and speak to Maurice de Londres about the growing Welsh threat.'

'You talk of Hywel ap Maredudd?'

'Aye. It is no secret that he has recruited an army in Brycheniog and I can only assume he does so with the intention of turning his forces upon the Crown. The threat is real and we have to prepare. Between us, Maurice and I can muster a formidable force but the numbers are spread out over too great an area and we need to coordinate our response.'

'The burdens of office are indeed great,' said Nesta.

Before Gerald could answer, the far doors of the hall burst open and one of the guards ran in unannounced.

'What is this?' started the steward, annoyed at the intrusion.

'My lord,' shouted the guard, ignoring the steward, 'the alarm has been sounded. Our men are under attack in the town.'

Several hours later, Gerald paced back and forth in the hall, his face a picture of controlled rage. To one side stood Salisbury, the man responsible for the debacle that had unfolded throughout the day, and the sergeant-at-arms who had led the counteroffensive against the rebels. Nesta stood at the back of the hall, alongside the castle steward, both watching with concern as the two men were questioned by the castellan.

'So,' said Gerald, as he walked, 'let's be clear about this, what you are saying is that during a completely legal execution, carried out in the name of the king, a band of unknown rebels attacked the execution party and released the prisoners from their bonds.'

'Only one of them, my lord,' said Salisbury. 'The rest were hanged as ordered.'

'If that is the case, why am I getting reports that there were two men released from the scaffold, both of whom made a clean escape?'

'The second man was not on the original list of condemned men, my lord. He was arrested only today and summarily condemned to death on the charges of brigandry against the Crown.'

'On whose authority?'

'On my authority, as vested in me by my position as Constable of Pembroke.'

'And do you have evidence of this man's guilt or are we nothing more than the barbarians that the Welsh already think we are?'

'I had a confession from the man himself,' said Salisbury, 'witnessed by many of our own men as well as some of the peasants around the scaffold.'

'So, you are telling me this man just walked up of his own free will and declared himself a rebel in order to be hanged. Why would he do that?'

'To save his son, my lord. One of the condemned men to be executed.'

'It still doesn't make sense.'

'He offered himself in his son's place, but I arrested him upon his confession and intended to hang them both.'

'But what made him think you would free his son?'

Salisbury glanced at Nesta at the far end of the hall. 'My lord, perhaps we could talk in private. There are matters that should stay between us only.'

Gerald followed his gaze before turning his attention back upon the constable. 'Nesta is both my wife and confidante, Master Salisbury. You can say what you have to say in front of her.'

'My lord,' said Salisbury, 'as Constable of Pembroke and in the interests of security I respectfully demand a private audience.'

'*Master Salisbury,*' shouted Gerald, 'at the moment you are in no position to demand anything. As far as I can see you are responsible for the deaths of ten of my men, another six grievously wounded and the release of two brigands whose heads should already be on spikes above the gate. Now, if you don't want to be charged with incompetence and possibly lose your very profitable station within this castle I suggest you start explaining yourself immediately.' Gerald paused and took a deep breath before continuing. 'So, I will ask you again. What did this mysterious man who confessed his crimes possibly offer that made him think you would grant his request?'

Salisbury paused and with another glance towards Nesta, raised himself up to his full height. 'My lord,' he announced, 'he told me he was the rebel prince of Deheubarth, Gruffydd ap Rhys.'

Gerald stared at Salisbury in silence, unsure what to make of his constable's last statement. Behind him, Nesta's eyes widened at the mention of her brother's name and she walked over to stand beside her husband, keen to hear more. Gerald's eyes narrowed as the information sunk in and Salisbury swallowed hard, realising how absurd his last statement must sound.

'Let me get this clear,' said Gerald eventually. 'You are telling me that some unknown vagrant came up to you out of nowhere and calmly announced he was one of the most wanted men across the south of the country.'

'Yes, my lord.'

'A man,' continued Gerald, walking around the constable, 'who has been dead for many years and whose body was clearly identified as being the one we sought.'

'I know it sounds absurd,' said Salisbury, 'but he told me his death had been faked for the sake of his family.'

'And you believed him?'

'It matters not, my lord, the very fact that he was admitting to being a rebel gave me the authority to pass instant sentence upon him, as well you know.'

'You may be correct in that sense,' said Gerald, 'but I am keen to understand what it was that made you think he was telling the truth, prince or no prince.'

'My lord,' answered Salisbury, 'any man who offers his life in the place of one about to die has an air of believability about him. He was honest in his manner and was desperate to save the life of his son.'

'Which prisoner was this?' asked Gerald.

'The one who was captured on your campaign against the rebels.'

'The one who worked at the manor at Llandeilo?'

'Aye, my lord.'

'So if this man who claimed royal blood was indeed the father of the condemned boy, that would make him the steward of that manor.'

'I assume so.'

'So you decided that this stranger was lying and sentenced him to death.'

'I did, my lord,' said Salisbury, 'but when we came under attack from the rebels, I realised he may be telling the truth.'

'Even though he was supposed to be dead?'

'If you recall, my lord, Tarw's body was badly smashed from the fall from the cliff.'

'But he was identified by one of our own men.'

'One who was descended from Welsh stock. It is possible he had been bribed to say such a thing.'

Gerald heard a noise beside him. Nesta's hand was over her mouth to stifle any noise but he could hear her gasps of breath through her tears of disbelief.

'Calm yourself, Nesta,' said Gerald. 'This may yet be a mistake.'

Nesta nodded silently but her gaze never left Salisbury.

Gerald turned back to the constable. 'So what are your thoughts now?' he asked.

'In what matter, my lord?'

'Do you now think he was telling the truth?'

Salisbury felt Nesta's eyes burning into him. He knew he was in a precarious position for he was being asked to admit he had condemned a Welsh prince to death and that was a power out of his jurisdiction.

'My lord,' he said eventually, 'at the time of sentence, I believed he was naught but a madman and I acted accordingly. However, after seeing the strength of the attack launched to save his life and that of his son, I can only assume he is someone of importance within the rebel camp. Whether he is the prince or not, I cannot say.'

'No,' replied Gerald, 'you cannot for there are few who would recognise him after all this time. The idea sounds like that of a madman but if there is the slightest chance that this absurd story carries even the tiniest hint of truth, then I need to know. However, now you have allowed him to escape, it is possible we will never find out.'

'There is one way,' said Salisbury. 'Send a message to Lord Bevan of Llandeilo. The man claimed to be his steward so Bevan of all people will be aware of his history. Bring him here for questioning and if there is any substance to the story, then he will be the one who knows.'

Gerald nodded, recognising the merit in the suggestion. He turned to his steward. 'Send an armed column to Llandeilo. Invite Lord Bevan to attend me immediately and if he offers any resistance, have him arrested. Bring him in chains if necessary.'

'Aye, my lord,' said the steward and he left the room.

'As for you, Master Salisbury,' he continued, 'I'm still not sure how to assess your actions today. If the man was a commoner, then your ill-thought actions have needlessly contributed to the deaths of our men. On the other hand, if he was indeed the prince, then his escape has the potential to reignite the dormant fire that is the rebellion. Withdraw to your quarters while I consider what is to be done.'

'Aye, my lord,' said Salisbury and he turned and left the room.

'*Is it possible?*' gasped Nesta. 'Could Tarw still be alive?'

'Anything is possible,' said Gerald, 'but you should not get your hopes up. Even if he is, it will be my duty to arrest him and present him to the king for a trial.'

'But he is my brother and a true Prince of Wales. Surely that affords him some leniency?'

'He is also the man responsible for leading a rebellion against the Crown for many years,' replied Gerald.

'But he has done nothing of the sort for so long.'

'That is not an excuse for an avoidance of justice,' said Gerald. 'But let's not worry about that at the moment. We will know more when Lord Bevan arrives. Either he will vouch for this man and prove his innocence or, if not, then there are questions to be answered.'

'In what way?'

'If this man was indeed your brother and Lord Bevan was aware of his identity, then he will be complicit in harbouring a rebel from the justice of the Crown. That in itself is a crime punishable by hanging.'

'Even though Tarw may have turned away from such a life?'

'Aye. Like it or not, the deed will have been done and will warrant punishment.'

'But, assuming it is Tarw, you don't know that he will go back to the way of the rebel.'

'Don't I?' asked Gerald. 'Men have already died in his name today and, besides, now he has been unmasked, where else could he go? However, it is not your brother who worries me. If this turns out to be true, then it begs another question, one of far more importance.'

'And what would that be?' asked Nesta.

'The whereabouts of his wife,' replied Gerald.

'Gwenllian?' asked Nesta.

'Aye, Gwenllian,' confirmed Gerald, 'for if she is still alive and decides to join her husband amongst the rebel camps, then whether we like it or not, our position in Deheubarth just became a lot more dangerous.'

The Cantref Mawr

December 20th, AD 1135

Tarw and his sons rode hard throughout the day, stopping only to rest and feed the horses. Night was closing in and Maelgwyn was strangely quiet, still processing the information revealed to him back in Pembroke. He led his horse over to a small stream in the copse and watched it drink heavily as his mind turned over and over again, absorbing the implications.

'Maelgwyn,' said Morgan from behind. 'Something bothers you.'

'Does it not you?' asked Maelgwyn without turning around. 'Or are you comfortable that we have all been living a lie, hiding away like chickens from a fox?'

'Do not allow this revelation to cast a shadow upon your view of our father, Maelgwyn. He is a good man and meant only to secure our safety.'

'By lying to us for all these years?'

'Yes. He had become the main target of the king and there was a fortune on his head. Not just his but ours as well.'

'But you must have only been a boy and me a mere child. Why would the English want us dead?'

'Because Tarw is our father and thus we are descended from Hywel Dda himself. Henry knew that if we were allowed to grow up into men there was the potential for us to rally the whole of Wales behind us and that was something he could not risk. Rhys wasn't born then, but as our father already had three sons, he decided to choose our safety over his continued campaign. That is a sign of a good man, Maelgwyn, not a bad one.'

'But you knew. Why didn't you tell me when I became of age?'

'Why? What would you have done?'

'I know exactly what I would have done. I would have sought men of a like mind to continue the fight.'

'And that is exactly the reason I never told you. It was too dangerous.'

'Yet you did exactly that.'

'I did, and look at the mess it has led us into. I'm not sure what is going to happen now but I do know it has all gone terribly wrong.' Before he could continue, Tarw rode his horse up behind them.

'Are your horses ready?' he asked.

'Almost,' said Morgan. 'How much further?'

'Another two hours of riding north-east,' said Tarw. 'Stick close to the river and eventually you will be challenged by the rebels.'

'Are you not coming with us?'

'I can't,' said Tarw. 'There is something I must do.'

'What is so important that you leave us out here?' asked Maelgwyn.

'The lives of the men who fought and possibly died to save us a few hours ago,' replied Tarw. 'Hopefully they all managed to escape but I cannot ride on to safety knowing they are still not accounted for. Fret not, you are safe from here on in. We are already being watched so when you are challenged ask for an audience with Taliesin, the rebel leader, and tell him the truth about what happened today.'

'And about your identity?'

'Aye. Tell him everything. I will explain more when I reach the camp tomorrow but, until then, tell him I claim the hospitality of a fellow Welshman to look after my sons.'

'So yet again you postpone telling me the truth,' said Maelgwyn.

'I know you are frustrated, my son, but you have to trust me on this. I promise the time is coming when I will answer all your questions. For now, there are men's lives at risk and I have to be true to my own conscience. Wait at the rebel camp and we will talk there.'

'It seems I have no choice,' said Maelgwyn, and he turned away.

'Go, Father,' said Morgan. 'We will be fine. Just make sure you return safely.'

'Aye,' said Tarw, and without another word, he rode back the way they had come.

Tarw rode his tired horse as hard as he dared through the night and the following morning he rested in a hay barn on the outskirts of the town. Wary of being recognised, he stayed hidden throughout the day until finally darkness came and he headed down into Pembroke.

Slowly he walked through the deserted alleyways, his feet ankle-deep in the cloying filth that had spread with the melting snow, an overflow from a nearby blocked drainage ditch. The smell caught his breath and, as he walked, he sought out the drier parts of the alleyways, finally finding what he was looking for: a busy tavern. The hour was late and raucous songs echoed from within. If there was news to be had, this would be the place, for no doubt the attack of the previous day would have been the talking point of the town; yet he hesitated to go in lest he was recognised. Even in places like this, the English would have sympathisers and news of his return would be at the castle within the hour.

Frustrated, he watched as two drunken men stumbled around outside the tavern, each hopelessly trying to hit the other, but their pathetic attempt at a fight ended with both sprawling in the stinking mud with hardly a blow landed. One eventually staggered away and Tarw saw his chance. Looking around to check he wasn't seen, he ran over and helped the other man to his feet. He led him over into one of the side streets and sat him against a wall.

'Leave me alone,' mumbled the man, swiping Tarw's hand away.

'I am a friend,' said Tarw, wiping the filth from the man's face, 'and just want to talk.'

'Do you have ale?' asked the man looking up hopefully.

'Alas no, but I do have coin and if you answer a couple of questions, there is a penny in it for you.'

The man stopped struggling and looked up at the prince. 'What sort of questions?' he asked, his speech far clearer than his drunken state implied. 'For I am no informer.'

'I did not say that you are,' said Tarw. 'I just want to know what happened at the hanging.'

'Oh that,' said the drunk. 'In that case you have come to the right man. I was right there and saw everything.'

'Good,' said Tarw. 'Tell me, did you see the assault?'

'Aye, I did.'

'And did you see the prisoners escape?'

'Aye. They ran into the streets and disappeared. By now they are probably on a ship to Ireland.'

'Why do you say that?'

'Because the word is it was Tarw and his sons. Where else could they go?'

'I thought they were dead,' ventured Tarw, surprised that news of his identity had already spread.

'Apparently not. It seems he had been living the life of a steward somewhere in Llandeilo. Where is this penny you promised?'

'In a moment,' said Tarw. 'So, assuming it was indeed the prince, how does that news sit with the people of Pembroke?'

'They think it's good news,' said the man. 'Especially with the king lying cold in his coffin. If it was indeed the prince back from the dead, hopefully he will rally the people and drive the cursed English from Deheubarth once and for all.' He looked up with a glint of fear in his eyes. 'You're not English, are you?'

'Fear not,' said Tarw. 'I am as Welsh as you.'

'Enough talk,' said the man staggering to his feet. 'I need a drink and you owe me a penny.'

'One last question,' said Tarw. 'The men who rescued the prince. Were any of them captured?'

'Not that I know of. Two were killed and one wounded but the soldiers kicked him to death in the square. The rest slipped away into the streets.'

'Thank you,' said Tarw. 'You have been very helpful.' He handed over the penny but as he did, the drunk grabbed his hand and pulled him close to stare into his eyes.

'I know you,' he said, his eyes squinting. 'I have seen you before.'

'You are mistaken,' said Tarw, pulling his hand away. 'I am just a traveller passing through and will now be on my way.'

'No,' said the man, walking backward, away from the prince. 'I always remember a face. It will come back to me. I'm sure.'

'Enjoy your ale, my friend,' said Tarw, and he turned away, satisfied that everyone who was able had managed to escape the clutches of the English. He reached the barn and was tightening the strap around the girth of his horse when he heard something outside in the darkness. Drawing his blade, he walked slowly out of the barn, worried that he may have been followed, but there was nothing. The night was silent.

He returned to his horse but hadn't gone a few paces when his head was pulled back from behind and he felt the cold steel of a blade pressed against his throat.

'Don't move,' hissed a voice, 'or you are a dead man.'

———————

Tarw froze, his heart beating rapidly. For a second he considered lashing out and hoping his attacker was inexperienced but the pressure on the blade told him otherwise.

'Who are you?' hissed the voice. 'And tell me no lies.'

'I am Carwyn of Llandeilo,' said Tarw, unsure whether to reveal his true identity, 'and I am here on business.'

For a few seconds there was silence and when the unseen man spoke again, there was a hint of amusement in his tone. 'Well, Carwyn of Llandeilo, I am about to remove my blade but, be aware, there is an arrow aimed at you as we speak and if you so much as twitch as I step back, it will cut your heart in two before you take a step. Understood?'

'Aye,' said Tarw and he felt the pressure disappear as the man stepped back.

'Turn around,' said the man a moment later, 'for if you tell the truth then I need to see if you are as ugly as they say you are.'

Tarw smiled as he recognised the jibe and turned to see his comrade from Llandeilo Manor standing before him with a huge grin on his face.

'Robert,' said Tarw with relief. 'What are you doing here?'

'We knew you would get yourself into trouble,' replied Robert, 'so we came to rescue you of course. Besides, you still owe me a purse of silver pennies from our last game of dice.'

'We?' replied Tarw. 'Who else is here?'

'I have thirty men at my back,' said Robert. 'Each man recruited on the journey here from villages still loyal to your father's name and each willing to die in their support of the quest I laid before them.'

'Which was?'

'To save your son from the gallows.'

'And not to save me?' asked Tarw in amusement.

'To be fair, I did not know about your involvement at the time,' said Robert. 'Not until the moment I saw you upon the scaffold, and by then I had become aware that Brynmore had deployed his archers so I had to let the situation play out.'

'You saw Brynmore?'

'I did, and we agreed that his men would secure the release of Morgan while our own waited outside of the town to thwart any pursuit by the English.'

'A good plan,' said Tarw. 'So how did you find me here?'

'That was the easy part,' said Robert. 'We had just arrived at the Cantref Mawr after the assault when we were told that Maelgwyn and Morgan had been taken into the protection of Taliesin but you had returned here to seek survivors. We changed horses and rode after you as quickly as we could. I left the men hidden in the trees a few leagues back and fortunately saw you skulking around the tavern like a common drunk. After that I followed you here in case I was mistaken in the darkness.'

'Hence the knife.'

'Yes,' said Robert, glancing down at the blade still held in his hand. 'Sorry about that, but I had to be sure.' He sheathed the knife and looked back up at his friend. 'Anyway,' he continued, 'there's no harm done.'

'I'll let you know in the morning,' said Tarw, gingerly feeling the slightest of cuts along his neck. 'That blade is very sharp.'

Robert grinned and held out his arm. 'Good to see you safe, my lord, but I think we should be getting away from here. It seems you've stirred up a right hornet's nest.'

'I agree,' said Tarw, taking his offered wrist. 'And besides, I don't think it will be long before that drunk remembers my face.'

'Then let's go,' said Robert. 'The men are waiting.'

Tarw nodded and led his horse from the barn. Within minutes, the two men were riding away from Pembroke and headed back towards the distant hills.

Half an hour later, Tarw and Robert dismounted and led their horses into a dense thicket. Robert whistled quietly and was rewarded with a similar whistle from deeper within the trees.

'This way,' whispered Robert and soon they reached a clearing containing thirty men and their horses. At the centre a small fire burned, carefully sheltered by a surrounding wall of upright logs driven into the ground.

'You found him,' said one of the men, stepping forward to greet them. 'Thank God himself.'

'Aye,' said Tarw, 'he found me and it is I that should be thanking all of you for undertaking such a task. You have my gratitude.'

'We did not do it for you, my lord,' laughed another man, 'but for someone far prettier.'

'What do you mean?'

'My lord,' said Robert, interrupting the prince, 'there is something else you should know. Back in the barn, I did not tell you the whole story. I was not alone on this quest and it was not in my name that these men left their families to risk their lives.'

'Then if not mine or yours, whose?'

'Mine,' said a gentle voice and he turned to see a beautiful woman emerging from the darker shadows.

'Branwen,' he gasped and he stepped forward to embrace his wife. For a few seconds they held each other tightly before Tarw kissed her lovingly on the lips.

For a few moments there was an awkward silence, broken only when one of the men spoke quietly. 'Who in hell is Branwen?'

Tarw and his wife pulled apart amongst the ensuing laughter. 'Branwen and Carwyn are the names we adopted to keep our true identities secret,' explained Tarw, looking over at the young man. 'That way it was easier to evade the English spies.'

'Oh,' said the soldier quietly. 'So how do you wish to be addressed?'

Tarw turned to his wife. 'What do you think?'

'I think we have worn the cloaks of anonymity for far too long,' she replied, 'and I long to return to my birth name.'

'Then that is what we will do. Comrades, allow me to reintroduce my wife, Gwenllian ferch Gruffydd, daughter of King Gruffydd ap Cynan and scourge of the English.'

'My lady,' mumbled the men, all nodding their heads in acknowledgement. Some had served under Gwenllian many years earlier but most had only heard of her exploits in the struggle for freedom.

'And you?' asked Robert. 'Am I reduced to now using your formal name after all these years at your side?'

'Tarw is fine,' laughed the prince, 'and, in truth, it is a weight from my shoulders.'

Robert withdrew his sword from its scabbard and embedded it in the ground before him. 'Then let me be the first to pledge my allegiance to the returned true heir of Deheubarth, my lord Tarw, and his first lady, Gwenllian ferch Gruffydd.' He dropped to one knee, and with both hands on the hilt of his sword, lowered his head in a sign of allegiance.

The rest of the men followed suit and Tarw glanced at Gwenllian. 'You do know there will be no turning back from this?' he said.

'I do,' she replied, 'but, like you, I feel as if I am released from a darkened cell. Who knows where this may lead but I think we should embrace it with all our hearts.'

Tarw nodded and turned to face the kneeling men. 'We accept your allegiance, and are humbled to do so.'

The men got to their feet and crowded around the prince and his wife, talking excitedly. Finally, they returned to the fire and sought the hot ale boiling quietly in the suspended pot.

Tarw turned to Gwenllian. 'What I still don't understand is how you came to be here?'

'To try to save Morgan of course.'

'But how did you know he was in trouble?'

'While you were away from Llandeilo, Lord Bevan had a dispatch from Gerald saying he was about to hang the steward's son and invited representation. Bevan replied but his appeals were declined so Robert and I came with the intention of releasing Morgan, by force if necessary. On the way we called into villages known to still be loyal to the house of Tewdwr and recruited these men to our cause. We had no idea that you had also been captured but, luckily for us, Brynmore had set out upon your rescue and we found him already embarked upon his plan. We helped in the withdrawal after the attack, and the rest you know. We headed to the Cantref Mawr but when we found out you had returned to Pembroke I insisted on accompanying Robert there. Upon his persuasion, I agreed to stay here amongst the trees while he sought you out. In his words, it would have been unforgivable if we were both to be caught by the English.'

'Understandable,' said Tarw. 'And for a while I really thought my days had come to an end. Still, that threat has been dealt with so all we can do now is decide where we go from here.'

'First of all, I think we should take the boys to the safety of my father's house in Aberffraw. At least they will be safe there.'

'Where are Rhydian and Rhys now?' asked Tarw.

'Still in Llandeilo. They are safe there.'

'No, they're not,' said Tarw quickly, his heart racing.

'What do you mean?' asked Gwenllian.

'I mean the English know my real identity. I was tricked into revealing it to Salisbury in an effort to save Morgan and, if they know that, it won't take them long to realise Lord Bevan was in on the subterfuge. If I was Gerald, I would have a column of men galloping to Llandeilo as we speak.'

'Oh, sweet Jesus, we have to do something!' gasped Gwenllian. She called out across the clearing. 'Robert, saddle the horses quickly. We are returning to Llandeilo.'

'Is there a problem?' asked Robert, his leather jack halfway to his mouth.

'Yes. The boys are in danger and we need to get back as soon as we can. Muster twenty of the men and be ready to ride as soon as possible.'

'I'll come with you,' said Tarw as Robert turned to carry out the command.

'No, you go on to the Cantref Mawr,' said Gwenllian with urgency in her voice. 'Find Morgan and Maelgwyn. Wait there for us and, God willing, we will return within a couple of days.'

Tarw stared at Gwenllian, recognising the steely resolve in her voice, a trait that had been the cause of so much fear amongst the English for so many years. Finally, he nodded, knowing it made total sense not to ride together in the face of so much danger. At least this way, even if things went wrong, half the family would be guaranteed freedom.

'Gwenllian,' said Tarw as his wife strode over to the men, 'when you get there warn Lord Bevan his involvement has been discovered and it is in his interests to evacuate the manor. Do not waste any time retrieving anything of value. Just collect the boys and return with all haste. Drag them from their beds if necessary; there is no time to spare.'

'Don't worry about me,' said Gwenllian. 'I will be fine.'

'Don't forget you haven't wielded a blade in anger for many years,' said Tarw. 'Avoid conflict wherever possible.'

'I have Robert at my side,' said Gwenllian, placing her own saddle upon her horse, 'and the strength of suppressed freedom in my heart. You just look after Morgan and Maelgwyn.'

Minutes later, Gwenllian leaned over from astride her horse and kissed her husband goodbye, not knowing if it would be the last time she would ever see him.

'We'll see you in a few days,' she said before turning her horse and riding out of the copse.

'Be safe, my love,' said Tarw quietly as she disappeared from sight.

'My lord, are we to camp here?' said one of the remaining men.

'No,' said Tarw over his shoulder. 'Saddle your horses. There will be no rest for anyone this night.'

———

Maelgwyn sat outside one of the huts deep inside the forested valley that hid the rebel camp. A bowl of half-eaten chicken stew lay on the ground beside him and he watched the frenetic activity throughout the valley as people came and went in a place as busy as any village.

Since arriving the previous day, he had been left to himself. Maelgwyn was frustrated; not least because his father had still not explained more about the situation.

Behind him in the hut, his brother slept soundly, having had his wounds treated by one of the camp women, and if it hadn't been for him, Maelgwyn would have considered taking his chances out in the forest and returning to Llandeilo Manor.

'Have you finished with that?' asked a voice to his side and he turned to see Bethan, the young woman who had dressed his brother's wounds, pointing at the bowl of stew.

'Aye,' said Maelgwyn. 'You can give it to the dogs.'

'Bones are for the dogs,' said the girl, carefully picking up the bowl, 'as are the rotten carcasses of anything found dead upon the road, but uneaten stew goes straight back in the pots.'

'Really?' said Maelgwyn. 'That sounds disgusting.'

'Says the voice of privilege,' said the girl. 'You may have been able to waste food back in Llandeilo Manor but out here, every mouthful counts.'

'How do you know I am from Llandeilo?' asked Maelgwyn.

'Everyone knows,' said Bethan. 'That's another thing about living here in the camp, everyone knows everyone else's business.'

'So do you know about my father?'

'Aye, I do. Why do you ask?'

'Because I seem to be the only one around here who doesn't know him.'

'What do you mean?'

'Until yesterday, I always thought that he was just plain old Carwyn of Llandeilo, the steward of the manor. We had a nice house, a good life and the respect of everyone in the village, but today, it seems he is someone else completely. A rebel, no less, and even perhaps the greatest rebel of them all, Tarw of Wales.'

'There is no perhaps about it,' said Bethan. 'He is who you say he is and I am shocked that you did not know.'

'No more shocked than I,' said Maelgwyn. 'It seems my brother knew, but apart from him it was a secret well kept. I'm not sure how my mother is going to take all this.'

Bethan stared at Maelgwyn, a look of surprise upon her face. 'You really have no idea what is going on, do you?' she said.

'No,' he replied, 'and to be honest, I am getting very angry about the whole thing. So tell me, what else do you know about my father?'

Bethan sat down on a log on the opposite side of the fire. 'What do you want to know?'

'Anything – everything. Whatever you can tell me.'

'Well there's not a lot,' said Bethan, 'for I am only repeating what I have been told these past few days. It seems that a long time ago your father was one of the most feared rebel leaders ever to ride these lands. For many years he and his wife led a rebel army based right here in the Cantref Mawr and attacked the English throughout Deheubarth. Every caravan that dared to venture between the English castles had to be accompanied by an armed column to ensure they were not ravaged by the rebels. Even then they were not safe, and after Tarw turned down the offer of amnesty in return for stopping his attacks, the king offered a huge reward, payable to any man willing to betray his whereabouts to the Crown.'

'And did that work?'

'No, he and his wife were very popular throughout Deheubarth. They shared whatever wealth they liberated from the English caravans and made sure the poor had enough food throughout the winters.'

'He was married?'

'Indeed, to a very beautiful woman called Gwenllian, the warrior daughter of the king of Gwynedd. Together they were the scourge of every Englishman from Ceredigion to Gwent.'

'What happened to them?' asked Maelgwyn.

'Well, therein lies the mystery. One day they were heralded as the greatest freedom fighters ever to raise a sword against the English crown, the next they had both disappeared. A few days later, the criers announced Tarw's body had been found shattered at the base of a cliff and his corpse would be hanged for treason. Of course, now it appears all that was false and he has been in hiding all these years. Many call him a coward but those still loyal to the house of Tewdwr hope he has returned to stoke the fires of rebellion that still smoulder amongst the backstreets of Deheubarth.'

'My father is no coward,' growled Maelgwyn. 'Just yesterday he offered his own life in return for that of my brother.'

'I did not say he was, but there are some who think differently.'

'So what about his wife?'

'She disappeared just after his death. Everyone assumed she was killed by the English for nothing more was ever heard of her, but if Carwyn is indeed Tarw then your mother must be Gwenllian, the daughter of a king and a true hero throughout the south. She was as beautiful as a sunrise yet could match any man in trials of arms. If the rumours are true, then both she and your father turned away from the life of the freedom fighter and sought obscurity, leaving a fractured rebel cause behind them. Nobody knows why but I suspect we will soon find out. I just hope the reasons were justified, for cowardice is given short shrift around here.'

'I told you,' growled Maelgwyn. 'My father is no coward and in my eyes my mother is no princess. She is just the daughter of a farmer in Llandeilo.'

'Well,' said Bethan, staring over Maelgwyn's shoulder, 'whichever one of us is right, we are about to find out.'

Maelgwyn turned and saw a column of horses riding into the camp, headed by his father. People started to emerge from their tents and huts, keen to see the man they had heard so much about, and soon a crowd had gathered in the central clearing.

'Are you he?' shouted one of the crowd. 'Is it truly you?'

'Are you the prince?' shouted another. 'Where have you been?'

The questions came thick and fast but before he could answer, a voice echoed out from the trees just above the camp.

'*Enough,*' roared Taliesin, commanding instant silence and respect. 'Give them some space and make sure they are well tended.' He turned to the unkempt warrior at his side. 'Dog, see that they are fed and watered.'

The warrior nodded and, as the rebel leader disappeared back into his hut, he descended the slope to stand before Tarw. The crowd started to talk amongst themselves again and several young boys came forward to take the riders' horses. Some of the women came over to offer food and hot ale to the weary travellers, leaving Tarw standing alone, staring at the man before him.

Dog looked him up and down, chewing on the edge of a stripped twig. Tarw remained silent, knowing the inspection would soon end and Dog would address him eventually.

'So,' said Dog, 'when we met a few days ago you claimed to be naught but a steward. Now you claim to be a prince. Which is it to be, stranger?'

'I am Tarw,' came the reply, 'and I know you are known as Dog, the mercenary my brother put so much faith in when he sought vengeance for his mutilation.'

'Ah, Diafol,' said Dog. 'He had my respect. A man that ignored the niceties of mercy and compassion as I recall.'

'He had good reason, so I will not judge his methods.' said Tarw.

'Alas, he is gone now,' said Dog. 'But perhaps his spirit lives on in you?'

'I seek freedom, not revenge,' said Tarw. He looked up towards the hut on the hill.

'Was that Taliesin?'

'Aye, and he will see you in his own good time. In the meantime, you will eat with me. Come.'

'I want to see my sons.'

'Eat first, then I will take you to them. Fret not, they are safe and well fed.' Dog led Tarw over to a waxed-linen canopy, stretched between the trees. Beneath the leaking shelter, several men sat at a rough log table eating stew served from a communal pot, casting nervous and judgemental glances in his direction.

'You are in luck,' said Dog, retrieving two used wooden bowls from one end of the table. 'Our traps secured a couple of squirrels this very morning.'

'Anything will do,' said Tarw. 'I haven't eaten since yesterday.'

Dog threw him a bowl before dipping his own into the rodent-flavoured potage. 'Eat while you can,' he said. 'Sometimes we go without.'

'Do you not hold stores?'

'Aye, but there are many mouths to feed and often the pots are empty.'

'Surely you can get food elsewhere.'

'Taliesin will not raid the farms,' said Dog with a shrug. 'A noble gesture but one beyond my understanding. He would rather see his own people go hungry.'

'What about the supply wagons of the English?'

'You saw with your own eyes what happened to our men the last time we attacked a supply caravan.'

Tarw thought back to the deathly scene he had stumbled across several days earlier. 'I did,' he replied. 'But surely that was through bad execution?'

'Aye. The raiding party got careless and thought Gerald would not follow due to the bad weather. They found out the hard way, and deservedly so, but now we hunger because of their stupidity.'

'It sounds like times are hard for those loyal to the Welsh kings.'

'I've seen worse times,' said Dog, 'but they need to organise before Gerald wipes them all out once and for all. Now eat before someone takes it from you.'

Tarw dipped his own bowl into the potage before turning to look around the camp. People wandered aimlessly, wrapped against the cold. The sound of coughing filled the air and many were obviously sick.

'Where are the men?' asked Tarw.

'Apart from those responsible for your release,' replied Dog through a mouthful of food, 'these few are about all there are. The others are dead through battle or the other challenges faced by desperate men. It seems that even if they avoid being killed by the English, the Welsh are intent on killing each other.'

'And thus it always was,' sighed Tarw before putting the first spoon of foul-tasting potage in his mouth.

Pembroke Castle

December 22nd, AD 1135

The first fingers of light were just creeping into the sky and the castle slowly stirring into daily life when the alarm first came. It wasn't the furious echoing of a sentry's horn signalling an attack that woke the garrison, but a blood-curdling scream of someone discovering something straight from one of her nightmares.

In the guardroom alongside the gates, two men sat up straight and stared at each other for a few seconds, their minds still foggy from the slumber they had stolen before the flames of the fire.

'What was that?' gasped one of the soldiers.

'I don't know,' said his comrade. 'Come on, grab your weapon.'

Both men left the guardroom and stood outside, wondering where the scream had come from.

'Over there,' shouted a voice from up on the palisade and another guard pointed towards the stables.

They ran over and as they approached, collided with a young girl running from behind the stables.

'Whoa,' said one of the guards, grabbing her as she tried to run away. 'What's going on here? Are you hurt?'

'No,' gasped the girl through her sobs, 'but there's someone there, in the goose hut . . . she's . . . dead!'

The soldier glanced at his comrade. 'You, step aside,' he said to the girl. 'Wait here. We'll see what's going on.'

The two men placed their spears against a wall and drew their swords before walking slowly around to the goose pen. A flock of geese paraded at the far wall, necks extended as if waiting to see what unfolded next.

'I see nothing,' said the first guard.

'The door is open. Look inside,' said the second.

'You look inside,' came the retort. 'I outrank you remember?'

The first man grumbled but walked carefully over to the door. He pulled it fully open and peered inside. At first he could see nothing but as a sliver of light eased through a gap in the wall, he could see a body on the floor.

'Can you see anything?' asked his comrade behind him.

'Aye, it looks like a young girl.' He placed his sword in his scabbard and dropped to his knees.

'Is she alive?'

'No, her throat has been cut. It looks like she has been dead for hours.'

'I know her,' said his comrade peering over his shoulder. 'Her name is Catrin and she collected the eggs for the kitchens every morning. Why would someone want to kill her?'

'Why do you think?' replied the first soldier and he moved to one side revealing the girl's dress was up around her waist. 'It looks like someone raped her before cutting her throat.'

'Oh, sweet Jesus,' replied the second soldier. 'You stay here. I'll alert the constable.'

As he left the hut, the first soldier got to his feet and looked around the room, suddenly aware that the perpetrator could still be there. Within seconds it was obvious he was alone but as he looked, the growing sunlight leaking into the goose shed reflected on something hidden beneath the straw upon the floor.

'Hello,' he said to himself. 'What do we have here?' He bent to move the straw and found the bloodied blade responsible for opening the girl's throat hidden beneath. Picking it up he turned it over in his hand and saw an arrow carved into the handle. Behind him, the duty sergeant came into the hut alongside another guard.

'What's going on?' he demanded. 'Who is she?'

'A servant from the keep,' said the first soldier. 'It looks like she's been raped and murdered. Here, I found this.' He handed over the knife and the sergeant examined the handle.

'An archer's knife; probably dropped by the man responsible.'

'You think one of our own men did this?' asked the soldier.

'I don't know but there's one way to find out. Get this girl covered up. The constable is going to want to see what happened here but there's no need to leave her exposed like that. Turn out the barracks. I want everyone formed up complete with their personal weapons.'

'Aye, my lord,' said the soldier at his back and he turned away to his task.

Half an hour later, the entire garrison lay formed up in the bailey – over a hundred men each stamping their feet or blowing on their hands in a vain effort to keep warm. To one side, fifty archers lined up in a straight line at the command of the duty sergeant. In the centre of the bailey, the constable talked quietly with the steward, glancing over at the archers, and as they waited, two men carried a bundle over to place it at the constable's feet. As the men fell silent, Salisbury reached down and removed the blanket, revealing the dead body of the scullery girl. A collective gasp rippled around the bailey. They had all seen a dead body before but the pretty girl was well known and popular amongst the men.

'Settle down,' ordered Salisbury and the men fell silent. 'Sometime last night,' he continued, 'this girl was raped and brutally killed. Her murderer stands amongst us and we are here to find out the man responsible.'

Another murmur rippled amongst the men.

'Unluckily for him,' said Salisbury, 'it seems that in his rush to flee the scene he dropped his knife and consequently, we are able to identify him.' He nodded at the duty sergeant.

'Every man here, draw your knives and present them for inspection,' roared the sergeant.

Slowly the order sunk in and after a lot of shuffling each man held out their knives before them. Eventually, silence returned and the sergeant walked slowly amongst the ranks. Finally, he stopped before one of the archers.

'Where's your knife?' he asked coldly.

'I don't know, my lord,' stuttered the young man. 'I had it last night. It must be somewhere in the barracks.'

'Step forward,' said the sergeant.

The archer took several paces and stopped, acutely aware of every set of eyes focussed on him.

'It wasn't me,' he said, looking around. 'I swear it.'

The constable walked over and held the murder weapon before him. 'Do you recognise this?' he asked.

'It is an archer's knife, true enough,' said the young man, 'but it could be anyone's.'

'Really?' said the constable. 'Look closer. Do you not recognise the mark?'

The archer's eyes looked down and his heart sank as he recognised his own mark upon the hilt. 'I don't understand. Someone must have stolen it in the night.'

'How convenient,' sneered Salisbury.

'I swear,' gasped the young man, looking around in panic, 'I was on duty on the palisade until midnight but after that I slept the night through.'

'Keep your story for your trial,' said the constable coldly. 'Sergeant, take him into custody.' The sergeant stepped forward and, as the young man started to protest his innocence again, punched him straight in the face with a chainmailed fist, knocking him to the ground.

'Shut your mouth, you filthy murderer,' he snarled, and he nodded to two waiting guards. Together they dragged the semi-conscious archer away as Salisbury addressed the garrison.

'It may have been that man's hand that murdered this girl,' he announced, 'but you men also share the blame. He is one of yours; a comrade, a brother. You allowed this to happen so will share the punishment. All leave is cancelled for ten days and there will be extra duties for all. There is no place in this castle for murderers.' He turned to the man at his side. 'Sir Walter, see to it that these men are worked hard today and get that girl buried.'

'Aye, my lord,' said the knight. 'What about the archer?'

'Detain him in the dungeons. Let him suffer for a while before we find him guilty. Death is too easy an escape.'

As Walter de Calais turned to address the men, Salisbury allowed himself the luxury of the smallest of smiles. It was early days but already his plans were coming together.

The Cantref Mawr

December 23rd, AD 1135

Dog squatted on his haunches outside the campaign tent. His ragged appearance meant he could walk through any village and be mistaken for a beggar but this was no carefully contrived image, it was who he was, a dirty and unkempt vagrant, who also happened to be the most talented killer in the south of the country.

As a well-travelled mercenary who had seen battle from Scotland to the Holy Land and every place in between, his services were often in demand by noble men from all sides but for the past few years he had made his home amongst the rebels of the south. Though he knew he would never die a rich man, as long as he was fed and enjoyed freedom to come and go as he pleased, his price was modest.

Below him, on the valley floor the camp laboured under a heightened level of excitement. The success of the rescue in Pembroke, the first such attack in many months, meant everyone was nervous, and extra guards had been posted on every approach to the camp for miles around. They knew that the attack would hurt the English and, though few men had died, the castellan would not let it go unpunished. Despite that, the mood was upbeat for though any strike against the enemy was good, the rumour that Tarw and Gwenllian had resurfaced after so many years lifted many hearts from the despondency they had suffered for so long.

Inside the tent, Tarw sat on a chair to one side of the entrance, waiting for his audience with Taliesin. He had been waiting for over an hour but, despite his royal heritage, Tarw felt no animosity to the common-born leader for though he had once borne the mantle himself, he had given up any privilege associated with the role many years earlier.

Opposite Tarw, half a dozen men-at-arms stood around a table, supping watered wine and talking amongst themselves. Tarw knew none of them and amongst the many looks of interest cast his way was the occasional grimace of distaste, for though they knew of his heritage, his disappearance from the struggle against the English so many years earlier left many questions unanswered. Despite his patience, Tarw felt his ire rising and he stood to confront the one man in particular who seemed to have a particular disliking for him.

'My friend,' said Tarw, returning the man's stare. 'Your manner suggests you may have swallowed something distasteful. Perhaps I can be of assistance.'

'Cut your fancy words, steward,' said the man, turning to face Tarw head on. 'The only thing I find distasteful around here is the presence of a coward amongst true warriors.'

Tarw breathed deeply, knowing this was not something he could let slide. 'If you are referring to me,' he replied, 'then you must know I cannot let that accusation pass.'

The soldier spat on the floor and took a step nearer.

'Tomas, leave it,' said one of the other men quietly.

'You are not amongst the skirts and servants of your castles now, Prince,' said Tomas Scar, ignoring his comrade's advice. 'Say your piece or hold your tongue, unless you want me to hand it to you on the end of my blade.' His hand went to the hilt of his knife and he took another step forward.

Tarw looked around the tent. Behind him he had ten of his own men but he had not witnessed their ability in conflict and those before him were obviously battle hardened.

'Well?' said Tomas. 'Do you have the mettle to back up your manner?'

Voices were raised on both sides and the mood started to turn ugly before a voice cut through the noise like a knife. 'What goes on here?'

Everyone turned to see the rebel leader standing inside the flaps of the tent. He was head and shoulders above the rest and the wolf-skin cloak around his shoulders was matted and dirty. Underneath, the visible parts of the hauberk covering his muscular body were rusty and damaged, the sign of much wear and conflict.

Gradually the commotion died down and the men parted to allow their leader through. Taliesin walked up to the table and drank straight from the jug before unfastening his cloak and throwing it onto a nearby bench. When done he turned around and faced the men in the tent, staring at each of them in turn.

'Well?' he said. 'Anyone care to explain?'

'It was nothing, my lord, just a disagreement,' said one of the men.

'A disagreement with someone who is here at my personal invitation,' said Taliesin.

'No one was hurt,' said the first man. 'Heated words only.'

Taliesin nodded and walked over to stand in front of Tarw. Tarw returned his gaze and waited patiently as the rebel leader walked around him, realising all this was for show in front of his own men.

'So,' said Taliesin eventually, walking away to get a drink, 'you are the famous prince, Gruffydd ap Rhys, commonly known as Tarw.'

'I am,' said Tarw, 'and you must be the famous Taliesin ap John, freedom fighter and leader of the rebels of the Cantref Mawr.'

'You have heard of me?' said Taliesin, pouring wine into two tankards. 'That surprises me.'

'Why? You are the leader of the southern rebellion. What man in Deheubarth does not know your name?'

'Perhaps many,' said Taliesin, turning around, 'especially those who hide from their fellows in times of national need.'

Tarw nodded gently at the ill-disguised jibe but kept his silence. Taliesin walked over and handed him one of the tankards.

'I apologise for the hospitality shown so far,' said Taliesin, glancing towards Tomas, 'but my men have fought the English for many years. They are tired and battle weary so perhaps it is understandable their tempers are as frayed as a well-used bridle.'

'Like your comrade said, there is no harm done,' replied Tarw. 'Perhaps we should start again.'

'I agree. Please, join me at the table.' He stood to one side to indicate the empty benches and waited as Tarw took his place.

'Tomas, you will join us,' said Taliesin, 'as will your men.' He turned to Tarw. 'Feel free to invite your own to sit alongside you.'

'Would you like some food, my lord,' asked a young voice from the rear of the tent as the men sought their seats.

'Aye, and bring fresh ale for I still have the mud of the road within my mouth.' He waited as everyone settled down and finally spoke to Tarw again.

'So,' he said, 'I think we can safely assume you are who you say you are?'

'Why would I lie?' asked Tarw.

'Who knows? Perhaps for personal gain, or perhaps you are a spy sent by the Crown.'

'I can assure you I am neither,' said Tarw.

'And I believe you,' said Taliesin eventually, 'for there are many in this camp who have already vouched for you, especially those whom you left behind.'

'I am honoured you take their word,' said Tarw.

'Oh, trust me, if I had any cause for doubt you would already be dead. However, that is but a small problem when compared with what comes next.'

'And that is?' asked Tarw.

'To ascertain why exactly it is that you have returned to the Cantref Mawr after so many years. Is it perhaps that you see an opportunity to regain that which was once yours now the king is dead?'

'What do you mean?' Tarw asked.

'Well, it is no secret that Henry's only male heir died at sea and there will surely be a struggle amongst the English nobles to choose the next monarch. Those of a suspicious nature could think that you have reappeared to take advantage of that situation and seek the leadership of the rebel cause for your own ends.'

'I can assure you, that was never my intention,' said Tarw, accepting a tankard of ale from a serving boy. 'As far as I was concerned, my rebel days were over a long time ago and it was only by unfortunate circumstance that I find myself back amongst these hills.'

'You speak of your son?'

'Aye, and that devil, John of Salisbury. He made me reveal my identity in return for my son's life but reneged on the agreement as soon as he knew who I was. Now I am uncloaked, I cannot return to the life I have been living these past years.'

'That still doesn't explain what you are doing here.'

'The reasoning is simple. I am here to collect my two sons only. If you are agreeable, I will also seek refuge while Morgan recovers from his wounds.'

'And your wife, is she going to make an appearance?'

'She is riding to Llandeilo as we speak. Our other two sons are in danger and if God is with us, she will return here in a few days. After that we will leave for Gwynedd as soon as we can.'

Taliesin nodded with interest and supped on his ale as he stared at the man before him. 'Tell me,' he said eventually, 'these men at your back. Are they seasoned warriors?'

Tarw glanced to either side. 'Some have seen battle before, but most are new to the saddle.'

'So they are not your own men.'

'I have maintained no army. My wife recruited them on the road from Llandeilo.'

'Interesting. And how many do you have at your call?'

'About thirty in total. A small force only yet each have sworn allegiance.'

'I am impressed,' said Taliesin.

'With such small numbers?'

'No, with the fact that you have managed to recruit as many men in just a few days. It takes us a year to find as many and often they are the dregs from the barrel. These men, despite their inexperience, look healthy and ripe for instruction. Are there more where these came from?'

Tarw paused, his drink halfway to his mouth. Slowly he replaced the tankard on the table, aware of where the conversation was leading. 'Taliesin,' he said. 'You have lived this life for over ten years. You are better placed than I to judge the mood of the people and I have heard many good things about you as a leader. The English stranglehold over our country tightens by the day but, even though children are going hungry, a living father is far more likely to bring home some food than one already dead from fighting a dying cause.'

'Profound words,' said Taliesin. 'Yet when you were at the head of like-minded men, they say your forces flocked like sheep upon the hills. Is this true?'

'On occasion,' said Tarw. 'Our standing army numbered around a hundred but the strength swelled whenever we needed extra sword arms. Add to that the money we spent on mercenaries and we often reached five times that amount.'

The tent flaps opened again and two serving boys brought in a large iron pot and a sack of wooden bowls. They placed the pot on the table and tipped out the sack before leaving the tent.

'Mutton,' said one of the men as he removed the lid. 'A feast fit for a king.'

'Or at least a returned prince,' said Taliesin with a sideways glance at Tarw. 'Dig in, my friend, you are our guest and will have the choicest cut.'

Tarw retrieved his knife and delved into the thick stew before retrieving a slab of meat. He placed it in a bowl and used the iron tankard hanging from the side of the pot to scoop some of the thick gravy over the top. The rest of the men passed the pot around and soon each had a bowl of steaming food before them. Another boy appeared with a jug of ale and walked around the table filling each of the warriors' leather jacks. For the next few minutes, everyone focussed on their food and the ale boy was kept busy.

'So, what are your ultimate plans?' said Taliesin as they ate.

'I don't know,' said Tarw. 'I hope that the death of Henry will distract the English long enough for us to make our way to Gwynedd, but beyond that I cannot see.'

'Is that what you want?'

'I don't know what I want. I have hardly had time to breathe these past few days.'

'You could stay here with us.'

Tarw didn't answer and just looked down into the remains of his stew.

'Is it such a bad suggestion?' asked Taliesin.

'The thought is not unpleasant to me,' said Tarw, 'but a few moments ago you seemed to be warning me against such a thing.'

'It was a line of questioning only,' replied Taliesin, 'not a preference. Indeed, I would have thought a prince of Deheubarth belongs in the south, not amongst the halls of a blind, subservient king.'

Tarw looked up.

'Be careful what you say, Taliesin, for he is my family, and though he is suffering the pains of extended age, he still maintains his own kingdom and an army that keeps the north free from the English fist.'

'He is your family by marriage only,' replied Taliesin, 'and I repeat only what many others are already saying.' He paused and took a drink from his jack, his gaze never leaving Tarw's eyes.

'What do you mean?' asked Tarw.

'You say he maintains a strong army, and hint that the English fear his strength, but why is it, when a fellow Welshman whose blood runs as true as his asks for aid against a common enemy, he pleads poverty and lack of resources?'

'And you have done this?'

'On three occasions. Twice he refused and once I did not receive a reply. Is this the mark of a strong man? I think not, Tarw. We are on our own down here and the struggle has been great, yet with Hywel ap Maredudd likely to campaign against the English then we have a great chance to rekindle the fire that once burned in the hearts of every man from here to Ceredigion. With you at my side we can rebuild those armies you speak of and once more strike fear into the hearts of the enemy. What say you, Tarw – is the sanctuary of an old man who accepts English coin so readily an attractive choice or would you rather take up your sword and tear away the yoke from the necks of our people?'

Tarw sat back and stared at the rebel leader before looking around the table at the rest of the men. Everyone was silent and all eyes lay upon him, waiting for his answer. Finally he took a deep breath and drained his jack before placing it on the table. 'What I say is this,' he said. 'I agree the death of Henry presents us with an unprecedented opportunity and the thought of wielding my sword against the invader is indeed appealing, but there are a lot of things to consider before I make a decision. I will sleep on the matter and come back to you with my answer in a few days.'

'What sort of things?' asked Taliesin, disappointed at the reply. 'Either you are with us or you are not?'

'I have to discuss it with my wife and sons,' said Tarw, 'for they are in the front line of my thoughts and their will is paramount. In addition, I see the light of mistrust in many of the eyes around this table. If I was to seriously consider your offer, I would need to be sure I have the support of you and your men. A comrade's back is an easy target in the heat of battle.'

'You insult us,' growled Taliesin, 'for though your absence has caused anguish and heartache, there is no one who would speak against a true blood prince of Deheubarth.'

'*I would*,' said a voice and all eyes turned to Tomas Scar. The warrior was staring down into his jack and it was obvious he had already drunk too much ale. Silence fell and eventually he looked up, his gaze passing between Tarw and Taliesin.

'You two make me sick,' he said eventually.

One of the men at Taliesin's side made to stand up, his hand going to his blade, but the rebel leader pulled him back onto the bench.

'Let him be,' said Taliesin. 'I value the word of every man in this tent. Our comrade will have his say and we will listen.' He turned to Tomas. 'Say your piece, my friend, but I hope you know what you are doing.'

'I will,' said Tomas, 'because if this man is really who he says he is, then you have invited a coward and a traitor into our midst. A man who ran like a scared child as soon as the Crown set a price upon his head. Is that the sort of leader we want, one who runs as soon as his skin is at risk?'

'It wasn't like that,' said Tarw quietly.

'Then what was it like, Tarw?' shouted Tomas, slamming his jack down onto the table. 'Because from here that is exactly what it looks like. Tell these men why it is that while they continued the fight against the English, often seeing comrades dangle at the end of a hangman's noose, you were lording it up at Llandeilo with a warm bed and a full belly. Explain to them why you ran like a scared child and if they offer understanding perhaps then and only then can you even dream we will accept you as one of our own.'

'He is the prince of our kingdom,' said one of the men behind Tarw, 'and does not answer to you or anyone else.'

'Yes I do,' said Tarw quietly. 'The man is right and even if our paths separate on the morrow, these men still deserve an explanation.'

'Then spit it out, Prince,' said Tomas with a sneer, 'for I am in need of light-hearted entertainment.'

'The truth is,' said Tarw, 'you are right, I did leave the rebellion without warning and I admit there was an element of selfishness in my decision, but it was not for myself, it was for my family. The king had put a price on my head and on that of my wife. While that was nothing new, he extended it to my sons and made it known it would be paid for any one of us, man, woman or child, dead or alive. Of course I had to consider their safety for, though Gwenllian and I had embraced the life of a rebel, they were innocent in all this.'

'So what is the difference between your children and ours?' asked Tomas. 'Are ours not also deserving of a warm bed and the chance to live in peace?'

'Of course,' said Tarw, 'and therein lies my point. Henry sent a message offering me and my family a total amnesty if we laid down our weapons and submitted to him the names of everyone involved in the rebellion. If we refused, he vowed to invade Deheubarth and burn every village to the ground, slaughtering man or beast without mercy. All land would be confiscated and awarded to his Flemish-born knights, men of renowned cruelty, and anyone left alive would be enslaved to the new landholders.'

'And you believed him?'

'I had no option,' snapped Tarw, his voice raising in frustration. 'The letter was signed and sealed by his own hand and if I had ignored it, I would have been responsible for hundreds of deaths, perhaps thousands. It would certainly have meant the end of Deheubarth as a kingdom.'

'We face such threats on a daily basis,' said another voice.

'I know,' said Tarw, turning around, 'but this was different. This time he was targeting the innocent. You men chose the burden of rebellion and all the risks that go with it, as did I, but those people out there who scratch in the earth every day for a mouthful of food did not. I had no choice and had to negotiate.'

'What did you do?' asked Taliesin.

'I refused to give the names of my fellow rebels,' said Tarw, 'but instead offered to disappear along with my family if Henry withdrew his threat. Negotiations were long and drawn out but eventually he agreed as long as he had my word that I would never again lead a rebellion in his or my lifetime. We agreed terms and when the document was signed, Gwenllian and I, along with my children left the Cantref Mawr and headed into obscurity.'

'Hardly obscurity,' said Tomas. 'More like the life of luxury.'

'The Lord of Llandeilo is an old family friend,' said Tarw, 'and he offered us sanctuary at his manor. Nobody knew our true identity there, so we remained and I took up the position of steward. That is where we remained for many years until a few days ago when circumstances dragged us from our shelter and forced us once more to face reality.'

'So do you still harbour resentment against the Crown?'

'With every fibre of my being,' said Tarw. 'And if it wasn't for my vow, I would join you in an instant.'

'But the king is dead,' said Tomas. 'Why withhold your sword arm if your resentment still burns?'

'My vow was to last as long as he or I still lived,' said Tarw. 'Henry may have died but I have not.'

'So what? He would know no difference.'

'I would and no man is better than his word.' He turned to Taliesin. 'So, now you know. Yes, I fled the Cantref Mawr but the reasons were sound and though I freely admit to protecting my family, there were other things to consider.'

'*We needed you*,' shouted Tomas Scar, getting to his feet and throwing his jack across the tent.

'*My family needed me*,' roared Tarw in response, getting to his own feet, 'and if that is such a crime then strike me down now for I have no regrets. If I had not done what I did, we would all now be in our graves including you. As it is Deheubarth still stands and with the English king dead, it yet has a chance to stand again.'

'Enough!' shouted Taliesin, getting to his feet. 'We are going around in circles. Tomas, you assume I have already made up my mind in this matter but nothing could be further from the truth. Yes, I am as frustrated as you about this man's absence but I owe it to everyone to hear all sides of the story. I suggest you go back to your hut and sleep off the ale before something is said we all may regret.' He turned to Tarw. 'You may be a prince, but you forfeited the right to lead these men when you left. I cannot deny that your desertion leaves me with a great feeling of unease. However, these are unique times and with the king dead there may be an opportunity to renew our struggle. I will consider your explanation overnight and we will meet again in a few days. Until then, you will remain in the camp under armed guard. Understood?'

'Aye,' said Tarw.

'Good, now everyone be gone.'

Kidwelly Castle

December 23rd, AD 1135

Lord Maurice de Londres, castellan of Kidwelly castle, stood atop the palisade watching the approaching column of knights. He had received word the previous day that Gerald of Windsor would be coming, and though he was preoccupied with preparations to attend London for the funeral of the king, he knew that, for Gerald to come himself, it had to be important. The winter wind whistled around his bald head while blowing his long beard against his mail-covered barrel-like chest. Though a small man, Maurice's reputation was huge and what he lacked in stature he made up for in aggression and ability. He was fiercely loyal to the Crown and hated the Welsh with a vengeance. Despite this, he had immediately accepted the posting as castellan of Kidwelly castle the moment the king had suggested it a few years earlier. Now that Henry was dead he couldn't help wondering what other opportunities might arise under the reign of the new monarch, whoever that might turn out to be.

His deep-set eyes stared at the scene outside the castle walls. Kidwelly town lay less than a few hundred paces distant across the river, and though it was largely peaceful, his men were forbidden from enjoying the few taverns in the town due to the risk of assault from the more patriotic of the locals.

Outside the palisade, fifty of Maurice's best men lined the track as a welcoming guard and the castellan nodded to Gerald in acknowledgement as the visitor passed through the gateway below. When everyone was inside, the giant gates closed and Maurice descended to greet his fellow knight.

'Sir Gerald,' he said, walking over. 'I trust you had a good journey?'

'As well as can be expected,' said Gerald. 'We came via Carmarthen, though stayed just the one night.'

'Was not the hospitality to your liking?'

'On the contrary, they were very welcoming but the main purpose of my journey is to meet with you.'

'I am intrigued,' said Maurice, 'and look forward to hearing what you have to say, but first you must accompany me to the hall to meet my wife.'

Gerald looked around at the rest of his men.

'You can trust they will be well catered for,' said Maurice, seeing his look of concern, 'both man and beast. Come, Marion is waiting.'

Gerald followed Maurice up the steps of the motte and into the lesser hall of the keep. Inside, a beautiful young woman was standing alongside an inviting fire. Her fiery red hair hung down to her waist, matching the silken dress that was clinging to her like a second skin.

'My Lord Gerald,' said Maurice, 'allow me to introduce my lady wife, Marion of Cork.'

'I am honoured,' said Gerald, taking the lady's hand and bowing gently. 'The rumours of your beauty were not unwarranted.'

'Thank you, my lord,' said Marion, 'but it is I who am honoured. Your reputation precedes you and we are lucky to have your influence in this dangerous country. Please, approach the fire and get some warmth back into your bones.' She looked over his shoulder. 'Is not the Lady Nesta with you?'

'Alas, not this time. This a visit of business, not pleasure. Your husband and I have matters of great importance to discuss over the next few hours.'

'Of course,' said Marion, 'and I will leave you to the business of men, but tonight we will dine in your honour. Please say you will accommodate us.'

Gerald smiled. 'Of course,' he said. 'Again, I am honoured.'

Marion smiled back and turned to one of her servants. 'Instruct the kitchens that we will eat at dusk,' she said, 'and ensure the best wine is served throughout the evening.'

The maid curtsied and went about her tasks as Marion turned back to face Gerald.

'My husband will show you to your quarters where there is hot water waiting for you as well as clean linen with which to wash the road from your skin. I look forward to hearing all about your daring exploits amongst the natives of this God forsaken land later but, in the meantime, please make yourself at home.'

'Thank you, my lady,' said Gerald.

Marion smiled at the two men and left the hall.

When they were alone, Gerald said, 'It has been a long time, my friend.'

'Too long,' said Maurice, walking over to the silver decanter on a nearby table. 'Is the Welsh winter treating you well?'

'I have been here for many years, Maurice,' said Gerald as he joined him by the fire, 'and I am used to anything it throws at me.'

'I wish I could say the same,' replied Maurice, offering Gerald a goblet, 'but alas the winds cut into my very bones like the sharpest blade.'

Gerald took the goblet and his eyes widened in admiration. It was made of solid silver and finely decorated with a detailed hunting scene.

'A fine goblet,' he said, turning it around in his hand. 'Did you have them made?'

'No, we confiscated them from a chapel down near the coast. Apparently they were a gift to the clergy from a local Welsh lord when his wife died. A sort of thank you for the ceremony, I suppose.'

'And you saw fit to take them?'

'The priest was a drunkard and a womaniser,' said Maurice with a sigh. 'He was no more pious than my horse, and after my constable was called out to deal with the results of his drunken temper for the third time in a week, I decided he should pay for the privilege. Any coins he had hidden in his church, and there were quite a few, we gave to his victims' families while the rest of his possessions we took as payment, including these goblets.'

'Where is he now?'

'I know not,' said Maurice. 'I had him thrown out and burned the hovel he called his church.' He took a swig of his wine before continuing. 'Anyway, you haven't come all the way down here to discuss some drunken varlet.'

'I only wish it was that simple,' said Gerald. 'But you are right, my reasons for coming are of a far more serious nature.'

Maurice nodded towards the two comfortable seats near the fire. 'Come, we have a few hours before Marion's obligatory hospitality. Let us talk while we have some privacy and tonight we can relax.'

Gerald sank into one of the chairs opposite Maurice and leaned forward to place his ornate goblet on the table. 'The problem is this,' he said eventually, 'I am getting very worried about the mood in Deheubarth. There is an up-swelling of anger amongst the population and our gaols are full of those found guilty of conspiracy as they wait to be executed. On top of that, there is a definite increase in the number of attacks on our supply columns, many from brigand groups previously unknown.'

'Surely a few brigands do not unduly worry you?'

'Ordinarily no, but their numbers are increasing across the kingdom and I worry that they may join together in common purpose.'

'Highly unlikely, I would have thought,' said Maurice. 'It is one thing to feed a handful of brigands with a stolen pig but quite another to feed an army of any size. Besides, who would lead such a group?'

'Well, that's the thing,' said Gerald. 'There is a chance that Gruffydd ap Rhys yet lives, as well as his wife, Gwenllian.'

Maurice paused with his goblet halfway to his lips. *'Tarw is alive?'* he gasped. 'But that is impossible.'

'Apparently not. It seems his death may have been a ruse and he has hidden himself away these past few years. Recently he has had cause to break his cover, and though he has again disappeared from sight, my spies tell me he has joined with the rebels in the Cantref Mawr. If this is true, I am concerned that all those brigands we just talked about could unite under his banner.'

'And you really think that is possible?'

'I don't know,' said Gerald. 'But what I do know is that we should not take the risk lightly. The mood amongst the people is ripe for a new cause and already we are finding it harder and harder to fill our food stores.'

'What do you mean?'

'It seems that, all of a sudden, those farmers who once begged to sell their produce within the palisades of our castles now have less livestock to sell. The rumours are that any spare is being diverted into the Cantref Mawr to feed the rebel camps. Consequently we are increasingly reliant on supply caravans from Carmarthen and beyond.'

'Why not just simply relieve these errant farmers of whatever goods they have before they can give them to the rebels?'

'I fear it will come to that,' said Gerald. 'But the day it does we will lose the goodwill of the people and that is a hornet's nest we should not poke.'

Maurice fell quiet and stared at Gerald for a few moments, his mind racing with the news. As far as he was concerned, Gerald was by far the strongest in Deheubarth and for him to voice his concerns over the threat of the Welsh meant it was a problem that must be taken seriously.

'Even so,' he said eventually, 'there remains the possibility that none of this may come to pass. Tarw could actually be dead and the rebel groups you speak of are nothing more than starving criminals spreading rumours. Hardly the makings of a credible army.'

'I agree,' said Gerald, 'and believe me when I say that I have thought long and hard about my concerns before coming here, but there is one more thing that forced my hand.'

'And that is?'

'The fact that Hywel ap Maredudd has already mustered an army to his banner.'

'I had heard the rumours but gave them little credence. Even if true, he will be given short shrift by the king.'

'The king is dead,' said Gerald. 'Remember?'

'Forgive me,' said Maurice, 'it was a shameful oversight but the sentiment still stands. Any Welsh noble raising an army is subject to the full weight of English law, and no matter who takes the throne, you can rest assured they will wipe out this threat within weeks.'

'Maurice, my spies say he already has over five hundred men-at-arms and is marching south as we speak. It will take weeks for the new monarch to settle in and by then it could be too late. Add this to the potential resurgence of Tarw and we have a serious problem on our hands. Now, I don't know about you but my garrison is nowhere near strong enough to fight a full-scale war.'

'Mine neither,' said Maurice quietly. 'Henry's castles all across Wales were depleted when he needed men for his war in France and I have fewer than a hundred at my disposal, including those in outlying fortifications.'

'My numbers are even smaller,' said Gerald, 'and that is why I am here. I believe you are going to London to pay respect to the king and to attend his successor's coronation?'

'Aye,' said Maurice. 'I leave tomorrow.'

'Then I have a boon to ask. When you are there I want you to press the court for extra men to be deployed in Deheubarth. Explain to them the danger we face and seek support to bolster our defences. With the death of the king and the challenges to the succession, we are facing the possibility of an all-out revolt while our attentions are focussed elsewhere. I cannot overstate the seriousness of this situation, and not a day goes by without our spies reporting another attack on the king's roads. Eventually these minor skirmishes will grow and when they do, we need to be ready.'

Maurice again looked thoughtfully at the man opposite him. Gerald was one of the most respected knights serving the king, yet for Gerald to seek aid from the Crown at such a tragic time meant exposing himself to ridicule from the barons who made up the court. However, to deny the request could possibly place the whole of the south at risk should the Welsh revolt.

'Gerald,' he said eventually, 'you ask a great deal and I am doubtful whether we will receive a supportive answer, especially at this time.'

'I realise that,' said Gerald, 'but they have to be made aware of the threat. That way, should the worst happen and we send for help, at least it will already be in their minds and perhaps they will afford it the urgency any such request deserves. I also have a document that you can take with you, signed by all the local castellans listing their concerns. This is very serious, Maurice, and I trust no one better than you to carry out this task. Our futures may be in your hands. So, will you do it?'

Maurice returned Gerald's intense stare before draining his goblet and placing it on the table. 'Aye,' he said, 'I will. Of course, I will need more detail before you leave and it would help if one of your seconds came along to relay your fears first-hand. Other than that, you have my word that I will do whatever I can.'

'Excellent,' said Gerald sitting back in his chair. 'I cannot ask for more.' He lifted his own goblet and drank it dry. 'Now,' he said, wiping some ale from the side of his mouth with the back of his hand, 'who else is coming to tonight's banquet?'

———⌣———

Ten leagues away a servant ran through the silent corridor and up the stairs to Nesta's quarters. As she approached the room, the guard stationed at the top of the stair stepped forward with his hand on the hilt of his sword.

'Stop right there,' he said. 'What's the rush?'

'I have an urgent message for the lady Nesta,' said the servant.

'She had a sleepless night,' said the guard, 'and is not to be disturbed. Give me the message and I will see she gets it.'

The servant looked around, not sure what to do. She had been instructed to give the castellan's wife the message herself but this was obviously not possible.

'Well,' he said, 'spit it out or be gone. Either way is good for me.'

'I will leave it with you,' said the girl. 'Tell her that the archer who killed mistress Catrin is no longer in his cell.'

'What do you mean?' asked the guard. 'Where is he?'

'Nobody knows,' said the servant. 'He has escaped!'

Kidwelly

December 24th, AD 1135

Colin of Monmouth sat against a gravestone in an overgrown cemetery, his dirty face lined with the tracks of his tears. Since being freed from his cell back in Pembroke castle, he had ridden hard with his rescuer, an English knight called Walter de Calais, and now found himself faced with a task that almost made him wish he was still there and facing the justice of Gerald.

Walter de Calais had said little since leaving Pembroke, insisting instead they had to be as far away as possible before the alarm was raised. Colin had little option other than to obey the knight and flee, despite his innocence. Throughout the arduous journey, his mind raced, going over and over the situation they had left behind in the castle, and though he had not known where they were headed, he clung on to the faint hope that someone would realise there had been a terrible mistake and he could soon head home.

For the past few hours they had hidden amongst the trees of the graveyard, safe from prying eyes and the worst of the weather. His rescuer had given him food, water and warm clothing and he had gone on to explain that Colin had been released at the orders of the constable himself, John of Salisbury.

Colin looked around the graveyard. To one side were the ruins of a church, most of its walls long since removed for building materials on nearby farms and houses, and within the shadows of the one wall still standing the remains of the night's fire smouldered silently. Just below the derelict church, a well-trodden path stretched southward and in the distance he could see a castle dominating the skyline.

'Here they come,' said a voice and Walter appeared from the shadows to stand before him. 'You know what you have to do?'

'Aye,' said Colin, 'but I still don't understand.'

'I have already told you,' said Walter. 'It was your blade found at the scene and the constable's hands are tied in this matter. Whether you killed the girl or not, the fact is that you will be found guilty and be hanged should you be caught. That means your soul will rot in hell for eternity. However, do this one simple task and he has granted me permission to set you free. After that, you are on your own but we will not pursue you for seven full days. By then you can easily be in another kingdom and free to continue your life.'

'But who is this man we target?' asked Colin, looking towards the approaching column. 'If he is guilty of a crime, why doesn't the constable arrest him?'

'Because our quarry is a cruel tyrant and has many allies,' replied Walter. 'The politics involved are complicated but, suffice to say, he is a threat to the Crown and needs to be killed. At least this way his death will be blamed on brigands and our land will be rid of a tyrant. Do this and you will be a free man to live your life as you wish.'

'But why me?'

'Because it is well known that despite your age, you are one of the best archers in the garrison.'

He threw an unstrung bow at Colin's feet. 'The rumours are that you killed four men on Gerald's last campaign.'

'Five,' said Colin.

'Well, there you are, killing one more will be as nothing. Just think of your target as another rebel. After all, it wasn't you who killed that poor girl was it?'

'No,' snapped Colin. 'Whoever did it stole my knife to lay the blame at my feet.'

'Perhaps so,' said Walter. 'But as I said, the Constable's hands are tied in this matter. Do this one thing and you will be free again. Do you understand?'

Colin nodded and got to his feet.

'Then come,' said Walter, 'you need to choose your place for the best shot.'

'I have already done so,' said Colin quietly. 'It is from the bracken on the forward slope.'

'Not from there?' asked Walter, pointing to some nearby rocks.

'No, it is too open to the wind. From the bracken the arrow will be protected and fly true. There is also a stream crossing the track at the base of the hill and the column will have to slow down to cross. It is there that the target will be most vulnerable.'

'See,' said Walter, 'you are already thinking like a true soldier.'

'What happens when the deed is done?' asked Colin.

'I will be waiting here with the horses,' came the reply. 'One arrow is probably all you will have time for; possibly two but no more. They will come after us but by the time they find our tracks we will be long gone. Now hurry or your neck will be stretched before the sun sets tomorrow.'

He handed over two arrows and watched as Colin made his way through the trees. The archer stuck them in the ground before him and strung his bow, the larger muscle in his right arm tensing under the strain. When he was ready he looked back at the man hidden amongst the trees behind him.

'Don't miss,' warned Walter, as Colin turned to face the approaching column.

Slowly they drew nearer and the archer could see his target in the third rank, riding beside the standard-bearer. As expected, the column slowed as the horses picked their way through the stream and for a few moments, everyone came to a halt.

Knowing he would not get a better chance, Colin notched his arrow and stood up amongst the bracken. Without hesitation he drew back the bowstring and took aim. For a second he paused, something didn't feel right.

'*Do it, damn you, or I swear I will hang you myself,*' hissed the man behind him.

With no other option, Colin calmed his breathing and pulled the bowstring to its furthest extent. Almost casually, he let the bowstring slip from his fingers and the released energy sent the arrow flying through the air to smash into the face of the victim. It was a perfect shot and the man was dead before he hit the ground.

For a few seconds, confusion reigned amongst the column down on the track, and expecting an imminent attack, each man quickly drew his sword as they all desperately scanned the landscape to find the assassin.

'*Does anyone see anything?*' roared the captain from behind his raised shield.

'No, my lord,' came the reply from two dozen voices.

The captain looked over at the man lying on the ground with an arrow through his head. Some of the riders had dismounted and formed a shield wall to protect the victim but the officer already guessed it would be of no use. No man could survive such an injury.

For a few seconds he stared in horror. As captain of the guard it had been his duty to protect his master from all assaults and it was obvious he had failed. The blood drained from his face as the implications sank in and he turned to face the rest of his men.

'*Whoever is responsible for this,*' he shouted, '*I want them brought to me before this day ends. Spread out and find him. A purse of silver to whoever brings me his head.*'

As one, the line of riders started forward over the rough ground, their shields held before them, but unbeknownst to them, the threat had long gone. Colin of Monmouth and Walter de Calais were already on the far side of the hill and galloping as hard as they could away from the scene of the ambush.

———

'We'll stop here,' called Walter less than an hour later.

'Why?' asked Colin. 'They can't be far behind us.'

'The horses need water and there is a stream over there.'

'But shouldn't we press on?'

'It makes no sense to ride our horses to death,' said Walter, dismounting. 'Fret not, our pursuers will also have to water their horses. We will take a few moments only and then continue.'

Colin rode over and dismounted before leading his horse down to the stream. When it had drunk its fill, he led it back to the track where Walter was waiting.

'Ready?' asked Walter.

'Aye,' said Colin. 'We should move.'

'Before we do, you should check your horse's rear leg, it looks like he is lame,' said Walter.

'Oh, no,' said Colin and he walked to the rear of his horse. Bending down, he checked the hoof before running both hands up the leg, checking for lumps or tears in the muscle.

'I can't see anything,' he said over his shoulder. 'You must be mistaken.'

'Aye,' said Walter, walking up behind him, 'perhaps I was.'

Before Colin could stand, Walter pushed him forward into the mud and dropped onto his back, pinning the archer to the floor with his knees.

'What are you doing?' panted Colin, trying to break free.

'I'm sorry, my friend, but if I let you live and they catch you, you could identify me and I cannot risk that happening.'

'No,' cried Colin as Walter's huge hands grabbed him around the head. 'Please, don't do this. Master Salisbury said I could live.'

'Salisbury?' sneered Walter. 'Who do you think ordered your death?'

'But you said . . .'

'Oh, I know what I said,' said Walter, 'but that was before you killed the castellan.'

'What castellan?' gasped Colin.

'Gerald, of course,' said Walter as he started to twist the archer's neck. 'You just murdered Henry's favoured knight.'

As the pressure increased, Colin finally realised he had been tricked and screamed both in fear and in pain. Walter gave one last twist and heard the sound of his victim's neck snap beneath his hands. Satisfied the boy was dead, he stood up and walked over to his own horse. He retrieved a bunch of bone-dry bracken from the saddlebag and, after tying it to the horse's tail, set it alight with a flint and a piece of dried lamb's wool. Within moments this had the desired effect and the horse lurched away from the flames, taking the attached flaming bundle with it.

Walter watched the terrified horse gallop away, satisfied that the ruse had achieved the desired effect. By the time the flames petered out, the horse would be a long way down the track, leaving an easy trail for the armed column to follow while he, in the meantime, would be leagues away in the opposite direction.

Quickly, he placed one end of Colin's horse's reins beneath the dead boy's body before running up a nearby hill away from the scene, taking care to only tread on the rocks. On the other side, he made his way to another nearby copse to collect the fresh horse a comrade had left for him that morning and, satisfied his task was done, he rode hard back to Pembroke.

Gerald of Windsor was dead and as far as anyone would be concerned the murderer lay dead in the mud of the track behind him.

Llandeilo

December 24th, AD 1135

Gwenllian and Robert rode side by side along a hidden path towards Llandeilo. They had pushed their horses to the limit and the journey had been hard going due to the need to avoid the main tracks frequented by the English and their allies. Behind them, the numbers of those accompanying them had swelled from twenty to almost fifty as word of her true identity had spread, and though some were inexperienced in the ways of war, the fact that their much beloved warrior princess was still alive made many swear allegiance there and then. At first she had tried to deny the rumours but it had soon become clear news of her return was spreading like wildfire, and eventually she succumbed to the inevitable.

Inside, her mind was in turmoil. Only days ago she had been enjoying a relatively peaceful life as the wife of a manor steward, yet here she was, days later, with an uncertain future before her and sitting astride a horse, riding to rescue her children from the clutches of an enemy she had long since stopped fighting. Her heart ached at the thought of the danger they might be in, but while she would rather the events of the past few days hadn't happened, deep inside, the tiniest spark of excitement struggled to ignite a fire she had long thought extinguished for good.

'Our numbers are increasing,' said Robert, looking over his shoulder. 'At this rate we will have an army to rival Hywel's before the month is out.'

'I desire no army, Robert, just a return to the days when the only conflict I saw was the daily fights between my sons.'

'What you desire and what you get are often rare bedfellows,' said Robert. 'And even if that is possible, which I doubt, what do you intend to do with those who ride behind you?'

'I don't know,' said Gwenllian. 'At the moment, all I care about is securing the safety of my sons. Beyond that, who knows what is going to happen?' Before she could continue, one of the two men riding a hundred paces before them reined in his horse and held up a hand, signalling a halt. Dismounting, he ran forward to a ridgeline ahead of him and lay down in the mud to peer over the top. Gwenllian and Robert also dismounted and, crouching low, ran forward to join him.

'What is it?' asked Gwenllian, dropping to the floor beside the lead rider.

'See for yourself,' he replied, pointing over the ridge to a distant plume of black smoke.

'Where is that?' asked Gwenllian, dreading the answer.

'My lady, it's Llandeilo.'

'Oh, sweet Jesus, my boys,' gasped Gwenllian. Before anyone could respond, she turned and ran back to her horse.

'My lady,' shouted Robert, running behind her. 'Wait!' He grabbed her horse by the bridle and held tight.

Gwenllian was already in the saddle and looking down at her comrade in disdain. 'Wait?' she said. 'For *what*? For those animals to have even more time to find and kill my sons? I think not, Robert. Now get out of my way.'

'Gerald's men could still be there,' said Robert. 'And we are no match for a column of English knights.'

'I don't care if there are twelve knights or a hundred,' said Gwenllian. 'I will not stay here while my sons are at risk. Now let go or I swear I will ride you down.'

Robert shook his head, knowing that in this mood there was no talking to her. 'At least wait a moment,' he said. 'I will come with you.'

'Do what you will, Robert,' said Gwenllian. 'I am beyond caring.' Before he could answer, she dug her heels into the flanks of her exhausted horse, forcing it into a gallop along the rough track.

'What are we going to do?' asked one of the men. 'What if the English are still there? She can't fight them alone.'

'No, she can't,' said Robert, mounting his horse. 'That is why we have to go after her.'

'And ride against trained knights?'

'Did you pledge allegiance or did you not?' said Robert, and he turned to face the rest of the men. 'Well, what are you waiting for? You swore fealty to that woman and now more than ever she needs you at her side. It is time to show your mettle or turn away for good. The choice is yours.'

He spurred his own horse to gallop after Gwenllian and, within moments, the rest of the men followed.

The sight facing Gwenllian as she rode down to the manor made her feel sick to her stomach. All the outbuildings were ablaze and the roof of the manor had already collapsed into the building. Smoke billowed into the sky and bodies lay everywhere, men and beasts alike. Four men hung from one of the trees, their bodies swinging like macabre puppets. She rode into the heart of the manor courtyard and jumped from her horse, closely followed by Robert.

'Where were they?' he shouted, running through the smoke.

'In the house,' replied Gwenllian. 'Quickly, the roof is on fire.'

Robert turned to the men now arriving in the courtyard behind him. 'Half of you form a perimeter around the manor,' he shouted. 'Let us know if anyone comes within a hundred paces. The rest of you, dismount and search the buildings for survivors. *Move!'*

As the men raced to their tasks, Robert ran after Gwenllian to the burning house. The door had already been kicked in and they stumbled into the dark interior, their hands over their mouths to filter the smoke. The floor was covered with charred timber and Gwenllian pulled away what she could, searching for bodies yet terrified of what she might find.

'It's no good,' shouted Robert, looking nervously up at the roof rafters. 'We have to get out of here.'

'I'm not going until I find them,' shouted Gwenllian.

'They may not even be in here,' replied Robert. 'Think about it. The English obviously knew who they were looking for so if they found your boys, they would more than likely have taken them hostage. They are worth far more alive to them than dead.'

'And what if they didn't?' said Gwenllian. 'What if they are still in here somewhere, under all this? They may be still alive, Robert, just waiting to be pulled out. I cannot simply hope that they are elsewhere.'

'We will search every corner of this place,' said Robert, 'I swear by almighty God, but you have to get out of here before the roof caves in.' As he spoke, one of the burning rafters above snapped, sending showers of sparks down upon her head. Robert grabbed her arm.

'There may well be a chance they are still alive but you will be no good to them if you are dead. Use your head, Gwenllian, we have to get out of here.'

Gwenllian nodded and allowed herself to be dragged from the building just as the roof collapsed. Clouds of smoke and ash billowed out through the door and they both ran spluttering to one side.

'I'll gather the rest of the men,' gasped Robert as soon as he could breathe. 'You point out where they should look. Don't worry, Gwenllian, if they are here, we will find them.'

For the next hour or so, all the men searched the ruins but to no avail. Finally, one of the men came over to speak to Robert. 'My lord, we have searched everywhere. The children are not here, dead or alive.'

'Thank you,' said Robert. 'Tell the men to grab what rest they can. I suspect we will be riding out soon.' He looked around at the devastated manor buildings. 'Have they left anything here to eat?'

'Not that I can see, my lord. All the stores have been removed and what little was left has been destroyed in the fire.'

'Take another look,' said Robert. 'We are short on food and the men need to eat.' He walked over to Gwenllian who was standing in the gateway with her back to the destroyed manor.

'They must have captured them,' she said quietly as he stood beside her. 'The English have my children and I have to go after them.'

'Do not decide such things in haste, Gwenllian,' said Robert. 'There is no sign of Bevan amongst the bodies. Perhaps it is he who carried them away. We have to wait and see.'

'No, Robert, you don't understand. Every moment I linger is an extra moment they are nearer Pembroke and once they are there, there will be little, if any, chance of freeing them. I have to ride after them and hope an opportunity arises to rescue them.'

'At least wait and have some food,' said Robert. 'Your horse needs rest and if your belly is full, you will be stronger for what lies ahead.'

Gwenllian looked at him and he could see the marks of tears amongst the soot on her face.

'We will find your sons, my lady,' he said. 'I promise.'

'We have to, Robert,' she said. 'I am nothing without them.'

As they turned to walk back into the manor courtyard a voice echoed through the ruins. 'My lord, I think we've found something.'

Gwenllian looked up at Robert before they both ran to the furthest part of the wrecked palisade.

'Over here,' shouted the voice and they could see two men near the pigsty. Gwenllian and Robert ran across to peer over the wall of the pen. At first, all Gwenllian could see was an enormous dead pig lying on its side, but then she noticed something red amongst the mud.

'What's that?' she asked.

'I think it's a headscarf, my lady. It looks like someone dropped it as they crawled inside.'

'Then what are you waiting for?' snapped Robert. 'Get them out.'

One of the men dropped to his knees and crawled through the filth into the darkness of the stone sty.

'There's someone here,' he shouted from inside. 'Help me.'

The second man dropped to his knees and reached inside. Robert joined him and taking an arm each, they dragged the body of a young woman out of the sty and into the light.

Gwenllian gasped as she recognised Gwyneth, the house servant from the manor. Her dress was soaked with blood and Gwenllian could see a snapped arrow in her side where the girl had bled out. For a few seconds she just stared in horror, her mind not comprehending what had happened but she was suddenly brought back to reality by the sound of a child's cry from inside the sty.

'*Rhydian*,' she gasped, recognising the sound, and she jumped over the wall just as the soldier inside passed a small boy out to Robert.

'Oh, sweet Jesus,' whispered Gwenllian, taking her five-year-old son into her arms and hugging him as tightly as she could.

Her son clung on to her, his body wracked with sobs. He was covered with pig filth and stank to high heaven but he seemed to be uninjured. Despite her joy, Gwenllian held back any further emotion and looked back down to the sty, praying for more good news from inside.

'Is anyone else there?' shouted Robert.

For a few moments there was no answer and Robert was about to go in himself when the head of the soldier appeared in the low doorway. He straightened up and they could see he was holding something in his arms.

'Aye,' said the soldier with a smile. 'I found this little man asleep on a cloak.'

Gwenllian broke into tears of joy and ran forward to take her youngest son from the soldier.

'It is a miracle,' said one of the men as Gwenllian held her sons tightly.

'If it is,' said Robert, looking down at the body of the dead girl, 'it was one administered by this poor soul. It seems that though she was wounded, she managed to grab the children and hide them out here away from the English. Take her back to the manor and we will see she has a proper burial. My lady, we should head back to shelter and get the children warmed up as soon as we can. Let me help you.'

'I can manage, Robert,' said Gwenllian. 'Thank you.' Holding both her sons, Gwenllian made her way back to the manor, walking past the rest of the men who had gathered at the wall.

'Someone find a cauldron,' shouted Robert, following her back through the palisade. 'There must be one around here somewhere. I want hot water and plenty of it. The rest of you, set up camp, we will stay here tonight. Bring in that pig and get it butchered.'

'What about the dead?' asked one of the men.

'We will bury them on the morrow,' said Robert. 'In the meantime, pile them behind that wall out of sight. There's nothing we can do for them tonight.' He turned to Gwenllian. 'My lady, one of the guard-rooms is still intact. Take the boys there and I will have someone come over to build a fire. Get yourselves clean and I will see if we can find anything for you to wear while we wash that filth from your clothes.'

'Thank you, Robert,' said Gwenllian. 'I am in your debt.'

'The fact that the boys are safe is repayment enough,' said Robert. 'After all, one of them may be a future king of Deheubarth.'

Gwenllian smiled and walked away to find the guardroom.

⌣

The following afternoon, all the men who had ridden with Gwenllian to Llandeilo lined up on their horses outside the burned-out manor. To one side, the mound of soil covering the large communal grave lay raw and silent, a testament to the slaughter that had happened there the previous day. Next to the communal grave, a smaller mound complete with a wooden cross and a surrounding circle of small stones marked the grave of Gwyneth.

'Where is she?' asked one of the men, referring to the absence of Gwenllian.

'She will be along shortly,' said Robert. 'She said she had something to do.'

Moments later, Gwenllian appeared from the nearby trees holding a wreath made from holly. She walked over to the grave and knelt down, placing it gently on the disturbed soil.

'I'm sorry it's not flowers, Gwyneth,' she said quietly, brushing her hands over the earth, 'but I promise that I will return in the spring to place a garland in your memory and, for as long as I live, I will return every year to pray for your soul and thank you for the lives of my sons.' She got to her feet and, after kissing her own fingers, placed them on the top of the cross.

The men watched in silence, respecting the moment. Finally Gwenllian turned back to face Robert.

'Are the boys in the cart?' she asked.

'Aye,' he said. 'The youngest is sleeping and his brother is playing with a wooden horse one of the men carved last night. Are you ready?'

'No,' said Gwenllian. 'There is one more thing I must do. Wait for me here.'

She turned away and walked back into the manor courtyard, making her way to the house where she used to live. The fires were out and she picked her way over the debris to the far wall that held the fireplace. Under some rubble, she found what she was looking for, the chest where she and Tarw had kept the few items of value they possessed. She reached in and, delving past the valuable books and personal items, she retrieved a pile of leather clothing from the bottom. With a deep sigh she stood up and started to undress.

———

Ten minutes later the men were standing around in a circle talking amongst themselves, each impatient to be leaving. One was boasting of a recent sexual conquest when suddenly he fell silent and stared towards the manor gates. All eyes followed his and they watched in awe as Gwenllian approached.

The woman of yesterday, who had cried at the thought of her sons being captured, was nowhere to be seen. The soot-covered face was now spotlessly clean and the hair that had been tied back with a dirty rag now hung loose about her shoulders, a waterfall of summer gold.

Instead of the dirty red dress she had worn earlier, she was now wearing black leather armour, reinforced with row after row of metal studs along the seams. The shoulders were heavily padded and the whole thing was pulled tight by two diagonal belts reaching from each shoulder down to the opposite hip. A high collar protected the back of her neck and a sheathed dagger hung from a wide belt around her waist.

Every man watched in silence as Gwenllian walked up to Robert, her golden hair blowing in the breeze.

'Now are you ready?' he asked.

Without answering, Gwenllian walked past her horse and over to the cart where the men had collected the weapons of the fallen. She lifted several swords, swinging them back and forth before finding one with a balance she liked. She fastened the scabbard to the side of her belt and walked back over to stand before Robert.

'Now I am ready,' she said, her face fixed in a stare of steely resolve. 'Take me back to the Cantref Mawr, Robert. There is work to be done.'

Pembroke

December 26th, AD 1135

Every person in the town stood silently on the sides of the road, waiting for the caravan to arrive. News of Gerald's death had travelled swiftly, and though his body was to be taken to the castle, it was being brought through the town square for the population to pay their last respects. Gerald had been a firm yet fair governor but some attended with a grudge in their heart, resentful that after so many years Deheubarth was still under English control.

In the distance, the first riders appeared, a double column of English knights bedecked in their best finery and carrying Gerald's colours atop their upright lances. Behind them came the cart bearing the castellan's coffin, pulled by a team of four horses and manned by two cart masters aboard the plate.

As the cortege passed, every person removed any headgear and bowed deeply, paying their respects, closely monitored by Salisbury's spies to ensure compliance until it left the town behind and wound its way up the short hill to the castle where the garrison was waiting.

All along the palisades, the remaining men-at-arms stood upright in respect while, down in the bailey, the staff and any remaining civilians stood in a semi-circle with many of the women crying quietly as they waited.

Eventually, the caravan entered through the palisade gates and the riders peeled off to either side to form a channel. A group of soldiers approached the tailgate of the cart and dragged the coffin off to place it on a nearby trestle. The castle priest walked over and said a prayer before stepping aside. Everyone stood still, waiting in silence for the appearance of the castellan's wife until, eventually, several minutes later, at the top of the motte Nesta appeared out of the keep doors accompanied by John of Salisbury. Together they walked down the steps and over to the coffin.

'It is closed,' said Nesta, her voice cold and emotionless.

'My lady,' said the captain of the guard, 'the castellan suffered terrible injuries to his face and we thought it would be better to spare you from the horror.'

'My husband suffered the ultimate horror,' she said quietly, 'and it would be remiss of me to fear the features of the man who shared my life, no matter how bad the state. Open the casket.'

The captain looked at the constable who nodded gently in agreement.

Two soldiers stepped forward and lifted the lid, carrying it back over to the cart.

Nesta stepped forward and looked down at the body of her murdered husband. For a second she caught her breath at the smell for, despite the cold temperature, the sealed coffin had allowed a build-up of the fumes associated with the rotting process as well as the faeces the body had vented at the moment of death. When she had gathered herself, she lifted her hand and softly touched her husband's hair, brushing it gently back into place as she looked at the face she had known for so long. The damage was substantial as the arrow had caught him high on the cheek, smashing the bone inward before bursting out of the back of his skull. On the cloak beneath, which made up his temporary shroud, she could still see the pools of congealed blood and brain that had leaked after he had been placed in the coffin and she turned to the captain with a look of concern on her face.

'He has not been washed or prepared for burial,' she said.

'No, my lady, we thought we should bring him home immediately. If we had returned to Kidwelly, we would either have had to bury him there or strip the meat from his bones to transport him in a barrel of salt. We thought you would want him home in one piece to say your goodbyes.'

Nesta nodded in understanding. 'Take him to the keep,' she said, 'and summon the castle ladies. We will wash him and dress him appropriately for a man of his stature.'

'Of course,' said the captain and he turned to give the orders.

'My lady,' said the constable, 'do you not think it appropriate that he is buried in consecrated ground?'

'Master Salisbury,' replied Nesta, 'my husband has been the castellan here since it was no more than a simple wooden palisade, a mere symbol of the English Crown's ambition. Over the years he has made it what it is and a lesser man would have failed where he has succeeded. As far as I am concerned, his place is here within his castle. The responsibility of burying my husband lies with me, you just concentrate on finding the man who did this.'

Salisbury inwardly flinched at the admonishment but kept his counsel. Now was not the time nor the place for argument. 'I am,' he replied, 'and I have just heard there is a patrol on the way back with the body of a suspect. If he is found guilty we will hang him for the birds.'

'The body? Is this man already dead?'

'It seems that during his flight from the scene of the ambush, his horse stumbled and threw him. My men found him lying on the path with a broken neck.'

'Then how do you know he was the one responsible?'

'The arrows within his quiver were the same and my men were already on his trail. He will be tried for murder upon his return.'

'Hanging a dead man hardly seems suitable punishment,' said Nesta.

'On the contrary, an uninterred body rotting in full view of the people is denied access to heaven and there is no fate worse.'

Nesta nodded and turned away.

'My lady,' said Salisbury, before she had gone a few steps, 'are you well?'

'In the circumstances, I am hardly well,' said Nesta, turning back. 'Why do you ask?'

'Because your husband lies dead before you yet you show not the slightest sign of upset. A more uninformed man may think you were not concerned.'

'Any concern or upset is between Gerald, me and God,' said Nesta coldly, 'and not for the consumption of anyone else in what is nothing more than a contrived outpouring of false sympathy.'

'I know not what you mean,' said Salisbury.

'Oh, come now, Constable,' said Nesta. 'Do you really think that the whole population of Pembroke would spontaneously burst into such outpourings of sympathy had it not been for the threats of your henchmen. No, of course not. Gerald was a good man at heart but let us not forget he was an extension of Henry's arm in an occupied country. He was my husband and I loved him but he was never, nor ever could be the natural leader of these people. Most of the tears shed down in the town were as a result of threats, not respect. Now if you don't mind, I will retire and prepare my husband for burial.'

Nesta turned away and made her way up the motte steps, followed by her maid. Behind her, two of the soldiers walked over to replace the casket lid.

'Wait,' said Salisbury as he walked closer to look down on the man whose life he had coveted for so long. Fully aware that many eyes were upon him, he was careful not to show any sign of satisfaction yet inside he was elated. For too long the castellan had kept him in his place and imposed boundaries upon the constable's role but, now he was out of the way, Salisbury knew that at last this was his opportunity and it was one that he intended to embrace with every fibre of his being.

He reached in as if to touch the forehead of the castellan but unseen by anyone else, his fingers lingered on the dry blood encrusted upon the knight's face.

'Goodbye, Gerald,' he said under his breath, 'and good riddance.' With the slightest of sneers, he stepped back and turned to the captain.

'Take the casket to the lesser hall.'

'My lord,' said the captain, 'many want to pay their last respects to the castellan. Should we allow them to approach?'

'No,' said Salisbury, 'not yet. After he has been prepared properly, we will allow the people to attend him but until then, they should return to work. Oh, and, Captain . . .'

'Yes, my lord.'

'From now on, you will not refer to him as the castellan, he is Gerald of Windsor, knight of Henry.'

'But I thought . . .'

'Then you thought wrong. Yesterday he was the castellan but today he is dead and that honour is passed on to the next man in seniority. That man is me, Captain, and with immediate effect, I am the castellan of Pembroke castle. Understood?'

'Yes, my lord,' said the captain and he turned away to make the preparations.

Salisbury watched the soldiers carry the casket up the steps, his heart racing at the opportunity now facing him.

'Don't worry, Gerald,' he said under his breath, 'your legacy is in good hands' – he paused and stared up at the windows on the highest level of the keep as he rolled the knight's dried blood between his fingers, before adding – 'as indeed is your wife.'

Up in her quarters, Nesta lay face down on her bed, sobbing uncontrollably.

The Cantref Mawr

December 27th, AD 1135

The early morning mist was still on the ground when Gwenllian and her men rode into the Cantref Mawr. They had ridden for almost two days via the hidden routes of the forest to avoid English patrols and were exhausted.

In the camp, Taliesin sat at a fire outside his hut alongside Dog, keen to witness the arrival of the woman he had heard so much about, while down in the valley, almost a hundred people hung around the early morning fires, waiting in expectation for the arrival of the fabled princess of Gwynedd.

On the opposite side of the valley, Tarw was already awake and tending his own fire when Robert's messengers arrived and told him his children were safe. Relieved, he went to wake his oldest sons and tell them the good news but, aware that they were both exhausted, decided to let them rest a little while longer.

Returning to the fire, he placed a few handfuls of kindling on the embers and blew the flames back to life. He added some dried wood from the pile at the back of the hut and waited for the fire to catch fully before adding the pot containing dried fruit and water. He added a few handfuls of oats and sat back to watch it boil, taking the opportunity to reflect on everything that had happened over the past few days.

As a younger man, he had sought the path of a warrior and, when he had met and fallen in love with Gwenllian, she had joined him in his life of rebellion, fighting alongside him as well as any man. Her prowess in battle had become renowned and, if truth be told, it was her story that had caught the imagination of so many people of Deheubarth, far more than anything he had done in many years of fighting. The sight of her riding against the English with her golden hair blowing in the wind behind her had inspired many tales, not all of which were true, but, as is the nature of such things, it wasn't long before her exploits had become legendary across the kingdom. It had been her idea to redistribute the wealth of the many captured English caravans amongst the poor and, though they often lived with little money themselves, the loyalty amongst the people of Deheubarth knew no bounds and they were never short of food or shelter whenever they were requested.

But that had been many years ago and, despite Taliesin's hints that they could regain that path, Tarw suspected that their swords had been sheathed too long to regain even the smallest share of the respect they once had. On top of that, despite his explanations to the rebel leader, Tarw knew that Tomas Scar had voiced a valid point and also enjoyed the respect of his fellow warriors. When all was said and done, Tarw and Gwenllian had once walked away leaving the rebels without a leader. That was possibly an obstacle too difficult to surmount and whatever happened in the next few hours, their fates would be decided one way or the other.

He stirred the pot and walked over to the cot where his two sons still slept. He looked down, reluctant to wake them up. Both had been through so much over the last few days, he knew that they needed to recover. Morgan's physical wounds in particular were bad, but it seemed there was no infection and he would make a full recovery. Maelgwyn, however, had wounds of a different variety and bore no visible scars.

He had joined the single men in the warriors' shelters at the end of the valley, drinking ale and listening to stories of exaggerated bravado and battles of kings long dead. By the time he had returned to the hut, he was heavily drunk and, though Tarw was waiting, it was obvious that it would be pointless talking to him in such a state. Consequently, the prince had let his son fall upon the cot and there he had stayed, hardly moving the whole night through.

'Morgan,' he said, shaking his eldest son by the shoulder, 'time to awaken. There is food on the table.'

Morgan yawned and sat up. He looked across at his sleeping brother.

'When did he return?' he asked.

'Just before dawn,' said Tarw, 'and he was full of ale. I suspect he will regret it when he awakes.'

'I am already awake,' mumbled Maelgwyn, 'and I regret not a single moment.' He sat up and placed his feet on the floor before standing up and walking over to the table, taking one of the sheepskin covers with him, still wrapped around his shoulders.

'It's cold,' he said, sitting at the table.

'Aye, the fire was almost out,' said Tarw as he and Morgan joined him. 'I'll bank it up shortly but eat first and get dressed. There are matters to attend.'

'What matters?' said Morgan as he peered into the pot and stirred it with the ladle.

'Your mother and younger brothers will be here shortly,' said Tarw, 'and I want to be there to greet them.'

'They are safe?' asked Maelgwyn, looking up for the first time.

'Aye, and are being escorted here as we speak by Robert. I understand that Llandeilo Manor has been burned to the ground by Gerald's forces and they were lucky to escape with their lives.'

'Another consequence of your uncovered secrets, I suppose,' said Maelgwyn.

Tarw stared at his son, concerned at the continued animosity hidden beneath his words.

'Maelgwyn,' he said, 'I know I haven't been truthful with you these past few days but . . .'

'Days?' said Maelgwyn, interrupting his father. 'Surely you mean years?'

'Maelgwyn, hold your tongue,' said Morgan.

'No,' said Tarw, 'he has a right to his thoughts.' He turned back to Maelgwyn. 'You are right; I have hidden the truth from you all of your life but it was for your own sake. The burden was already heavy enough for your mother and me so we wanted to shield you from it for as long as we could. We always intended to tell you the truth one day but it wasn't the time. Unfortunately, events overtook us before we could carry out that task so here we are. Ask me whatever you will and I promise I will speak truthfully.'

Maelgwyn spooned some potage into his mouth and chewed quietly, his eyes never leaving his bowl.

'Maelgwyn,' said Tarw, 'for the past few days I have hardly seen you. For an age you held anger in your heart at my failure to tell you the truth yet now I am here, you avoid me like a leper. Ask whatever questions you want and I swear by almighty God I will be truthful with you.'

'I have nothing to say,' said Maelgwyn. He stood up to leave the table.

'Sit down,' said his brother. 'Our father is talking.'

'He is not my father,' said Maelgwyn. 'My father is the steward of Llandeilo Manor, not some liar who claims to be descended from Hywel Dda himself. I am done here.' He turned to leave but Morgan jumped to his feet and grabbed his brother by the throat.

'*No!*' he shouted. 'You are not done here. You will stay and discuss this like a man.'

'Leave me be,' growled Maelgwyn, 'or I swear I will forget you are my brother and strike you dead.'

'Strike me dead?' laughed Morgan. 'So now you are a man who speaks of killing when only a moment ago you were sulking like a beaten child.' He released his brother's throat, pushing him back towards the table. 'Make your mind up, Maelgwyn,' he continued. 'What do you actually want? To be treated like a man and accept the burdens that title brings or return to the comfort of our mother's skirts alongside Rhydian and Rhys?'

'Don't bring them into this,' shouted Maelgwyn. 'This is between me and him.' He pointed at Tarw.

'He is our father,' shouted Morgan, 'and will be treated with respect. Now grow up and act like a man or it is I who will be doing the beating.'

'*Enough*,' roared, Tarw. 'Sit down, the both of you.'

For a few moments the young men stared at each other before taking their seats again and waiting in silence.

'This has to stop right now,' said Tarw. 'There are dangerous times before us and if we are to survive we need to stand alongside each other as family, not against each other as enemies.' He turned to face his younger son. 'Maelgwyn, you have my apologies for not telling you the truth but what's done is done and there is no turning back. I will tell you everything you want to know but I will not pander to your hurt feelings like a nursemaid. I am Gruffydd ap Rhys, son of Rhys ap Tewdwr and true prince of Deheubarth. Your mother is Gwenllian ferch Gruffydd, daughter of Gruffydd ap Cynan, king of Gwynedd. That makes you royal born and a descendant of Hywel Dda. If that is too much of a burden, then feel free to ride away but your brother has made a good point. This should not be about you, me or even your mother, it is about your younger brothers, those two little boys who were almost killed at Llandeilo. The future is uncertain for all of us and even tomorrow is not promised. Do what you will but enough of your whining. Stand up with the rest of your family and be the man you are so desperate to become or be gone and never darken any doorway of ours again. The time for acting like a child is over, Maelgwyn, but the choice is yours.' He stood up and fastened his sword belt before retrieving his cloak and heading towards the door. He left the hut leaving his sons shocked at the anger in his manner. Finally, Morgan got dressed and also headed towards the door.

'Where are you going?' asked Maelgwyn, looking up.

'To meet the caravan from Llandeilo,' said Morgan. 'I have family upon it.'

Without another word he stormed out of the hut, leaving his younger brother alone at the table, staring into his potage. For a few moments, Maelgwyn glowered at the bowl before finally picking it up and hurling it across the hut to break against the door frame. His mind was in turmoil but he knew, he had a serious decision to make.

———

Tarw walked down the hill to the valley floor. In the distance he could see Gwenllian's column approaching. For a few moments, he stopped dead in his tracks, shocked at what he saw. At the head of the column rode his wife, sitting upright and proud in the saddle with an air of power and ability about her, an authoritative and almost arrogant presence that he had known and loved for so many years. Despite not losing any of the love for her during their time in anonymity, he suddenly realised he had missed this woman, the one who had commanded so much fear and respect from friend and foe alike. With a grin on his face he walked onto the path and waited for his wife to arrive.

A few minutes later, Gwenllian reined in her horse and slid from the saddle to stand before her husband. Tarw looked her up and down, recalling the last time he had seen her in full armour, and for a few seconds there was silence as each looked deep into the other's eyes, remembering the many campaigns they had embarked upon in the pursuit of freedom. Tarw's heart was racing with love, desire and admiration. His princess, the one whom he had eloped with all those years previously, was once again standing before him, as large as life and ready to stand against any man who crossed her.

'Well,' she said eventually, 'what do you think?'

'I think,' he said, after a few moments, 'that you have never looked more beautiful, more regal or more damned scary in all the years I have known you.'

As they embraced the population of the rebel camp gathered around, many remembering the couple from years earlier.

'My lady,' called a voice, 'welcome back.'

'Remember me?' called another. 'We rode together at Wetwall Bridge.'

Gwenllian laughed as she disengaged from her husband's embrace and turned to acknowledge all of the best wishes. A little girl came up and gave her a holly sprig complete with berries.

'From my mother,' she said sweetly, and Gwenllian turned to see one of the young women who had ridden alongside her all those years earlier, now an older mother with another child held tightly beneath her shawl.

'Karin,' shouted Gwenllian as the crowd gathered around her in excitement. 'How are you?'

'As well as I can be,' replied the woman over the noise of the crowd. 'Though these two keep me busy.'

'My boys are the same,' shouted Gwenllian as she was jostled by those eager to touch her. 'Come and see me when all this has died down.'

'I will,' laughed Karin as Gwenllian was swept away by the crowd, 'and give my love to your family.'

For the next ten minutes or so, Gwenllian was kept busy saying hello to old friends and meeting others who had only heard stories about her exploits fighting the English all those years earlier. Finally, the crowd started to thin out and Gwenllian turned to see a rather frightening and dirty warrior standing before her.

'Hello,' she said slowly, 'and you are?'

'They call him Dog,' said Tarw, walking up to join his wife, 'and he is the voice of Taliesin. I assume the leader wants to meet you.'

'He does,' said Dog. 'Be done with your reunions and when you are ready, he will be waiting for you in the campaign tent.'

'We will,' said Tarw and they watched as Dog turned away, leaving the prince and his wife alone.

'Where are the boys?' asked Gwenllian, looking around.

'Here,' said a voice and Gwenllian turned to see Morgan standing behind her. At first her face fell seeing the extent of his injuries but she was soon reassured when he stepped forward to embrace her warmly.

'Is this the work of John Salisbury?' she asked, stepping back to look at him again.

'Him and his henchmen,' said Morgan. 'But that is a story for another time. Worry not, I will be fine.'

'And what about Maelgwyn? Is he here?'

'He is back at the hut,' said Morgan. 'Sulking like a spoilt child.'

'Why?' asked Gwenllian. 'Is he hurt?'

'Only his pride,' said Tarw. 'He thinks we have been lying to him and nurses a grudge.'

'Then I must go to him and explain,' said Gwenllian.

'No, not yet,' said Tarw. 'Let it all sink in and then we will talk as a family.' He looked over at the cart. 'Are the children in there?'

'They are fast asleep,' said Gwenllian. 'And we should let them rest. We have been travelling the whole night.'

'What about you?'

'I am as awake as a morning lark,' said Gwenllian. 'So shall we see what this Taliesin has to say?'

'Aye,' replied Tarw. He turned to Morgan. 'Are you coming?'

'Am I invited?'

'You are my oldest son, Morgan, and as such have just as much say in this family as anyone. You should be at our side.'

'Then let's go,' said Morgan and he led the way up the path leading to the campaign tent.

———

'They are here,' said Dog simply, entering the campaign tent and walking over to sit on one of the benches.

Tarw, Gwenllian and Morgan followed him in and stood side by side, staring at the ten men lined up against the far wall of the tent. The air seemed tense and there was none of the hospitality Tarw had experienced a few nights earlier.

'So,' said Taliesin, stepping forward, 'you must be the famous Gwenllian. I must say, you certainly look the part.' The men either side of the rebel leader laughed at his taunt but Gwenllian remained unmoved.

'If that is supposed to be an insult,' said Tarw, 'then you demean yourself. We are here to discuss what happens next so why don't we just get on with it?'

'Not so fast, prince,' said Taliesin as he walked over to stand before Gwenllian. 'We are still waiting for your accuser and, besides, first I need to be introduced to your wife for the rumours of her beauty have certainly not been exaggerated.'

'If you have anything to say, you can say it directly to me,' said Gwenllian, meeting his stare, 'and not through my husband.' As Gwenllian and Taliesin stared at each other, more men entered the tent and stood behind the newcomers. Amongst them was Tomas Scar.

'Ah, here they are,' said Taliesin, looking over Gwenllian's shoulder. 'Now we can begin.' He turned and walked to the far side of the table and dropped into the large carved chair like a self-assured monarch. 'Tomas Scar,' he said, 'I trust you are sober?'

'As the day as I was born,' said Scar.

'And do you still hold the view that the prince and his wife are nothing more than cowards?'

'I have had a chance to digest Tarw's explanations and if what he said is true, then it dulls the blade of my accusations but it still leaves me uneasy about allowing someone back into the fold who once rode away so easily.'

Taliesin turned to face Tarw. 'And what say you to these concerns?'

'First of all,' said Tarw, 'I have not said I want to ride with you at all. I said I will discuss it with my family.'

'And have you?'

'Not yet, they have only just arrived.'

'Then this is your chance.' He turned to Gwenllian. 'Let me explain. It appears to me that fortune may have smiled upon the Welsh cause these past few days. With the death of the king, not only is there unprecedented turmoil amongst the halls of Westminster, there is also great fear and confusion amongst the barons and castles across Wales. This alone offers great opportunity, but when you realise that Hywel ap Maredudd has amassed a huge army and already defies English rule across Brycheniog, it does not take a clever man to realise there is a chance to seize the moment and take back what is ours.'

'Then why don't you do it?' asked Gwenllian.

'Because we don't have the numbers,' replied Taliesin. 'And while I am a stubborn man, I am not stupid. You two, on the other hand, seem to have an attraction that draws men to any cause you may support.'

'I feel you may be insulting those very men you speak of,' said Gwenllian, 'for you do not credit them with any patriotism. No man risks his life for a single man or woman, be they pauper or prince. Someone like me, or indeed my husband, can only be a figurehead in such things. The men that wield the swords have to do so with the intention of either winning something or defending something. Often, it can be the same thing.'

'Explain?'

'Freedom. Once won, it will always have to be defended and that is what makes a man fight. Those at the head of the armies are figureheads only, no more than human representations of a nation's colours.'

Taliesin fell silent and sat back in his chair. The woman before him was certainly beautiful and indeed striking in her studded leather armour but more than that she was intelligent and engaging, a trait he seldom found in other men, let alone women.

'I can see why you were so revered by your people,' said Taliesin.

'So what is all this about?' asked Gwenllian with a sigh. 'Why are we here, Taliesin? Spit it out.'

'You are here,' said the leader, 'because there is a suggestion you could re-join the rebellion. Your husband has recently indicated that in his heart of hearts he would gladly take up the sword but alas his agreement with the dead king prevents him from doing so.'

'A man is only as good as his word,' said Gwenllian.

'And therein lies the problem. I hear you have about eighty men-at-arms between you, and while that is impressive in such a short time, it isn't anywhere near enough. If we are going to take advantage of the turmoil amongst the English, we need to rally a nation and to do that we need a prince.'

'Or a princess,' said a voice, and everyone turned to stare at Dog, sitting casually on the side bench using the point of his knife to pick his teeth. For a few moments there was silence until eventually someone spoke from just behind Gwenllian's shoulder.

'Arguing about the merits of a Welsh prince leading the rebellion is one thing,' said Scar, 'but to consider riding under the command of a woman is beyond contemplation.'

'Why?' asked Dog simply.

'Because battle is men's business,' said Scar. 'She may ride into this camp as a daughter of a king but that carries no weight with me. I see no wounds or scars of conflict. All she has is her fancy armour and a haughty bearing. This is the badge of battle,' he said, drawing his knife and resting the point on the vivid scar running down his cheek, 'not fancy hair and a reputation gleaned from oft exaggerated stories.'

'A scar is not a badge of honour for the man who carries it but the man who inflicted it,' said Gwenllian without turning around. Scar lowered his knife to rest it on Gwenllian's shoulder, so the blade was just within her sight.

'If you are implying you are a better warrior than I, then feel free to challenge me. I distinguish not between foes of any sex; they all die the same way.'

A murmur rippled around the tent at the implied threat and Morgan's hand strayed to his own blade, only to be stopped by his father.

'Don't,' said Tarw quietly. 'This will be played out.'

'But . . .' started Morgan.

'Do as you are told,' said Tarw menacingly, 'and stay out of it. Your mother is fine.'

'Nobody is dying here today,' snapped Taliesin. 'The meeting is to decide where we go from here, but you and your husband need to make your minds up as to what your intentions are. If you want to leave, then go but if your hearts are as patriotic as you claim then state your expectations for we are getting nowhere.'

'I am happy to do so,' said Gwenllian. 'But first, you can tell your court jester here that if he does not remove his blade, I will cut his throat with his own knife.'

For a few seconds there was silence and then the tent erupted into laughter.

'Really?' said Taliesin eventually. 'I heard you had a fierce reputation but for one so slight I wonder if such words can be backed up with suitable actions.'

'Try me,' said Gwenllian, meeting his stare.

Taliesin looked over her shoulder at Tomas Scar. 'Tomas, you can stand down. We wouldn't want you to get hurt.'

The warrior sneered before sheathing his blade. 'I suspect hell would freeze over before this wench would hurt me, unless of course, she refused my bed and then I would be extremely hurt.' As the tent burst into laughter again, Tomas Scar placed his chin on Gwenllian's shoulder and whispered into her ear. 'What about it, Princess. Fancy trying a real man instead of a coward?'

Gwenllian turned around and smiled up at Tomas. He loomed tall before her and his foul breath swept down upon her face. Tomas Scar leered back, his eyes widening in pleasant surprise as her hands lifted his hauberk to seek his crotch.

'I'll tell you what,' she said, her voice colder than her actions implied, 'you keep your filthy thoughts to yourself and in return, I'll let you keep these.' Before he could respond, Gwenllian grabbed his crotch in a vicelike grip and twisted as hard as she could, forcing the warrior to cry out in unexpected pain. For a few seconds he just stood there, bent over in agony, but despite the pain, his fist lashed out to knock the woman away.

Gwenllian stepped quickly back away but as Tomas Scar followed up his unsuccessful punch with a lunge, she kicked out with the sole of her boot, connecting with the warrior's knee, sending him crashing to the floor. Before anyone could move, she followed up by dropping onto his chest, drawing a blade from her boot and pressing it against his throat. The whole thing had taken seconds only and everyone else looked on in shock.

'Well,' said Gwenllian, without taking her cold eyes from those of the man beneath her face, 'do I kill him or not?'

No one answered and the tent fell silent.

'Gwenllian, you have made your point,' said Tarw quietly. 'Let him up.'

For a few seconds, her blade remained where it was before finally she eased the pressure and jumped to her feet.

'Do not judge me, my friend,' she said as the man staggered up from the floor, 'for I have killed bigger and better men than you.'

Tomas Scar turned to face her and she braced herself for another assault. Instead, after a moment's pause, he nodded his head in acknowledgement. 'I have to admit you got the better of me this time, Princess, but be aware that if ever we need to do this again, you will not find me so unprepared.'

Gwenllian nodded back and Tomas Scar returned to his comrades, growling at the inevitable teasing, having been bettered by a woman.

Gwenllian turned to Taliesin. 'You were saying?'

Taliesin breathed deeply and nodded his own head in admiration. 'I admit I am impressed,' he said, 'but a scuffle in a tent is not warfare. Tell me what you want and your terms.'

'Two days ago, I wanted nothing but my boys safely home and to enjoy the peace to which we had become accustomed. Since then, my eldest son has been beaten by the English and almost hanged alongside my husband. The place I have called home all these years has been burned to the ground and many of those I called friends, slaughtered like cattle. I found my two youngest sons hiding amongst the filth of the pigs yet thanked God I did for they were the only survivors.' She paused and looked around the tent. 'But none of this had as much effect on me as the poor girl who saved their lives. It was obvious she had been raped and left to die but somehow, she still managed to find my children and hid them from the murdering bastards who would see them dead. Even as she breathed her last, she kept them warm with her dying body.'

She stared into the eyes of each man in turn as she continued. 'She did this not because of who they were, for their true identities were kept secret, but because they were innocent children and as such represented the future of our kingdom. To me that is an act of bravery greater than any campaign I have ever ridden upon or heard about.'

She turned back to face Taliesin. 'So, you ask me what I want to do, well here is my answer. I want to take the fight to the English. To strike them down wherever we find them until every last one is dead or flees beaten and bloody back through the Marches to England. But this is not for me, or my husband or even my sons. I want to do this for a poor girl who lies rotting in her grave outside the ruins of Llandeilo. Someone who, despite her pain, sacrificed her life for the future of this country and if every man here has even a portion of that girl's courage, then Deheubarth could see a Welsh king within months.'

A murmur of support and admiration rippled around the tent and Taliesin watched with interest at the effect she was having on his men. She had only been in the camp for an hour yet she was already inspiring those who had faced so much hardship and danger.

'So,' he said, returning his gaze to the princess, 'you want to join us?'

'Aye. Give us shelter and time to train those who have followed us here and we will ride alongside you as allies. We will send out word to everyone still loyal to the crown of Deheubarth and swell our numbers. By spring we could have an army capable of engaging most of what Gerald can send against us.'

'Even if this was possible, we are in the depths of winter and can hardly feed ourselves. How do you suggest we feed an army?'

'We have many contacts, Taliesin, lords and commoners alike, and when we preyed upon the English columns, it was they who profited from our attacks. No one went hungry during those winters for we made sure there was bread for all. Now it is time to call in those debts and, though some may struggle, I am confident many will give what they can. Add this to carefully planned attacks on English interests and I'm sure we can live well until spring.'

'And what if Gerald responds with knights?'

'I doubt he will for he cannot risk defeat while the Crown mourns for Henry. If he does, we will strike like adders and flee back amongst the forests like frightened deer, leading them a merry dance until such a time when we are strong enough to face them as equals.'

Taliesin sat back again and stared at Gwenllian. Her ambition was huge and he foresaw many problems but for the first time in years, he felt the stirrings of excitement in his gut. 'And you think we can do this?'

'We have done it before,' said Gwenllian.

Taliesin turned to face Tarw. 'And what say you, Prince?'

'I agree with my wife,' said Tarw. 'I will not break my word to the dead king and lead any rebellion but it was a promise about leadership only, not participation.'

'So you will ride amongst us?'

'Aye, and be proud to do so.'

Taliesin took a deep breath and looked around the tent. Every eye was upon him and he knew he had a big decision to make. Finally, he turned back to face Tarw and Gwenllian. 'I will talk to my men and come to a judgement,' he said. 'Go to your hut and await me there.'

Gwenllian and Tarw nodded in acknowledgement and left the tent, closely followed by their son.

'Well, the matter is now out of our hands,' said Tarw as they walked down the slope. 'How do you think the dice will fall?'

'Only Taliesin and God know,' said Gwenllian. 'But I will tell you this. Even if he sends us away, I will not leave Deheubarth before Gerald and his murdering knights feel the weight of my retribution and if we have to ride alone, then so be it.'

Later that day, Tarw, Gwenllian and Morgan sat at the table in their hut eating a stew made from wood pigeon and root vegetables. Maelgwyn was still absent and Gwenllian was worried for his safety.

'What if he has ridden from here?' she asked. 'He is not yet able to live his life as a man, especially in such dangerous times.'

'He will be back,' said Morgan, delving back into the pot for more meat. 'He just needs time.'

Tarw looked across at his two youngest sons playing happily in the corner. Rhydian was tickling his brother and both were hysterically laughing. 'It's those two I am more concerned about,' said Tarw. 'If we are to join this rebellion then it is they who will suffer most.'

'In what way?' asked his wife.

'You know the demands of warfare,' said Tarw. 'And it is likely we will both be away from camp for long stretches of time. They will see us very seldom and that is not a situation they are used to.'

'I will engage one of the women to look after them in my absence,' said Gwenllian. 'They will be fine and it is a small price to pay towards the freedom we seek.'

'And if we die?' asked Tarw. 'What then?'

Morgan looked between each of his parents thoughtfully. The thought of death in battle wasn't a stranger to him but the aftermath was a scenario he hadn't considered.

'Well we are still a long way from that possibility,' said Gwenllian, 'but I will leave instructions and money to pay for safe passage to my father's house in Aberffraw. They will be safe there and can make their own choices when they are men.'

'Perhaps it is wise to send them sooner rather than later.'

'Let's not get ahead of ourselves,' said Gwenllian. 'We don't even know if this Taliesin will allow us to ride with him yet. Once it is clear what is happening, we will decide.'

'Well, whatever the outcome,' said Morgan, looking over his parents' shoulders, 'we are about to find out.'

Tarw and Gwenllian turned to see the figure of Dog standing quietly in the doorway.

'We are ready,' said Dog and he turned away before anyone could ask him any questions.

'What does he mean?' asked Morgan.

'There's only one way to find out,' said Tarw, standing up. 'Come on.'

He walked over to the door followed by Morgan and Gwenllian and ducked under the low lintel. Outside, he stopped dead in his tracks and as his wife and son joined him, they all stared in silence at the astonishing sight below them.

Down on the valley floor, every member of Taliesin's small army was lined up in ranks. Behind them stood the civilians of the camp, men, women and children alike, who were too young, too old or too infirm to carry a weapon. To either flank stood the men Tarw and Gwenllian had recruited to their cause over the past few days, again, each fully armed. In all there were over two hundred individuals looking up at the family and at their head stood Taliesin, towering above them all.

'What is this?' asked Morgan quietly. 'What are they doing?'

Before Tarw could answer, Taliesin's voice echoed around the hidden valley. 'Gruffydd ap Rhys, Gwenllian ferch Gruffydd. You have been accused of leaving the rebellion at a critical time. In a council of your peers you have been found guilty as charged and will be sentenced forthwith.'

Morgan's hand went to his blade but again it was his father who reached out to stay his arm. 'Wait,' he said. 'Let's hear him out.'

'You have given your reasons,' continued Taliesin, 'and some find them adequate but there are others who struggle to find merit in your actions. Consequently, the views differ widely amongst the people of this valley.' He paused and looked around before returning his gaze to the three on the slope. 'However, we all agree that what is done is done and there is no going back. We have an opportunity before us that needs to be grasped but to do that, we need a leader, someone who can rally the whole of Deheubarth behind them.' He paused again and took a deep breath. 'That person cannot be me.'

Tarw's eyes widened in surprise and he guessed what was coming next.

'I have done what I can,' said Taliesin, 'and have led to the best of my ability but my time as leader cannot continue while there is even one person left alive with the blood of Hywel Dda running through their veins. Tarw, you have stated that you cannot and will not break your word and that is an admirable trait in any man so we turn to you, Gwenllian ferch Gruffydd. You are the daughter of a king and he too is descended from the great Hywel Dda. This means that though you are not a direct descendant of the house of Tewdwr, your pedigree is just as strong. It is you we turn to, Gwenllian, and charge you with leading these people out of the dark of servitude and fear, into the light of laughter and freedom.' He paused to stare deep into her eyes. 'This is your sentence, Gwenllian, this is the will of the people. Do you accept your penance?'

Gwenllian swallowed hard, looking around the large gathering and realising each and every one held hope in their hearts, dreams that she may or may not be able to deliver.

'And is this the will of you all?' she asked.

For a few seconds, nobody moved until finally Taliesin drew his sword and plunged it into the ground before him. 'It is mine,' he said as he dropped to one knee in a show of allegiance.

Behind him another man drew his sword and followed the example of his leader. 'And mine,' he shouted.

'I too pledge my fealty,' shouted another.

Within seconds, everyone started pledging allegiance and soon almost everyone was on their knees, man and woman alike. One man, however, was still on his feet, staring at the princess. Gwenllian returned his gaze with a steeliness of her own.

'What about you, Tomas Scar?' she said eventually. 'Do you still contest my right to lead?'

For a few seconds there was silence until the warrior slowly withdrew his knife and walked up the slope towards her. Everyone held their breath as the warrior and princess stood toe to toe. Finally, Tomas Scar spun the knife in the air and caught it by the blade before offering it to the princess, hilt first.

'Aye, I will ride with you,' he said, 'but know this, the moment you leave us standing alone, or I see you flee in the face of the enemy, it will be this blade that brings you down, not some lance born by an English mercenary. Is that understood?'

'Understood,' said Gwenllian with a smile.

'In that case,' said Tomas Scar, dropping to both knees, 'I too swear fealty.'

Gwenllian returned the warrior's knife and looked at the camp of rebels before her. She was about to speak when Tarw's arm shot out and grabbed her own. 'Look,' he said and Gwenllian turned to see a familiar young man walking towards her.

'Maelgwyn,' she said quietly, her voice almost breaking, 'I have missed you.'

'And I you,' said Maelgwyn, 'but the time for such sentiment is over. The mother I have known all my life has long gone, I realise that now, but in her place stands another. Someone who I now realise holds the best interests of not only me and my brothers at heart but a whole nation. I have wronged you and the rest of my family by doubting your intentions but the fog has lifted from my mind and the way is clear. If you will have me back, I too pledge my lifelong fealty as a son, a brother and as a warrior, until the day I draw my last breath.' Like the others he drove his sword into the ground and bowed his head.

Gwenllian swallowed hard, and placed her hand on his shoulder, knowing it would not be good to cry in front of so many people. 'Stand up, Maelgwyn,' she said, 'and take your place alongside your brother. You too, Tomas Scar, you are a respected warrior amongst these men and should bow to no one.' Scar got to his feet and stepped to one side as Gwenllian walked forward to address the rebel camp.

'I am honoured that you have gifted us a second chance,' she called loudly, 'and make no mistake, if we are to do this then there will be many hardships along the way. Some of us will die on the journey but the destination of freedom is a glorious one and something our fathers could only dream of since William the Bastard first stormed these shores.' She looked around again. 'So,' she called, her voice rising to be heard at the far side of the valley, 'before I accept your charge, I ask you this. Will you follow me through the dark days before us, even though they may lead to your graves?'

'*Aye*,' they roared in unison.

'Then get to your feet,' she shouted. 'For from this day hence, no person Welsh born will take a knee in subservience before me. I may bear the title, but it is all of us who carry freedom in our hearts.' She drew her own sword and held it high. 'In the name of Hywel Dda the lawmaker, I hereby decree that we will not stop until we have driven out every invader from these sacred lands. Tyranny ends here, today. Tomorrow we take the first steps to freedom.'

'*Freedom*,' roared every voice in agreement and as her family looked on, the crowd surged forward to engulf their new leader.

Tarw and Morgan were joined by Maelgwyn and both men embraced him, knowing that no words of explanation were needed.

'I have never seen mother looking so glorious,' said Morgan eventually.

'Oh, you have seen nothing yet,' said Tarw, placing his arms around the shoulders of his two sons. 'This is the woman I fell in love with and, trust me, this is just the beginning.'

Pembroke Castle

December 28th, AD 1135

Nesta sat on a chair at the end of her husband's sealed coffin in the castle's chapel. All around the walls, Gerald's favoured men stood silently, waiting for the priest to finish his prayers over the casket. The windowless chapel was lit by hundreds of candles and incense burners hung in each corner, adding to the already oppressive atmosphere caused by so many people in such a confined space. Behind the casket, the floor slabs had been removed and a grave dug for the internment.

Nesta had decided that, though the body would be buried within the chapel itself, it should have no formal markings in case the castle was ever taken in conflict and the aggressors sought to take any vengeance on Gerald's remains. Consequently, everyone present had been sworn to secrecy and they had already buried an empty coffin in the castle graveyard the previous day in an effort to mislead any prying eyes as to the location of the castellan's grave.

Nesta stared at the coffin, her eyes cold and dry. Since her husband's body had been brought back from Kidwelly, she had done her mourning in private and now she was all out of tears.

She looked up as the priest approached to give her a simple wooden cross. After saying a silent prayer, she kissed the cross and placed it on the coffin lid, knowing that everyone present was waiting for her to say something.

'Goodbye, my love,' she said eventually, deciding to keep it simple. 'I shall see you one day in the house of the Lord.'

As she backed away from the coffin, four knights approached and lifted it from the trestle to pass it down to two more men already waiting in the grave. Carefully, they laid the casket down before climbing out and joining their comrades. The priest sprinkled a handful of soil down into the grave and, stepping aside, allowed the rest of the men to do the same. Each man in turn walked past the grave to repeat the gesture but, as they did, Nesta started to sweat and she knew that she had to get out.

'Master Salisbury,' she said to the constable, 'I regret I have to leave. The air in this room is becoming heavy and I fear I will faint.'

'Your husband is being buried, my lady,' he said quietly. 'You should stay until the coffin is covered.'

'I have said my goodbyes,' said Nesta. 'There is nothing more for me to say. Besides, that is not Gerald in that box – it is an empty vessel that once held his soul, nothing more. Now if you don't mind, I am leaving.'

Much to his disdain, Nesta brushed past the constable and walked along the corridor towards the keep doors. Behind her the knights waited until the coffin was covered before leaving the chapel and heading up to the grand hall to feast in their comrade's name.

Nesta stood in the doorway looking out over Pembroke towards the distant hills. The air was cold upon her face but she breathed it in, clearing her lungs and mind of the despondency of the chapel. As she stared, she knew her life was about to change. She didn't know what changes would come about but whatever they were, she suspected they may not be to her liking.

'My lady,' said a quiet voice and she turned to see Emma standing behind her.

'Hello, Emma,' said Nesta with a forced smile. 'You should go back to your room; it is cold out here.'

'Not as cold as it is in my heart,' said Emma. 'These are indeed dark days the devil has sent upon us.'

'They are,' said Nesta, turning to look out over the hills again. 'Oh, I wish life could be simple once again.'

'A wish we all share at times,' said Emma, walking over to stand beside her mistress. 'Are you well? Your face is pale.'

'It's just the chill and the upset of the past few days. Now Gerald has been buried, I can begin to look forward, though what the future holds is anyone's guess.' She turned to her maid. 'But enough about me. You have your own burdens to bear. When is Catrin's burial? I will attend on behalf of the garrison.'

'She was buried two days ago, my lady – in a graveyard outside of the town.'

'Oh no,' said Nesta. 'I am so sorry. Had I known . . .'

'You had other things to attend to,' said Emma. 'The main thing is she is now at rest, as is your husband. All we can do now is pray for them.'

'Indeed,' said Nesta, 'and also for the soul of the king.'

'Henry?'

'Yes. Don't forget, Emma, he is the father of my eldest son and despite what he did to this beautiful country of ours, there was a time when I loved him more than life itself.'

'It is a strange and complicated life that our Lord lays before us,' said Emma.

'Come,' said Nesta, 'let's go in and sit before the fire.' She turned to walk inside but Emma remained, staring down into the bailey. A man had just ridden through the gates and was talking frantically to one of the guards. As she watched, the guard pointed up the motte to the keep and the rider dismounted before running up the steps as fast as he could.

'My lady,' said Emma. 'There is someone coming.'

Nesta turned back and waited for the young man to arrive.

The door guard stepped forward, presenting his pike, but Nesta held up her hand.

'Let him approach,' she said. 'He is no more than a boy.'

The young man reached the last step and after a nervous glance at the scowling guard, turned to address Nesta. 'My lady,' he panted, still trying to catch his breath, 'I have ridden direct from Worcester and have important news. I seek an urgent audience with Gerald of Windsor in the name of the king.'

Nesta swallowed hard. Obviously news of her husband's death hadn't reached Worcester yet.

'My husband is dead,' she said eventually. 'Killed by an assassin's arrow just a few days ago.'

The young man's face dropped and he stared in disbelief. 'Oh, sweet Lord,' he gasped, crossing himself. 'These are challenging days. May he rest in peace.'

'What is your message?' continued Nesta. 'I will see it is passed on.'

'I'm not sure I should give it to you,' said the young man slowly. 'It is of national importance and I was instructed to give it only to the castellan. Has a replacement been appointed?'

'No,' said Nesta calmly. 'I doubt that news of Gerald's death has even reached London yet but I am his wife, and until such time Westminster appoints a new castellan, I hold authority here. Now state your message or be gone for I have other matters to attend to.'

Again the young man hesitated and peered over her shoulder into the interior of the keep.

Nesta could feel herself losing her temper and turned to the guard. 'This man is wasting my time,' she said. 'Throw him out.'

'Wait!' shouted the young man, delving into a pouch around his waist. 'I cannot leave without passing the message on to someone.' He retrieved a rolled-up parchment sealed with red wax and handed it over to Nesta. Without waiting, Nesta broke the seal and unfurled the parchment, reading it silently to herself. When she was done, she looked up at the young man and he could see she was visibly shocked.

'Is this true?' she asked. 'For the seal is that of Worcestershire not Westminster.'

'The parchment was written in Worcestershire for redistribution,' said the messenger, 'but the news came straight from Westminster via carrier pigeon and the encryptions were authenticated by the clergy. The news is true and needs to be transmitted to all those in the service of the Crown as soon as possible. Criers will announce it to the people within days.'

'Leave it to me,' replied Nesta. She turned to her maid. 'Emma, I have to go to the great hall. Please see this man gets a penny for his efforts.'

'Of course,' said Emma and she watched as Nesta went inside to climb the stairway.

Moments later, Nesta entered the hall and saw that all of Gerald's knights were present, as well as his trusted sergeants and officers, each sharing their memories of Gerald, and all held a tankard of wine or ale, depending on their preference. Down the middle of the hall ran three lines of trestle tables complete with linen covers and adorned with the castle silverware. Silver candelabras decorated the tables and a band of minstrels played subdued music as servants scurried amongst the men, filling their tankards wherever needed.

Nesta looked around the hall. The civility of the proceedings was welcome but she knew it wouldn't last. The whole point of the wake was for Gerald's comrades-in-arms to remember their fellow warrior and that meant getting blind drunk as quickly as possible. Soon the hall would be filled with the sounds of drunken men loudly recalling distant deeds of valour – some real, some false, but all exaggerated. With a sigh she walked up to the top table where John of Salisbury was talking quietly to one of his trusted men.

'My lady,' said Salisbury turning in his seat to face her, 'I am glad you have seen sense. Please, sit beside me and we will invite our guests to take their seats.'

'I am not here to drink, Constable,' said Nesta. 'I have come to relay a message from Westminster to the garrison.'

'A message,' said Salisbury, his eyes opening in surprise.

'It is addressed to my husband and, as such, I have taken possession of it,' said Nesta.

Salisbury's face hardened and he stared at Nesta with ill-disguised anger. 'I have told you before,' he said, 'until Gerald's successor is appointed, I am the senior man here and any messages should be relayed through me.'

'It was addressed directly to him, and not his station,' said Nesta coldly, 'so if you don't mind, please call the hall to order.'

Salisbury stared again, but as several of the nearby knights had already overheard the conversation, he knew there was little he could do. Most had been fiercely loyal to Gerald and, indeed, Nesta.

'Of course,' he said eventually with a forced smile and he got to his feet.

'Gentlemen,' he called, banging his tankard on the table. 'Quiet please.' One of the knights signalled for the minstrels to stop playing and gradually the hall fell silent. 'Thank you,' said Salisbury. 'If we can have your indulgence for just a few minutes, I promise the remembrance feast will start shortly but in the meantime, the Lady Nesta has something she wants to say.'

Nesta nodded her gratitude and walked to the centre of the hall. 'Gentlemen,' she said, 'I am in receipt of a dispatch from Westminster and it is incumbent upon me to deliver it to you good men.' She unfurled the scroll and took a deep breath before reading the contents aloud.

'"*To all men of the cloth, barons, lords, castellans and knights of the realm. Let it be known that on this day, the twenty-sixth of December in the year of our Lord eleven hundred and thirty-five, in the presence of their Excellencies, the bishops of Winchester and Salisbury, and witnessed by Lord Hugh Bigod, first earl of Norfolk, Stephen de Blois, first count of Boulogne, was crowned king of England by William of Corbeil, Archbishop of Canterbury. All subjects are to send declarations of fealty to the Crown upon return. Let all men bless the choice of the people and the judgement of the Lord.*"'

Nesta looked up before reciting the last line.

'"*God save the king.*"'

For a few seconds there was silence as the news sank in but then one of the knights raised his tankard and roared his allegiance. 'God save the king!'

'God save the king,' responded the rest of the men in similar fashion, and picking up on the change of mood, the minstrels started up again, though this time with a celebratory tune.

'Very interesting,' said Salisbury, approaching Nesta as the noise continued.

'Not a word that I would have chosen,' said Nesta.

'No? Then what would you call it?'

'I was thinking more of *travesty.*'

'Are you not happy?'

'It is common knowledge the crown was promised to Henry's daughter,' said Nesta. 'It was witnessed by many barons.'

'Yes, but there is another witness who swore that he recanted that promise on his death bed.'

'You talk of Hugh Bigod?'

'You know I do.'

'Yet he is a known ally of Stephen de Blois and stands to profit greatly from this appointment. Don't you think that in itself is a coincidence too many?'

'Perhaps, but it is not for the likes of you and me to second-guess the bishops. I, for one, welcome his appointment for he is known to be in favour of allowing the recognised local authorities to administer justice as they see fit without constant recourse to the Crown.'

'And that will suit you no end,' said Nesta.

'Oh yes,' said Salisbury, 'it certainly will. Now, if you don't mind, I have a celebration to attend.'

Nesta nodded and left the room. Behind her, another knight walked over to stand at the constable's side. 'A fascinating development,' he said quietly, 'and one which you should exploit to the full.'

'Oh, I intend to,' said Salisbury, still staring at the departing figure of Nesta. 'Tell me, what is the latest news about the second assassin, the one that escaped?'

'I sent word to Kidwelly Castle that as the trail led into Pembroke, we would take over the hunt,' said the knight. 'In honesty, I think that Maurice was secretly relieved to have the burden taken from his hands. To have such an important guest murdered in view of your castle is one thing but to have one of the assassins escape is even more embarrassing.'

'And there is no chance of him being found?'

'Of course not,' said the knight. 'I was very careful.'

Salisbury smiled. Walter de Calais was nothing if not thorough and he knew there would be no loose ends leading any suspicion of Gerald's death to his door.

'Good,' he said eventually. 'In that case, tell the grooms to prepare the horses. Tomorrow we ride to London.'

Pembroke Harbour

January 1st, AD 1136

The dock was busy, as it was on most days, but today the taverns were particularly full. Three ships had already been unloaded and another lay at anchor offshore waiting for space at the wharf. Labourers scurried down the gangplanks, their backs bent under the weight of provisions, and a line of covered wagons lay waiting along the dock, ready to take the much-needed provisions up to the castle. Well-wrapped whores prowled the shadows, keen to do business with the sailors, always a good source of easily obtained coin. To one side, a group of soldiers stood around a brazier talking quietly about the recent news regarding the new king. Though their role at the dock was one of protection, the day had been long and there was no sign of their relief. Consequently, they were hungry and tired, and their attention to what was going on around them waned as the day progressed.

'This is getting ridiculous,' said one, blowing on his hands again. 'We should have been relieved hours ago, and when we get back I'm going to make someone pay, you see if I don't.'

'What are you going to do, Gilbert?' laughed his comrade. 'Strike an officer or a sergeant? That will at least lose you your hands if not your life. Besides, you could do with missing a few meals.'

The rest of the men laughed and stared at the tight hauberk already stretched over the soldier's enormous gut.

'I'm a big man,' said Gilbert, 'and need my food.'

'It looks like we won't be here much longer,' said another of the guards. 'There are just two carts left empty. Anything left after they have been loaded will have to wait until tomorrow.'

'I can't wait that long,' replied Gilbert. 'I'm going to get myself some food.'

'Don't be a fool,' warned one of his comrades. 'If any of the sergeants come back you'll be charged with leaving your post.'

'I don't care,' said Gilbert, leaning his pike up against the wall. 'You just look after this. I'll be back before you know it.'

Despite his comrade's warnings, the obese soldier walked across the dock towards the nearest tavern. Moments later he was inside and pushing his way through the many drunken sailors towards the bench holding two open barrels of ale.

As he entered, the noise level dropped and many eyes turned to stare at him, but this didn't put him off; he was used to the bad feeling in the town and he knew that if any man raised even a hand against one of the king's men, then they would be hunted down like wild pigs and hanged before the rest of the town.

'What are you staring at?' he sneered at a man standing in his way. 'Do you want some broken teeth?'

'Sorry, my lord,' said the man, meekly backing away.

'So you should be,' said Gilbert and he turned to seek the landlord.

'You there,' he shouted at a man wearing a leather apron and ladling ale into some tankards from a bucket. 'Do you have hot food in here, preferably some meat or pasties?'

'Aye, we have pies and bread, freshly baked,' said the landlord, finishing his task. 'What do you want?'

'Both,' said the soldier. 'Half a loaf and two pies. Quick about it and none of your rubbish. I only pay for good food.'

'My food is the best on the dock,' said the barman. He turned to one of the serving girls. 'There are pies on a shelf in one of the ovens. Bring two and a whole loaf – our friend here is a big man and needs feeding.'

Gilbert's eyes lit up but then narrowed again in suspicion. 'I'm only paying for half a loaf. That was agreed.'

'Of course. The other half is free as a gesture towards the great work you and your friends do around here.'

A confused smile played around Gilbert's mouth for it was rare any native of Pembroke paid an English soldier a compliment, let alone gave them something for nothing.

'How long will she be?' he asked.

'A few minutes only,' said the landlord.

The soldier looked around nervously. The tavern had grown strangely quiet, and whereas that was quite common, the way many of the men met his gaze wasn't and he started to feel uncomfortable.

'Where is she?' he snapped. 'I have to go.'

'A little while longer,' said the landlord. 'You asked for them hot, did you not?'

'Aye, I did, but you said they were already in the oven. I think you are jesting with me.' Without warning, Gilbert walked past the ale table and out towards the back room.

'Wait,' shouted the landlord as he went. 'You can't go in there.'

'I can go where I want,' said Gilbert and he continued through the door. As soon as he entered, he stopped in shock. Instead of a single girl tending an oven, what he found was a scene of carnage. Eight armed men, sweating and bloodied, turned to face him as he entered, but what made him gasp in shock were the six bodies lying dead upon the floor, each covered in blood and each wearing the uniform of an English foot soldier. For a few seconds nobody moved, and with horror, Gilbert realised this was the reason the relief had not come – they had been murdered en route and their bodies hidden in the back room of the tavern.

Despite his size, he turned and bolted for the door, knocking aside the landlord as he went.

'*Stop him,*' roared a voice but it was too late – he managed to make it into the tavern, barging aside both men and women as he fled for his life.

'*Stop him,*' the voice roared again and two men drinking ale at the door tried to bring him down but to no avail. His strength and size meant he managed to get out of the doorway and call the alarm to his comrades on the far side of the dock.

'*Stand to,*' he roared as he ran. 'We are under attack,' but within seconds, he stopped dead in his tracks as he stared at the devastating scene before him. All around the brazier lay the bodies of his five comrades, one still on fire where he had fallen into the flames. Others moaned as they died and one looked up in false hope, desperate for the help that could never come. The dozens of arrows sticking out of their bodies paid witness to the terrible events that had happened only moments earlier. It was clear they had stood no chance against their attackers. Frantically Gilbert looked around, his stomach churning with fear. Many of those who moments earlier had seemed nothing more than interested bystanders now stood in defiance of him, many with swords or knives in their hands. Others bore the bows responsible for the deaths of his comrades and it was clear he was trapped.

'What's going on?' he stuttered. 'Who are you? What do you want?'

Nobody answered but one man stepped out from the crowd before drawing a blade from the sheath on his belt. Gilbert recognised him as the one who had backed meekly away when he had first entered the tavern.

'No,' said the soldier, looking around in panic, 'you can't do this. Stay away from me.' He drew his sword and turned on the spot, brandishing his weapon towards any who came close. 'I'll kill you,' he shouted, his voice shaking in fear. 'I swear I will.'

'I think not,' said the man and before Gilbert could answer, he felt a thud in his back and he fell to his knees in pain, knowing he had been struck by an arrow. All around him, more men emerged from the crowd, each carrying weapons and each keen to end the fat man's life.

'Wait,' called a voice and the crowd parted to let a dozen riders through. At their head was a beautiful woman and within seconds a name rippled around the crowd like a gentle wind. Gwenllian ferch Gruffydd. The people formed a circle to watch as the woman dismounted to stand before the severely wounded man.

'What is your name?' she asked coldly.

'Gilbert Bones,' he gasped with tears in his eyes. 'I am a respected man and the castellan will pay well for my return.'

'We have no need of gifted English coins,' said Gwenllian. 'We take what we need.'

'Then just let me go,' gasped Gilbert. 'I will tell no one what happened here, I swear.'

'A futile gesture,' said Gwenllian. 'For the quicker your people know I am back the better. Until then we will send them the only message they understand.' She pushed back her wolf-skin cape and drew her sword from its scabbard.

'No,' he cried with tears running down his face. 'Don't do this I beg of you.'

'I suspect a poor girl named Gwyneth once begged for mercy at Llandeilo,' said Gwenllian, 'and all she got in return was to be raped before being used as target practise and left to die amongst the filth. Tell me why you are more deserving than her.'

'I was not at Llandeilo,' gasped the soldier, sensing the slightest of hope. 'I was on duty at the castle.'

'Wrong,' said Gwenllian. 'You may not have been there personally but those animals who took it upon themselves to rape, torture and kill so many innocents did so beneath the same colours that you wear on your gambeson. By doing so, they represented you and anyone else who serves alongside you. You may have not wielded the bow that killed her, Gilbert Bones, but your black heart was there in spirit. Now I seek vengeance on her behalf.'

Gilbert shook his head and closed his eyes as he sobbed. 'Please don't do this,' he begged again. 'Show mercy I beg of you.'

'I have none to show,' said Gwenllian and with an arcing swing of her sword, she decapitated Gilbert with a single blow.

Such was the sharpness of the blade and the force of the strike, the body stayed where it was as the head thudded onto the floor and rolled against Gwenllian's feet. Blood spurted skyward from the arteries in the body's neck and as it slowly toppled over, Gwenllian bent over to pick up the soldier's head by the hair before holding it up for all to see.

'Let it be known,' she shouted, 'my name is Gwenllian ferch Gruffydd and I demand the English leave Deheubarth while they still can.' She turned slowly on the spot so everyone could see. 'This is just the first of many,' she continued, 'and before this year is out, I swear this town will be adorned with many heads such as this.'

A gasp of astonishment rippled around the crowd.

'The time is here, my friends,' she shouted. 'The English are there for the taking but we need your help. Let every man, boy or woman who can wield a blade come to the Cantref Mawr and join us in the fight. You will be trained and fed but better than this, you will be free. We need cooks to feed the hungry and nurses to tend our wounded. The stores on these wagons will see us through a few months but we need more. If you have had enough of the English yoke, bring what you can and join the struggle. Weapons, clothes, food, tools, anything you have will be greatly received. Horses in particular are in short supply and we will buy any offered of good stock. Also, any livestock will earn good coin and though our coffers are currently bare, I give my word you will be paid in full before this month is out.'

'Where do we go to join, Gwenllian?' asked a young man, caught up in the fervour.

'Just ride northward on the main road through the Cantref Mawr,' replied Gwenllian. 'Worry not about finding us for we will find you. This is the first day of the year, my friends, let it also be the day that signals our freedom.' To a roar of approval, she walked to the dockside and hurled the decapitated head as far as she could into the water.

Some of the armed men climbed aboard the carts and drove them from the dock, heading for the Cantref Mawr, knowing they had only a few hours before the castle realised their soldiers were missing.

When the last cart had left, Gwenllian turned to the rest of her foot soldiers. 'Get rid of the English bodies,' she said. 'Leave them for the wolves in the forest. When you are done, we will meet back at the camp but make sure you are not followed.'

'Aye, my lady,' said one of the men and left to make the arrangements.

'Well,' said Gwenllian, turning to the rider at her side. 'Now do you believe we can do this?'

'Oh, yes, Gwenllian,' said Taliesin, staring at the woman with intense respect. 'For the first time in many years I actually believe we have a chance.'

With a nod of her head and the sound of the people's cheering still echoing around the dock, Gwenllian ferch Gruffydd dug her heels into the flank of her horse and rode back towards the Cantref Mawr having struck the first blow of the new rebellion.

The Cantref Mawr

January 2nd, AD 1136

Five leagues away, Tarw and a force of thirty warriors lay hidden amongst the trees above a narrow forest path. Down below, a column of over fifty men rode slowly along the track, each watching the trees to either side, obviously wary of an ambush.

'Who are they?' whispered Robert.

'I have no idea,' replied Tarw, 'but they might be mercenaries hired by the English to seek us out.'

'They look like experienced warriors,' replied Robert, 'and more than a match for anything we can field.'

'Agreed,' said Tarw. 'At the moment all we can do is watch and ensure they do not pose a threat to the camp. Send a runner and warn Gwenllian to prepare the defences in case the need arises.'

'Aye,' said Robert, but before he could go, Tarw's hand shot out to hold him back.

'Wait,' he said. 'Something's happening.'

Down below the column had come to a halt and the lead rider dismounted. Leaving his horse behind, he walked towards the forest edge and climbed up on a rock. Even from so far away, Tarw could see the man was enormous, a size exaggerated by the heavy cloak around his shoulders.

'I know you are there,' the man shouted suddenly, 'and you have been watching us since daybreak. Come out from hiding for I would parley with those in charge.'

'He must have seen us moving,' hissed Tarw.

'Perhaps he was waiting for favourable ground before confronting us,' said Robert.

Tarw peered through the branches. 'No,' he said, 'they are enclosed between two forested slopes and the only way out is at both ends of the path. If these are mercenaries, they are poor ones.'

They waited as the man below turned slowly on the rock, his arms outstretched.

'Send a man down to meet me,' shouted the warrior, 'and I will discard my weapons. I just want to talk.'

'What do you think?' asked Tarw.

'It may be a trap,' said Robert. 'We should stay where we are.'

'Or we could take him at his word and see what he wants. If we just stay hidden, we will never know.'

'You can't go down there, Tarw. You could be killed.'

'I have to,' said Tarw, preparing to stand up. 'I am intrigued as to his purpose.'

'Then let me go,' said Robert. 'If it is a trick, at least you will be safe. We have already come far and cannot afford to lose you in an act of stupidity.'

'I can't let you risk your life for me,' said Tarw.

'Yes, you can. The forthcoming campaign is just too important to lose you now. If you want to see what this man wants, then you must let me be the one. Surely you can see that?'

Tarw paused, staring at his comrade. Finally, he saw sense and nodded his agreement. 'So be it,' he said, 'but take no risks. At the slightest sign of trouble, turn around and get out of there. We will cover your

escape with archers from the trees but we are few and will have to withdraw before they can attack.'

'Don't worry about me,' said Robert. 'Just make sure that if they do,
you get away safely.' Without waiting for a response, he got to his feet
and turned to face the warrior down on the path. 'I hear you, stranger,'
he shouted. 'Tell your men to withdraw and I will join you.'

The grizzled warrior nodded in silence to the rest of the men. The
column turned and retreated several hundred paces before dismounting
and taking the opportunity to feed their horses with handfuls of grain.

Robert walked down the slope and onto the path as the warrior
climbed down from the rock to wait for him. Soon they stood face-to-
face and Robert stared at the biggest man he had ever seen.

'Well met,' said the stranger. 'Do I address the leader of the
rebellion?'

'You do,' lied Robert, 'I am Tarw, true prince of Deheubarth. Who
is it that leads an armed party through our lands with such disdain?'

'My name is Heinrich Bernhard of Saxony,' said the warrior. 'I
am the leader of these men. We seek employment with the freedom
fighters.'

'Mercenaries?' asked Robert.

'Aye. We were in the employ of the English but that agreement has
come to an end.'

Robert tensed at the revelation but the warrior seemed quite calm
and no obvious threat.

'So where have you ridden from?'

'The place you call the Marches,' replied Heinrich. 'We were stationed there and told we would be fighting against a man called Hywel
ap Maredudd but that is a task now withdrawn.'

'Why?' asked Robert. 'Have you changed loyalties?'

'We fight for coin not loyalty,' said Heinrich. 'When the English
king died, we were told there would be no contract, no fighting and
no money.'

'So you came here?'

'We have already made enemies of this Hywel,' said Heinrich, 'and killed some of his men in skirmishes, so joining him was not an option. We were then told of a prince and his woman who have sent word far and wide that they are recruiting. So here we are.'

'So you want to fight alongside us?'

'Aye. Our price is modest and you will benefit from men already battle hardened.'

'You do realise that if we do this, you could be fighting the very men who hired you in the first place?'

'If that is what it means then so be it. We were hired by the king and brought here to join his army before sailing to France, but were sent to the Marches when Hywel's threat was first realised. We have been away from our homes for six months with little pay and seek an opportunity to fill our saddlebags before returning home.'

'How do I know this is not a ruse and you have been sent here by the English?'

'A point well made,' said Heinrich, 'and one hard to prove false so I suggest you pit us against an English target of your choice and watch us do what it is we do. After that, I assure you there will be no doubt as to our frustration and ability.'

Robert paused and stared at the big man. The opportunity to enlist such a force was very tempting but the decision lay in Tarw's hands, not his.

'You say your price is modest,' he said. 'What are the terms?'

'Food and ale for my men, fodder for the horses and a place to camp. In addition, one silver penny for every Englishman killed by my men and a tenth share of any bounty taken from the field of battle.'

'That seems reasonable,' said Robert. 'But there is much to consider. How long will you wait?'

The warrior looked up at the darkening sky. 'We will camp here tonight,' he said, 'and wait until the sun is at its highest on the morrow.

After that we will ride on and seek employment elsewhere. Be aware that if we do, you could end up seeing us on the opposite side of a battlefield.'

'Understood,' said Robert. 'I will withdraw and speak to the rest of my people. I will return at dawn with my decision.'

'Tell your prince that if he is serious about taking on the English, he would be a foolish man to turn down my offer. I have seen their numbers and seen them fight. They are a formidable enemy.'

'I told you,' said Robert tensely, 'I *am* the prince.'

'You seem an honest man,' said Heinrich, 'but you are no prince. Like I said, he has until tomorrow.' Without another word the warrior turned and walked back to his men, leaving Robert staring at his back.

Several minutes later, Robert rejoined the rest of the men amongst the trees on the higher slopes. In the distance, the mercenaries could be seen making camp and Robert relayed the contents of the conversation to Tarw.

'An interesting proposal,' said Tarw, 'yet one that could easily be a ruse to get inside our camp.'

'It could be,' said Robert, 'but he seemed like an honest man and I think we should give it some thought.'

'Agreed,' said Tarw. 'We'll withdraw for the night but leave some men to watch their camp. In the morning we will return with the answer.'

———◡———

The following morning, Tarw and ten of his men rode slowly along the track towards the mercenary camp. It was still dark but the first tendrils of light were just creeping over the distant hill. They had discussed the risks through most of the night but had finally decided they were risks worth taking and the prince now headed the men to open talks with Heinrich.

'Perhaps we should wait here,' said one of the men. 'To ride unannounced into a camp of experienced fighters invites trouble.'

'There will be no surprises,' said Tarw. 'Look.'

His men stared forward and in the gloom they could see a group of heavily armed warriors standing across the path. On the slopes to either side, more could be seen standing amongst the rocks, ready to sweep down to engage the Welshmen should the need arise.

'It looks like they were expecting us,' said Robert quietly.

'Come, let's get this done,' said Tarw. He urged his horse forward again and when they were only a few dozen paces from the impressive warriors, he and Robert dismounted to walk towards them.

'You must be Heinrich,' said Tarw, looking at the mountain of a man.

'I am,' said Heinrich, 'and you are the prince I have heard so much about.'

'I am,' said Tarw, 'and my second here has told me about your offer. I assume it still stands?'

'Aye,' said Heinrich, 'but only until noon. After that we will be on our way.'

'Understood,' said Tarw. He looked around at the silent men spread out across the landscape. 'It looks like you were expecting us.'

'You make enough noise to wake the dead,' said Heinrich, 'but my scouts reported to me when you left your camp. You cannot blame a man for taking precautions, especially in a strange country.'

'You had someone watching our camp?' asked Tarw.

'I did. They followed you back and watched through the night. A precautionary measure only.'

'I had men on guard all night,' said Robert. 'Nobody reported anything suspicious.'

'Perhaps they fell asleep,' said Tarw, 'and if so I will whip them myself.'

'Blame not your men,' said Heinrich. 'They did what they were tasked to do. My scouts are as silent as the night itself and well versed in such things. A thousand men would not have seen them.'

'That's quite a boast,' said Tarw.

'It is no boast,' said Heinrich simply. 'But we waste time. What is your answer?'

'I am inclined to do business with you, Heinrich, but you must understand my concerns,' said Tarw. 'Even with your offer of proving your skills in battle, I cannot be certain that it is not some ruse to aid the English.'

'In what way?'

'Perhaps you are still under contract and wait for the opportunity to kill us in our sleep.'

'That is not the case,' said Heinrich.

'I know that is what you claim, but how do we know for certain?'

'Because if that was my wish, you would already be dead.'

Tarw's eyes narrowed and he met Heinrich's stare. 'Again you make bold statements,' he said, 'but perhaps you only stay your hand because you don't know how many bows are aimed at your men as we speak.'

'You have ten bowmen,' said Heinrich, 'no more. You also have another twenty or so men-at-arms including those at your back – most poorly armed. The rest are deployed amongst the trees on the southern slope. Your horses are beyond the hill.'

Tarw swallowed hard. The giant warrior seemed to know everything about them.

'Enough talking,' said Heinrich. 'I will offer you one more thing as proof that I do not seek your death. After that, this conversation is done.'

Tarw nodded, unsure what proof the strange warrior could possibly have that would ease his mind. 'Go ahead,' he said.

Heinrich turned to the bearded man at his side. The grizzled warrior reached beneath his heavy cloak and produced a knife, stepping forward to offer it to the prince.

Tarw took the knife and stared at the blade for an age before looking back up at Heinrich. 'I accept your terms,' he said simply, 'and you will be welcome at the Cantref Mawr. Pack your camp and I will leave men here to guide you in.'

Heinrich nodded and turned away, followed by the rest of his mercenaries.

'My lord, are you sure about this?' said Robert as they walked away.

'Aye,' said Tarw, staring at the receding Germanic warriors. 'They will be a great asset.'

'Why?' continued Robert. 'All he did was give you a knife.'

'I know,' said Tarw. 'But this is the blade I keep beside my sleeping furs in my tent. Someone was close enough last night to steal this without awakening me. If they wanted me dead, Robert, I would already be cold. Summon the rest of the men – we are heading back to the Cantref Mawr.'

The Cantref Mawr

January 10th, AD 1136

Gwenllian stood outside the campaign tent looking down at the activity below. Since acquiring the carts from the docks at Pembroke ten days earlier, the numbers at the camp had increased threefold. Word had obviously started to spread and there wasn't a day that went by when dozens of men, both in groups and alone, found their way onto the forest roads to be picked up by the rebel guards and shown into the camp. All were eager to join the rebels, many were young and fit but few were experienced in the way of warfare.

In addition, several families had also turned up at the camp, frustrated at the harshness of life under the English. Some brought handcarts containing the few possessions they owned while others came unburdened, owning nothing but the clothes they stood up in.

The contents of the stolen carts had already gone a long way to help feed the rebels, especially the many sacks of salted pork and dried oats. There were also fifty heavy-duty tents in the haul, a very welcome addition to the camp, though the fact that the English had deemed it necessary to procure such quantities suggested to Gwenllian that they must be planning some sort of campaign, possibly when the weather broke in the spring. Other bounty included gambesons and cloaks, and baskets of geese, a valuable source of eggs and meat, but to her disappointment, there had been no weapons.

'Impressive,' said Taliesin, joining her outside the tent.

'I have to admit it is happening quicker than I thought,' said Gwenllian. 'The numbers are growing but many are new to this life and it will take time to train them. Even then, skill at arms is no match for battle experience. This may be the last chance we get so we need to ensure our victories are certain, no matter how small. Success begets success, and with every skirmish won, these men will get better.'

Taliesin nodded and they both watched the bustling activity in the camp below for a few moments before returning to the campaign tent. Upon the table lay a large piece of white linen marked with the positions of every known road, village, castle or town throughout Deheubarth. In addition, the trees were clearly marked, as were the rivers and mountains. The map had been Gwenllian's idea and though at first Taliesin had been sceptical, preferring to rely on local knowledge, he had soon seen the merits as it had developed and become more detailed.

'So what's the situation so far?' she asked, walking over to the map. 'Are there any updates?'

Taliesin picked up a small carving of a horse and looked at it closely. They had found several such figurines in a velvet sack amongst the wagons.

'It's a playing piece from a game called chess,' said Gwenllian. 'A pastime popular with Henry. Obviously he had sent it as a gift to someone in the castle.'

'Children's games for grown men,' said Taliesin. 'A strange concept.'

'On the contrary,' said Gwenllian. 'It is based on the tactics of battle and enjoyed by all the barons of the court. Would you like me to teach you?'

Taliesin looked up and sneered. 'I have no time for such nonsense. The only tactics I need to know are the ones that result in real men dying, not wooden representatives.' He reached over and placed the horse on a junction of two roads between Pembroke and the cathedral of Saint David. 'My men are camped amongst the forests here,' he said. 'We have heard there may be a payment of tax being sent to Pembroke over the next few days. If our information is right, they will seek to relieve them of the money.'

'How many did you send?' asked Gwenllian.

'Twenty.'

'Twenty? I thought you had fifty at your disposal.'

'I do, but they are spread out around the Cantref Mawr guarding the approach roads. It was all I could spare.'

'Twenty is not enough,' said Gwenllian. 'If the money is a substantial amount there will be at least that many English riders guarding the caravan and your men are not yet equipped to face such a foe.'

'Then what do you suggest?' asked Taliesin tensely. 'You saw for yourself, those new to our cause are not yet ready and you are reluctant to use the mercenaries recruited by your husband. What is the point of them being engaged if we are not using them?'

'I want their first target to be one worth taking,' said Gwenllian. 'If we reveal them against smaller targets then the English will increase the strength of their defences accordingly and we will not have the luxury of surprise.'

'But how long do we wait? News of any likely targets is scarce at the best of times and even when our spies manage to find anything out, it is often wrong and we waste time chasing shadows.'

'I know,' said Gwenllian, 'but worry not. That is about to change.'

'How?'

'I cannot say yet,' said Gwenllian. 'But trust me, if what I have planned comes to pass, we will have all the targets you want within the month.'

Back in Pembroke, Nesta's maid walked through the graveyard on the outskirts of the town, her cloak tied tightly against the January air. The murdered girl from the castle had been her niece and, as there was no other living family, Emma had decided to pay her respects as soon as circumstances had allowed. Her feet crunched through the brittle grass as she negotiated the many wooden crosses and headed to the far wall. She stopped before a freshly filled grave and knelt in the frost to say a prayer. When she was done, she placed a simple decoration of entwined twigs and pine cones at the base of the cross before getting to her feet and gazing down at the last resting place of the murdered girl.

'Oh, Catrin,' she said quietly, 'what has this world done to you? You had so much to live for and it has been taken away by the devil himself. I pray you are now walking the fields of heaven alongside your mother.'

She crossed herself before turning away but cried out in fright when she almost walked into a man standing directly behind her.

'*Who are you?*' she gasped, stepping backwards onto the grave. 'Get away from me.'

'Calm yourself, woman,' said the man. 'I mean you no harm.'

'Then what do you want?' she said again, her heart racing with fear. 'I have nothing of value and if you touch me I swear I will scream like all the demons of hell.'

The man laughed. 'I may not have enjoyed the company of a woman for many months, old hag,' he said, 'but trust me, not even I am tempted by what you may have to offer beneath that cloak.'

'Save your insults, stranger,' said Emma, 'and be gone before I call for help.'

'Listen to me,' said the man, holding up his hand. 'I apologise for my foul mouth but please listen. I am looking for the lady's maid known as Emma. Are you she?'

'Who wants to know?' asked Emma.

'Please, indulge me,' said the man. 'I was told she was going to be here today by a friend of hers and I just want to talk to her. So I ask again, are you she?'

Emma paused and stared at the man. Her heart was still beating fit to burst and she knew it would be better if she just said no and left for the safety of the castle but she was intrigued as to why this man wanted to speak to her. Finally, she nodded and confirmed his suspicions. 'Yes,' she said. 'I am Emma.'

'And you work at the castle as maid to the wife of the castellan?'

'Aye, I do but please afford me the courtesy of knowing whom I am addressing.'

'Alas, I cannot tell you my name,' said the man, 'but I have an urgent message for your mistress and I want you to take it to her.'

'I will do no such thing,' said Emma, 'for it is a dangerous occupation in these troubling times. Secret messages suggest illegal activities and the constable is a cruel and suspicious man. If I was found to have such a thing I could be on the scaffold by morning.'

'I offer no parchment,' said the man, 'just a simple message to be passed from my lips to her ears.'

Emma stared at the man again. 'Speak it,' she said. 'But be quick for I have to return.'

'All I want you to do is tell your mistress *her calf will be in the usual stall on the last day of the month.*'

Emma's face screwed up in misunderstanding. 'That makes no sense,' she said. 'My lady has no dealings with livestock. What sort of message is this?'

'Please,' said the man, 'ask no more questions for it is too dangerous for all of us. Suffice to say, your mistress will understand. Can you do this for me?'

'But why?' asked Emma. 'Is there a reason for this?'

'Oh yes, Emma, a reason far greater than you or I. So, will you do it?'

'Aye,' she said with a sigh. 'If I remember. I have a lot to do so can't promise anything.'

'That's all I can ask,' said the man. 'Now be gone and here is a penny for your trouble.'

Emma looked down at the coin in his hand and then back up into his face. 'Keep your money, stranger,' she said. 'I came here to pay respects to my niece, not barter like a marketplace whore.'

'So be it,' said the man and he put the coin away before stepping aside. 'Don't forget, her calf will be in the stall on the last day of the month.'

'Aye,' she sighed as she walked past him, 'but a more stupid message I have never heard.'

'Fare ye well, Emma,' said the messenger and he watched her walk back towards the town. When she had finally gone, he climbed over the graveyard wall and ran back to the cover of the nearest trees where another man was waiting with two horses.

'Well, will she do it?' said Tarw.

'I think so, but her mind seems slow. Time will tell.'

'Then we have done what we can, it is now out of our hands.'

Without further ado, they mounted their horses and headed back into the dense forests.

Pembroke Castle

January 31st, AD 1136

Emma was brushing Nesta's hair, looking over her mistress' head to gaze at her in the mirror.

'Emma,' said Nesta, 'is there something on your mind? You seem distracted.'

'Yes, my lady,' replied Emma with a sigh. 'I have heard that the constable is on his way back from London and will be here by midday tomorrow.'

'He is,' confirmed Nesta, 'and who knows what new and oppressive ideas he will bring back from London with him.'

'Mistress,' said Emma eventually. 'Can I be open with you?'

'Of course,' said Nesta. 'What is it?'

Emma walked around to face Nesta and took her hands in her own. 'My lady,' she said earnestly, 'I worry for your safety. That constable is a cruel man and I have seen the way he looks at you. With the master gone, I think it won't be long before he tries something with you and my heart would surely break in two if he should ever hurt you.'

'I share your worry, Emma,' replied Nesta quietly. 'I really do, and if truth be told, I am scared of what will befall us both when he returns.

But there is nothing I can do except hope he sees reason and turns his attention elsewhere.'

'That will never happen, my lady,' said Emma, 'as well you know. That man is the devil himself, and since the master died, this whole place has changed. There is an air of fear and oppression within these walls, a build-up of anticipation as if there is a dam waiting to burst. Everyone is afraid of what is going to happen but it is you who are at risk most of all. He sees you as the ultimate prize. My lady, you have to get away from here.'

'And go where?' asked Nesta.

'Can you not seek refuge amongst those who still hold your father's name in good esteem? Surely there must be many across Wales who would offer you shelter, especially in Ceredigion or Gwynedd?'

'I'm not sure, Emma. My life is here and always has been. Deheubarth is my family's kingdom, the place where I grew up and the place where I want to be laid to rest when I die. Despite my fear, I think I should stay a while and see what happens. Perhaps, when the new castellan is appointed by the king I can share my fears and curtail the constable's attentions.'

'I hope so, my lady,' said Emma, 'for it is only a matter of time before that man does something terrible. You mark my words.'

The maid continued brushing her mistress' hair. For a few moments there was a shared silence until eventually Nesta spoke again.

'Emma,' she said quietly, 'you have always been a good servant to me and to my mother before me. Not only are you my maid and confidante, I also count you as my friend. Perhaps the only true one I have.'

'Nonsense, my lady,' replied Emma. 'You are well respected by all the people of Pembroke and right across Deheubarth.'

'Respected?' said Nesta. 'Not the first emotion I would have chosen, given the choice.'

'Respect is good, my lady,' said Emma, 'and I'm sure that if things had been different you would be as loved as your dear mother was. As it is, well . . .' The rest of the sentence went unfinished as both women stared at each other.

'You mean if I had been married to a Welshman,' said Nesta.

'What I think is irrelevant,' said Emma, 'and the politics of royalty is often beyond me. All I know is you are the daughter of Rhys ap Tewdwr and should have been living a life suitable to your station, not married off to an English knight.'

'Well, that situation has come to an end,' said Nesta quietly.

'Oh, my lady,' said Emma, 'I did not mean to disrespect your husband so soon after his death I just meant you deserved so much more. But God works in mysterious ways and it is obvious he had a different path chosen for you.'

'Is this it then?' asked Nesta. 'Is this where that path ends? For if it is, it just doesn't make sense.'

Emma walked over to a table and picked up a small hand mirror to show Nesta the back of her hair.

'Whatever happens,' she said as her mistress inspected her work, 'you are still a beautiful woman and when your heart has stopped aching, I'm sure there will be suitors queuing from here to London to take your hand.'

'I don't want any other man,' said Nesta, 'at least not yet. I would just like a few months to gather my thoughts in peace while I try to work out what my future holds.'

'Nonsense,' said Emma. 'No woman should be alone. It's not natural.'

'You are, and as far as I know, always have been.'

'That's different,' said Emma. 'I had a calling and devoted my life to your mother and now you.'

Nesta smiled. 'What did I ever do to deserve you?'

'Oh, stop it,' said Emma. 'You are making me blush. Right, I am done here, I'll just go down and collect your cloak from the kitchens and we can be going. It should be nice and warm by now.'

'I hope so,' said Nesta. 'It looks freezing out there.'

'It's even colder in the cemetery,' said Emma. 'It's as if the souls of the dead linger there, extending their spirit fingers into your soul.'

'Stop it,' said Nesta with a shiver. 'I don't like those places at the best of times.'

'We don't have to go,' said Emma. 'We can go in the spring.'

'No, I missed Catrin's burial,' said Nesta, 'and it is only right I pay my respects.'

'If you are sure,' said Emma.

'I am. Come, I will go to the kitchens with you.'

'If truth be told,' said Emma as they walked to the door, 'I will be glad of the company. The last time I went I thought my heart would stop in fear.'

'Really? Is it that bad?'

'Well, it is quite scary but it was no spirit that made me jump but a stranger who crept up behind me.'

'Oh, no,' said Nesta, 'did he hurt you?'

'No, my lady, he just rambled something about calves and stalls.'

'Calves and stalls,' said Nesta as they descended the stairs. 'How strange.'

'Aye,' said Emma. 'It was. That is why I didn't bother telling you before. The man was obviously drunk so I didn't want to burden you with his nonsense.'

'Burden me? Why would it affect me?'

'Because he insisted I pass the message on to you. Obviously he was a simpleton and, anyway, it was over a week ago and he has no doubt long gone.' Emma went down the last few steps before realising her mistress was no longer beside her. She turned to see Nesta standing halfway up the stairs, her face pale with shock. 'My lady,' she said, 'what's the matter?'

'Emma,' said Nesta, 'tell me exactly what the man said, word for word.'

'I think it was a calf will be in the stalls,' said Emma. 'Why? Is it important?'

Nesta ran down the steps and grabbed Emma's arm. 'Yes it is,' she said earnestly. 'Think hard. What *exactly* did he say? It is essential you get it right.'

Emma took a deep breath and thought back. 'His exact words were: "*her calf will be in the stalls*", referring to you. That's why I thought he was a simpleton, you have no calves.'

'Oh, I do,' said Nesta. 'One very important one. When did he say it will be there?'

'On the last day of the month,' said Emma.

'That's tonight,' said Nesta. Her mind raced with the implications before she looked back at her maid.

'Emma,' she said, 'please accept my apologies but I can no longer accompany you to the graveyard. At least not today. Would you be heartbroken if we put it off for a few days?'

'Of course not,' said Emma. 'But I do not understand. Where are you going?'

'I'll tell you, Emma,' she said, 'but not here. Let's go back to my quarters.' Nesta turned and ran back up the stairs with her maid following as fast as she was able. Moments later they were in Nesta's room and Emma closed the door behind them.

'Lock it,' said Nesta. 'We need to ensure nobody else overhears us.'

Emma did as she was told and turned back to her mistress. 'My lady, I have not seen you so excited in a long while. What is it about this message that has you in such a state?'

'Emma,' replied Nesta, 'you have met my brother on several occasions, yes?'

'I have,' said Emma, 'but not for many years.'

'Neither have I, for we thought he was dead. But recently he reappeared along with one of his sons down in the town. It is rumoured his wife is also alive and they hide out amongst the rebels of the Cantref Mawr. Did you know this?'

'I have heard the rumours,' said Emma, 'but believed they were no more than that.'

'As did I,' said Nesta, pacing the floor. 'Since then I have hoped he would get in touch but, alas, no contact was forthcoming. I then thought perhaps the stories were false and he really was dead but this message proves differently. He is alive, Emma, and he wants to see me.'

'I don't understand,' said Emma. 'If you are referring to the message, then I can assure you it was not your brother who gave it to me.'

'No, I expect not and it was good planning on his behalf in case the English got wind of his appearance and trapped him there. The messenger was obviously one of his men and used in case of treachery.'

'But I still don't understand. What is it in the message that proves he is alive?'

'Emma, what do they call my brother?'

'I have always called him my Lord Gruffydd,' said Emma.

'No, I mean the people, his men, his enemies, what name is he known by?'

'Tarw, the bull of Wales.'

'Exactly, and he has born that name since he was a babe in arms. When we were growing up, I used to tease him and say he wasn't a bull but a little calf, my little calf. Since then it has always been our way of ensuring any messages from him were genuine.'

'Oh,' said Emma, 'I didn't realise.'

'That's the whole point, but it matters not. I have the message now and I still have time.'

'Time for what?'

'To meet him of course. That's what the message is about. He wants to meet me on the last day of the month and that is today.'

'My lady, you cannot leave the castle. The steward will insist on guards.'

'I know, but luckily I don't have to. The stall he refers to is built into the castle walls – a room to which we both have access.'

'The postern gate,' said Emma quietly as she recalled a memory. 'I remember you used to meet him there many years ago. I had spare keys made for you in the town.'

'You did, and I met Tarw several times there without discovery.'

'Do you still have the key to the inner door?'

'I do and I assume he also has his key to the outer door.' She paused and stared at the maid. 'Oh Emma,' she said, walking over to take her maid's hands in hers, 'I know I am putting you at risk by telling you this but I have no one else to talk to and I will need your help to make it happen. Please say you will keep this between ourselves.'

'My lady,' said Emma, stepping back in shock, 'I have never betrayed even the slightest of trusts placed upon me and I swear, I would suffer the depths of hell itself before I said anything to anyone that may put you at risk.'

'I know,' said Nesta, 'and I would entrust this information to no other person. You are truly the greatest friend any woman ever had.'

'So,' said Emma, 'what do you want me to do?'

Pembroke Castle

January 31st, AD 1136

Tarw kept close to the timber palisade of the castle walls as he sidled through the darker shadows to the postern gate. The small doorway, designed for secret access and egress during any potential siege, was hidden in the corner where one of the defensive towers met a wall and though in times of war it would be heavily defended from above, during peacetime its robust nature and the fact that it led into a room secured on the opposite side by another heavily locked door meant it was not seen as a risk to the garrison. To either side of the outer door were a series of very narrow arrow slits and in the room itself murder holes were incorporated into the ceiling above, allowing defenders to assault any intruders who managed to find and access the hidden entrance.

Tarw knew that the murder holes themselves would be covered with trapdoors on the floor above – not only to stop anyone turning an ankle as they passed but also to stop any draughts affecting the room where many men were stationed. Despite this, he also knew that once inside, he had to be as quiet as death itself. Slowly he approached, regularly glancing upwards at the ramparts. Though it was dark, the clouds were fleeting and the moon meant that if any guard looked down, it was quite likely Tarw would be seen.

Eventually he reached the door and retrieved a key held on a leather thong from around his neck. Carefully he placed the key in the lock and turned it slowly. At first it refused to budge and for a few moments he feared the lock had been changed but finally the key turned and the locking bar withdrew with a faint but satisfying thud. Quickly, he leaned against the door but it wouldn't move and he realised that it must be barred on the inside.

'Damn,' he cursed to himself but he knew there was nothing more he could do. He was relying now on the intervention of Nesta from the inside.

———

'Right,' said Nesta, up in her room. 'You know what to do.'

'Aye,' said Emma. 'Tell the guard that you are ill and have refused your food. Offer it to him but ensure he leaves the keep door unattended.'

'Right,' said Nesta. 'When I have gone, keep an eye out for me down at the stables from my chambers. I will signal you when we are done and you can distract him again to let me back in. Agreed?'

'I'll try my best, my lady,' said Emma.

'Good. Let's see what you have for him.'

Emma uncovered the tray and revealed half a loaf of warm bread with a pot of rich butter, a whole chicken still steaming from the oven and a bowl of boiled root vegetables.

'Quite a feast,' said Nesta, 'and one difficult to turn down. The poor man will think I am a glutton, there is so much food.'

'Are you ready?' asked Emma.

'Wait,' said Nesta. 'There is something missing.' She walked over to the side table and came back clutching a flask of good wine. 'It was the master's favourite,' she said, 'but he has no use for it now.'

With all preparations done, the two women crept down the stairs and approached the main doorway to the keep. As planned, Emma placed the tray in the guardroom to one side before opening the outer door and addressing the guard outside. Nesta hid around the corner, listening to the muffled conversation. At first she thought the ruse was not going to work but finally the guard came inside, banging his hands against his sides to restore some circulation. Emma came behind him and glanced towards Nesta's hiding place.

'You had better not tell the constable about this,' he said to the maid, 'or he will have my hide.'

'You have my sworn word,' said Emma, 'and besides, even if I did I would surely be in just as much trouble as you.'

'And you are sure the lady Nesta said I could have it?' he asked again, glancing through the door to the guardroom and seeing the uncovered feast upon the tray.

'She told me to get rid of it as she is so sick but I have already eaten. Of course, if you don't want it I can give it to the dogs.'

'No, you stay where you are,' said the guard, 'and keep an eye on the bailey out of the window. If anything should even move, you call me straight away. Understood?'

'Aye,' sighed Emma, 'but make up your mind for I am growing tired and that hot chicken is beginning to look quite tempting.'

The soldier laughed and headed into the room. 'Too late for that, old girl,' he said as he dragged a chair over to the table.

When he was settled, Emma nodded to her mistress, still hiding in the shadows. Nesta quickly walked across the corridor and eased the door inward before slipping out into the night. Behind her, Emma kept the guard distracted before going over to her agreed position at one of the windows. The first part of the plan was done.

———

Nesta walked quickly down the steps of the motte and across the bailey towards the stables. Up on the palisades she could see some of the castle guards standing around the braziers, their attention focussed on the warmth of the flames rather than anything else. She kept to the shadows and was soon at the inner door of the postern tower. Retrieving her key, she let herself inside before locking the door behind her. The darkness was absolute and she fumbled in the pouch around her waist to find the items she needed to light a fire. Soon she had a small flame in a ball of lamb's wool kindling and she carefully lit the half-candle she had brought with her.

Now able to see where she was going, she walked over to the outer door and was shocked to find it secured with a wooden bar sitting across the frame. Placing the candle to one side, she lifted the bar and slid it to one side and was about to try the lock when the door eased inward. Quickly, she retreated across the room, and watched as a man's head appeared around the frame. Even in the faint light given off by the flickering candle, she recognised the features of her younger brother.

'Tarw,' she whispered. 'Is it truly you?'

'Aye, Sister,' he whispered back, 'it is. Come and say hello.'

Needing no further invitation, she flew across the room and into her brother's arms, the man she had thought dead for so many years.

'I can't believe it, Tarw. After all this time, God has seen fit to return you to me. I am truly blessed.'

'Me too, Nesta,' he said, 'but I cannot linger more than a few moments. It is too dangerous.'

Nesta disentangled herself and looked up at her brother while wiping her eyes. 'Of course,' she said, 'but even the fleetest of moments are the sweetest.'

'They are,' said Tarw, 'and one day there will be many such times but until then there is work to do.'

'And that is why you are here?'

'It is. I am up against an impossible hurdle, Nesta, and I need you to help me overcome it. I need help and you are the best placed to grant me the aid I speak of. I ask not for myself but for the future of our father's kingdom. What say you, Nesta? Will you help?'

Nesta stared at her brother and recalled the earlier conversation with Emma about God having a different plan for her. Whatever Tarw wanted was obviously dangerous but she knew she could no more refuse him than become queen of England.

'Aye, Tarw, I will,' she said. 'And if I should be found out by those who surround me, then I will gladly suffer whatever fate they deem necessary. Ask your favours for if it is within my power to grant them, I will do so with all my heart.'

'Thank you, dear sister,' said Tarw. 'I had no doubt otherwise. What I need is this.'

For the next ten minutes they talked quickly and quietly until Nesta was absolutely clear what was required and by the time she replaced the locking bar over the inner frame of the postern gate, her heart was already racing.

Ever since she had been a child her life had been laid out for her, right up to when she had been married off to Gerald, but with her husband now dead, any loyalties she had for him or indeed the privileged position that she found herself in were at an end and her future was in her own hands. For as long as she could remember, her life had been moulded by men from a different country, men who bore no affinity to her, her family or her people and for too long she had allowed that situation to continue unhindered. But now that time was over, and with Tarw back on the scene with a plan to rebuild her family's name, her path had never been clearer. Her life amongst the English was coming to an end, and though she could not yet easily leave the castle, it was time to start fighting for her own people, using whatever means she could.

Feeling a resolve within her heart colder and harder than any steel blade, she made her way back up to the keep, a new and dangerous ally to the rebellion.

Pembroke Castle

February 1st, AD 1136

The following day, Nesta was talking in her locked room with Emma. She had not slept a second the whole night, her mind racing as she considered the favours her brother had asked. She knew it would be dangerous to meet his requests but she was excited at the opportunity to help the Welsh cause. Unfortunately, it had soon become obvious that she could not do it alone and would have to involve a third party if she was to have any chance of success. Consequently, she had taken the opportunity to explain the situation to Emma and now she sat quietly, waiting for her trusted friend to speak.

'It is a lot to ask,' said Emma, 'and the whole thing is very dangerous.'

'I know and I would rather take all the risk myself but the constable would never let me frequent the town without some sort of escort and that would make it impossible for me to carry out the task.'

'I'm not pointing out the danger for myself, my lady. You know I would gladly die for you, but this road can only lead to heartache and possibly death. I just wonder if you have thought this through.'

'I have, Emma, and I want this more than anything. My station precludes me from doing anything else. Even if I was to run away and join the rebels, the cosseted life I have led up until now would make me more of a burden than an ally. At least this way, I can be of help and perhaps, when all this is over, we can all be free again to come and go as we please.'

Emma smiled at her mistress's enthusiasm. The thought of freedom for Deheubarth had long been a dream for everyone in the south and there had been many uprisings but they were always put down with great brutality.

'What makes you think they will succeed this time?' she asked.

'Many things,' said Nesta. 'The coronation of Stephen has split the loyalties of the English barons in two, and if Matilda sails from France to claim what is rightfully hers, you can wager she will come with an army to challenge Stephen. I think England is heading for a civil war, Emma, and when it does our countrymen must be ready to act. With our help, they will be in a better position than they ever have been before, and with Tarw and Gwenllian at their head, they can drive the English from these blessed lands.' She paused and looked deep into her maid's eyes, taking her hands in her own. 'So,' she said finally, 'it is indeed a great ask but I need to know: will you do it?'

'Of course I will,' said Emma with a smile. 'For you, my lady, anything.'

Nesta smiled back and embraced the servant as if she were her sister. 'When all this is over, Emma, you will go down in the history books as one of those responsible for the freedom of our country.'

'I don't know about that, my lady,' said Emma, 'but I'm just happy to see you smile again.' She pulled away and looked at her mistress. 'So, how are we going to do this?'

For the next hour or so, they plotted in Nesta's chambers, discussing options, methods and possible allies until, finally, they were interrupted by a loud knock on the door.

'Who is it?' asked Nesta.

'My lady,' said a voice, 'I have been instructed to tell you that the constable has returned from London and has requested your presence in the lesser hall.'

'Tell him I will be there shortly,' she said with a sigh. 'So, Emma,' she continued, 'it looks like we are ready. I'll go down and play the part of dutiful host while you get some rest. It has been a long day and you have my heartfelt gratitude.'

'Do you not want something to eat?' asked Emma, standing up. 'It won't take me but a few moments to arrange it.'

'No, I'm sure the constable has already demanded to be fed after his journey so, if necessary, I will join him.'

'As you wish, my lady,' said Emma, and she left the room.

Nesta walked over to the mirror on the wall and tidied up her appearance. Her eyes looked tired but apart from that there was nothing to suggest she hadn't slept for almost two days. Finally satisfied she was looking as good as she could hope, she donned a shawl and headed down into the lesser hall.

Salisbury was standing by the fire, still dressed in his riding leathers, when Nesta entered. In his hand was a large tankard of ale and he was laughing and joking with the castle steward. All around the hall, most of those soldiers who had accompanied him to London weeks earlier were also enjoying refreshments after their arduous ride.

'Ah, here she is,' said Salisbury and he turned to greet her as she made her way across the crowded hall.

'Master Salisbury,' she said, 'I trust you had a good journey?'

'We did,' said Salisbury, 'and also enjoyed the hospitality of the new king, who, may I add, is a most excellent host.'

'I'm glad to hear it,' said Nesta. 'Did you achieve what you hoped?'

'Indeed,' said Salisbury. 'That and more. In fact, I have an announcement to make and I was waiting for you to arrive before making it.' He turned to one of the men at his side. 'Master Steward, perhaps you could summon the rest of the castle staff.'

'Of course,' said the steward, immediately dispatching some servants to round up anybody not in the hall.

Ten minutes later, the steward climbed up onto a table and called for quiet. At the far end of the hall, all the servants, cooks, maids and other staff were gathered against the wall, unsure of what to expect. It was very rare to be summoned for an announcement.

'Thank you,' said Salisbury and he waited for the steward to descend before taking his place upon the table. The room fell silent as the constable looked around at the expectant faces. 'As you are aware,' he announced loudly, 'I have just returned from pledging our allegiance to the new king at Westminster. While I was there, my seconds and I managed to get a private audience with him and brief him as to the situation here in Deheubarth. I reported that this garrison was strong, loyal and well placed to continue serving the Crown as we always have done. I also told him about you people, the very heartbeat of this garrison, who provide a safe haven from which we rule this kingdom on his behalf and he asked me to extend his gratitude. In fact, he has authorised me to grant every civilian employed in this castle an extra penny as a sign of his satisfaction.'

A murmur rippled around the room. No man, king or castellan, had ever authorised such a thing and everyone was shocked at the unexpected bounty.

'He also asked about the threat from the brigands who call themselves rebels,' continued Salisbury, 'and I was happy to inform him that the situation is well in hand. He has promised us extra supplies and men when the time is right and he will support us in ridding the hills of those brigands once and for all.'

Another murmur circulated around the hall, though this time without as much excitement.

'Finally,' announced Salisbury, 'I informed him of the circumstances surrounding the death of our beloved castellan, Gerald of Windsor. He expressed his sincere condolences and sends his respects but more importantly focussed on the need to replace the castellan as soon as possible in order to continue the good work already carried out by Gerald. Consequently, a few days ago he summoned me to his private rooms and presented me with this scroll, the contents of which are a royal decree, effective immediately.' He unfurled the parchment and started reading out loud.

'"*To all citizens of Deheubarth and the surrounding territories. Let it be known that with immediate effect the honourable John of Salisbury, in recognition of his services to the Crown, is hereby awarded the title Lord of Pembroke and is recognised by the Crown as its senior representative across the kingdom known as Deheubarth. It is demanded that all his subjects honour this award and recognise his authority and actions in the name of the king.*

John of Salisbury is also awarded ownership of all lands east of Pembroke town as far as, and including, the commote of Dinefwr, his in perpetuity for his family and heirs.

Signed His Majesty the king, Stephen de Blois, this twentieth day of January in the year of our Lord 1136."'

John of Salisbury looked around the hall, barely able to contain the grin struggling to emerge across his face. 'What that means,' he said, 'is I am now in charge of all Deheubarth and, as such, automatically become the recognised castellan of Pembroke Castle.'

For a few seconds there was an awkward silence but then Walter de Calais removed his cap and held it up in the air.

'Three cheers for the new castellan,' he shouted and immediately everyone responded, each knowing full well that to hesitate invited scrutiny and possible punishment. As Salisbury looked around, he noticed that Nesta was nowhere to be seen.

'Where is she?' he said down to Walter as the last of the cheers subsided.

'She left as soon as you finished reading the decree,' replied Walter. 'I think she went back to her rooms.'

Salisbury laughed quietly to himself. He had expected such a reaction from her but he knew there was nothing she could do. His lobbying of the king and exaggerated claims of success as constable had achieved exactly what he had hoped for. Indeed, he had still another surprise for the beautiful Nesta but that would wait until later. For now, he was happy to enjoy the fact that he had at last achieved the position he had coveted for so long and bask in the many declarations of loyalty coming from the mouths of knights and servants alike.

Up in the room, Nesta sat on her bed, horrified at the scene she had just witnessed. She had always known the constable was a sly and calculating man, but to do what he did and acquire her husband's office so soon after his burial was an immoral depth not even she had expected of him. Her mind raced, trying to work out what it meant for her. Some of the lands now gifted to Salisbury had been owned by Gerald and, as such, should have passed to their sons but if the king's decree was valid, and she had no reason to doubt that it was, that inheritance now lay in tatters and Gerald's sons would receive next to nothing from his estates in Wales. There were other interests in England that would ensure they never wanted for anything but Nesta held no such investments in her name and Salisbury's gain would leave her almost penniless.

The door knocked and she turned to see Emma peering around the door frame.

'Can I come in?' she asked.

'Aye,' sighed Nesta.

'I saw you go,' said Emma, 'but could not join you until he allowed us to leave.'

'I understand,' said Nesta.

'I suppose this means you are no longer in charge of the castle?'

'That and more,' said Nesta. 'To all extents and purposes I am now destitute except for my clothes, my jewellery and the purse of coins beneath my bed.'

'What are you going to do?'

Nesta looked at Emma with a steely gaze. 'Do?' she said. 'I know exactly what I am going to do. I intend to carry out the plan we agreed with Tarw. Salisbury is a merciless man and his cruelty will reach right across Deheubarth. Our people need Gwenllian to succeed more than ever and I intend to help her as much as I can. If that means seeing him revel in his new-found authority as he smirks at me, then so be it. It is a small price to pay.'

Another knock came at the door and both women turned to see Salisbury enter the room. The new castellan stopped and stared at them both in silence, as if waiting for something to happen.

'Well,' he said, 'is that how you welcome your new lord and master?'

For a second, Nesta almost forgot her station and had to bite her lip not to say anything inappropriate. Instead, she got to her feet and bowed her head slightly, acknowledging his new position. Emma curtsied low and stayed on the floor, her eyes lowered.

'That's better,' said Salisbury. He glared at Emma. 'You,' he said, 'get up. If you ever pass me by without an acknowledgement again, your time here will be over. Understand?'

'Yes, my lord,' she said.

'Good. Now leave us and see we are not disturbed.'

Emma left the room and closed the door as Salisbury turned to Nesta. 'So,' he said, walking across and sitting in her chair, 'here we are.'

'What do you want, Salisbury?' said Nesta. 'If you have come to gloat you are wasting your time. I will not lower myself to react to such sewer politics.'

'Oh, come, come,' said Salisbury, 'is that the way to address your new master?'

'You will never be my master,' said Nesta.

'But I am the castellan, Lord of Pembroke. I believe that gives me domain over you.'

'Perhaps in public,' she said, 'but never, ever in private.'

'We shall see,' said Salisbury with a cold smile.

'What do you want?' she asked again. 'For this is my private room and I am busy. So if you don't mind . . .'

'Ah, yes,' said Salisbury, 'this room.' He stood up and wandered around the substantial quarters, peering into each nook and cranny as Nesta watched. 'Correct me if I am wrong,' he said eventually, 'but this room was Gerald's quarters before he married you, which means it comes with the station, not the personality.'

Nesta shook her head slowly as the implications sunk in. 'No,' she said. 'This room is mine and will remain so. If you think you can take this away from me then you are mistaken.'

'That's exactly what I think,' said Salisbury. 'In fact, you have one day to remove your things to the room on the top floor. If they are not out by tomorrow at sundown, my men will move them for you, and indeed you, if needs be, without ceremony.'

'You can't do this,' gasped Nesta.

'I think you will find I can do whatever I want,' said Salisbury. 'In fact, your life here is about to become far less comfortable than it has been these past few years.'

'Then I will leave,' said Nesta.

'No, you won't,' said Salisbury. 'You will stay here, under house arrest if needs be. And consider this: the room on the top floor, albeit small, is far better than the lodgings offered in the castle gaol.'

'You wouldn't dare,' said Nesta.

'Try me,' said Salisbury, holding her stare. 'Of course,' he continued, 'there is another way. A proposal that may not garner your favour in the first instance but one that is far more sensible for both of us in its outcome.'

'And that is?'

'You become my wife and regain all the privileges you enjoyed with Gerald.'

Nesta's mouth dropped open at the suggestion and she stared at him in shock.

'Surprised?' asked Salisbury. 'Surely you must have noticed my attention these past few years. Not even you are that stupid.'

'If you think for one second that I will marry you,' gasped Nesta, 'then you truly are as mad as I have always thought you were. I would *never* consent to being your wife as long as I draw breath.'

'I thought you might say that,' said Salisbury with a grimace, 'so I have made certain preparations to avoid any unnecessary animosity between us.' He reached into his inside pocket and withdrew a leather wrap, throwing it on the bed at Nesta's side.

'What is that supposed to be?' asked Nesta.

'It is a personal letter from the king to you,' said Salisbury, 'expressing his expectation that after a suitable period of mourning you will become the first lady of Pembroke, my wife.'

'*What?*' gasped Nesta.

'Go ahead,' said Salisbury. 'Read it. It is genuine enough.'

'I don't care if he hand-wrote it in his own blood,' gasped Nesta. 'He has no right to dictate who I marry.'

'I think you will find he does,' said Salisbury, removing a stopper from a jug to smell the contents. 'You see, the political situation here in Deheubarth is very fragile and, as you know, the union between you and Gerald went a long way to contain any potential upset. Now Gerald has gone, but there is no need to lose your influence, so it was suggested we simply replace one castellan with another while keeping our pretty Welsh princess in place so the peasants are appeased.'

'That's not going to happen,' she said. 'I would rather die first.'

'I'm sure you would,' said Salisbury. 'But I think you wouldn't want the same fate to happen to any of your children.'

'*What?*' gasped Nesta again.

'Accidents happen around here,' said Salisbury pouring some wine into a goblet, 'and it would be such a shame if one or more of your children, say, got stuck in a burning building, or accidentally drowned in the river. Now wouldn't that be tragic?'

Nesta stared in horror at the implied threat.

'Of course,' he continued, 'none of that is likely to happen if you just do what the king has commanded. What is one more marriage of convenience to you, anyway? The last one was exactly the same.'

'Do not compare yourself to Gerald,' said Nesta. 'You were never fit to clean his boots.'

'Whatever you say,' said Salisbury. 'Think about it and I will talk to you in the next few days. You can mourn for exactly three months from the date of Gerald's burial. After that we can be wed within weeks.' He walked over to the doorway before stopping and turning around. 'Oh, I forgot to say: your youngest son has gone fishing with one of my men, but I'm sure he will be fine.'

The angry look on Nesta's face turned to horror at the veiled threat.

'Can I take this with me?' he said holding up the goblet. 'I have to say it is the most excellent wine.'

Without waiting for an answer, he left the room and closed the door, leaving a dumbstruck and horrified Nesta staring after him.

The Outskirts of Pembroke Town

February 2nd, AD 1136

Gwenllian stood back amongst the trees overlooking the town in the distance. Her husband was beside her and they were relatively quiet as they waited for Robert to return from his task.

Two ships lay at anchor outside the dock in the distance, a tempting but unreachable target. Since her audacious attack the previous month, security had been heavily increased whenever a ship docked to unload stores. The English were taking no chances.

'Are you sure about this?' asked Gwenllian.

'Absolutely,' said Tarw. 'There were two candles in the tower window last night, and that was the agreed signal.'

'I hope you are right,' said Gwenllian. 'The men are chomping at the bit to take the fight to the English and if we don't feed their blades soon we risk dulling their spirit.'

'We'll soon find out,' said Tarw, 'but we are wasting time here. Robert will find us when he is done.'

They both retreated from the tree line to find their horses and return to the temporary camp back in the forest.

———————

Down in the market, Emma walked through the busy street pausing to look at the wares on each stall. Sometimes she picked up a piece of cloth or a utensil to check the quality and the price but invariably put them back. As she went, she bought some small things for herself and when she came to the pie and bread stall, her mouth watered at the wonderful aromas blowing towards her in the morning breeze.

'Emma,' said the lady on the stall, 'how are you this frosty morning?'

'Cold,' said Emma, 'but nothing that a hot pie won't cure.'

'Then let me get you one of my best,' said the seller. 'It has extra fat so it tastes wonderful.'

Emma smiled. Sian was a lifelong friend and, though she had a reputation as the best pie maker in Pembroke, her great belly and poor clothing suggested she ate far more than she sold.

'Have you been busy?' asked Emma as Sian retrieved a pie from the clay oven built into the wall of the house behind her.

The seller paused momentarily to carefully phrase her answer. 'No more than usual,' she said eventually.

'What about yesterday?' asked Emma.

Sian paused again, her heart racing at the agreed code. 'The same as always,' she said, turning around to place the pie on the table.

'Good,' said Emma and she held out her hand to make the payment.

'Thank you,' said Sian, taking the penny while staring knowingly at her lifelong friend. 'And a very good day to you.'

'And to you,' said Emma and she scurried away, her focus on a stall selling leather straps further down the road.

For a few moments, Sian watched her go, her heart racing as she felt the hidden folded message in her fist. Quickly she placed it into the pocket of her apron but soon her attention returned to the steady stream of customers treating themselves to her well-known delicacies.

Five minutes later, a man she had never seen before approached and greeted her with a big smile.

'Good day,' he said.

'And to you,' she replied. 'What can I get you, a nice hot pie perhaps?'

'No, I am about to go out on a hunt so I would prefer some of that warm bread.'

'Of course,' said Sian and she turned to the basket of bread sitting on a table to one side.

'Have you been busy?' asked the stranger, causing the woman to stop dead in her tracks again.

'No more than usual,' she said slowly, repeating the words she had used with Emma just a few minutes earlier.

'What about yesterday?' asked the man. Sian swallowed hard. This was the man she had been told to expect. Without turning around, she retrieved the folded note Emma had given her and pushed it deep beneath the crust of the bread.

'The same as always,' she said as she turned back around. She placed the bread on the table and looked up at the man. 'Anything else?'

'No, that will be fine.'

'Then you owe me a penny if you please,' she said, 'and I hope it is all you wish for.'

'I'm sure it is,' said the man as he placed two pennies into her hand. 'For your trouble,' he said.

Sian felt the two coins in her fist but said nothing. Instead, she moved on to the next customer as if Robert didn't exist. 'So, what can I get you, young sir,' she said to the boy. 'You look like you need fattening up.'

Robert walked away quickly, his bread already in the food pouch about his waist. With the transaction completed as planned, he made his way back to his horse and rode out of the town to meet up with Gwenllian and Tarw.

Twenty minutes later, they all stood together amongst the trees and Gwenllian waited in expectation as Tarw broke apart the bread to reveal the hidden message. Hurriedly he unfolded the parchment and read the contents to himself.

'Well,' said Gwenllian. 'Is it what we wanted?'

'Oh, yes,' said Tarw, his voice heavy with anticipation. 'That and a whole lot more.'

'Let me see,' said his wife and she took the parchment from her husband. As she read the details, Robert turned to Tarw.

'So,' he said, 'what's happening?'

'What is happening, Robert,' replied Tarw, 'is in five days' time, we take the fight to the English.'

The Road Between Pembroke and
Kidwelly

February 7th, AD 1136

Gwenllian rode calmly at the head of sixty handpicked horsemen along a shallow but steep-sided ravine carved out by the actions of a relentless stream over many millennia. For the past few days, she and the rest of the rebel leaders had used the information sent from Nesta to plan an attack that would leave the garrison at Pembroke reeling. When everything had been confirmed, all those involved were deployed to various areas on the Kidwelly road, each fully briefed as to what was expected of them, and at last, the target was confirmed. A heavily laden and valuable caravan heading from Pembroke to Kidwelly.

Gwenllian's role in the attack was simple: to lead a full frontal attack on the well-guarded caravan and, with the help of reinforcements, inflict a devastating defeat on the English that would take an age to recover from.

For over a day they had lain low, hidden away from prying eyes amongst the trees, waiting for the caravan to appear on the road and at last, when her scouts had confirmed it was no more than a league away, she had urged her men into action and led her column along the ravine towards the selected ambush site. All she had to do now was wait.

———

Wilhelm Berman, a Flemish knight in the employ of the English, rode along the coastal path at the head of twenty men on horseback. Behind him came a caravan of four carts, each heavily laden with stores for the garrison at Kidwelly castle. Behind the carts came sixty foot-soldiers and finally another twenty heavily armed horsemen.

The increasing threat from the rebels meant most caravans were now escorted by experienced soldiers, and this one in particular enjoyed a very strong escort. While Wilhelm was certain they could defend against anything the Welsh could throw at them, just to be sure, they had left Pembroke while it was still dark and had since kept off the main tracks, away from the threat of ambush that the proximity of the forests often brought.

Despite the lack of cover, Wilhelm saw the openness as an ally, for it would afford him plenty of opportunity to deploy his men should they come under attack.

'If the weather holds, we should be there by nightfall,' said Wilhelm to Rowan, a fellow knight and his second in command, 'and perhaps we can relieve them of some of that swill they call ale.'

'That does not excite me,' said Rowan. 'It is like drinking straight from the sewer. Give me corn brew, anytime, or even some of their foul wine, but the ale makes my stomach drop out.'

'We noticed,' laughed Wilhelm. 'Perhaps you are right – we will keep you away from that devil's fluid, if only for our own sakes.' Wilhelm laughed again but suddenly stopped as Rowan held up his hand and ordered the caravan to stop.

'What's wrong?' asked Wilhelm, all thoughts of laughter gone.

'Over there,' said Rowan, pointing forward. 'I thought I saw a rider disappear beyond that slope.'

Wilhelm stared but could see nothing. 'A lone rider worries me not,' he said. 'In fact, I am rather hoping some brigands chance their arm for I have not exercised my sword in many weeks.'

'Be careful what you wish for, comrade,' said Rowan, 'for you may just get the chance.' Again he nodded towards the path to his front and, this time, the Flemish knight could see that they did indeed have company.

Several hundred paces away, a column of riders emerged from behind a natural fold in the ground. At their head, one of the riders held a flag that blew defiantly in the sea breeze.

'Who are they?' asked Rowan.

'I do not recognise the colours,' said Wilhelm, 'but whoever they are, they certainly do not represent the English Crown.' He looked at the riders, counting them as they appeared, and despite the distance could see they were poorly armoured with only a few chainmail hauberks between them. The rest were protected by gambesons and leather armour.

'I count sixty,' he said, 'and they are of poor stock. I see not a single knight amongst them.'

'Brigands?' suggested Rowan.

'I know of no brigands who ride under colours,' said Wilhelm. 'Unless I am mistaken, these could be the rebels we have heard so much about. If truth be told, I see nothing to make me sweat.'

'I'll alert the men,' said Rowan and he turned his horse to ride back along the caravan.

Gwenllian led her men out from the protection of the ravine and waited as they spread out across the field, blocking any further progression for the caravan. On their right was rocky ground, strewn with the waste from an old flint mine – impossible to pass with wagons and dangerous to any horse travelling at speed – while to their left the way past was bordered by the cliff dropping down into the sea. If the English wanted to pass, there was only one way and that was through her lines.

Though she remained calm, her heart was beating fast. Decapitating a wounded man was one thing but a full-scale battle with a tried and tested enemy was completely different and, though she had been training hard in the Cantref Mawr to hone her long unused fighting skills, it had been many years since she had swung a blade in anger. To either side of her were those warriors who had kept the fight going in the intervening years and though poorly equipped they were the most experienced men she had available and she knew they would not let her down. Besides, she had something else up her sleeve, hopefully something the English would never expect.

'Their leader is approaching,' said Taliesin by her side. 'Do we pander to his request for parley?'

'We will hear what he has to say,' said Gwenllian. 'If we can take this caravan without shedding Welsh blood then we will.' With a kick of her heels, she urged her horse forward, leaving the line under the command of Taliesin. A hundred paces or so later, she reined in her horse and the Flemish knight did the same.

'I am surprised,' he said eventually, 'that it is a mere woman who deems to deny me the king's path.'

'I am Gwenllian ferch Gruffydd,' she replied, 'and this path has belonged to the kings of Deheubarth since before the time of Hywel Dda.'

'I know not of the man you speak,' said Wilhelm, 'nor do I care. However, I have heard your name mentioned over jugs of ale in the castle quarters and I have to admit that much mirth was expressed at the thought of a woman leading a rebellion. Tell me again why you think you have the right and strength to lead such a meaningless cause.'

'I will justify myself to no man,' replied Gwenllian, 'least of all someone born in a different land. All you need to know is my name and that my claim is just.'

'I have to admit you are a fair-looking woman, Gwenllian,' he replied, 'but if you seek the path of conflict in a man's world then you will be treated like any other foe and I will keep this simple. Cede the path or suffer the consequences.'

'Your threats do not sway me, stranger,' she said, 'but I will grant you the same courtesy and keep my stance easily understood. We will not cede this path and hereby reclaim it in the name of our fathers. However, you are welcome to pass on the payment of a toll.'

'A toll?' said Wilhelm with a smile. 'Surely you jest with me.'

'It is no jest,' said Gwenllian. 'If you pay the toll you may continue on your way unhindered.'

Again Wilhelm smiled and looked at the woman before him. She was slightly built and, though well protected in quality armour, he had no doubt he could easily better her in combat.

'Tell me,' he said eventually, 'even if I was inclined to pay this toll, what would be the cost?'

'Those carts,' replied Gwenllian, 'and everything they contain.'

This time the Flemish knight laughed aloud and Gwenllian waited until his mirth had subsided.

'You are a funny woman, Gwenllian,' he said eventually, 'and in different circumstances I think I would like you very much. However, we have business to attend. You know as well as I do that I will not give up these carts so I suggest you return to those peasants you call men and prepare them to fight. Unless, of course, you are willing to withdraw.'

'There will be no withdrawal,' said Gwenllian, 'neither will there be quarter shown. If you refuse my terms, then this is where it will end for one or both of us.'

'So be it,' said Wilhelm quietly. 'Your renewed leadership of this so-called rebellion will be recounted by your countrymen as the shortest in history.' Without waiting for a reply, he turned his horse and rode back to his men.

Gwenllian returned to her own line and reined in her horse next to Taliesin.

'Well,' he asked, 'did it work?'

'No, it did not,' said Gwenllian, 'nor did I expect it to, but I wanted him riled up and determined to teach us a lesson. That way, he may forget our obvious low numbers and fail to consider it may be a ruse.'

'Well, I think you succeeded,' said Taliesin. 'Look.'

Gwenllian looked back at the caravan. The rest of the enemy had all ridden forward to join their leader and, despite their slightly fewer numbers, it was obvious that everyone was well equipped and well trained. Behind those, Gwenllian could see another fifty or so foot soldiers forming up into a double line.

'It is no more than I expected,' said Gwenllian and she rode forward a few paces before turning to face her own men.

'Fear not their numbers nor their manner,' she called, 'for you have been well briefed as to how this will develop. Let our people's suffering strengthen your arm this day and with God's help we will prevail, and if you should fall go to God in the knowledge that you have right on your side.'

With the sound of her men cheering in her ears, she returned to her place beside Taliesin and drew her sword from the scabbard.

'Let it begin,' she said, and with a click of her heels, she urged her horse forward, her sword laying across her lap.

'Here they come,' said Wilhelm to Rowan. 'I will lead the first charge and we will ride straight through them. When they turn to defend themselves from the return assault, lead our foot soldiers against the rear of their lines.'

'Aye, my lord,' said Rowan.

'Remember,' said Wilhelm, 'no prisoners and no quarter.'

'Aye, my lord,' said Rowan again, drawing his own sword. 'Leave it to me.'

With his lancers impatient to start on either side of him, Wilhelm stood up in his stirrups. He removed his own steel-tipped lance from the leather socket attached to his saddle and held it up so the pennant could be seen right across the battlefield.

'This witch has deemed to think she can better us with naught but street vermin at her side,' he shouted. 'So let us show her what real warriors are capable of. Men of Flanders, *advance!*'

As one, the line of horsemen adjusted their grips on their lances, dug their heels into their horses' flanks and advanced in line abreast to meet Gwenllian on the field of battle.

Across the frosty grass, Gwenllian could feel the blood racing through her veins and for the first time in years felt the familiar rush of excitement tinged with fear. With a deep breath she raised her own sword and sounded her own charge.

'*Men of Wales,*' she roared. 'This is our day. For Deheubarth and for freedom. *Advaaaance.*'

With an almighty roar the men spurred their own horses forward and galloped into the attack, each knowing that the odds were stacked heavily against them. Unlike the enemy, they had no lances or metal armour; all they had was their swords, their hearts and their inspirational leader.

Gwenllian galloped hard towards Wilhelm, sword in hand. She wore no helmet or coif and her golden hair flew out behind her like a pennant. Wilhelm singled out the leader and, anticipating a quick victory, met her gallop head on, his lance lowered and aimed directly at her heart.

With no lance of her own, Gwenllian knew she was out-powered, especially with a trained knight, but the last few days she had trained specifically for this moment. With everything depending on the next few seconds, she drove her horse even harder, knowing that speed and momentum were critical if she was to succeed. At full tilt, both leaders met at the centre of the field, and just as it seemed she would be impaled on Wilhelm's lance, she lowered her sword arm and dropped her body tight to her horse. The lance sailed harmlessly over her back while at the same time she forced her sword upwards towards her opponent, resulting in a heavy blow under the knight's forearm. Though there was no strength in the impact, her momentum meant the edge of the sword smashed through his chainmail into his flesh.

To either side, both lines crashed into each other with deadly effect. Many of the Welsh had deployed the same tactic but, though it had caught some of the Flemish unawares, the knights' greater experience and training bore fruit and far more Welsh than English fell.

Shocked at the fact he had missed his target, Wilhelm continued riding through the Welsh lines before reining in his horse to turn for the follow-up assault.

'*Reform*,' he shouted at the rest of his men as they arrived. 'And this time do not fall for their trickery.' He discarded his lance and drew his sword. As he did, he felt the pain in his arm for the first time and looking down, saw the blood oozing between the broken links of his chainmail hauberk.

'My lord,' said one of his men, 'you are injured.'

'A scratch only,' said Wilhelm, knowing full well that some of the links had been forced into the wound. 'Reform the line and prepare to charge.'

In front of him, Gwenllian's own riders had also turned to ride back into battle. In between them, several men of both sides lay dead or wounded on the freezing ground while others tried to limp away, nursing wounds or broken bones.

'Those with lances to the fore,' shouted Wilhelm. 'The rest of you will ride behind and engage with swords. This time, we will not ride through but stay and engage what remains of her pathetic little army.' He turned to look at one of his own men riding a bleeding horse towards him from the battlefield. 'Are you wounded?' he asked.

'No my lord but . . .'

'Then dismount,' ordered Wilhelm. 'Find another horse.'

'Look, my lord,' said the horseman, pointing to the ground beyond Wilhelm.

Wilhelm stared behind him, his heart sinking at what he saw. All along the shallow ridge where Gwenllian had first emerged, another line of riders had appeared, but this time they were obviously far better equipped and far better organised.

'Who are they?' asked one of the men as his horse fidgeted beneath him.

'They fly no banners,' said Wilhelm, 'Welsh or English. I suggest they are mercenaries.'

'My lord,' said one of his officers, 'we now have foe on both sides. What are your orders?'

Wilhelm thought quickly. His men had suffered few casualties in the first encounter and the easier targets were indeed the Welsh, but he knew that even if they were routed in the second attack, he would still have to deal with the newcomers and he couldn't risk losing any more men before then. Quickly he looked around, assessing the situation. Rowan was an experienced, battle-hardened commander and Wilhelm knew that he and his foot soldiers could easily deal with the Welsh, or at least hold them at bay for a while. That would leave his own men to concentrate on this new threat before returning to finish off the woman and her comrades. With no time left, he made his decision.

'Reform,' he shouted suddenly. 'Face the rear. The Welsh can wait while we teach these newcomers a lesson and if they are still here when we return, we will cast them into the sea. On my command, *advaaance!*'

Back at the caravan, Gwenllian's men were also reforming. With a sinking heart, she could see at least ten had fallen with several more bearing heavy wounds, some of them fatal. It had been a far costlier first encounter than she had wanted but now was not the time to mourn. In the distance she could see the Saxon mercenaries forming up to engage the Flemish and, with immense relief, she could see that Wilhelm had decided they were the greater threat. If he had made a different choice, then this fight would already be lost. She looked around and saw the English foot soldiers had formed a shield wall, ready to defend against her anticipated assault on the wagons.

'Dismount and form up,' shouted Gwenllian. 'Wounded to the rear.'

The remainder of her command did as ordered and they formed a line facing the shield wall, a force of less than thirty against sixty.

'They outnumber us at least two to one,' said Taliesin. 'If they decide to advance, we will have to retreat.'

'Then let us even the numbers,' said Gwenllian. She turned to a young man at her side. 'Give the first signal.'

The man immediately lifted a horn to his mouth and sent a haunting tone through the air, the signal that a certain hidden warrior had been waiting for.

A hundred paces away, Dog grinned at the sound of the horn. He and his men had been waiting for hours, sitting on the ledges of the cliff above the sea like nesting gulls. He had been peering up over the cliff edge, watching the battle develop with increasing frustration and he knew his men were desperate to get involved.

'That's the signal,' he hissed, turning to waiting men beneath him. 'Prepare to move and I swear that if one man turns away in the assault I will kill him myself.'

The men climbed up over the edge of the cliff face and quickly formed up. In front of them they could see the wagons and the rear of the strong shield wall. As soon as they were ready, Dog drew his own sword. 'They are distracted,' he said, 'and do not know we are here. Let's keep it that way until the first of our blades tastes blood.'

In the English defences, Rowan crouched behind his men peering over the top of the shields. He was half expecting to see Gwenllian's warriors leading an assault but she just stood there, a hundred paces away staring at the wall as if expecting something to happen.

'What's going on?' asked one of his men after a few moments' silence. 'Why doesn't she attack?'

'I have no idea,' said Rowan. 'It doesn't make sense, unless . . .' He turned suddenly to look behind him and his face fell as he saw the swarm of Welsh warriors racing towards them, their faces full of rage.

'*Alarm*,' he screamed, raising his sword, but it was too late. Before any of the soldiers knew what was happening, Dog's blade smashed into Rowan's face, cleaving his head in two. Seconds later, the rest of the warriors fell on the panicking defenders, unleashing generations of pent-up aggression upon their terrified victims.

At the far end of the battlefield, Heinrich had already lined up his Saxon mercenaries and lost no time in preparing his charge. He needed no rousing speech or fancy words for this was what they were paid to do, and after so long waiting in the Cantref Mawr, the chance to at last unleash their frustration on an enemy made their mouths water in anticipation. On top of that, the promise of rich pickings from the caravan made it a perfect opportunity.

'Wedge formation,' he ordered, seeing the Flemish knights coming at them in line abreast. 'Present shields, *advance.*' The riders kicked their horses into action. Every one of the mercenaries held a heavy shield in one hand and a sword in the other. Their preference was close-quarter battle but with an enemy who preferred the lance, the shields were necessary for the initial contact.

'You know what to do,' shouted Heinrich. 'Take the blow and strike for the horses.'

'Aye,' shouted the men in response and as one they kicked into their horses' flanks again to increase speed.

The two lines of horsemen thundered across the battlefield, each force supremely confident in their own abilities. Seconds later, they clashed at full speed with horses and men falling on both sides. Flesh and bone were torn apart as Flemish spears and lances ripped through the Saxon armour and the air was filled with the sounds of battle intertwined with cries of pain. The Flemish impact had been brutal but they did not have it all their own way. The Saxon tactic of targeting the horses paid immense dividends and more than half of Wilhelm's men were unhorsed, with many crashing into the floor as their mounts were mortally wounded or killed outright.

The animals' screams of pain and fear mingled with the cries of wounded men. Wilhelm turned to see the Saxons had dismounted and were closing in on his comrades. Knowing that to go back in on horseback meant risking the last of the mounts they had, he ordered his own men to dismount and raced into the battle on foot. Within moments,

Flemish and Saxon warriors clashed in a brutal struggle between equally matched forces. Tall, strong warriors, used to the brutality of warfare, were hacked down with blows from double-handed swords, their chain-mail hauberks little defence in such close quarters. Blood and flesh flew everywhere and, though the Flemish were better trained, the mercenaries had fought in far more battles and employed every dirty trick they knew to their advantage. The battlefield was swiftly becoming a scene of depraved brutality and unrelenting carnage.

———⌣———

Back at the wagons, some of the English foot soldiers had managed to break from the doomed shield wall and were now fighting for their lives with the less-experienced Welsh warriors. Dog fought like a demon at the battle's midst, his very appearance and manner striking fear into any man who came close: friend or foe. His eyes had glazed over and he killed indiscriminately, his blade responsible for the deaths of many men.

Despite their surprise attack, the Welsh had since lost the advantage and it was obvious that the English could well carry the day against such an inexperienced foe. Gwenllian spotted the risk and turning to Taliesin, ordered the last of her men into attack.

'My lady,' said Taliesin, 'we should hold back. If the mercenaries are defeated, then we will be needed against the English horsemen.'

'Taliesin,' shouted Gwenllian, 'those men have great hearts but little experience. They need good leadership and not that maniac you call Dog. If we hold back, they are at risk of being bettered. Stay if you will but I am not going to let that happen.' Without another word, she ran across the open ground and drawing her sword, hurled herself deep into the midst of the battle, hacking at any Englishman who came within range.

For a few moments her men were dumbstruck at the sight. For the first time since she joined the rebellion, they now witnessed how effective Gwenllian was with a sword and they had seen few men better skilled.

'Well,' shouted Taliesin suddenly, 'are we going to let a woman show us how it's done?' He drew his own blade and raced after Gwenllian, closely followed by the rest of the men.

Over the next few minutes the battle swung both ways but with Gwenllian taking command, the Welsh quickly regained dominance and the few remaining English foot soldiers threw down their weapons in an act of surrender. Some of the Welsh forced them to the floor, making them lie face down in the mud with the points of bloodied swords resting against the backs of their necks.

'Give the word, my lady,' shouted Taliesin, 'and I will have them run through right here.'

Gwenllian stared at the men lying in the mud, each one shaking in fear as they contemplated their imminent death. She had sworn no quarter would be given but the blood lust was receding quickly and she saw no further need for killing.

'No,' she said eventually. 'Let them live.'

'But I thought you said . . .'

'I know what I said, but we are freedom fighters not murderers. To execute these men in cold blood makes us no better than them. Tie them up and I will deal with them later.'

The men holding the swords backed away and soon the prisoners were tied back-to-back on the ground.

'My lady, you are wounded,' said one of the warriors.

Gwenllian looked at him confused and he pointed at her face. She lifted her hand to her cheek and saw it was smeared with blood. 'It's nothing,' she said. 'Just a glancing blow. How goes the other fight? Is it over?'

'Aye it is,' said Taliesin joining them, 'and a more brutal battle no man has ever seen.'

'Did we prevail?'

'The mercenaries took the day, but not without serious casualties. We will offer aid to their wounded.'

'No,' said Gwenllian. 'Those Saxons are a strange race and have their own traditions outside of our understanding. If they want us they will send for us.' She turned to one of the sergeants. 'Have our men see to our own wounded. If any are beyond help, then use your blade to send them on their way with a prayer. I would rather see them die quickly than spend their last few hours in pain.'

'Well,' said Taliesin, when the sergeant had gone, 'shall we see if your source was correct?'

Gwenllian nodded and they walked over to the first wagon. They opened the rear flaps and saw the inside was piled high with sacks of food including flour, onions, beets and whole sides of smoked ham wrapped in linen.

'A goodly haul,' said Gwenllian. 'Our supplies are running low.' They walked back to the second wagon and peered inside. This time, Gwenllian's eyes lit up as half of the wagon was taken up with weapons of all sorts, from pikes and swords to unstrung bows and barrels of arrows. The rest of the cart was full of hauberks and coifs, the chainmail armour so desperately needed by the rebels.

'It seems your source is good,' said Taliesin. 'This is indeed a treasure, but where's the money?'

They walked to the third wagon and were about to open the flaps when Taliesin's hand shot out and he dragged Gwenllian back away from the cart.

'Wait,' he said, noticing the flaps were already untied. 'There's somebody in there.'

Gwenllian drew her own sword and faced the cart.

'Whoever you are,' she said, 'come out and you will be spared.'

When there was no answer Taliesin stepped forward.

'You heard the lady,' he said. 'Throw out your weapons and come out slowly. Refuse and we will burn the cart from beneath you.'

Someone moved inside the cart, and both Gwenllian and Taliesin braced as they waited for the guard to emerge. The flaps opened but to their surprise it was not an armed guard but a young boy of about ten years old.

'Please don't kill me,' he said, looking between them both. 'I have no weapons.'

For a few seconds, they both stared in shock but then burst into laughter. Gwenllian sheathed her sword and beckoned him forward.

'Wait,' said Taliesin, sheathing his own sword, 'let me just check.' He walked forward and searched the boy for any knives. 'We can't be too careful,' he said.

'What were you doing in there?' asked Gwenllian.

'My father is one of the soldiers,' said the boy. 'He said there was a witch leading an army of murderers in the forests of Pembroke so he was taking me to live with my grandfather at Kidwelly.' He looked around the scene of devastation. 'Is he here?'

Gwenllian glanced at Taliesin who shrugged his shoulders. 'We don't know who is alive and who is dead yet, boy,' he said, 'but you will find out soon enough.' He turned to one of his men. 'Take this boy away and watch over him.'

'Find him some food and water,' added Gwenllian as the warrior led the boy away, 'and keep him safe until I send for him. We wouldn't want any evil witches to cause him any harm.'

When he was gone, Gwenllian and Taliesin walked back to the cart and peered inside. At first they could only see some sacks, each tied tightly. The warrior pulled his knife from his belt and slit one open, standing back as the contents spilled onto the floor. Gwenllian squatted down, picking up some of the many fabulously decorated items at her feet.

'What are all these?' gasped Taliesin. 'And where have they come from?'

Gwenllian picked up a bejewelled goblet and a crucifix. 'I think they are sacred items looted from churches and manors across Deheubarth,' she said. 'They must fear for their security at Pembroke and are transferring them to Kidwelly.'

'There are another six such sacks,' said Taliesin. 'And look, there is a chest.'

He climbed aboard the cart and tried to open the lock but it was solid. Not to be thwarted he dragged the small chest from the cart and with some of the men gathering around, picked up a bloodstained pike from the floor.

'Stand back,' he said, and with an almighty swipe smashed the heavy blade down onto the timber around the lock. The wood splintered but did not give way.

'Hit it harder,' laughed one of the men. 'Imagine it is an English skull beneath your blade.'

Taliesin smiled at the jest and took another swing. This time the timber shattered and he inserted his knife beneath the lid to prise it open. Everyone leaned forward to see the contents and they were amazed when he dug in his hands to lift fistfuls of gold and silver coins, letting them pour through his fingers like water. Every man started cheering and Taliesin turned to look for Gwenllian but she was nowhere to be seen.

'Where's the princess?' he said. 'She needs to see this.'

'She is at the final cart,' said one of the men. 'Perhaps she is looking for her own treasure.'

Everyone laughed again and Taliesin grabbed a handful of coins to take to Gwenllian.

'It seems your source was good,' he said as he approached. 'It looks like the caravan contained half of the treasury from Pembroke.'

He stopped mid-sentence as he rounded the corner and saw Gwenllian staring into the back of the cart with a huge smile on her face.

'What is it?' he asked as he approached. 'Is there even more treasure?'

'Oh, there's treasure here all right,' said Gwenllian, 'and one with a value far exceeding all else in these carts.'

Taliesin peered inside, but if he was expecting chests of coins or sacks of jewels he was sadly mistaken. All he could see was an old man, gagged and tied to an anvil at the front of the cart.

'I see no coins or treasure,' said Taliesin. 'Is he sitting on a chest?'

'Oh no,' said Gwenllian, 'that old man *is* the treasure for he is one of the most trusted friends I have ever had. Taliesin, meet Lord Bevan of Llandeilo.'

Several hours later, all the English and Flemish dead lay in two rows, each covered with lengths of linen retrieved from the many rolls found on one of the wagons and weighed down with rocks to stop unwanted attention from the gulls and crows. The Welsh dead had been loaded onto two of the carts and had already been taken for burial in the nearest graveyard.

Gwenllian sat next to a fire sharing warm broth with Lord Bevan and hearing the terrible story of how the English had attacked his manor. He recounted how many of the women had been raped before being killed and every man caught, whatever his age, had been put to the sword. The only person spared, as far as he knew, was himself and after being taken to Pembroke for hanging, it subsequently turned out that he was to be shipped to Bristol to be hanged in the presence of the king. When he found out that Gwenllian's children had been found alive, he wept tears of joy.

'So what now for you?' asked Gwenllian.

'I have nothing left except the love of my country,' he replied, wiping his eyes. 'That and the friendship garnered over so many years with you and your husband.'

'Then come with us,' said Gwenllian gently. 'Be part of this movement and help regain that which was lost.'

'I am happy to come,' said Bevan, 'but I fear I will be more of a hindrance than a help. It has been years since I held a weapon of any sort and if truth be told, even then I was no better than a novice.'

'We need minds as well as swords,' said Gwenllian, 'and I know of no man as loyal or as clever as you. Your knowledge of the English system of government, their structures and their tactics are second to none and I will welcome you to my campaign tent in a heartbeat.'

Bevan smiled up at her with gratitude written all over his face, but remained silent.

Taliesin walked over and dipped a mug into the pot of broth amongst the ashes.

'How bad is it?' asked Gwenllian.

'Fifteen dead,' he said. 'Another dozen wounded with some unlikely to survive. The bodies have been taken for burial.'

'My lady,' someone shouted. 'Look.'

Gwenllian turned to see a line of men approaching from the far side of the battlefield, each leading a horse. Across some of the horses' backs, she could see their dead, draped like carcasses of hunted deer. At the fore she could see the corpse of Heinrich of Saxony, his enormous frame tied securely inside his huge fur cloak.

Gwenllian swallowed hard. This was not how it was supposed to have turned out. The mercenaries were supposed to have routed the Flemish horsemen with ease but, though they had been victorious, it had come at a great cost with over half either dead or wounded. She got to her feet and walked over to meet Heinrich's second in command.

'Did he die well?' she asked simply.

'He died a true warrior,' replied the Saxon, 'and he will be remembered by his people for many generations.'

'We will give him a Christian burial,' said Gwenllian, 'as we will for all your fallen.'

'No,' said the Saxon. 'We will strip the bodies of the flesh and leave it out for the birds. The bones will be burned in our fires and ground back to the dust whence they came. We will return it to the villages where each man was born.'

Gwenllian nodded in deference. It was a strange custom but one she had heard of before. 'When will that be?' she asked.

'This was our last battle,' said the Saxon. 'As soon as we have been paid and our dead have been prepared, we will be leaving.'

Again Gwenllian nodded. She turned to Taliesin. 'Break open the boxes,' she said, 'and give these men half.'

'The agreement was for one tenth,' said Taliesin.

'I know,' said Gwenllian, 'but if it was not for these men, we would not have carried the day. We owe them much more than any treasure chest can hold but perhaps this will go some way in compensation.'

It was the Saxon's turn to nod in appreciation. 'I will see that the family of each man who fell today gets his share. Now, we have to tend our wounded so, if you don't mind, you will find us back at your camp.'

'What about your money?' asked Taliesin. 'Do you not want to see it counted?'

'We trust you,' said the Saxon quietly, 'and will receive it on the morrow.' Without another word, he led the giant horse away, followed closely by the rest of his men, each leading their own horses heavily laden with dead or wounded comrades.

'We should be going ourselves,' said Taliesin quietly. 'We need to get distance between us and Kidwelly Castle before they realise something is wrong.'

'Agreed,' said Gwenllian. 'Slice the muscles on the backs of the wrists of the prisoners and set them free. At least that way they will never again fight against us.'

'So be it,' said Taliesin.

'The rest of you,' called Gwenllian to the remaining men, 'cut as much meat as you can carry from the dead horses and make your way back to camp. We will celebrate our victory with our families.'

The men moved away to collect the unexpected bounty as Gwenllian turned back to Bevan. 'Well,' she said, 'are you coming with us?'

'Aye,' he said, after a pause. 'I am, and will be proud to do so.'

'Then let's find you a horse,' she said. 'We have far to go.'

Within the hour, everyone was making their way back to the distant hills in small groups, making it harder for anyone to follow their trail. Each had been briefed to take circuitous routes and to lay several ambushes along the way in case they were followed. Gwenllian, Bevan and Taliesin started out along the coastal path towards Brecon, when Gwenllian suddenly stopped and looked around.

'Wait,' she said. 'Someone is missing.'

'Who?' asked Taliesin.

'Tomas Scar and Dog,' she replied. 'I have not seen either since the fight at the shield wall.'

'Tomas Scar was wounded,' said Taliesin. 'I sent him to the rear. He might have made his way back to camp.'

'And Dog?'

'That is a different matter,' said Taliesin. 'During the rush of battle he is taken over by demons unknown. He is likely to be gone for many days but, if I know him, he will return.'

'He is a dangerous man, Taliesin,' said Gwenllian. 'Possibly more than either of us realise.'

'Time will tell, Princess,' said Taliesin, 'but for now, let's just be grateful that his contribution helped get us to where we are now.'

Gwenllian nodded in silence and with a kick of her heels, urged her horse back towards the Cantref Mawr.

Pembroke Castle

February 9th, AD 1136

Salisbury stood in his quarters reading the dispatch delivered by one of the castle knights only moments earlier. His face was white with shock and he had to read the parchment twice to take in the terrible news.

'This is impossible,' he said. 'I sent the best we had. How under God's heaven can an unruly mob of peasants better such a force armed with little more than rusting swords and pitchforks. It makes no sense.'

'It's worse than that, my lord,' said the knight. 'If you recall, last year's taxes were also on the caravan intended to be forwarded to the king's treasury. In addition, one of the carts was laden with a shipment of weapons bound for the armoury at Kidwelly. Whether the attackers had pitchforks or not, they now have the latest swords and armour.'

'What about survivors?' asked Salisbury, looking up from the letter. 'Surely some managed to escape?'

'There were a few,' said the knight, 'though they have been muti-lated and will never fight again.'

'I care not about their wounds,' spat Salisbury. 'I want to know what happened out there. What fool enabled this to happen and why is his head not on a spike outside my window?'

'My lord,' said the knight, 'forgive me but I am led to believe that it is you who gave the final order to proceed.'

'I know I agreed the order,' snarled Salisbury, 'but I did so after taking advice from men used to battle. Why are they not here to answer for this disgrace?'

'If you talk of the Flemish knights,' said the knight, 'they both died defending the wagons, as did their men. Everything possible was done to prevent this happening and the outcome was unforeseeable.'

'No,' said Salisbury, walking back and forth across the room. 'We are missing something here. We fielded a strong force under experienced leadership. We even changed the route and left after dark so they wouldn't be seen. There is no way this happened by coincidence, we must have a spy in our midst and I swear I am going to find out who it is.'

'My lord,' said the knight, 'I trust every man under my command and would vouch for each and every one of them. There are no traitors in this garrison.'

'*Then how do you explain the ambush?*' roared Salisbury, throwing the document across the room. 'For I am at a complete loss.'

'I can't, my lord,' said the knight patiently. 'As yet I have no answers.'

'Then you had better start coming up with some,' said Salisbury, 'for I have many questions that need answering.'

'Of course,' said the knight. 'If there is nothing else, I need to withdraw. There are wagons approaching with our dead and I need to arrange the burials.'

'Put them in a mass grave,' said Salisbury. 'They are deserving of little more.'

'My lord, these are loyal and pious men,' argued the knight, 'surely they deserve separate graves and suitable ceremonies.'

'*Most were Flemish,*' shouted Salisbury, 'and they have let me down. Now dig a mass pit and cast them in or I swear you will join them.'

'Yes, my lord,' said the knight, and he left the room, passing Walter de Calais coming in.

Salisbury poured himself a jug of ale and drained it in one before refilling it again and drinking half.

'I have just heard the news,' said Walter, 'and it is hard to believe. The deaths of those men leaves us severely undermanned and with the rebels now in possession of quality armament, we could be at risk of attack.'

'I know,' said Salisbury. 'I need to think. What spies do we have in the enemy camp?'

'We have two men who ride with the rebels,' said Walter, 'each paid to report back on anything they plan.'

'Yet they failed to warn us of this attack.'

'I can only think it was too short notice,' said Walter. 'They have never failed us before.'

'More excuses,' said Salisbury. 'It's just not good enough. Send them a message from me. Tell them that if they value their lives and those of their families they will find out who the traitor is within my garrison. I want to know and I want to know now.'

'Understood,' said Walter. 'Anything else?'

'Aye,' said Salisbury. 'Send me the scribe and prepare two riders with the best horses we have. I need to send a message to London immediately.'

'Of course,' said Walter, and he left the room.

Salisbury watched him go and wondered if he could be trusted. There were very few men who had known about the importance of the caravan and most of them were dead by Welsh steel. Walter was one of the very few who had access to every detail and he also had Welsh heritage in his background, a grandfather who had sought his fortune and settled in France many years earlier.

'Is it you, my friend?' he said quietly after Walter had left the room. 'For if it is, I swear I will tear out your heart with my own bare hands.'

Several leagues away, Tarw stood in the campaign tent and read a message of his own. It was very short and had come via the same route as the message a week earlier, but this was different: it consisted of just one sentence. With a heavy sigh he turned to the man at his side. 'Robert,' he said, 'pass the word to the camp, there will be a meeting at last light. Everyone is expected to attend.'

'Is it really necessary?' asked Robert. 'Many are nursing their wounded or grieving for those that fell.'

'Aye, it is,' said Tarw. 'Especially for those who have lost loved ones over the past few weeks.'

'Understood,' said Robert and left the tent. Tarw turned to Gwenllian.

'You should see this,' he said and he handed over the note.

Gwenllian read the message and looked up at Tarw. 'Is she sure about this?' she asked.

'She was right about the caravan to Kidwelly,' said Tarw, 'and I see no reason to doubt her now.'

'If you are sure,' said Gwenllian, 'then I will back you up whatever path is taken.'

Several hours later, most of the camp inhabitants were gathered together, murmuring amongst themselves. Up above, Gwenllian and Tarw stood on the slope alongside Lord Bevan and Taliesin. Robert had been sent on an errand by Tarw, and when he eventually returned he whispered into the prince's ear as he handed him a leather purse. Tarw held up his hand and the crowd fell silent.

'I know the hour is late,' he said loudly, 'and I promise I won't keep you long but there is justice to be done.' He held up the piece of parchment he had received earlier in the day. 'In my hand, I have a message from a trusted source. This message reveals the names of two men amongst us that spy on behalf of the English.'

A gasp rippled around the crowd and people started looking at each other nervously, each wondering if they stood next to a traitor.

'This note,' continued Tarw over the noise of the crowd, 'has come from someone trusted within the castle, however, it holds no proof and is an accusation only. If I name these men, they will be allowed to defend themselves before you, a people's court. If found innocent or if there is little proof, they will be allowed to leave with assurances they will not be harmed. However, if the opposite is found to be true, then they will face punishment as befits an enemy spy.'

'Who is it?' called a voice. 'Name them.'

'The men accused are Giles the Miller and Dafydd ap Cenyn, the armourer from Brycheniog.' Tarw looked up and scanned the crowd. 'Make yourself known and face the court.'

'Here's one,' shouted another voice and a man was pushed out into the clearing in front of the people.

'And the other?' asked Tarw looking around.

'He was here a few minutes ago,' said one of the rebels. 'He must have fled.'

'Go after him,' ordered Taliesin, 'and bring him back alive.'

Four of the rebels ran from the camp while Tarw addressed the first accused man.

'Giles the Miller, there is an accusation that you are guilty of being a spy. Is this true?'

'Certainly not,' spluttered the man. 'The accusation is ridiculous. I am loyal to the cause.'

'Is your father not English born?' asked Tarw.

'Aye, he was, but that does not make me a traitor. I was born and bred in Pembroke.'

'He was,' said a man behind him. 'I can vouch for that.'

'So how did you end up here?' asked Tarw.

'For the same reason as most,' replied the Miller. 'The English killed my family and left me destitute. I want them gone as much as any man.'

'So you are a poor man?'

'Aye, yet I am the first to share my bread. Just ask any man.'

There was a murmur of agreement at the claim for Giles the Miller was indeed a generous man.

'Tell me,' said Tarw, 'I am told you often go to the local farms and villages.'

'As do many of us,' said the Miller. 'We seek roots and corn for the pots. There is no crime in that.'

'And how do you pay?'

'We barter or pay with coins from the common purse. Your wife will vouch for that.'

'I don't doubt the source of the copper coins,' said Tarw, 'but I wonder where you obtained these.' He held up the purse given to him by Robert and tipped it upside down. A rain of silver coins fell to the ground and the crowd gasped in shock.

'Silver pennies,' said Tarw coldly, his eyes not leaving the accused man's face, 'found under the mattress in your tent.'

The crowd fell silent and all eyes turned to the Miller.

'Well,' said Tarw, 'would you care to explain how you have suddenly become so rich while those around you have often gone hungry?'

'It is mine,' said the Miller slowly. 'Fairly earned and saved over time.'

'How?' asked Tarw.

The man struggled for words and looked around the crowd nervously. 'By being frugal,' he said. 'And by negotiating favourable deals.'

'Even though you were trading on behalf of your own people?' replied Tarw. 'If this is true, do you not think that any profit belonged to the cause?'

'There was no crime committed,' said the Miller. 'Every copper coin that was taken from the communal purse was repaid in full or used to buy the stores we needed.'

'Perhaps so, but, even if you are telling the truth, not only did you take advantage of the circumstances to better your own wealth, you also took profit from those least able to afford it.'

'You don't understand,' said the Miller. 'I have a wife and three children to support in Kidwelly. My responsibility is towards them, first and foremost.'

'But you just claimed your family are dead,' said Gwenllian. 'Which is it to be? Are they dead or not?'

'Yes,' said the man, 'I mean, no, but . . .'

Before he could continue one of the crowd stepped forward and spat in his face. Another drew a knife from a sheath and ran towards him.

'*Hold*,' roared Tarw. 'Give him space. No one has been condemned as yet and we will not become the same as those who seek to rule us.' The crowd died down and Tarw turned back to the Miller. 'Giles the Miller,' he continued, 'the coins are proof of greed and avarice only. They will not condemn you but neither do they prove your innocence. You remain accused of spying and if you tell us the truth of your actions then there may be clemency but if you should be found out in a lie, then you will suffer whatever sentence I impose upon you. So I ask again. Are you, or are you not a spy?'

'No,' gasped the man, looking around. 'I am one of you, I swear. If this is about the money then keep it, let me go and you'll never see me again I promise.'

'And that is your last word?'

The accused nodded vigorously, sensing a favourable outcome.

Robert handed Tarw a folded parchment. The prince opened it up and read a series of numbers out loud before handing it back to Robert as the crowd watched in confusion.

'For those of you that do not recognise those numbers,' he said, 'let me enlighten you. They correspond almost exactly to the numbers of archers, foot soldiers and horses we currently have in the Cantref Mawr. In addition, the bottom row lists the amount of swords and number of trained men able to use them.' He turned to face the Miller. 'This list would be invaluable to the English,' he said, 'and was found in the lining of your cloak. You are lying, Giles Miller, you are no more than a treacherous spy in the pay of the enemy.'

For a second everyone froze and suddenly the Miller made a futile dash for freedom. Within seconds he was hauled to the ground and dragged back to face Tarw.

'Comrades of the Cantref Mawr,' he announced, 'this man has been accused before you and stands ready to hear your verdict. How say you, guilty or not guilty?'

'*Guilty,*' roared the crowd and though Tarw held up his hands, it took a while for them to settle down, such was their ire.

'Giles the Miller,' he said eventually, 'you have been found guilty by your fellow men. You had your chance to lay your crimes clean before God but chose the path of deceit. Thus you are hereby sentenced to death with immediate effect.'

As the condemned man's head dropped to his chest in despondency, Tarw summoned every woman of the camp who had been raped, injured or had lost someone to the brutality of the English and they circled the scared man, staring at him intensely.

'Women of the camp,' said Tarw. 'Many of the men have already sampled the sweet taste of revenge upon the battlefield and in the months to come will do so again. You, on the other hand, carry out important roles here in the Cantref Mawr, unable to vent your anger on those responsible for your suffering. The man in front of you is one of those and has been sentenced to death. His fate is now in your hands, do with him as you will.'

For a moment nobody moved but slowly all the women turned to face the spy and as he started begging for mercy, they moved in.

Tarw, Gwenllian and Taliesin turned away as the first of his screams echoed through the camp but before they entered the campaign tent, they could see a familiar face coming towards them on horseback through the trees.

'Dog,' said Taliesin in surprise as he recognised the warrior. 'I was wondering when you would return.'

'As was I' said Dog. 'But this seems as good a time as any.'

'Welcome back,' said Taliesin. 'If you had been but moments earlier you could have led the hunt for a man who escaped justice.'

'I watched from the trees,' said Dog, 'and saw him make his run.'

'So do you know where he is?'

'Aye,' said Dog, 'I do,' and after retrieving something from behind him on his saddle, he threw it to the ground in front of Gwenllian and Tarw. It was the still bleeding head of Dafydd ap Cenyn, the second traitor.

The following morning, the people of Pembroke awoke to see the heads of both spies impaled on spears outside the gates of the castle. A crowd gathered, intrigued as to why they had been put there but up on the palisade, John of Salisbury knew exactly why and he was furious.

'They were the last of our men amongst the rebels,' said Walter de Calais. 'We are now blind to the enemy's plans and movements.'

'Perhaps,' said Salisbury. 'Perhaps not.'

Walter turned to face the new castellan. 'Are you saying there may be another?'

'I am saying nothing,' said Salisbury, 'for there is none I will trust amongst all this, not even you. Let me just say this. If that northern witch thinks she can better me, she is sadly mistaken. I am nothing if not resourceful, my friend, and already there are things afoot that will scratch this itch once and for all.'

He climbed down from the palisade before making his way back up to the keep on the motte. Despite the loss of the wagons and the real threat of a rebel attack, deep inside there was a feeling of excitement and he knew that before him lay a game of chess, though this time with real lives as pieces.

'You have made your opening move, Gwenllian,' he said quietly as he reached the keep. 'Let the game begin.'

The Cantref Mawr

February 10th, AD 1136

Gwenllian walked throughout the camp, talking quietly to the people as she passed. The younger children played happily between the tents while those a little older focussed on the many tasks that needed doing around the camp. Water was brought from the nearby stream, wood collected for the many fires and the increased numbers of horses carefully groomed, ready for the next time they were needed.

Despite the recent losses everyone seemed happier, not least because there was at last enough food to go around. In addition to the stores already plundered from the English wagons, regular supplies were coming in from outlying farms and villages, all keen to play their part in the rebellion. The wounded were being cared for in the few huts already built and new men were arriving in the Cantref Mawr every day, encouraged by the continued success of the hit-and-run tactics carried out by Gwenllian and her men across Deheubarth.

'Good morning, Karin,' said Gwenllian, seeing her old friend sitting at a fire.

'And to you, my lady,' said Karin, standing up.

'Oh, don't get up,' said Gwenllian. 'And when we are alone, please address me as you did when we rode alongside each other all those years ago.'

'I'd like that,' said Karin. 'Perhaps one day we will ride again.'

'You have children, Karin,' said Gwenllian, sitting on a tree trunk placed alongside the fire. 'Your place is here.'

'You also have children,' said Karin, 'yet did you not lead our men into battle just a few days ago?'

'That's different,' said Gwenllian. 'It is a role expected of me. Anyway, tell me of your life since we rode together, and the man you wed.'

Karin smiled but before she could say anything a commotion at the far end of the small valley drew their attention and both got to their feet.

'What's happening?' asked Karin, stepping up onto the log for a better view.

'I don't know,' replied Gwenllian. 'Let's go and find out.' Together the two women walked through the camp, joined by many of the others each keen to see what the commotion was all about.

'Make way,' called Gwenllian when she reached a crowd of people gathered around a man upon a horse. 'What goes on here?'

'My lady,' gasped the rider, 'I have wonderful news. Hywel ap Maredudd's army has engaged the English at Gower castle and emerged victorious.'

'*What?*' asked Gwenllian.

'It's true,' said the rider, struggling to control his horse, 'I heard it from one who was involved. He said the English landed a great force upon the Gower shore but Maredudd was waiting for them. The battle was a terrible thing but the enemy were routed and any survivors ran for their lives.'

The crowd broke into spontaneous cheering and hugged each other in celebration as Gwenllian looked on in astonishment. She had known that Maredudd had left Brycheniog with his army but had no idea he had campaigned so far west. To find out now that not only had he dared to confront an entire English army but, also, deep within the territory they considered safely under England's control was the most encouraging news she could have hoped for.

'Is there anything else?' asked Gwenllian, looking up at the messenger. 'What about casualties?'

'His own casualties are heavy,' said the messenger, 'but the English have lost over five hundred men. It was truly a great victory and surely unprecedented in our lifetime.'

'Where is he going next?' Gwenllian asked. 'Is he going to campaign further north?'

'I know no more,' said the messenger. 'I rode here as soon as I found out. No doubt more news will follow.'

'I appreciate it,' said Gwenllian. 'You are welcome to stay here while your horse recovers and will find hot food at any fireplace.'

'Thank you, my lady,' said the rider and he dismounted as the crowd gathered in to ask him more questions.

'I take it this news makes you happy?' said Karin as the two women walked quickly back through the camp.

'Oh yes,' replied Gwenllian, 'for it is more than just the death of a few Englishmen – this changes the whole landscape right across Deheubarth.'

'In what way?'

Gwenllian stopped walking and turned to her friend. 'In so many ways,' said Gwenllian. 'If this news is true then, for the first time in generations, a Welsh army has defeated the English in full-scale battle. Not only is that a victory in itself, it also gives us credibility. The English will have to take us seriously and any of our countrymen still undecided will flock to our banner. In addition, it gives us credence with the other kingdoms throughout Wales. With news that the English are not invincible, it strengthens their resolve and could lead to alliances across the country, not just in Deheubarth. Hywel ap Maredudd has done more than just give the English a bloody nose, Karin, he has given a country hope.'

———⌣———

Over in Pembroke castle, Walter de Calais had already briefed Salisbury about the shocking news and stood looking at the castellan's back as he stared out of the window in his chambers and across the rooftops of Pembroke town.

'I have increased the guards along the palisade,' said Walter, 'and instructed the steward to fill the castle stores with anything he can get hold of. As we speak, our men are clearing the markets of anything they can carry and our herds are already being brought back from the fields.'

'Why?' asked Salisbury without turning.

'In case of a siege of course,' said Walter. 'With this victory it is entirely possible Maredudd may turn his attentions on us.'

'I don't think so,' said Salisbury, turning around. 'His army is one for open warfare and not one suitable for a siege. To engage in such an action would mean he would have to be able to sustain an assault perhaps over many weeks, and as his men hail from Brycheniog, I see no reason why they would undertake such a task in a Deheubarth. There would be little benefit.'

'Yet they just fought a battle on the coast, does not that indicate Maredudd holds no such reservations?'

'I think not,' said Salisbury. 'Gower castle was an easy target and weakly defended. I would guess that was his primary target and it was chance that he was in the right place at the right time when the fleet landed. Besides, I suspect that despite his victory the Welsh casualties must also be substantial and no doubt he will return to Brycheniog to lick his wounds.'

'Forgive me, my lord, but is that a risk we can take?'

'You can continue making your preparations,' said Salisbury with a sigh. 'After all, it won't hurt to let the locals suffer a bit in retaliation, but trust me, these events are nothing more than minor victories in the greater scheme of things and plans are afoot to crush this rebellion once and for all. Now be gone and report back to me if there are any updates.'

'Of course, my lord,' said Walter. He left the chamber, closing the door behind him.

'Why didn't you tell him?' asked a voice from behind Salisbury and he turned to see Maurice de Londres coming out of a side chamber.

'There is a spy amongst us,' said Salisbury, pouring wine into two goblets, 'and at the moment I am not sure who it may be.'

'But I thought Walter de Calais was one of your trusted men,' said the castellan of Kidwelly castle, 'and has been at your side for years.'

'He has, and his loyalty has been second to none, but the news you have just shared with me is too precious to entrust to anyone.' He picked up a parchment from the table and reread the contents. 'When did this arrive?'

'Yesterday,' said Maurice, 'and was sealed by the king himself. I brought it over as soon as I could so you could make any necessary preparations.'

'It is much appreciated,' said Salisbury. 'And indeed, it seeds my mind with a plan not only to weed out my spy but also to put an end to this nonsense in the Cantref Mawr.'

'I hope you envisage a part for me in all this,' said Maurice. 'My own caravans have suffered badly at the hands of the rebels these past few months and I would welcome the chance to seek revenge.'

'Oh yes,' said Salisbury, 'you have a part to play. In fact, probably the most important part of all.'

'I'll drink to that,' said Maurice as he raised his tankard in a toast. 'To the end of the rebellion.'

'To the end of the rebellion,' agreed Salisbury and he raised his own goblet in salutation.

Several hours later, Nesta sat at her table in her new quarters at the top of the keep. Despite her protestations, Salisbury had insisted on having her original room and as he was now confirmed as the castellan, there had been nothing she could do about the situation. In her lap she held a small, framed tapestry and she sewed quietly, her way to temporarily forget the upset of the world around her. A knock came on the door and she looked up with a sigh, disappointed at being interrupted.

'Come in,' she said and was surprised when John Salisbury entered with a tray upon which was a covered bowl and a flask of wine.

'Master Salisbury,' she said in surprise, 'since when have you waited for an invitation to enter my personal rooms? Usually you would just barge in unannounced.'

'I think you will find that this room belongs to the king,' he replied coldly.

'You know what I mean,' she said. 'What do you want?'

'If I was you, Lady Nesta, I would perhaps ease my tone. My patience will last only so long and if you continue to treat your new castellan with such scorn then I may be forced to take action.'

'You lay a hand on me and I swear I will claw out your eyes,' she replied.

Salisbury sighed and looked at the tray. 'Lady Nesta,' he said, 'you will have to come to a decision sooner or later. We both know our union will make total sense and the sooner you accept it the better. However, I did not come here to discuss that issue but to offer you a gift. I see now that perhaps I was mistaken and will leave you alone to ponder what little future you have.'

'After everything that has happened, do you really expect me to soften my tone just because you have brought some sweetmeats and wine?'

'To be honest, this tray was already being brought up by one of the kitchen staff and I relieved him of it on my way from the stables. Hence my attire.'

Nesta looked at the light cloak the castellan used for any business within the castle grounds. The collar was fox fur and there was some snow still upon the shoulders.

'It's cold out there,' said Salisbury, 'but nothing a good fire won't sort out.' He lifted the cloth off the bowl and looked over to Nesta. 'Some dried berries, too,' he said. 'It's almost a banquet.'

'Enough of the pleasantries, Master Salisbury,' said Nesta. 'You came here for a reason so why don't you spit it out.'

Salisbury walked over to the fireplace, holding out his hands to the welcoming warmth. 'I take it you have heard by now of the success of one of your fellow Welshmen?' he asked over his shoulder.

'I assume you speak of Hywel ap Maredudd?'

'I do, and though the very fact of his heritage makes him my enemy, I admire the way he emerged victorious in such a vicious battle. Do you know him?'

'No,' said Nesta, 'though I have heard of him. Apparently he is a very short-tempered man and fiercely patriotic.'

'Obviously,' said Salisbury. 'And his victory has reminded us that nothing can be taken for granted in these dangerous times.'

'Forgive me,' said Nesta, 'but I am taken aback by your admiration of a Welshman who has apparently killed over five hundred of your fellows. How does that sit comfortably with you?'

'Mainly because most of those killed were French and Flemish,' said Salisbury, 'and tactical excellence is a trait to be admired in any man, no matter what banner he lives beneath.'

'So you would not kill him given the chance?'

'Oh, in a heartbeat,' said Salisbury, 'but that is not the same thing.'

'Are you not worried he may turn his attentions upon you?'

'Not at all. We are behind solid walls, Kidwelly has a full garrison just a few leagues away and Maurice de Londres has pledged his immediate support should any attack come to pass.'

'Yes, I saw him earlier. Is that why he was here?'

'He brought me a message from London,' said Salisbury, tapping the left side of his cloak indicating the inner pocket, 'one I had been expecting for many weeks.'

'So is that the gift you bear?' asked Nesta.

'Unfortunately no, but after he delivered the dispatches, he also conveyed an invitation from his wife for you to spend some time with her at Kidwelly Castle. In the circumstances I totally understand if you wish to decline her offer but at least I can say I passed it on.'

'When is the invitation for?' asked Nesta.

'Anytime,' said Salisbury. 'I am going there myself tomorrow with Maurice de Londres and you are welcome to join us on the journey. You will, of course, be completely safe and have your own quarters at the castle. You could even stay there for a while when I return if it pleases you.'

Nesta looked thoughtfully at the castellan. This was so out of character and though she wasn't convinced of his intentions, the thought of spending some time away from Pembroke was very enticing.

'I'll give it some thought,' she said, 'but I am intrigued, what sort of message is so important that the castellan of Kidwelly has to bring it to Pembroke himself?'

'It is from the king regarding imminent reinforcements for the garrisons but more than that I cannot say, I'm sure you understand.'

'Of course,' said Nesta, 'my heritage prevents me knowing such things lest I pass them on to my fellow Welshmen, correct?'

'Something like that,' said Salisbury. 'Anyway, let me know when you make up your mind. Go or stay, I care not either way.' He turned and strode towards the doorway.

'Master Salisbury,' said Nesta, 'I need no time for consideration. The thought of spending time with Marion appeals to me so, if the offer is still open, then yes, I will go with you to Kidwelly.'

Salisbury nodded. 'Have your maid pack a trunk and I will have it collected in the morning. We will be leaving at noon.' Without another word he left the room leaving Nesta alone in her room.

She watched him go with interest. She did not trust him but at least in Kidwelly she would be safe from his attentions, if only for a couple of weeks.

The following morning Nesta looked out of the window of her room and saw the two castellans both mounting their horses before riding out of the castle along with a column of well-armed horsemen.

'I wonder where they are going?' asked Nesta.

'Who?' asked the maid over her shoulder as she packed Nesta's trunk.

'Salisbury,' said Nesta. 'He has just left with Maurice de Londres.'

'Oh, him,' said Emma. 'I heard the men talking this morning. It seems he is going to extract some overdue taxes from some unfortunate landowner.'

'That must be why we are not leaving until noon,' said Nesta. 'I expect he will be gone some time.'

'To be honest, my lady, I wouldn't lose any sleep if both ended up on the wrong end of an assassin's arrow.'

'Don't speak like that, Emma,' said Nesta quietly. 'It will get you in trouble.'

'I don't care anymore, my lady,' said Emma. 'The man is the devil himself.'

Nesta turned suddenly and walked towards the door.

'Where are you going?' asked Emma.

'Down to my old room,' said Nesta. 'This may be the only chance I get to see what he is up to.'

'But why go to his room?'

'I'm hoping he left something there that I need to see.'

'It'll be locked,' said Emma.

'I know,' said Nesta, 'but I still have a key. Don't worry, I'll be back before you know it.'

'Be careful, my lady,' said Emma, but Nesta was already out of the door.

Back in the rebel camp, Gwenllian, Tarw and the rest of the leaders sat around the table, discussing the momentous news they had received the previous day.

'This is an opportunity too good to miss,' said Taliesin. 'The English will be rocked to the core at such a defeat and with a reduced garrison at Pembroke, they are there for the taking throughout Deheubarth.'

'How?' asked Robert. 'Our strength may be growing but we are nowhere near strong enough to capture Pembroke, let alone Kidwelly.'

'Perhaps not alone,' said Taliesin, 'but could we send messengers to Hywel ap Maredudd and seek an alliance?'

'I don't think that will work,' said Tarw. 'Maredudd suffered heavy casualties at the battle and is headed back to Brycheniog.'

'What about Gwent or Morgannwg?' said Taliesin. 'I heard there are a few groups there that prey on the English lines. Perhaps they could be tempted to join us.'

'No,' said Tarw again. 'There are not enough and too many smaller groups will be disruptive. What we need is a large force, similar to Maredudd's. That way the tactics will be far easier to command.'

'Apart from Maredudd,' said Robert, 'I know of no other man with such an army.'

'Not in the south,' said Bevan, 'but in the north there is a man who has the biggest army in Wales under his command. Gwenllian's father.'

The tent fell silent and everyone stared at him before turning their attention to Gwenllian.

'I don't think that is an option,' said Taliesin. 'We have been refused help in the past.'

'Let the princess answer,' said Bevan. 'What say you, Gwenllian? Your father's strength is renowned across Wales and even the English fear him. Do you think he would be willing to listen?'

'Perhaps,' said Gwenllian. 'The English Crown is in disarray, there is talk of a civil war between the barons, the occupation across Wales is creaking and Maredudd has just proved it is possible for a well-trained army to defeat them on the field of battle. There has never been an opportunity such as this and I think that if I was to go and ask for his support, he would look on it favourably.'

Again there was silence as all the men in the tent looked between each other.

'I'm not sure it is such a good idea,' said Robert. 'To invite another king to fight your battles is courting trouble. What's to stop him declaring himself king of Deheubarth if he is successful?'

'He is my father,' said Gwenllian, 'and he would not do that. Besides, he has a son-in-law and four grandsons who have a claim to the throne of Tewdwr; not even he would be so bold as to try to steal their heritage.'

Taliesin looked at Tarw. 'What do you think? Could it work?'

'Gwenllian knows her father better than any of us,' said Tarw with a shrug. 'He certainly has the numbers and they are a very well-trained army. Even putting aside the blood ties, the chance of defeating the English while they squabble amongst themselves will be very attractive to him. If we are successful, it could take the English a generation to rebuild what they had and, in that time, we can get ourselves organised across Wales. It could be our only chance.'

'Well that settles it,' said Taliesin, turning to Gwenllian. 'You should ride immediately and ask for his support. Go down on your knees and beg if necessary, but we can't do this without him.'

'No,' said Tarw, looking around the tent. 'My wife has become a loved and valued leader and we can't afford for her to be lost now. The road to Gwynedd is hard and beset with brigands so it is safer if she stays in the Cantref Mawr.' He turned to his wife. 'Gwenllian, if you write a note of explanation, I will carry it on your behalf and explain the situation to your father.'

'It makes sense,' said Bevan. 'An absence of even a few days may affect the morale of the camp such is your stature. Allow your husband to go in your place and if your father is agreeable, Tarw can be back within a month with an army at his back. We have waited all these years for such an opportunity so another few weeks is going to be as nothing in comparison.'

Everyone looked at each other again and there was a palpable air of excitement in the tent.

'Are we all agreed?' asked Taliesin.

'Aye,' responded the men and they all turned to Gwenllian, the only person present who had remained silent.

'Gwenllian?' asked Taliesin. 'What say you?'

'I am agreeable,' she said, 'but on one condition. If we are to take the fight to the English, then the boys need to be safe at the palace of Aberffraw.'

'I am going nowhere,' said Morgan from his seat at the end of the table.

'Nor me,' said Maelgwyn. 'My place is here at your side.'

'I understand that you are now men and choose your own path,' said Gwenllian, 'but your brothers are still children and do not have that choice. If we do this, and we all die, then it is possible they could be made orphans with no family left to protect them. At least in the north they will be protected by my father.'

'A fair point,' said Tarw. 'I will take them with me and leave them at Aberffraw when I return.'

'Then it is agreed,' said Taliesin standing up. 'If God is with us and with the support of Gruffydd ap Cynan and his army, before this month is out we will fall upon the invaders like a storm tide.'

Back in the castle, Nesta turned the key and entered the room where she had lived for so many years. It looked much the same except for some extra tables and chests along with a rack containing an assortment of different swords.

Quickly she looked around, moving some discarded clothes from the bed and checking amongst the many dispatches on the table. The chests were locked and there was nothing of interest on the shelves. Disappointed, she turned to leave but stopped suddenly as she saw Salisbury's cloak hanging on the back of the door, the same one he had been wearing the previous night.

'No,' she said to herself, 'surely he wouldn't be that stupid.' She walked across and reached into the inner chest pocket, her heart missing a beat as she felt something within. Quickly she withdrew the parchment and unfolded it to read the contents, her face dropping as the implications of the message became clear.

'Oh, sweet Jesus,' she murmured, reading the message again before folding the parchment back up and replacing it in the pocket. She looked around to make sure the room was exactly as she'd found it before leaving and locking the door behind her. Quickly she ran up the stairs and into her own quarters.

'My lady,' said Emma, 'what's the matter? You look like you have seen a ghost.'

'Not yet, Emma,' she said, her voice shaking, 'but if what I have just read comes to pass, there will be a lot of new ghosts in Deheubarth before this month is out, mostly Welsh.'

'What do you mean?'

'There is an army en route to Deheubarth, Emma, sponsored by the king himself. It seems that during his trip to Westminster, Salisbury begged Stephen for help to put down the rebellion and now the king has seen fit to honour that commitment. If the letter is accurate, there are two forces en route to help stamp out the rebellion – one via horseback from Bristol and the other by sea. My brother needs to know as soon as possible, Emma,' said Nesta, 'but I cannot entrust this information to a letter. I need to speak to him myself.'

'You could meet him again in the postern tower,' replied the maid. 'Do you want me to send him a message?'

'There is no point, I will be on my way to Kidwelly before nightfall. To change my mind now will raise suspicion.'

'What are you going to do?' asked Emma.

'I don't know,' said Nesta, pacing the floor, 'but I have to do something. If this army arrives before Tarw and Gwenllian have time to prepare, they will stand no chance.'

'Let me take the message,' said Emma.

'What do you mean?' asked Nesta.

'I said let me take the message to Tarw,' replied Emma. 'I am allowed outside the castle walls unescorted so just tell me what he needs to hear and I will go myself.'

'But how?' asked Nesta. 'Can you even ride?'

'I was brought up on a farm, my lady, and though it has been many years, it will soon come back to me. All you need to do is tell me what to say and arrange a horse. The rest I can do myself.'

'Do you even know where the Cantref Mawr is?'

'You know I do,' replied Emma, 'but you should make your mind up quickly for the master will be back soon and it will be too late.'

'You are right,' said Nesta, and she ran over to her bed to retrieve a small box.

'These are worth a fortune,' said Nesta, handing over a necklace of precious stones. 'First thing tomorrow morning, go into town, buy a good horse and hire someone you trust to protect you. Head north to the Cantref Mawr but stay on the main tracks. Eventually someone will challenge you. All you have to do is request an audience with Tarw and pass on my message.'

Emma nodded.

'You do know,' said Nesta, 'that if you do this, you can never return here, it will be too unsafe. Stay with Tarw until all this is over and when it is, with God's blessing, I will send for you again.'

'Worry not for me, my lady,' said Emma. 'You just take care of yourself. Now, what is the message you want me to take?'

The Cantref Mawr

February 12th, AD 1136

Gwenllian walked around the clearing with Taliesin, watching the men practise their sword drills. Some struck stakes driven into the ground to increase their power while others fought each other with wooden weapons.

'They improve quickly,' said Gwenllian. 'I am impressed.'

'It is amazing what a few victories and a full belly can do for a man's confidence,' replied Taliesin. 'We have come a long way in a short time.'

'Perhaps,' said Gwenllian. 'Though drills are poor substitutes for the real thing.'

'It is the best we can do at the moment,' said Taliesin, 'but hopefully by the time your father's army arrives we will be more than ready.'

Gwenllian nodded her approval and turned to head back towards the camp. As she walked along the track, she saw Maelgwyn coming towards her.

'There you are,' he said. 'I have been looking everywhere for you.'

'I've been at the training fields,' said Gwenllian. 'Is there something wrong?'

'I don't know,' said Maelgwyn. 'We picked up a woman on the road through the forests and she said she has an important message.'

'From who?'

'I don't know – she refuses to talk to anyone apart from Father or you.'

'Then let's go and see what she has to say,' said Gwenllian with a sigh.

They walked back to the camp and up to the campaign tent where an older woman was waiting with one of the camp guards.

'Hello,' said Gwenllian as she entered and removed her cloak. 'I am Gwenllian ferch Gruffydd. I understand you have a message for me.'

'Not for you, my lady, for your husband.'

'Well my husband is not here,' said Gwenllian, 'so unless your message will wait, I suggest you share it with me.'

The woman looked agitated and glanced between Robert and the princess.

'You look uncomfortable,' said Gwenllian. 'Is there a problem?'

'My lady,' came the reply, 'the message is of vital importance to you here in the Cantref Mawr and will not wait, yet I was instructed it was for Tarw's ears alone.'

'What is your name?' asked Gwenllian, seeing the woman's distress.

'Emma, my lady,' she replied with a bow, 'and I am here on behalf of my mistress.'

'Your mistress being?'

'The lady Nesta ferch Rhys,' said Emma to everyone's surprise. 'I am her personal maid.'

'If you are,' said Gwenllian eventually, 'that means you must have come from Pembroke castle. That's quite a ride through dangerous territory. Why would the lady Nesta risk your life on such a task?'

'Because she would entrust this message to nobody else lest it fell into the wrong hands. The two men currently being guarded by your soldiers were employed for my safety and are loyal to Nesta.'

'I'm sorry, Emma,' said Gwenllian, 'but that is quite a claim. How do I know you are who you say you are?'

'I can vouch for her,' said Robert, walking into the clearing. 'She is the one who passes the messages from Nesta to the pie woman for me to collect.'

'Is this true?' asked Gwenllian, turning to Emma.

'It is, my lady. My mistress was not allowed to leave the castle without an escort so I became the go-between.'

'Then I must give you our thanks,' said Gwenllian. 'You undertake a dangerous task on behalf of Welshmen everywhere.'

'That matters not, my lady,' said Emma. 'The important thing is that you are now all in peril and my mistress sent me here to warn you.'

'Even so, your journey will be in vain if we do not know the nature of the threat.' She paused before continuing. 'Emma, your loyalty to your mistress is admirable but if we are in danger, we need to know. Where is the message?'

'Up here,' said Emma, tapping the side of her head, 'and in the circumstances I think she will be content that I share it with you.' She glanced briefly at Robert and Maelgwyn before continuing. 'She said to tell you that five days from today, a column of three hundred well-trained men-at-arms under the command of ten English knights will arrive at Kidwelly castle on the road from Carmarthen. At the same time, another two hundred men will meet two cargo ships at the dock in Burry. Their task is to supply a caravan of empty carts to take the ships' cargo and bring it to Kidwelly with all haste.'

'Do you know what this cargo consists of?' asked Robert.

'We do,' replied Emma. 'There will be all the weapons, armour and stores needed to support a lengthened campaign of aggression against the Welsh. Apparently when they all muster at Kidwelly Castle, they will join forces to form the vanguard of a bigger army to be drawn from all the garrisons across Deheubarth. When they are at full strength they intend to fall upon the Cantref Mawr and wipe out the rebellion once and for all. It is estimated they will number in excess of three thousand men, all well armed, well trained and well supplied, with more to follow as needed. She said to tell you, my lady, it is nothing short of a full-scale invasion.'

Everyone stared in shock at the news and for a few moments there was silence in the tent.

'How do you know all this?' asked Robert eventually.

'My mistress read it herself on a document signed by the king's hand. The new castellan has already ridden to Kidwelly to make preparations with Maurice de Londres to receive the two forces.'

'Where is your mistress now?' asked Gwenllian. 'I need to talk to her.'

'You can't,' said Emma. 'She has gone with John of Salisbury. That is why I had to come. She could not withdraw from the journey without raising suspicion.'

'It could be a trick,' suggested Maelgwyn, 'designed to lure us out of hiding.'

'No,' said Emma. 'I was with her moments before my mistress found the document. It was locked in the castellan's rooms and she risked her life to find it.'

'Nesta has never let us down before,' said Gwenllian, 'and I see no reason to disbelieve her now.'

'So what do you want to do?' asked Robert.

'I need to think,' said Gwenllian. 'Summon all the leaders to meet us here at dusk.' She turned to Emma. 'You have provided a great service and possibly prevented a massacre. You are welcome to stay with us in our family hut as a guest until this is over.'

'Thank you, my lady,' said Emma. 'Is there anything else you require of me?'

'No, go and rest. Maelgwyn will show you where to go.'

Her son led the maid from the tent leaving Gwenllian alone, and for the first time in her life, the princess felt the icy needles of genuine fear creeping through her veins.

——— ———

Later that night, Gwenllian stood behind the table in the campaign tent, waiting for the chatter to die down. Those she had appointed as leaders had already been briefed as to the risk and now they were in the midst of a full-blooded and robust debate. Though it was noisy, Gwenllian was astute enough to know that the men had to be allowed to vent their shock and anger before she could address what really mattered. Eventually the ruckus died down and she nodded slightly towards Robert, letting him know she was ready to begin.

'Comrades,' he said loudly, 'enough. We have all had our say and there have been many points of view expressed on both sides of the argument. Everyone here has a valid point but we need to stay focussed and come through this with a plan.' He turned to Gwenllian. 'My lady, throughout this you have remained silent. Perhaps you can share your own thoughts with us.'

Gwenllian nodded and walked around the table to stand in the middle of the tent as the men formed a circle around her.

'The way I see it is this,' said Gwenllian. 'We have three options. First of all, we pack everything up, strike camp and retreat to the safety of Ceredigion. No matter how big their army, they will struggle to find us amongst the forests and mountains and we can continue to fight a war of attrition. We will have to keep moving, staying in one place for short periods only before moving on. This is by far the safest choice and it will ensure our families are unlikely to be put at risk.'

She looked around the room as the men considered the option. 'The second option,' she continued, 'is that we wait until Tarw returns with my father's army. We hide here in the Cantref Mawr, and as soon as they arrive, we face the English on a battlefield of our choice and seek the sort of victory recently experienced by Hywel ap Maredudd at Gower. However, at the moment we don't know how many my father will send, if indeed any. Even if they do come and they are a thousand strong, that makes our numbers just under two thousand in total, still less than the full English army once they have mustered.'

'I would put a Welshman fighting for freedom against any two English fighting for coin on any day,' said Taliesin.

'Let's not let our hearts rule our heads, Taliesin,' said Gwenllian. 'We all know your passion but many of our men have never wielded a sword in anger.'

'I will not run, Gwenllian,' said Taliesin, 'no matter what words are spouted this night. You can run and hide if you want but me and my men intend to take the fight to the English and if we die while doing so, then so be it.'

'Nobody is talking about running,' said Gwenllian above the voices raised in support of Taliesin, 'but we have to know the options before we set out upon a path that cannot be changed once taken. Now, I said there are three options, and if you listen to me I will explain the third.'

'Quiet!' roared Lord Bevan over the noise. 'You are acting like unruly children, not men of war.'

Shocked at the outburst from the slight man, everyone fell silent and turned back towards Gwenllian.

'The third option,' she continued with a sigh, 'is my preferred choice, though it is the riskiest of all three. We know that they aim to muster all the garrisons across Deheubarth and will have in excess of three thousand men within weeks. If we allow them that luxury, any chance of victory for us will vanish as quickly as the morning mist. What we have to do is to prevent them doing that and, in the process, keep them under pressure until Tarw returns with the northern army. If we can keep them fragmented and guessing as to our numbers and tactics, we will have a chance. When Tarw returns, our forces can link together while the English cower behind palisades and shield walls. That way, before they have a chance to muster the rest of their army, we can fall upon them with all our might.'

'I see the sense in the idea,' said Bevan, 'but there are two armies to confront, one in the south with the ships and another riding from Carmarthen on the same day. You said yourself, our men are not battle-hardened and will struggle without your father's army to support them.'

'I know,' said Gwenllian, 'but my plan does not include any frontal assaults on either force.' She walked back to the far side of the table. 'Gather around,' she said, 'for you need to see the chart.'

Once everyone was in place she indicated the map dominating the table. 'This is Burry Dock,' she said, pointing at a location drawn on the map. 'The place where we suspect the ships' stores will be unloaded. We know they will be escorted by experienced men, but two hundred we can deal with. I suggest we send three hundred of our men to harry the caravan from the moment the ships dock to the time they reach Kidwelly and do everything we can to delay them, felling trees across the road and diverting streams onto the tracks to bog down the wheels of the carts. Our archers can attack from the tree line and target the oxen before disappearing like frightened birds back into the forests. If they decide to pursue our men, others can attack from a different direction and do the same. The enemy may be prepared for battle but they cannot fight men they cannot find.'

'Why can we not just kill them and be done with it?' said Taliesin.

'That would take too many men,' said Gwenllian, 'and we would no doubt suffer casualties. By doing it this way, we will wear down those guarding the supply wagon and hold up the supplies. Without those it will be far more difficult for them to organise their army.'

'My question still stands,' said Taliesin. 'Why not fall upon them with everything we have, slaughter the English and keep the stores for ourselves? Without those supplies there can be no war.'

'Because you are forgetting the second column,' said Gwenllian, pointing at a row of chess pieces representing the mounted column on the road from Carmarthen. 'If we focus all our attentions on the ships, this column will reach Kidwelly unchallenged and join with Maurice de Londres' men. We all know Kidwelly already has a strong garrison, and if those two forces combine, they will be a formidable foe and hard to defeat, even with my father's army.'

'So what do you suggest?' asked Bevan.

'What I propose,' said Gwenllian, 'is that while our men harry the supply wagons on the coast, the rest will lie in ambush somewhere along this road and attack the main column. The trees on the higher ground alongside the road give us a huge advantage and we can be amongst them before they know we are there.'

'It sounds like they are a well-armed foe,' said Robert.

'I know, but we will outnumber them at least two to one and we will use the best of our men in the attack. With the advantage of surprise, I am sure we can emerge victorious, and even if we do not kill them all, their numbers will be decimated and it will delay their plans long enough for Tarw to return. When he does, I propose we immediately press home a full-scale assault on Kidwelly and burn it to the ground.'

She stopped and looked around the tent. Some of the men were talking quietly between themselves, discussing the various advantages or drawbacks of the plan.

'I have a question,' said Taliesin. 'The assault on the horsemen is by far the more dangerous of the two and the chances are we will suffer heavy casualties, even with the advantage of surprise. Who do you intend to lead these men?'

'I will be at their head,' said Gwenllian without a pause, 'and will be proud to do so. The first assault is the most important and sets out our stall. We need to summon the berserkers within us and strike fear right into the Englishmen's hearts, for after that they will be on their guard.'

'And the other men?'

'I am happy for you to make your own decisions about who is responsible,' said Gwenllian.

'I will also be amongst those who fight the second column,' said Taliesin. 'I suggest Robert here has the necessary mettle to undertake the task, accompanied by Dog.'

'Are you comfortable with the role, Robert?' asked Gwenllian.

'Aye,' came the reply.

'Dog?'

The warrior shrugged his shoulders, indicating his indifference.

'So be it,' said Gwenllian. 'In that case, although there is much to plan, can I assume that we are all in agreement and it is the third option that we will pursue?'

The men in the tent looked around, each nodding and asserting their approval.

'Make no mistake,' said Gwenllian, 'this enemy will present a formidable challenge, especially the column on the Carmarthen Road, and many of our own men will die in this campaign, but we have been hitting stakes with wooden swords for too long. It is now time to put our training to good use.'

'Aye,' shouted the men in unison.

'Tomorrow we will muster the men,' she continued, 'and go through the finer details, but tonight we will allow ourselves a taste of freedom.' She looked towards the flap of the tent as two young men carried in a cask of ale and removed the lid.

'Fill your jacks, my friends,' said Gwenllian, 'for there will be no more celebration until Kidwelly Castle lies in a pile of ashes.'

The men in the tent each took one of the many tankards out of a sack and dipped them in the cask.

Gwenllian walked over and dipped her own jack into the ale before turning back to face the men.

'Only God knows what outcome lies before us,' she said, 'so this toast is for every soul who will stand beside us on the field of battle.' She looked around at the many warriors, recognising the hungry look in their eyes. For too long they had plied their trade amongst the forests and shadows. Now it was time to step out and do what every one of them believed they had been born to do: regain freedom from the invaders. She raised her jack into the air. *'To those about to die,'* she shouted, *'and those about to live!'*

'Gwenllian,' roared the men in response as the princess downed her ale, and as one, they emptied their own tankards. The decisions had been made and their path was set before them.

The Carmarthen Road

February 16th, AD 1136

The lack of cloud cover meant that the night was even colder than Gwenllian could have expected. However, the extra light afforded by the half-moon meant the journey down past Dynevor Castle and through the hills of Deheubarth had been made a little easier along the hidden pathways known only to those locally born. Behind her came over four hundred men, each wrapped in heavy furs against the cold and weighed down by their weapons. Due to the nature of the route, they had no horses and were relying on whatever they carried. There would be no resupply, no extra food and no reinforcements. The commitment was total.

Some men relished the chance to at last strike a serious blow against the occupying forces but most were nervous, unsure about their chances against men both better armed and trained. Their preparation had been intense but skills against comrades with practise weapons were little use against a ferocious enemy experienced in the way of killing.

During the frequent rest stops, the younger men whispered amongst themselves, talking about the forthcoming fight, and while their zeal was encouraging, those more experienced in warfare kept themselves to themselves, taking the opportunity to eat or sharpen their blades knowing full well that warfare in any form was a terrible thing and, even if they were victorious, many of those sat around them would not be coming back.

As they sat, sergeants walked amongst them, offering encouraging words and advice, keeping the men's minds focussed on why they were setting out upon this mission: to help secure the freedom of their kingdom for their families and generations to come. The odd few were scared, their eyes staring into the night as they contemplated the blood-bath that was to come, and it was these men that took up most of the sergeants' attention. The last thing they needed was scared men fleeing wildly into the night, not only because it weakened their strength but it also risked them being discovered before a blow could be struck in anger.

Eventually, they continued through the forests and over the hills, staying away from the skyline wherever possible to avoid being seen by anyone foolish enough to be out in the biting cold.

Due to the distance and the numbers involved, they had taken three days to get to the ambush area, travelling only at night and lying up in dense undergrowth during the day, hidden from man and beast alike. It was imperative they reached the ambush position without being seen.

For what seemed like the hundredth time that night, Gwenllian put up her hand and one by one, four hundred men behind her dropped silently to the ground as she waited to see what the returning scouts had to say.

'*Over here,*' she whispered as they approached and within seconds, two men dropped to their knees beside her.

'The road is on the far side of this hill,' said one of the scouts, 'and is lined on this side by trees and heavy undergrowth. I think it is as good a position as we can hope to find.'

'Show me,' she said and together, the two scouts, Bevan and herself made their way to the top of the slope, dropping down onto all fours as they neared the ridge. The final approach was done at a crawl and finally she peered out over the flatlands that led down to the coast.

In the distance she could see the dim glow of the fires from the town of Kidwelly and on a spur of land above it, the wooden fortress that was Kidwelly castle. Though she could see no one upon the palisade, the several burning torches moving along the wall indicated it was well manned and well guarded. Between her position and the castle was a wide open plain, the trees long gone, not just for timber for the fires and for building but also as a necessity to enable a clear view from the castle palisade in case of assault.

Silently, the scout pointed down the slope to their front and, in the starlight, she could see the road stretching away in both directions. A few hundred paces to her right, it forked, with one track heading towards the castle while the other continued westward. The attack would have to be made before the column reached the junction or their targets would have a straight escape down the road to Kidwelly.

'Over there,' she whispered, pointing to her left. 'The trees are denser and closer to the path. We will lie up there and set the trap.'

'Are you sure?' asked Bevan. 'The fields below the road are an easy retreat should they decide to run.'

'It is open ground,' said Gwenllian, 'with no cover. Any that run will be easy pickings for our archers, besides, they can't run far.' She pointed to the far side of the fields and Bevan could just about make out the reflection of the moon on the surface of some water.

'It's a stream feeding the Gwendraeth River,' said Gwenllian, referring to the watercourse on the far side of the castle. 'It's not wide but it is at least chest deep and will slow down anyone stupid enough to try to cross it.' She looked up and down the position again before indicating they should withdraw.

Several minutes later they were back amongst the relative safety of the bushes on the reverse side of the hill.

'It looks fine,' said Gwenllian, 'and I want to be in position before dawn. Pass the word to the men: they are to eat what they can now. It may be the last chance they get before the battle.' Bevan nodded and crept down the line to brief some of the lesser commanders as Gwenllian turned to her scouts.

'Have your men head towards Carmarthen,' she said. 'Stay off the road and make sure they are not seen. I want early warning of when the enemy approach.'

'Consider it done,' said the scout and he disappeared into the night.

Gwenllian looked up at the sky and reckoned they had about four hours of darkness left. She reached into the food pouch on her belt and withdrew a chunk of dried pork, chewing quietly as she contemplated that if it was going to be her last meal, it was a humble one.

Several leagues to the south, Robert and Dog had taken no such precautions. They and their men were on horseback and had ridden hard through the day to cover the ground needed if they were to reach the dock at Burry before the resupply ships landed. They had made good time and were now camped in the forest near the village, hidden from sight behind a row of hills.

Several communal fires warmed pots of hot ale along with some hastily concocted broth from dried meat, and though the men were tired from the hard ride, not one of them was willing to lie down and sleep. Every moment of life was treasured as a soldier, especially the night before battle.

'Are they there yet?' asked Robert, standing up from his fire as Dog approached.

'No,' said Dog, 'neither are they anchored offshore.'

'Good,' said Robert. 'Then they obviously haven't arrived yet. We will have time to prepare properly.'

'I'm not so sure,' said Dog. 'There is no sign that they are expecting any ships.'

'What makes you say that?'

'There are no carts upon the dock,' said Dog, 'and the taverns are empty. The whole place just seems a bit quiet.'

'The information from our contact hasn't been found wanting yet, Dog,' said Robert. 'They will be here.'

The Carmarthen Road

February 17th, AD 1136

Gwenllian was fast asleep wrapped in her heavy furs when Taliesin shook her gently by the shoulders.

'Gwenllian,' he said quietly, 'dawn is here, drink some of this.'

Gwenllian opened her eyes to see Taliesin holding a leather jack.

'What's that?' she asked.

'Hot broth,' he said quietly. 'There's not much but at least it will warm your insides.'

'I said no fires,' said Gwenllian sitting up.

'Gwenllian,' said Taliesin, 'there are over two hundred armed men along this tree line and another two hundred behind the hill to our rear. Each have been here since yesterday morning with no food and only honeyed water to drink. They are freezing to their bones and needed something hot else they will be no good to us on the field of battle. Don't worry, the fires were well shielded.'

Gwenllian looked at Taliesin realising he was right. The expected column had not turned up the previous day and without fires or food, her men were suffering badly.

'Is there any sign of the column?' she asked, sitting up and taking the broth in both hands.

'Not yet. One of the scouts came in a little while ago and said they rode almost halfway to Carmarthen but there was no sign. How long do you intend that we stay?'

'I don't know,' said Gwenllian. 'Nesta hasn't been wrong before, so I am reluctant to withdraw.'

'Then I would recommend staying until dusk only,' said Taliesin. 'We can leave scouts upon the road from here to Carmarthen and at the first sign, return with all haste. We will be in no fit state to do ourselves justice unless the men get properly fed and well rested.'

'Understood,' said Gwenllian. 'If there is still no sign by dusk, we will withdraw.'

Taliesin sat down beside her and sipped on his own drink.

She looked across to a nearby thicket. Both Maelgwyn and Morgan sat with their backs against their own trees, talking quietly between themselves. Gwenllian smiled to herself. Though the circumstances were unfortunate, it was good to see them getting on.

'They are good boys,' said Taliesin seeing her gaze. 'You must be very proud.'

'I am,' said Gwenllian, 'and though I know they will do themselves justice, I just can't help wishing they didn't have to go through all this.'

'Is it not what you have lived for all your life?' asked Taliesin, chewing on the end of a twig.

'For *my* life, yes,' she replied turning to face the warrior, 'but they have spent most of theirs thinking warfare was for other people. Especially Maelgwyn, he remembers nothing of the last time we rode as rebels.'

'He is proud of you, Gwenllian,' said Taliesin, 'they both are. Just revel in the fact that they are good men, true and proud. Whatever God has in store for them today or in the future, their paths are now their

311

own and they are here beside you because they want to be, not because you told them to.'

Gwenllian smiled at Taliesin and returned her gaze towards Kidwelly Castle in the distance.

'Do you really think we can take it?' she asked quietly.

'If we can emerge victorious from the battle before us,' replied Taliesin, 'I see no reason why not, especially with your father's army at our side. Victory begets victory and should we win, the rebellion will be like a ball of snow rolling down a mountain, gathering speed and strength with every second that passes. Everything relies on today, Gwenllian. The future will belong to whoever carries the day.'

'Then let us hope that God is with us,' said Gwenllian.

Gwenllian sipped on the welcoming broth and peered through the foliage to her front. The determined focus of the previous few days was waning due to the discomfort of the wait and she knew that if she was feeling it, her men must be suffering far worse. She had experienced this a hundred times over the years but most of those hidden amongst the trees around her were new to warfare.

As the warmth of the hot drink seeped down into her innards she allowed herself to think again of her sons. The two youngest should soon be safe at Aberffraw and even if the day went against her, at least she would die knowing they would be safe growing up amongst her family in Gwynedd.

As for the other two, she worried about what lay before them in the next few hours. Neither were experienced but they were both were well trained with their weapons and, as much as she had wanted to send them away to safety, they were both grown men and had committed to the cause.

She knew the first few moments were crucial in any battle but once they had seen their first men killed, the initial shock would pass. After that their fate was in their own hands, and those whom they called comrade.

———————

Several leagues away, Dog and Robert stood on a hill high above the village of Burry.

'This is ridiculous,' said Robert from his vantage point. 'There are no ships as far as I can see and we were told they would be here yesterday.'

'I told you,' said Dog at his side, 'something is wrong. Do you want me to go into the town and find out what's going on?'

'Yes,' said Robert, 'but keep the reasons to yourself. We have no idea who is or isn't loyal to the cause.'

'Understood,' said Dog and he walked back down the hill to retrieve his horse. Half an hour later, he tied his horse to a hitching rail outside a tavern near the dock and walked in to the stifling heat from the huge fire roaring in the stone hearth.

'A good day to you stranger,' said the landlord. 'Hot ale?'

'Aye,' said Dog, looking around the room.

The landlord went to the pot hanging over the fire while Dog sat at a table in the corner.

'Here you are,' said the landlord, placing the full tankard on the table. 'Do you want food? We have crabs and fish freshly caught just yesterday. They make a fine soup with plenty of meat.'

'Aye, it sounds good,' said Dog.

The landlord disappeared into the back room while Dog sipped on his drink, quietly minding his own business.

'You're not from around here,' said a voice and Dog looked over to a man sitting at a table near the fire.

'No, I'm from Llandeilo,' said Dog. 'I'm here looking for work.'

'Work?' laughed the man. 'You'll be lucky. In case you haven't noticed, it's winter out there and the dock is quiet. Not many boats to unload in this weather.'

'I was led to believe there may be a few due in,' said Dog, 'and was hoping to earn a few coins unloading.'

'No ships due in as far as I know,' said the man and he shouted through the door leading to the rear room. 'Gwyn, do you know of any cargo ships due to dock in the next few days?'

'No,' replied the landlord from the back. 'Why?'

'Our new friend here was asking.'

'Nothing for two weeks,' shouted the landlord again. 'At least, nothing scheduled.'

'Sorry, my friend,' said the first man with a hint of a smirk, 'it seems you are unlucky.'

Dog's mind worked furiously. Either Nesta's intelligence had been wrong or they had the wrong dock. He decided to enjoy the hot ale so as not to arouse suspicion before taking the worrying news back to Robert.

'So what do you do around here when there is no work?' asked Dog.

'Look after the swine,' said the man with a shrug, 'catch fish, whatever we can do to keep death from the door.'

'Shouldn't you be out there?' asked Dog sipping the hot ale. 'It's cold but the sun is out. Is it not a good day for fishing?'

'Indeed it is,' said the man. 'However I still have some coins left from the last ship that docked and it is a while since I enjoyed such wealth.' He guffawed at his own joke before draining his tankard and banging it on the table. 'Landlord, more ale,' he roared and followed it up with another laugh.

'So when was the last ship?' asked Dog.

'Five days ago,' said the man. 'In fact there were two ships. There wasn't much work to be had in truth but I was one of the lucky few.'

'But you said there were no ships,' said Dog.

'I said there were none due,' said the man. 'You didn't ask me about those that had already landed.'

Dog stared at the half-drunk man, his heart racing. 'What did you unload?' he asked.

'Why do you want to know?' asked the man. 'They've gone, you've missed out and that is all there is to it.'

Dog's patience ran out and he drew his knife before kicking away the table and lunging for the man, pressing his knife against his throat. 'You listen to me,' he hissed. 'You will tell me everything I ask or I swear you are a dead man.'

The man's eyes bulged with fear and he nodded vigorously.

'Right,' said Dog, 'I want to know what you unloaded and which way the carts went for there is no sign upon the road.'

'There were no carts,' gasped the man. 'There were riders only.'

'You are lying,' said Dog, increasing the pressure on his blade. 'I was told there would be a cargo of supplies and two hundred soldiers here to escort them. That will take a whole column of carts. Now where are they?'

'No,' said the man, his voice shaking with fear, 'you are wrong. Both ships were carrying men and horses only. They docked and were away within hours headed inland. Check the northern path, you will see for yourself.'

'The northern path?'

'Aye, it is a hidden path and leads inland for two leagues before swinging north. It is of poor quality but hidden from the eyes of most.'

'If it is a hidden path, how did they know which way to go? Did you tell them?'

'No,' gasped the man, 'they were met by a guide. He was here for two days, talking little and keeping himself to himself. When they had disembarked, it was he who led the way.'

'And do you know this man's name?'

'No, my lord. He was a stranger.'

Dog grimaced, realising that somehow they had missed their quarry. 'How many?' he asked, determined to get what information he could.

'How many what?'

'Men,' roared Dog, 'horses, weapons, anything. Tell me what you saw!' He increased the pressure on the blade drawing a thin line of blood.

'About five hundred in all,' gasped the man, 'each mounted and heavily armed. There were also about another fifty pack horses with heavy burdens.'

'What were the riders wearing?'

'Heavy cloaks but I could see the coifs of many as they rode past. It looks like they were ready to fight.'

Dog withdrew his blade and glared at the terrified man sat on the bench before him. 'If I find out you were lying,' he said, 'I swear I will be back to finish the job.'

'He is not lying,' said a voice and he turned to see the landlord standing in the doorway holding a fishing gaff threateningly in his arms. 'There were about five hundred in all and each armed to the teeth. Like he said, they rode directly north away from the coastal path so if you want to know more, go and ask them yourself, just get out of my tavern.' He lowered the gaff so it was aimed at Dog's stomach.

For a few seconds Dog was tempted to kill them both, a task he could easily accomplish alone but finally he realised this situation was not of their making and he had far more important things to do.

'One more thing,' said Dog, turning back to the first man. 'You may not know his name but was there anything about the guide that looked familiar?'

'No,' said the man, 'he was a stranger to me, but I did notice one thing about him.'

'And that was?'

'He had a deep scar running down his right cheek.'

Dog stared for a moment, absorbing the implications.

'You have what you came for,' interrupted the landlord, 'now get out.'

Dog tossed a silver penny onto a nearby table.

'That's for the ale,' he said, 'and give the soup to my friend there.' Without waiting for a reply, he walked quickly out of the tavern.

———

'What do you mean five days ago?' asked Robert, back on the hill. 'That is not possible, we would have seen them.'

'There are other roads back to Kidwelly,' said Dog. 'Apparently they are more difficult to find but they had a guide and if I am not mistaken, it was Tomas Scar.'

'*Tomas Scar,*' gasped Robert. 'I thought he was dead?'

'As did we all,' said Dog, 'but the coincidence is too great. He knows all the hidden pathways of Deheubarth and has exactly the same scar as the guide was said to have had. I think someone knew we were coming and sent him here to lead the soldiers away from conflict.'

'But why?' asked Robert. 'Even if that is true, with such a powerful army at their disposal, why lure us here only to avoid us when they could have set an ambush? It just doesn't make sense.'

'It does if you had a different target in mind,' said Dog.

Robert stared at the warrior. 'By the devil's teeth,' he said eventually as the full horror struck home. 'You mean . . .'

'They've gone for Gwenllian,' said Dog. 'The princess is walking into a trap!'

The Carmarthen Road

February 17th, AD 1136

The day was quiet, unnaturally so, and despite the temperature, the skies were clear. Gwenllian sat with her back against the trunk of one of the few giant trees amongst the forest edge. Her cloak was wrapped tightly around her body and she stared out across the plain towards the distant Kidwelly Castle. She started to doze as the afternoon sun warmed her face and was slipping into a much-needed deeper sleep when she was jerked awake as suddenly as if falling from a horse. For a few seconds she just looked around, unsure about what had woken her.

'What was that?' she gasped looking over to Taliesin.

'I don't know,' said the warrior as he got to his feet. 'It sounded like a scream.'

Gwenllian looked across at her sons. It was obvious that they too had heard something and were peering back up the slope to their rear. Another scream echoed through the trees and she jumped to her feet as more voices joined the first. Within seconds, the deathly silence of the previous two days was torn apart as the unmistaken sound of fighting filled the air.

'*We're under attack*,' roared Gwenllian. 'Look to your weapons.'

Everyone in earshot jumped to their feet, and as the warning spread, two hundred armed Welshmen stared nervously into the thicket above them.

'Where are they?' shouted Maelgwyn. 'I see nobody.'

'It's coming from up there,' shouted Morgan pointing his sword up the hill. 'It sounds like our rear lines are under attack.'

Gwenllian spun around to stare down at the Carmarthen Road, half expecting to see the English column but the road was clear in both directions, as was the open countryside stretching away to Kidwelly Castle in the distance.

'I don't understand it,' she gasped. 'How are they behind us, there are no paths back there?'

'There are if you know where to look,' said Taliesin. 'Either we were seen getting into position or we have been betrayed by someone who knows the lay of the land. Whatever the reason, now is not the time to consider such things, we have to do something and fast.'

Gwenllian looked up the hill to the sound of the battle. The choices raced through her mind like galloping horses. Should she lead the men at the bottom of the hill in a counteroffensive without knowing who they faced, should they retreat onto the road and make their escape, thus leaving their rear unprotected, or should they go firm here and make a stand?

'*Gwenllian*,' shouted Taliesin above the noise of the battle, 'we need to do something. If we remain strung out like this, they will pick us off one by one. What are your orders?'

Gwenllian looked in both directions and could see all eyes focussed on her, waiting for her to give a command. She knew that the men were nervous and looking for leadership. A few dozen paces up the hill she could see the grass-covered line of an old embankment, now no more than a fold in the slope but it was something and she needed a focus.

'Pass the word,' she shouted, 'everyone to merge on me. Move yourselves and form a defensive line on that mound. Shields to the fore and lances in the second rank.'

Those in earshot shouted down along the tree line while those further up the hill retreated back to the embankment. For several minutes there was chaos as men ran from every direction while Taliesin and Gwenllian tried to make sense of the situation. The noise of battle from further up the hill got closer and Gwenllian was sorely tempted to lead those still alongside her into the fray but it was an uphill slog against a force of unknown strength.

Finally the men formed themselves into a defensive formation facing up the hill, shoulder to shoulder, protected by a shield wall. Behind them was a line of lance bearers, each resting their weapons on the shoulders of those in the front rank. Behind those were the sword bearers, the men who had excelled on the training fields before, finally, the archers formed the rear rank.

Taliesin and Gwenllian marched back and forth behind the defences, barking orders and forming the men into a strong position. The human wall curved backwards on either end to protect their flanks and with the ground being unsuitable for cavalry, they knew that it was unlikely anyone would pass them by to attack their rear. As long as the road stayed unoccupied, they could focus their attention up the hill.

Morgan and Maelgwyn stood shoulder to shoulder in the third rank, each with swords drawn. The noise from above was getting louder and they looked at each other nervously.

'Look to your weapons,' shouted Gwenllian again. 'I know not what has happened up there but they will not find us unprepared. If they attack, lean into the shields with all your might. Archers, do not wait for any commands. If the enemy attack you are to loose your arrows as fast as you are able. Make every one count and when you have no more, join the rest of us in the struggle.'

Taliesin ran over, his breath laboured after running along the lines.

'How many do we have?' asked Gwenllian quietly.

'About two hundred,' said Taliesin, 'no more than that.'

'It will have to do. You take the left, I will take the right.' She looked around at the defensive line, now rock solid and silent in their demeanour, each man focussed on the slope above.

'Listen,' said Gwenllian. Taliesin turned to face the hill. Gradually the noise was dying down and though they could hear the commands of unseen men echoing through the trees, the sounds of battle had all but disappeared.

'What do you think?' she asked.

'I think we are in deep trouble,' said Taliesin as one voice repeated itself over and over again on the hill, 'because that man, whoever he is, is speaking in Flemish and if my poor command of the language serves me at all, he is readying his men for a second assault.'

Gwenllian swallowed hard. If Taliesin was correct, then over half of her force must lie dead or dying high amongst the forest trees. 'They must have taken them by complete surprise,' she said eventually, 'but they will find no such complacency here. Keep the men sharp, Taliesin, this is going to be the fight of our lives.' She drew her own sword and walked along the rear of the defensive position, giving encouragement and advice, her words strong but calm. Taliesin did the same in the opposite direction. The unseen Flemish man's voice eventually died away and soon quiet returned to the forest, an eerie, unnatural silence that promised many dreadful things.

'Do you think they have gone?' asked Maelgwyn.

'No, lad,' said Taliesin from behind, 'they are up there and probably watching us as we speak. You just focus on what is expected of you.'

Gwenllian stopped walking and looked back up the hill. Her attention had been caught by movement and as she stared, a fully armoured soldier walked into view, clad in a heavy chainmail hauberk, a coif and the sort of helmet favoured by the Norman knights. In his hands she could see a large sword, already bloodied from an unknown number of victims.

As she watched, similarly clad men emerged from the trees to stand alongside him and soon there was over a hundred, each staring at the Welsh defensive line below. Further movement could be seen amongst the trees beyond and Gwenllian knew that her own men were probably vastly outnumbered.

'Steady,' she shouted to her lines. 'Hold firm. There is no room for them to manoeuvre amongst the trees so they cannot all attack at the same time. Stay steadfast and we will prevail.'

As every pair of Welsh eyes stared at the men forming up on the hill above, one of the enemy stepped forward and hurled something in the air to fly over the defensive lines and land at Gwenllian's feet. When she looked down to see what it was, her heart sank as she recognised the severed head of Lord Bevan of Llandeilo. Feeling sick to her stomach, she turned and glared at the grinning knight above. A few minutes ago she had contemplated trying to negotiate a withdrawal but at the sight of her friend's head on the floor of the forest, all such thoughts disappeared.

'Stand firm, men of Wales,' she shouted, still staring at the knight. 'They bleed like any other men.'

Up above, the Flemish knight raised his bloody sword and shouted his own commands. His warriors roared their support and banged their swords against their shields. The noise was intimidating and as they started to run down the hill, Gwenllian knew that the odds were stacked heavily against her own army.

'*Ready,*' she shouted.

'*Aye,*' roared her men in response.

'*Then let this be the day we change our world,*' roared Gwenllian. '*Lock shields.*'

The front wall of Welshmen locked together as tightly as they could and as each said a silent prayer, the front wave of the enemy smashed into them like the winds of a winter storm.

The Carmarthen Road

February 17th, AD 1136

'*Hold firm*,' roared Gwenllian as the force of the assault pushed the Welsh line back. 'Rear ranks, add your weight.'

All along the defensive line, men leaned their shoulders against the backs of those before them, locking their legs against the frozen ground, desperate to provide a solid buttress, but the attackers already impaled on the Welsh lances proved their undoing and those coming behind used their bodies as macabre ramps to leap over the front line and land amongst those at the rear. Others just smashed straight through the shield wall, carried by their momentum and aided by the relative inexperience of the defenders.

Immediately Gwenllian knew they faced vastly experienced and battle-hardened men, and as the Welsh swordsmen turned to defend their backs, one-on-one fights broke out all along the line. The immediate weakening of the shield wall meant even more attackers broke through and within moments the lines collapsed and the fighting turned into a full-scale battle between two desperate armies, one brutally efficient, the other, inexperienced and fighting for their lives.

Gwenllian raced into the fray, lashing out at the unprotected faces of the Flemish warriors. Her sword cleaved its way through flesh and bone and she fought ferociously beside Taliesin. Her fervour inspired fresh efforts from those around her and men stunned by the initial ferocity of the enemy assault found renewed strength. Inspired, they followed their leader in a counter-attack, their initial shock being replaced with the pent-up anger and frustration from so many years of depravation.

All along the forest edge, warriors fought to the death and blood flew everywhere as antagonists fought without quarter. For several minutes the battle was shapeless with no side taking overall advantage. The attack of the Flemish had been ferocious with the added momentum of the downhill assault but the Welsh defensive line, despite its disintegration, had served its purpose and had absorbed much of the initial impact.

Gwenllian ducked to avoid a swinging blow from a Flemish axeman and swung her sword in an arc, slashing through the tendons at the back of both his knees. The attacker screamed in agony and collapsed like a felled tree amongst the blood-sodden undergrowth. Taliesin jumped to Gwenllian's aid and stamped his heavy boot over and over on the wounded man's face until the skull collapsed beneath his brutal onslaught.

Gwenllian got to her feet and looked around for her sons.

'Where are they?' she shouted, wiping a stream of blood from her face.

'Over there,' replied Taliesin, and Gwenllian saw Morgan and Maelgwyn fighting alongside each other. Others fought at their sides and she could see their formation was tight, keeping many of the enemy at bay. For the first time in several minutes her hopes soared, for the enemy had lost all momentum. If she and her men could regain a structure, the day may not be lost.

'We are too fragmented,' she shouted. 'Pass the word to reform. Use Morgan's position as the centre for a new line.'

Taliesin rallied the men as Gwenllian ran back into the fight. The battle was fragmenting into isolated pockets, and as men heard the message they broke off to run back towards Morgan's position. Within minutes the Welsh had reformed into another defensive line albeit a poor semblance of what they had been before.

'Is this it?' asked Gwenllian, looking at her decimated army.

'It's all I could find,' gasped Taliesin. 'We have lost over half.'

'We will lose the rest if we remain here,' said Gwenllian, hearing the enemy commanders shouting throughout the trees in the distance. 'It sounds like they are reorganising for another attack.'

'We can't go back up the hill,' said Taliesin. 'Our men are already exhausted and the Flemish have the advantage of the high ground. We have to go down onto the road, at least we will have more options.'

'I don't know,' said Gwenllian. 'To retreat to the road leaves us with no cover and there will be no coming back.'

'We have no other option,' replied Taliesin. 'Staying here will get us all killed. At least on the road we will have room to manoeuvre.'

Gwenllian stared at Taliesin, her mind working furiously. A few hours ago they had both agreed that the road was a killing zone with little chance of escape, yet here they were contemplating it as their only hope.

'And what about their archers?' she asked. 'Once we are down there they can pick us off like rats in a barrel.'

'They can't if we are not there,' said Taliesin. 'Once we hit the road, we must head east as fast as we can.'

'You mean run away?' asked Gwenllian. 'We did not come here to flee, Taliesin, we came to fight, remember?'

'*That option has gone*,' shouted Taliesin. 'Their army has already taken us by surprise and half of our men lie dead amongst the trees. If you want the rest to join them then, fine, we will stay here and fight to the death for that is what will happen, Gwenllian, make no mistake about it.'

She looked at the men behind her, each looking to her for guidance and leadership. Many already carried wounds and she knew they were in no state for a full-scale battle.

'Gwenllian,' said Taliesin, his voice lowering, 'there is no shame in withdrawing. We have been bettered but that is what happens in war. It is what you do now that will decide if this day is wasted. If we all die then it will all have been in vain but if we can save these men then they will live to fight again, possibly alongside your father's army. Stay or go, the command is yours to give but whatever it is, give it soon before it is too late.'

'So be it,' she said and she turned again to the men. 'Get down to the road,' she ordered. 'Take the walking wounded with us. The rest of you, take whatever weapons you can find from amongst the fallen, I suspect they will be needed before this day is done.'

The last of her army turned to scramble down the bank and out onto the Carmarthen Road. Gwenllian followed but as she reached the frozen ruts of the well-travelled highway, her heart sank as one of her men called out. 'My lady, look.'

Gwenllian looked along the road and saw dozens of English also climbing down the bank to the east, effectively blocking their escape route. She spun around only to find a similar situation to the west. They were hemmed in with no route to escape. Taliesin came sliding down the bank along with the rear guard.

'They are coming,' he gasped. 'We have to move.'

'We have nowhere to go,' said Gwenllian. 'Look.'

Taliesin looked along the road in both directions, taking in the situation, before gazing out over the open field. In the distance he could see a rise in the ground, the site of an ancient burial mound.

'There,' he said. 'The rear of the mound will protect us from archers and if it comes to a fight at least we will have the higher ground.'

'I'm not sure,' replied Gwenllian. 'We will be exposed.'

'*Gwenllian*,' shouted Taliesin, 'we are out of options. Our plan centred on us being the ambushers with our quarry upon the road. Now that role has been reversed and we are hemmed in on three sides. To stay here is to die; at least out there we have a chance, no matter how slight.'

Gwenllian hesitated a moment more. Despite her concerns, she knew she had no other options. With a deep breath she turned to the remainder of her army. 'Head to that mound,' she shouted, 'and form a shield wall along the top.'

'*You heard the Princess*,' roared Taliesin. 'Get moving or die where you stand.'

Exhausted, the men staggered across the field towards the burial mound. Behind them the rest of the Flemish army emerged from the forest but stopped on the road as their archers sent volley after volley after the Welsh.

'*Keep moving*,' shouted Gwenllian as men fell all around her. 'The mound is our only hope.'

Minutes later the remainder of her devastated army collapsed behind the burial mound in exhaustion. The rain of arrows had stopped but they were in a terrible state. Another fifty or so men had fallen during the flight and of those that remained, another dozen or so had been hit by arrows.

For a while nobody spoke, they just lay on the damp grass trying to regain their breath. Eventually Taliesin crawled back up to the top of the mound to see what the enemy were doing.

'Well?' asked Gwenllian.

'They're just waiting there,' said Taliesin. 'It doesn't make sense. Surely they can see what state we are in.'

Gwenllian joined him and stared over to the enemy reforming on the road. She did a quick head count and was surprised how few there actually were.

'Unless there are more amongst the trees then it seems we have acquitted ourselves well,' she said. 'Our numbers look about even.'

'They still have the advantage,' said Taliesin. 'We have many wounded and they have the road. Even if we wanted to counter-attack, we have too much space between us.'

'We should have stayed where we were,' said Gwenllian, 'at least the odds were even.'

'There was no way to know their strength,' said Taliesin. 'Still, at least we are safe here for a while. Even if they decide to follow up their advantage, they will have to cover the open space and the threat from our own archers.'

Gwenllian looked around. 'We have no more than a handful left alive, and their arrow pouches are almost empty.'

'Agreed, but they don't know that. The longer they wait the closer night-time gets,' he continued, 'and if we can last until then, we can slip away under the cover of darkness.'

Gwenllian nodded. It was an ambitious goal but at least it gave them something to hope for. She turned to the men. 'We will go firm here and make the best defensive position that we can. Get the shields to the top as well as whatever lances we have left. Archers, share your arrows between you. The rest of you – do what you can for the wounded and see what we have to drink. You have fought well, every last one of you, but I ask just a few more hours. Do this and we can be back in the Cantref Mawr by nightfall tomorrow. Be of stout heart, my friends, this day is not yet lost.'

The men rallied to the inspiration of her voice and soon they had yet another defensive position along the brow of the mound.

'It's the best we can do,' she said to Taliesin a few minutes later. 'All we can do now is wait.'

Kidwelly Castle

February 17th, AD 1136

Nesta was sitting in Marion's quarters along with her hostess and two of the other castle ladies. The mood was jovial and they were listening to one of the bards regaling them with a song about the excesses of London life when the door burst open and one of Marion's maids ran in unannounced.

'*My lady*,' she gasped with a quick curtsey. 'You should come quickly. There is a battle under way on the northern fields.'

'*What?*' said Marion, getting to her feet.

'It's true,' said the maid. 'Everyone is gathering on the palisades as we speak to get a better view.'

Nesta swallowed hard. She had an idea as to what might be going on, but she had never guessed any confrontation would take place so near the castle.

'We should also go to the palisades,' said one of the women, 'and see what unfolds.'

'No, I've got a better idea,' said Marion. 'There will be a clearer view from the keep roof. Come, grab your cloaks.'

The women followed Marion out of her quarters and hurried up the stairs to the top of the keep. They ran over to the castellated wall and stared across the fields.

'Look,' gasped one of the women. 'There is an army encamped on Arthur's Mound.'

'Who's army?' asked Marion. 'I see no colours.'

'It must be the Welsh,' replied the first woman, 'for the others fly the flag of England.'

'Oh my,' said one of the women. 'How exciting.'

'There's nothing exciting about men dying,' said Nesta coldly, 'no matter whose banner they fight beneath.'

'No, I only meant . . .' started the woman, but her words fell away in silence.

'Be careful with your words, Elisabeth,' said Marion, 'for, don't forget, our guest here is from Welsh stock.'

'I know,' replied Elisabeth, 'but surely not from those monsters. She is royal born, a true princess.'

Nesta glared at Elisabeth but did not respond. Instead she peered at the Welsh lines, desperate to see if her brother was amongst them.

'My lady,' said another voice from the side of the keep, 'look down in the bailey.'

The women ran across the tower and peered down. The courtyard was a hive of activity as men prepared their horses. Sergeants barked their orders and men raced to collect their weapons and equipment as the garrison responded to the developing events out on the battlefield.

'What are they doing?' asked Elisabeth. 'Surely they should be manning the walls?'

'We are not under threat here,' said Marion, 'and unless I am mistaken, it looks like they are heading out to join the fight.'

Nesta gasped in horror and her hand flew to her mouth. If that was what was happening, then the besieged Welsh lines had no hope.

'Ah,' said a male voice from behind them. 'I see you have heard the news.'

The women turned to see John Salisbury striding across from the door. 'Keep watching, ladies,' he continued, 'for I suspect you are about to witness the ending of the so-called rebellion right before your very eyes.'

The women moved back to the castellated walls, pulling their cloaks tighter around them. Nesta stayed back, staring out into space.

'Are you not joining us, Lady Nesta?' said Salisbury with a knowing sneer. 'Surely you were anticipating this as eagerly as I?'

Nesta stared back, not knowing how to react. The way he was behaving it was almost as if he knew this was going to happen, which was impossible, unless . . .

'I don't know what you mean,' she replied with a stutter.

'Oh, come on,' said Salisbury. 'Do you take me for a fool? I have long known about your rekindled allegiance to the rebel cause for my spies reach into every corner across Deheubarth. Even as far as market places where bakers pass secret messages hidden in loaves of bread.'

Nesta stared in horror. The arrangements with the market woman had obviously been uncovered.

'Oh don't look so surprised,' said Salisbury. 'There is hardly a conversation that goes on between anyone of note without it being eventually reported to me. It has been a long time in its development, Nesta, almost a lifetime, but a network of informers is often more powerful than the strongest army.'

'You are mistaken,' started Nesta.

'Save your arguments,' snapped Salisbury. 'The baker talked and is already hanging from a gibbet. As I have stated, I have long known about your treachery but have allowed you your little victories in pursuit of a bigger goal' – he nodded towards the battlefield – 'the crushing of the rebellion once and for all.'

'That's impossible,' she said. 'There's no way you could have known about . . .' She stopped suddenly, realising she had been about to incriminate herself.

'About what?' asked Salisbury. 'About you reading the note in my cloak back in my quarters in Pembroke?'

Again Nesta was rocked at the revelation. Unless Emma had been caught or had betrayed her, he could not have possibly known.

'Enough of the games,' growled Salisbury. 'I had my suspicions and used that letter as bait. You took it like a starving fox.'

Nesta was horrified. If he was telling the truth then the terrible situation unfolding out on the battlefield was all down to her. She had not only fed Gwenllian with inaccurate information, but actually lured them into an ambush of Salisbury's making.

'Come,' said Salisbury, and grabbing her arm, he dragged her over to throw her against the wall. 'Take a good look,' he snarled, grabbing her jaw and forcing her to stare towards the slaughter a few hundred paces away. 'This is of your making, Nesta. Those men are dying because of your stupidity.'

Nesta stood pressed against the wooden wall, numb with fear and self-loathing. As she watched, the sound of the gates opening in the bailey below echoed through the air and over a hundred horsemen thundered across the drawbridge and out onto the field of battle.

Over on the burial mound, Taliesin stared towards the road, momentarily unaware of what was happening back at the castle.

'*Stand to*,' he roared as the lines of foot soldiers descended onto the field. 'Here they come.'

The Welsh sprang to their feet and lined up behind the few dozen shields they had remaining, but as they did, Taliesin could see Gwenllian staring towards the castle.

With a sinking feeling in his gut he turned and saw the column of horsemen galloping along the castle road and heading for the bridge across the river.

'Oh no,' he said quietly. 'What are we going to do?'

'I'll tell you what we are going to do,' said Gwenllian. 'We are going to take the fight back to them. Prepare to advance,' she shouted. 'Drop everything except your shields and swords.'

'*What are you doing?*' gasped Taliesin. 'There is nowhere to go.'

'I'm not going to stay out here and be cut down like summer hay,' she said. 'We have a few minutes, no more. In that time, if God is on our side, we can reach the trees.'

'But you have to go through them,' said Taliesin, pointing towards the advancing Flemish foot soldiers.

'It's either that or be killed here,' said Gwenllian, 'and I for one intend to go down fighting.'

For a few moments Taliesin stared at the princess realising she was deadly serious. Finally, he grinned and, drawing his own sword, he too turned to the remnants of their army.

'You heard the woman,' he shouted. 'Prepare to advance. We are headed to the trees and will be stopping for nobody.' He waited atop the burial mound as the rest of the men joined him. One by one they lined up, each with a sword in hand.

'Ready?' asked Gwenllian.

'As ready as we'll ever be,' replied Taliesin.

'*Men of Deheubarth*,' roared Gwenllian. 'Advance.'

———

Up on the keep, Nesta stared with horror as the two armies raced across the field towards each other. From her position she had an excellent view of the battlefield and, in the moments before they clashed, her heart seemed to stop and she felt physically sick. The sound of men roaring their challenges reached the tower on the breeze, and as they finally crashed into each other, she turned away in dismay but Salisbury grabbed her and dragged her back to the wall.

'Oh no you don't, Princess,' he snarled. 'This is all of your making and you will witness every last moment. Let it be a lesson to you that no one, no matter how highborn, gets away with treachery under my watch. Men will die screaming in pain today, Lady Nesta. More will take days if not months to die from their wounds. Their families will go hungry and children will cry night after night for lack of food in their bellies. This is your legacy and you will pay witness or by God I will cut you down where you stand.'

As the other women stared at the unfolding drama upon the keep, Salisbury grabbed Nesta's chin and forced her head around to stare out over the battlefield. 'Open your eyes,' he shouted, 'and witness the carnage you have caused.'

'No,' cried Nesta. 'I can't.'

'*Open your eyes, God damn you,*' roared Salisbury.

Nesta gasped as the castellan slammed her into the wooden wall surrounding the tower, and as the sobs began, she realised that the tears rolling down her face were not from the pain: they were tears of shame.

'*Keep moving,*' screamed Gwenllian as she fought her way forward. 'Do not stop. Fight for your lives.'

'It's no use,' shouted Taliesin. 'They are too strong.'

Gwenllian glanced over to the road and realised the horsemen were far closer than she had thought. If they continued to fight, there was no way they could make it to the road before they arrived.

'*On me,*' she roared and the remaining Welsh made their way to her position. 'Form a wedge,' she cried, 'and head for the trees. Do not stop for anything. *Go!*'

The remains of the Welsh army ran for their lives towards the road, with many breaking through the enemy lines. Gwenllian fought like a madwoman and men fell around her. Her mind became a blur and she screamed like a wounded animal every time her blade met flesh. Some of the Flemish soldiers hesitated to engage her, and for a few moments, it looked like she would make it to the road, but as she and her sons fought their way through, one of the enemy launched a spear at close range.

'*Look out*,' shouted Morgan, and he hurled himself at his mother to knock her out of the way.

Gwenllian was knocked to the floor, uncertain as to what had just happened. For a moment she was stunned but quickly regained her feet only to see Morgan lying on the ground with a spear sticking out of his chest. For a few seconds the princess stared in shock, and then the reality hit her and she dropped to her knees beside him, oblivious to everything around her.

'Morgan,' she gasped. 'Morgan, my son.'

She took his head in her hands and kissed him gently as her tears dropped to mingle with the blood on his face.

'*Protect the princess*,' someone roared, 'at all costs.'

Taliesin and some of the men had reached the road, but when he heard the cry, he turned to see several men desperately defending Gwenllian as she sat on the floor nursing her wounded son.

'You men carry on,' he shouted. 'Get yourselves into the trees and keep running.'

'Where are you going?' panted one of the men beside him.

'I came here with a princess,' said Taliesin, 'and one way or another I am leaving with one.'

Without another word he raced back across the battlefield. As he did, he became aware that every other man who had managed to escape the carnage with him had followed him back, each determined to stay and fight alongside their comrades.

Gwenllian sat on the ground, cradling her son's head in her lap. He clung to life but she knew he was dying. Blood oozed from his mouth as he coughed and he stared up at his mother with fear in his eyes.

'Mother,' he gasped, 'leave me. Get away while you can.'

'Never,' said Gwenllian gently. 'I will stay with you while you set out on the great journey. Fear not, my son, for God and the angels are waiting to take you into heaven.'

'It hurts,' said Morgan.

'The pain will soon be gone, Morgan,' said Gwenllian through her tears. 'Be brave, my beautiful little boy.'

'*Form a circle*,' roared Taliesin beside her. '*Backs to the princess.*'

The remnants of the Welsh army stood shoulder to shoulder facing outwards to protect Gwenllian. As they did, they saw the column of riders racing towards them with lances lowered. Knowing there could be no defence against such force, Taliesin raised his sword and roared in defiance, his face contorted in rage. The men around him did the same, and as their battle cries echoed around the field, they faced their imminent deaths with a defiance born from generations of servitude.

The Flemish foot soldiers raced out of the cavalry's path, and as Morgan passed into oblivion in his mother's arms, the first of the horses smashed into the pathetic Welsh defensive lines.

Men screamed as they were knocked down by the armoured horses and many were run through with lances or struck down with heavy swords. Some threw themselves out of the way as the horses galloped past before jumping back to their feet and reforming in another, tighter circle.

Taliesin struggled to his feet with blood pouring from a deep wound in his shoulder and turned to stare at the cavalry less than a hundred paces away, already reformed and ready for the second charge.

'Everyone close in,' he shouted. 'Those of you with swords, take the horses' legs from beneath them as they ride through.'

'My lord,' shouted one of the men, 'surely we should open up the lines. If we stay as we are, we present too easy a target.'

'*No*,' roared Taliesin. 'I will not expose our princess to their blades. We will hold this line to the last man. We may be defeated but we will go down fighting as warriors. Now look to your weapons. Here they come again.'

Again the English cavalry smashed through the lines and again many men fell to the unrelenting assault. This time Taliesin was on his knees with a lance through his side and he knew his day was done.

'My lady,' he gasped as the cavalry formed up yet again, 'forgive me. I have let you down.'

'No,' said Gwenllian, shaking her head, 'it is I who bear that shame. The loyalty of you and your men has been more than anyone could ever dream of. Be proud, Taliesin, history will judge you as a great man.'

As she spoke Taliesin fell to one side and lay dead upon the ground. For a few moments she stared at him before looking up at the remaining men, each one again shuffling into position to protect her. Amongst them all she could see Maelgwyn, bloody and beaten but still alive.

'*Reform*,' roared Maelgwyn, realising that they had lost Taliesin. 'Lances to the fore.'

Gwenllian's heart almost burst with pride at the sound of her son's voice. No more was it full of the joyous playfulness that she had heard for so many years; now it had the timbre and authoritative air of a grown man.

'This time,' he shouted while facing away from his mother, 'we will not stand like sheep waiting to be slaughtered. When they are no more than twenty paces away, we will charge forward to meet them. They will not be expecting such a manoeuvre and we may find some of them wanting. Ready?'

'No,' said a quiet voice and he turned to see Gwenllian standing behind him.

'Mother,' he gasped. 'How is Morgan?'

'He has gone, Maelgwyn,' said Gwenllian. 'He has taken the same path as many such men before him in the pursuit of freedom.'

'Then they will pay for this,' shouted Maelgwyn with tears in his eyes. 'I swear I will avenge my brother.'

'No,' said Gwenllian again. 'Enough is enough. We cannot prevail against such numbers, and too many men have already died. I will seek a surrender and save who we can.'

'No,' gasped Maelgwyn. 'We will fight on to the last man.'

'There is no point,' said Gwenllian. 'The day is lost and the killing must come to an end. These men have families and I will seek their freedom.'

'But, Mother . . .' started Maelgwyn, but Gwenllian had already pushed past him and begun walking alone towards the line of enemy cavalry.

As she walked, one of the riders detached and walked his horse forward to meet her.

'Are you in command of these men?' she asked.

'Aye,' he replied. 'I am Maurice de Londres, castellan of Kidwelly Castle. I assume you are the witch.'

'I am Gwenllian ferch Gruffydd,' said Gwenllian, 'but am aware that I have often been called such names by the English.'

'What do you want, Gwenllian,' asked Maurice, 'for there is still blood to be spilled?'

'I have come to seek a surrender on behalf of my men,' she said, 'and will submit to your custody if you let them go.'

'Let them go?' laughed Maurice. 'Why would I do that?'

'Because they have no guilt in all this. They are honest men who have followed their leader without question. I am the prize you seek, Maurice. Take me and allow them to return to their families.'

'Another two attacks and they will all be dead anyway,' said Maurice, looking over her head at the shattered defenders, 'as will you. I see no reason to let them live to fight another day.'

'They are soldiers just like you, Maurice, and have fought bravely. Surely they deserve your recognition as a fellow warrior.'

The knight nodded slowly as he considered her request. Finally he looked down at Gwenllian. 'I have made my judgement,' he said, 'and your words have merit. These men are rebels and deserve death under the laws of England. However, there is one scenario where I will allow them to leave unharmed. Agree to my terms and I give my word we will set them free.'

'What are these terms?' asked Gwenllian.

'You will not like them,' replied Maurice.

'Try me,' she said. 'For if it secures the freedom of these men, there is nothing I will not consider.'

'Then listen carefully, witch queen,' he said, and as he made his demands, Gwenllian's heart sank with despair.

Across the field, Maelgwyn and his men watched his mother walk back towards them.

'What's happening?' asked one of the men. 'The English are withdrawing.'

Sure enough, the riders had turned their horses and were riding over to the burial mound at the centre of the plain.

'Mother,' shouted Maelgwyn, running over to her, 'what's happening? Were you successful?'

'I was,' said Gwenllian quietly. 'You are all free to leave but first there is a price to pay. Come, we must gather at the burial mound.'

'But the enemy are heading over there,' said Maelgwyn.

'I have their commander's word as a knight that this battle is over, Maelgwyn. There will be no treachery.'

'And you believe him?'

'I do. Say what you will about the English but their knights' vows are as solid as the strongest steel.'

'But why?'

'All will be revealed, Maelgwyn. Now come, muster the men and help me meet our side of the bargain.'

'What about Morgan?' asked Maelgwyn.

Gwenllian looked over at her dead son. 'He has gone, Maelgwyn,' she said. 'His soul is with God now.' Without waiting for a reply, she turned to walk back across the field to the burial mound.

A few moments later, the remainder of her army discarded their weapons and followed her.

The battle was over.

Kidwelly Castle

February 17th, AD 1136

Fewer than fifty wounded and exhausted Welshmen gathered at the base of the ancient burial mound. To either side stood the Flemish and English warriors, each watching them carefully. Up on the mound stood Maurice de Londres and three of his men. Maurice had removed his helmet and coif and his bald head shone in the late afternoon sun.

'You men have fought well,' he said, 'and by agreement with your princess, have earned the right to live. But there is a price to pay and you shall bear witness.' He turned towards Gwenllian standing at the front of her men. 'You know what you have to do, Gwenllian. Let's not make it worse than it is.'

Gwenllian turned to her son and looked deep into his eyes. 'Maelgwyn,' she said gently, 'you have turned into a fine man. Go forth into the world and make it know your name.'

'What do you mean?' asked Maelgwyn. 'What's happening?'

'Listen to me,' she said, 'for we have little time. Tell your father what happened here today. Tell him enough is enough and no more blood should be spilled. I love you, Maelgwyn, and always will. Never

ever forget that.' She tiptoed up and kissed her son on the cheek before turning and walking up the slope to the top of the mound.

'Wait,' said Maelgwyn. 'Mother, what's happening?' He stepped forward but two men armed with pikes stepped before him, blocking his way.

'Be brave, Maelgwyn,' said Gwenllian. 'And worry not for me, for I will soon stand alongside your brother in heaven.'

Maelgwyn's face fell as one of the men beside Maurice drew his sword.

'*No*,' roared Maelgwyn as he realised what was about to happen and he tried to rush up the mound.

More soldiers leapt forward to force him to his knees while another stood behind him with his blade pressed against Maelgwyn's throat. Others joined the initial pike men to provide a wall between the mound and the angry Welsh.

'*Hold there*,' shouted Maurice, 'or you will all die where you stand, agreement or no agreement.'

'Do as he says,' shouted Gwenllian. 'I choose this fate of my own free will, and not for you or for me, but for your children yet unborn and the families of every man who gave their lives this fateful day. Your task is not to mourn those who fell but nurture those that still live.'

'*No*,' gasped Maelgwyn, as tears started to flow. 'Don't allow this, Mother, it is too great a price.'

Two men pushed Gwenllian to her knees before grabbing her wrists and stretching her arms out wide. Another soldier pushed her head forward exposing her slender neck. The executioner stepped forward and took a few deep breaths before adjusting his grip on the sword.

'Make it clean,' said Maurice. 'She deserves no less.'

At the last moment, Gwenllian raised her head once more and looked into the eyes of the stunned Welshmen below the mound.

'*Let history know of this day*,' she shouted through her tears. '*And I ask no more than this, that generations yet unborn know the name I bore. I, Gwenllian ferch Gruffydd, beg only one thing . . . that you remember me!*'

The soldier pulled her head forward by her hair, and as the remainder of her army looked on, the executioner cut Gwenllian's head from her shoulders, killing the most effective and loved rebel leader that Wales had ever known.

Maelgwyn broke free from his captors before running up the hill and collapsing to his knees before his mother's mutilated corpse.

For a few moments everyone stared in shock, including the English. Right up until the last moment, nobody thought for a second that Maurice would go through with it but they were wrong, and Gwenllian now lay dead at the feet of Maurice de Londres, castellan of Kidwelly castle.

'You men,' said Maurice, turning to the Welsh. 'I gave my word that you would be released. Be gone from this place by nightfall and if I ever set eyes on any one of you again I shall burn you alive.'

The men mumbled amongst themselves and turned to walk away.

'What about him?' asked one of the other knights, nodding towards Maelgwyn still kneeling at the side of his mother's body.

'I have no time for the futile quests of children seeking revenge,' said Maurice. 'Cast him in chains.'

'I thought you promised . . .' began one of his men.

'What I promised was between me and Gwenllian,' said Maurice. 'She is now dead so will not judge. Do as I say and tomorrow at dawn, I will hang him from the battlements.' He turned to his cavalry. 'Escort these filth to the tree line in safety,' he said. 'After that, any who shows his face is free game. Let us leave this place forthwith for this day is done.'

Without another word he turned towards his own horse and, within ten minutes, the last of the combatants left the burial mound, leaving the slaughtered Welsh army and the decapitated corpse of the most famous female leader since Boudicca lying cold on the field of battle. The rebellion was finally over.

Kidwelly Castle

February 18th, AD 1136

Nesta lay bruised and beaten on the bed in one of the rooms of the keep at Kidwelly. The door was locked from the outside and her aggressor, John of Salisbury, had long gone after subjecting her to a night of beatings and sexual assault. For an age she had lain motionless on the bed, her horrified mind going over and over what she had witnessed throughout the day. Compared to the slaughter and the brutal execution of Gwenllian, the past few hours were nothing and her heart ached at the fate of so many good men who had suffered so much worse.

She got to her feet and staggered over to the window, looking down into the courtyard below. The drop was inviting, tempting her to end her pain, both physical and mental. All she had to do was push open the window and let herself fall. Her eyes glazed over and her hand unconsciously stretched out to push the windows wide. She climbed upon the chair, her breathing coming faster and deeper. How sweet were the last few moments of life? With her heart racing, she sought the courage for the final movement, the action that would start the journey to peace she so desperately craved, but just as a calmness came upon her, someone knocked on the door and a voice called her name.

'Nesta.'

She turned her head slowly to look at the door.

'Nesta,' came the voice again. 'I have a message for you. Come to the door.'

Nesta hesitated and looked back down into the beckoning courtyard.

'Lady Nesta,' hissed the voice. 'Please come to the door. There is little time.'

Nesta climbed down from the chair and walked over to the door, sliding down the wall to sit alongside the door frame.

'What do you want?' she asked.

'I have a message for you,' said the young girl's voice.

'From whom?'

'I cannot say, nor do I know the contents, but here it is. My mistress asks that you burn it as soon as it is read. Now I must go before I am discovered.'

Nesta looked down to see a piece of parchment slide beneath the door. She picked it up and limped over to the single candle in the dark room. Nervously she broke the seal and opened the message. It consisted of just one sentence.

'Your brother was not amongst the dead.'

Nesta's hand flew to her mouth to mask the gasp of joy begging to be released from deep within her soul. Whatever had happened out there that day, no matter how brutal or how depraved, the fact that her brother may still be alive gave her hope renewed.

She looked up at the open window – the perceived route to everlasting escape only moments earlier – now nothing more than the source of a bitterly cold breeze. She walked across the room and stared out, the icy-cold westerly wind washing over her like a cleansing waterfall, and all thoughts of killing herself evaporated like a mist. If the note was correct, and she had no reason to believe it was not, then Tarw still lived, and if that was indeed the case, she knew he would never rest until he had avenged the death of his beautiful wife.

It may take years to rebuild, but if she knew her brother, and as long as Gwenllian's name remained upon the voices of the people of Deheubarth, the rebellion could never be over.

Indeed, it had only just begun!

Author's Note

Though historical dates for famous battles and coronations are often recorded from so long ago, the finer detail of an individual's life usually disappears with the passing of time. Consequently, it falls to authors to use their imaginations to fill in the detail of their characters' lives.

As is usual in these types of books, there is little documented evidence as to the facts and details of what really happened so far back in history. This often includes the names of some of the main characters, for example, in this case, the names of Gwenllian's sons are often different depending on which source is used. In such cases I have opted for the version that seems more popular or, indeed, used a different name if it helped the flow.

In addition, as it was common for boys to be named after their fathers, it was often the case that several men in the same family were called by the same name. Obviously, this would be far too complicated to follow in a novel so, where needed, I have changed names to help the storyline read a little easier.

Finally, the notes below indicate the rough brushstrokes of what is known or surmised from the little data available. It also contains my own theories and understandings along with a liberal sprinkling of artistic license. For those who are more enlightened than I in such things, if I have misrepresented anything either in error or in the pursuit of a smoother storyline, then I can only apologise.

Nesta ferch Rhys

Nesta ferch Rhys was the sister of Gruffydd ap Rhys (Tarw) and lived with her husband, Gerald of Windsor, in Pembroke castle. As a young woman she had a passionate affair with Henry the First and bore him a bastard son. Eventually she was married off to Gerald of Windsor, a well-respected knight of the English Crown and lived at Pembroke Castle for many years, bearing Gerald several sons.

Gruffydd ap Rhys

Gruffydd ap Rhys (known as Tarw in our tale) was the son of Rhys ap Tewdwr, the last king of Deheubarth. When he was young, Gruffydd was sent to Ireland for his own safety and was brought up by one of the Irish kings. When he was old enough he returned to Deheubarth and often stayed at Pembroke castle with his sister Nesta and her husband Gerald of Windsor before turning to the life of a rebel.

John of Salisbury

Around this time, Gerald disappears from the records. In our story, he is obviously replaced by John of Salisbury and though Nesta eventually did end up marrying the constable of Cardigan, John of Salisbury is a character made up for the continuation of the storyline.

Gwenllian Ferch Gruffydd

In the early years of the 12th century AD, a young princess of Gwynedd in North Wales fell in love with a southern prince and eloped to live with him in the kingdom of Deheubarth in the south, living the life of a rebel and freedom fighter. Using the homes and castles of those still loyal to her husband's family, they lived for years amongst the forests and hills of South Wales, basing themselves mainly in the vast area known as the Cantref Mawr, a wild and lawless place covered with dense forests and hidden valleys. It was a perfect hiding place for those outside the law and they used it as a base for their constant harrying of the English, French and Flemish forces that had occupied Deheubarth for so many years. Over time, Gwenllian became famous for her prowess in battle and she became the figurehead for the rebellion across South Wales, despite being constantly outnumbered and hunted by the Crown.

Gwenllian's life with Gruffydd ap Rhys

During this time, Gwenllian bore at least four sons to Gruffydd and as they grew older, her thoughts became more and more concerned with her family's safety. Henry I, King of England at that time, placed a price on both Gwenllian and Tarw's heads but, though many sought to collect the reward, those around the fugitives were fiercely protective and they were relatively safe within the Cantref Mawr.

It seems that during this time, Henry was so concerned with the continuing struggle in France, he offered Gwenllian and Tarw an amnesty in return for abandoning the life of rebels. Worried for the safety of their sons, some records seem to indicate that they accepted the amnesty and, for a while, lived a quiet life in a village somewhere in the Cantref Mawr. Eventually, however, circumstances forced them to return to their previous lives as rebels and they once more took up the sword of freedom.

The Death of Henry the First

In December 1135, King Henry died and though the crown had been promised to his daughter, Matilda, many of the barons were unhappy and turned against the idea of having a woman on the throne. During the confusion, Stephen de Blois, the grandson of William the conqueror, took the opportunity of sailing to England with his army and claiming the throne for himself. Matilda was livid and set out with her own army to confront Stephen and reclaim what had been promised to her. The situation was confused and dangerous and led to the period of English history known as 'the anarchy', a period of civil war stretching over the next nineteen years.

The Battle of Gower

Early in 1136, an army of Welshmen led by Hywel ap Maredudd confronted and defeated a large English force near the coast of Gower in modern-day South Wales. The implications were enormous and it gave great hope to those still embarked upon the path of rebellion, especially with English attentions being taken up with the political struggle in London. Knowing they needed more men, Tarw rode to North Wales to ask Gwenllian's father, Gruffydd ap Cynan, to send his army south and take advantage of the situation. Tarw also took his two youngest sons with him on the journey, leaving his two eldest behind with Gwenllian.

The Death of Gwenllian

While Tarw was away, it seems Gwenllian became aware of another English army preparing to attack the Cantref Mawr. Various sources seem to indicate that even though she was outnumbered, in order to gain her husband time to return with reinforcements, she decided to confront the English. She split her forces in two with one half targeting the supply lines and the other half lying in ambush for the main force. However, they had been tricked, for the army had landed days earlier and many were hidden amongst the hills and forests behind Gwenllian's ambush position having been led there by a traitor. Without warning they fell upon Gwenllian's position and forced them out onto the open plain. Seizing the opportunity, Maurice de Londres, castellan of Kidwelly Castle, led his own garrison from the castle to join the battle. Gwenllian's army had no chance and were slaughtered.

During the fighting, Morgan, Gwenllian's son, was killed and when she saw that defeat was certain, she surrendered, hoping the enemy would show mercy.

Maurice de Londres accepted her surrender but in a cold-blooded message to anyone who dared to rebel against the Crown in the future, he had Gwenllian beheaded right there on the battlefield in front of her men. Gwenllian's last words are reported to have been 'Remember me', and for centuries after the terrible defeat, the battle cry of the Welsh in their never-ending search for freedom became 'Remember Gwenllian!'

About the Author

Photo © 2015 Steve Powderhill

Kevin Ashman is the author of eighteen novels, including the bestselling Roman Chronicles and highly ranked Medieval Sagas. Always pushing the boundaries, he found further success with the India Sommers Mysteries, as well as three other standalone projects, *Vampire*, *Savage Eden* and the dystopian horror story *The Last Citadel*. Kevin was born and raised in Wales and now writes full-time. He is married with four grown children and enjoys cycling, swimming and watching rugby. Current works include the Blood of Kings series: *A Land Divided*, *A Wounded Realm* and *Rebellion's Forge*. Links to all Kevin's books can be found at www.KMAshman.co.uk.